FEB 1 2 2020

LARGE
PRINT
LONDON

London, Julia

The Devil in the
saddle

The DEVIL *in the* SADDLE

Center Point
Large Print

Also by Julia London and available from
Center Point Large Print:

The Charmer in Chaps

**This Large Print Book carries the
Seal of Approval of N.A.V.H.**

The
DEVIL
in the
SADDLE

JULIA LONDON

CENTER POINT LARGE PRINT
THORNDIKE, MAINE

This Center Point Large Print edition
is published in the year 2020 by arrangement with
Berkley, an imprint of Penguin Publishing Group,
a division of Penguin Random House LLC.

The text of this Large Print edition is unabridged.
In other aspects, this book may vary
from the original edition.
Printed in the United States of America
on permanent paper.
Set in 16-point Times New Roman type.

ISBN: 978-1-64358-484-3

The Library of Congress has cataloged this record
under Library of Congress Control Number: 2019951745

Chapter One

The dreams that happen just before waking, the ones that take weird turns into hippie-dippie landscapes, are the strangest of all. When Hallie Prince could recall her dreams, which wasn't often, as she was not a morning person and her first thought was usually coffee, it seemed she was always looking for something. Like her ballet shoes in a stranger's house. Her phone in a foreign country. Sometimes she was in the company of people she seemed to know well, but then again, knew not at all. Sometimes she was in places unrecognizable to her, but that she seemed to know.

Other times, she was doing something out of character, like hiding in a warehouse. That was the dream that was waking her this particular day. She didn't know where the warehouse was, or why she was there, but she knew she was hiding from Anna, a friend she'd known long ago in New York, and had not had occasion to see in several years. She also knew that it was imperative she hide, even though she was going to be late. She was supposed to dance, she was supposed to be at the theater, but she was folded into a small dark space, pressed up against something scratchy and sort of soft. But also hard. Soft and hard and scratchy.

Hallie opened her eyes, and the warehouse fluttered into the ether. She tried to blink away what looked like a caterpillar that draped one eye, but it stubbornly held on. *Oh.* Not a caterpillar. A strip of false lashes.

"Are you okay?"

The deeply masculine voice startled Hallie, and with a gasp of surprise, she pushed up to her elbows. The scratchy part of her dream was a plaid wool shirt. The soft and hard part of her dream was apparently the body of a man. And though a tangle of hair covered half her face, she could see she'd slept in the heavily beaded gown she'd meant to wear to her wedding reception.

But there wasn't going to be a wedding reception, so why . . .

Oh.

The memory of last night slowly began to seep into her brain. *Damn tequila.*

"Hallie?"

Hallie knew that voice. She slowly turned her head and pushed hair from her face. *"Rafe?"* Her old friend, handsome, sexy-as-hell cowboy and ex–Army Ranger Rafe? She thought he was in Chicago or somewhere.

"Good morning."

A sudden image of Rafe came roaring back to her. Rafe, standing in the driveway, illuminated by the headlights of her car, his weight shifted to one hip, holding a saddle on his shoulder and looking bemused. And she remembered thinking how relieved she was that Rafe had come. Rafe would fix things. Rafe knew what to do.

Oh please, dear God, she hadn't actually gotten behind a wheel, had she? *Yes.* Yes, she had. But wait! She remembered—she'd never left the garage. She'd never even put the car in gear.

Rafe's handsome face came into view. He used to be so skinny, a scarecrow of a boy, but now he was all filled out with a square jaw covered by the morning growth of a beard. He squinted caramel-colored eyes at her, examining her face. "You look like crap," he said, and plucked the strip of lashes from her eye.

"I *feel* like crap."

"Are you going to make it?"

No. She was most definitely not going to make it. A swell of nausea made her whimper.

"Oh no. Please don't—" A small trash can appeared in her line of vision.

It was too late—she retched into the trash can. "Nononono!" Rafe exclaimed. "Oh, man!" he said desperately as she retched, and then he made a hacking noise like he was trying to keep from vomiting, too.

When she had emptied the contents of her stomach into that can, Hallie collapsed, face-down, onto her pillow. "I thought you were supposed to be a tough army guy."

"I *am* a tough army guy. But my gag reflex is a baby."

She felt his weight lift up off the bed with the can. "Don't throw up until I get back," he warned her. She heard him go into her bathroom, heard water running, heard him muttering.

Why was Rafe still here? What was good ol' Rafael, the ranch majordomo's very hot oldest son and Hallie's lifelong friend, doing at Three Rivers at all? She thought he split his time between San Antonio and Chicago. Wasn't he moving there soon?

When they were children, Martin would bring his kids—Rafe, who was her brother Nick's age; and Rico, who was the same age as Hallie and her twin, Luca; and Angie, the youngest of them all—to the main compound on weekends, and they would swim or her dad would grill burgers for them. Rafe was a lot like Nick, the steady, dependable son in the family. Rico was a party animal, and if he were around last night, he would have told her to move over and let him drive to Houston. Angie was the squirt some adult was always shouting at them to watch.

Thank God it was steady Rafe who'd happened upon her last night. Hallie couldn't begin to

8

remember what she'd done, but whatever it was, she was pretty sure she was going to want to open the window and dive headfirst into the bushes below.

Rafe reappeared, sans can, and stood over her, studying her very closely, like a lab specimen.

"Stop looking at me like that. I'm hideous. I could die," she said, mortified.

"You're not *hideous*," he said, as if she still had a few steps to go before she reached the certifiably hideous level. "You just look a little beat up. I think the dark circles under your eyes—"

"Okay," she said, weakly waving her hand at him. "Don't tell me."

He patted her shoulder. "Look at the bright side—you're probably going to live."

"Do I have a choice?"

"No."

"What's the dark side?"

"The dark side is you won't believe you're going to live until tomorrow."

Great.

"Maybe you should have a little hair of the dog that bit you. You might feel better."

"Nooo," Hallie moaned, and squeezed her eyes shut as she swallowed down a swell of nausea. "Don't even *say* it."

"How about food? Do you think you could keep something down?"

"Stop talking." She rolled over onto her back and squinted up at him. "What happened last night?"

Rafe smiled. Very slowly and very sexily. That smile used to drive her friends crazy with lust. "I don't even know where to begin."

"Must have been epic." No wonder her head was pounding.

"Pretty spectacular," Rafe agreed.

Hallie groaned and rolled onto her side, away from him. She wasn't much of a drinker, so she would lay the blame for however she might have humiliated herself squarely at the feet of her recent *ex*-fiancé, Christopher. Everything was his fault. Her terrible, piteous mood was his fault. Her five-pound weight gain was *definitely* his fault. She wouldn't be the least bit surprised if even the Israeli-Palestinian conflict could be traced back to him.

She could clearly remember rambling around the twenty thousand square feet of the main house at Three Rivers Ranch, where she, a grown woman of thirty years, was living with her mother (God help her), and her grandmother (adding salt to the wound since 1936). Nick and Luca came by a couple of times a week to check on things, but all of them, *all* of them, had been out last night and left Hallie alone in abject peril, because without any good reality TV to distract her, she had only her thoughts to keep her company.

Anyone who knew her knew that being alone with her thoughts was a train wreck waiting to happen. Well, she'd pumped that locomotive right into a ditch.

Oh, but she'd worked herself into a good lather over Chris. She could remember coming up with the brilliant idea that she ought to drive to Houston and confront him and her supposed bridesmaid, Dani, whom she'd last seen naked beneath Chris. Hallie could even remember convincing her weakly responsible self that she wasn't *that* drunk, that she could make the three-hour drive to Houston, *no problema.*

She could vaguely remember putting on her reception dress with the dumb idea that Chris ought to see what he would be missing—her looking exquisite on her wedding day to be precise, but not in her *actual* wedding dress, because he'd lost that privilege when he pile drove his body into Dani's. But she hadn't been able to fix her hair, and this was not the sort of dress one could don without assistance. In fact, she could feel the cool air the ceiling fan kept pushing against her bare back.

Who really understood the power of tequila until one had empty shot glasses up to her elbows? She couldn't remember much of anything after squeezing herself into this dress. Mostly just snatches of Rafe, now that she thought about it.

"Want me to get Frederica?" Rafe asked.

Frederica had been cooking the meals at Three Rivers Ranch since Hallie was a little girl. "She's probably not here. Mom cut her to three days a week."

"You're kidding," Rafe said flatly.

That's what everyone said—Frederica was like family. But when Hallie's father had died so unexpectedly earlier in the year, things changed. The Princes were having to do a lot for themselves around the ranch, which none of them were really accustomed to doing. "I'm not kidding," Hallie said. She wrapped her arms around a pillow and lay on her side. "Did you really stay with me all night?" she asked, feeling immeasurably pathetic.

"You insisted," he said. "But now that I have assured myself you are breathing, I'll just tiptoe on out of here." He made a move toward the door.

"No, wait," she said. "Don't go yet."

Rafe hesitated.

"Please, Rafe."

He glanced at her sidelong, clearly debating. She didn't blame him—babysitting hungover debutantes was probably not his cup of tea. But Hallie didn't want to be alone again. Not until she could at least drag herself to the bathroom by her own power. "At least tell me how we ended up in my room."

"You want to hear the truth, huh?" he said, smiling a little. "That might take a minute."

"What else am I going to do while I die my slow and agonizing death?"

He chuckled softly. "Okay," he said, and turned around, easing himself onto the foot of the bed. "Shall I start with the cows?"

"Great," Hallie moaned. "It's even worse than I feared. I don't remember any cows."

Rafe gave her foot a squeeze. "Last night, Mr. Creedy's cows got out."

"Again?" Hallie was immediately struck with the realization that her world had gone from high-society parties and charity events to knowing how often the Creedy cows got out. *Oh, how the mighty have fallen.*

"Yep. About a dozen of them sauntered through a hole in the fence, I presume because they thought the eating would be better on the other side of the road. But they must have taken a moment to contemplate just how small they were in the vast cow universe, because they were bunched up on the road and wouldn't move."

In spite of herself, Hallie smiled. "Can't blame them—it *is* a pretty big universe. And besides, I don't know why Mr. Creedy won't fix that fence, because those cows keep getting out."

"Mrs. Bachman wondered the same thing," he said, and crossed one booted foot over his knee. Had he left his boots on all night? Rafe had to be the most respectful man she'd ever known.

"By all accounts, she was pretty upset," he said.

"Those cows were blocking her path to bridge club."

"Oh, no. Mrs. Bachman does *not* miss bridge club."

"No, she does not. She was fit to be tied and called the new sheriff. What's his name?"

"Sam Richards."

"That's right. Well, Sheriff Richards called Dad. He said he'd drive a patrol car down here to take care of it, but they were all tied up at the Broken Wagon."

The Broken Wagon was an old-style honky-tonk on the highway to San Antonio. They had live music most nights, a washer's pit, a pool hall, and a dance hall where they still sprinkled sawdust on the floor for all the scooting boots that went round it. "Why?" Hallie asked. "What happened?"

Rafe leaned forward and said, "Now, this is all secondhand, as told by Sheriff Richards to my dad, who, I have to tell you, doesn't always appreciate the nuance of a well-told tale. But the sheriff said they had their hands full putting down a brawl."

"A *brawl?*" Hallie asked, perking up. "That sounds juicy. What started it?"

"If I had to hazard a guess, I'd say it was probably a woman. Saturday night brawls at the Broken Wagon are usually about a woman."

Hallie smiled a little. "Spoken like someone with personal experience."

"I am man enough to admit that I may or may not have gotten tangled up by a woman on occasion," he said with a wink.

She would love to hear *that* story. In high school, Hallie and her friends would openly swoon as they lay around the pool while Rafe walked around with a weed eater in his hand. He would roll his eyes at them and tell them to get a job. Kara Mapplethorpe was absolutely tongue-tied whenever she saw him in a sweaty, threadbare T-shirt and jeans. She definitely would have thrown down for a chance with Rafe. "I haven't been to the Broken Wagon in ages," Hallie said through a yawn.

"It's a good thing you didn't choose last night for your return," Rafe said.

He was right. "So far you've told me about a brawl, some contemplative cows, and a mad Mrs. Bachman," she said, lifting three fingers as she counted them off. "But what has that got to do with me?"

"Nothing," Rafe said. "But that's why I happened to be close by last night. Dad and I saddled up a couple of horses and rode out to move the cows and patch the fence. When I brought the horses back, there weren't any lights on in the house and it looked like no one was home."

"Just me and the blues," Hallie muttered.

"You and a blue streak, you mean," Rafe said.

"When I first heard it, I thought it had to be Miss Dolly. No disrespect, but your grandmother can get a little salty."

Hallie snorted. "Tell me about it."

"But Miss Dolly doesn't generally cry. And whoever was cussing was sobbing."

"Okay, thank you, that's all I need to hear," Hallie said, and, mortified, turned her face into the pillow. "Just shoot me, Rafe. Find a gun and take me out back and shoot me."

"Nah," he said, and shifted on the bed. "You're too pretty to shoot. Anyway, I went to have a look," he continued, "and as I got closer, who should I see but Hallie Prince hobbling out to the garage like she had a peg leg."

"I wasn't *hobbling*," Hallie said. Give her a little dignity in this tale, please.

But Rafe leaned over and picked something up off the floor. He held up one of her wedding shoes. The heel was broken. *Broken?* Oh, right— she'd slammed the sparkly silver shoe against a brick wall.

"That wasn't all," Rafe said.

"How did I know that? Let me guess—you also noticed I was quite inebriated."

"Well, sure. I could smell that from thirty steps away. But what I thought was a little strange was that you were wearing your wedding dress. And as far as I knew, you weren't getting married last night."

16

She wasn't getting married at all. The spread in *Bridal Guide* magazine, the feature and registry on theknot.com, three hundred guests, followed by the reception at the Sky Room in San Antonio, and that followed the next day by another reception at the River Oaks Country Club in Houston, where Chris was from. "It's not my *wedding* dress," she said. "It's one of my reception dresses."

"That's not the first time you've said that, and honestly, I have no idea what that means. All I know is that it looked like a wedding dress, and I thought it was a strange fashion choice. That's when things got interesting."

He was enjoying this, she could tell. Drawing out the torture. Hallie was fairly certain she didn't want to hear the rest.

"Now, I didn't believe you could actually pour yourself into the driver's seat of your car, especially after you practically nose-dived into the hood of it trying to walk around it. But you always surprise me, Hallie. Somehow, you managed to put yourself in the driver's seat. So I walked up and stood in front of the car, because, obviously, I wasn't going to let you drive."

"You realize it's a miracle I even saw you and didn't run right over you," she said. "You risked your life and all your limbs."

Rafe laughed. "Oh, you *saw* me, Hal. You were so pissed I wouldn't move that you laid on the horn and sent everything from cattle to baby rabbits running across Texas. And then you got out and Frankensteined your way over to me and started shouting something about a whore and a wedding cake."

She groaned with mortification. "I don't remember any of that."

"You got really mad when I said you were going to have to walk if you were that determined to get to Houston. That's when you went all King Kong on me and started smashing buildings and hurling cars."

"You're exaggerating!"

"You threw your broken shoe at me."

"Rafe! *Did* I? I am so sorry!"

"You were wide by a mile." He smiled.

She let out a sigh of relief.

"But then you took a swing at me, and you had some velocity behind it." He sounded almost impressed.

"Ohmigod," she muttered. "I had no idea I was one of those girls who fights when she's drunk."

Rafe laughed. "For what it's worth, you're a horrible fighter. Your swing was so wild that it knocked you off balance, and you crashed into me and then grabbed on to cry some more."

"Do me a favor and open the window, will you? I'm going through," she said, and buried her face in the pillow. It was sort of impossible to believe . . . and yet entirely possible to believe . . . that

18

she could make such an ass of herself. She didn't know who she was these days. *"Rafe* . . . I am so, *so* sorry," she murmured tearfully, and lifted her face. "I'm a horrible drinker. I mean I *don't* drink. Until I do, and apparently, I'm about as gifted at that as anything else."

"It's okay, Hal," he said with a kind smile, and caressed her arm. "You're entitled to let loose once in a while. Hey . . . I haven't talked to you in a few weeks. I didn't know about your, ah . . . wedding," he said carefully.

For years, she and Rafe had gone through periods of intense texting to very little texting, depending on what was going on in their lives. Over the last few months, Hallie had been caught up with wedding planning. Rafe had been caught up with school and some project in Chicago. She glanced at him sidelong. "Did I tell you?"

"You told me. And included some very vivid imagery." He smiled and squeezed her arm affectionately. "I'm sorry, Hallie. That really sucks."

Hallie closed her eyes. He had no idea. "Thanks," she whispered. "Then what happened? How'd we end up in my room?"

"Let's see. I suggested maybe you ought to go to bed, and you decided that was a good idea, because the fight had gone out of you. Unfortunately, no one was home, and I couldn't trust you not to stab yourself in the eye, so I hung out for a little bit."

"You mean you saved me. Again."

"I don't mean that at all. I did what any friend would do. Especially if their friend was drunk out of her mind stumbling around in a wedding dress."

"*Reception* dress. But you know what I mean, Rafe. You're always there for me. Remember the time you pulled me out the bathroom window at Alexandra Ferguson's graduation party?"

He looked puzzled.

"You don't remember? I was sixteen and had that ridiculous crush on Jonathan Peavey."

"Oh, *that* time," Rafe said, nodding. He rearranged himself so that he was sitting beside her now, propped against the headboard of her bed; one leg stretched long, one foot on the floor. "I hate to say I told you so—"

"Really? You hate to say it? Because you said it like a thousand times, as I recall—"

"Well, come on, Hallie, *everyone* knew he was gay. That is, everyone but you."

"It's not like he wore a shirt that said 'I'm gay.' I made the biggest fool of myself that night," Hallie said. "There was no way I could have walked through that party with my head up after I tried to kiss him in front of everyone and he almost fainted with terror. You saved me from even more humiliation, Rafe. You were there for me."

"Hallie. You were halfway out the bathroom

window when I found you. I just helped you land on your feet instead of your head."

"And what about that time in middle school, when Melissa Rodriguez took her parents' car without permission and we were going to go on a joyride? You told her if she didn't get out of here, you'd jujitsu her butt back home. I was *so* mad at you."

"I don't believe it was jujitsu," he said. "I think I threatened tae kwon do. She was thirteen. So were you. You had no business being in that car."

"Well, I know that *now*," Hallie said. "The point is, you saved me then, too, because Melissa ended up backing that car into a light pole. If I'd been in that car, my mother would have killed me."

"Okay, I helped you out a couple of times. It's no big thing."

"It is." She eased herself up to sit beside him, propped against her headboard. She glanced down at her reception dress. "You were also there for me when I found out my dad died. Remember?"

Rafe took her hand in his. "I definitely remember."

The day her dad dropped dead, Hallie had been in Houston. Nick called her and told her he was on his way to pick her up. All he would say was that something had happened to Dad. He didn't have to say more—Hallie just knew. She'd tried

21

to get hold of Chris, but he was in surgery, could not be reached. For some reason, Hallie had called Rafe's cell. He'd been in Chicago, but he answered immediately, and he stayed on the phone with her until she could collect herself and gather her things.

After a long moment, he let go of her hand and rubbed his palms on his jeans. "So it's really over with you and the doc, huh?"

An image of Chris's handsome face danced in Hallie's mind. His pale blue eyes. His golden hair, streaked by the sun after days spent on the open waters of the Gulf of Mexico in his enormous boat. His naked body on top of Dani's naked body, who, if memory served, was still wearing her stupid stilettos. "Oh yeah, it's over," she said, willing the image away. "He keeps calling and texting, but for me, it's dead and buried. Beaten and burned. Hacked and—"

"I'm truly sorry, Hallie."

Her eyes welled. "Thanks, Rafe." It had been almost a month. She felt a lump of hardness in the pit of her stomach when she thought of Chris. She wasn't even sure if she missed him anymore. But she was beginning to despair of whether she would ever get over his betrayal. Over the utter humiliation of it. The terrible, soul-consuming feeling of realizing you'd been a colossal fool. Chris had destroyed the last little bit of faith in herself that she'd had. Hallie attempted to choke back a sob, but it sounded more like a honk.

"Okay," Rafe said, and patted her leg. "I'm going to go. Try and find something to eat to soak up all that gin."

"*Tequila,*" she murmured tearfully.

"*Ouch,*" he said, grimacing. "That *is* a mean hangover."

He stood up and walked out of her room, giving her a last, reassuring smile before disappearing into the hall.

Good ol' Rafe. He'd stayed all night with her. After all these years, he was still one of her best friends.

Her eyes felt heavy and her stomach felt queasy. She should get out of this stupid dress, but she didn't have the energy. She'd do it in a minute, she thought, as she drifted into the dead sleep of a hangover.

Chapter Two

As a boy, Rafe had learned to navigate the service stairs in the mansion at Three Rivers Ranch. Even though the Prince children were their friends, the Fontana children had never been welcome to go traipsing about the main house. That was the law, set by Mrs. Prince. She was not a mean woman, as his sister Angie had believed. On the contrary, Mrs. Prince had always been supportive of Rafe. But she had certain expectations of how things should be, and it was her expectation that her majordomo's children remained unseen by her and her friends.

The house seemed awfully quiet. It was just past seven, and he supposed people were still sleeping. But it seemed odd to him—work on a ranch started when the sun came up.

The mansion had always been at the nexus of a lot of activity beyond the workings of a modern ranch. It had seemed to him that people were constantly coming and going, and that at any given time, one could hear a loud argument or laughter.

In his youth, the Princes seemed to constantly entertain, throwing parties and events on the terrace—charity events, political fundraisers, anniversary parties, what have you. Sleek cars lined the long brick drive, and music of all types—country western, string quartets, jazz trios from New Orleans—would fill the night sky and drift downwind across the pastures and undeveloped ranch land.

Those parties had been legendary. Celebrities and high-placed politicians would put in appearances. The Texas registry of Who the Hell Was Who would fly in from around the state just for a good time. And come hunting season, forget it—the ranch had a hunting lodge, and it remained filled with men (mostly) and a lot of booze. Rafe knew this because one of his after-school jobs one year had been to drive out to the lodge and clean it up after a hunting party had come through. He could easily say that even after two tours of duty in Afghanistan, that job was one of the most disgusting.

But Rafe understood from his father that things had changed since the patriarch, Charlie Prince, dropped dead of a heart attack on the golf course a few months ago. His dad said the ranch was different now. Somber. Other than the funeral reception for Mr. Prince, there'd been only one event here since, and that one was put on by Luca for his conservation project.

His dad had also said that there were money problems. That seemed hard to believe—the house and grounds looked like they'd walked right out of a glossy magazine about the lifestyles of the rich and famous. Money had never been an issue for the Princes. But according to his dad, there were some big gambling debts. The family had been laying off staff, and his dad was worried.

Rafe slipped out a side door and into the cool morning mist. The air felt heavy—a norther was supposed to sweep through tonight. The morning sun was only a thin line of yellow on the horizon, hemmed in by a weak gray sky.

It wasn't the prettiest sunrise Rafe had ever seen, but this was the part of the day that he liked best. The peaceful moments when the day was still full of promise.

It was this quiet that he'd missed most about living at Three Rivers Ranch when he'd gone off to join the army. He'd missed summer nights under the stars with no sound but the distant call of a coyote, or a mother cow bellowing to her calf. Cool winter mornings that were so still one could hear the distant thrum of a truck on the highway several miles away. The world could be a very noisy place. Especially places like Afghanistan.

He'd been raised a mile from here, the two houses separated by a well-worn path through cactus and cedar and along a riverbank. His father, Martin Fontana, was afforded the use of the ranch-held property for his family as part of his compensation. The house was a modest three bedroom, two bath. Rafe and his younger brother Rico had shared a room and plastered the walls with posters of baseball and basketball idols. Angie, his kid sister, had the room next door to them, her walls painted bubblegum pink, and her bedspread ice blue. His mother was a stay-at-home mom, always puttering around the kitchen, attending every school function, and sewing patches on the knees of his jeans. Until he was thirteen. That was when his mother suffered through her first bout of cancer. She was so sick, none of them thought she'd make it. Rafe's dad was a great ranch manager, but he was a horrible caregiver, and the burden had fallen to Rafe. There wasn't much worse than seeing your mother sick and weak and helpless.

Rafe yawned as he walked down the side of the house. He'd slept very little through the night, too self-conscious and absolutely terrified of getting comfortable in Hallie's bed. So he'd read most of the night while she slept. When he and Hallie were kids, they'd shared a love of reading that the others didn't have. They'd liked to exchange books—Harry Potter, *The Lord of the Rings*, the Chronicles of Narnia, to name a few. Rafe still loved to read, although he didn't have as much time for it as he would have liked. Apparently, Hallie was still a voracious reader, because the bookshelf in her room was stuffed so full it was practically bowing at the seams.

He turned the corner of the house to walk down the brick path that led to the garages and, beyond that, the stables. As he passed the expanse of lawn on the west side, he saw Miss Dolly, the mother of the late Charlie Prince. He'd spotted her in town recently and had been surprised to see that she'd colored her silver hair a shade of blue he was going to have to classify as interesting. But today it was pink and blue, and from a distance, she looked like a county fair snow cone in her white sweats. She was in the company of two women and a gentleman, all of them probably fellow octogenarians, judging by the way they were bent at the shoulders. The four of them were silently and solemnly moving through a series of tai chi poses.

Rafe couldn't help but smile—he was a little proud of himself, to be honest, because he was the one who'd taught Miss Dolly tai chi a few years ago when he'd been home on leave. He was a martial arts fanatic—it was his juice. He loved practicing and teaching it.

Miss Dolly had come to see his mother, whom he'd been tending after another bout of cancer. Miss Dolly had complained about her balance and held on to the wall as she'd walked down the hall to his mother's bedroom. After a friendly discussion, she'd agreed to go to a tai chi class with him. After that class, she'd challenged him to design a training program for her. Well, Miss Dolly walked without needing a wall to hold on to now. His father said she was out here most mornings, going through the poses.

Rafe ducked behind a hedge so as not to disturb them, and emerged onto the drive in front of the multicar garage. The door behind which Hallie's Range Rover was parked was still open. He'd neglected to shut it last night after picking up her shoe and then dragging her inside. He walked over to the garage and pushed the button to close it.

"Hey, Rafe."

Rafe jerked around to see Hallie's older brother, Nick, standing a few feet away. "Dude, you startled me," Rafe said. "Where were you hiding?"

Nick grinned. "I wasn't hiding. I just came up from the shed," he said, gesturing with his chin to one of the nearby outbuildings.

Nick had dark brown hair like Luca, and when he smiled, his unusually dark blue eyes took on a sparkle. Rafe had always thought Nick looked like Mr. Prince, whereas the twins looked more like Mrs. Prince. "What are you doing here?" he asked, clapping Rafe genially on the shoulder.

"Home for the holidays," Rafe said. "I

promised Dad I'd stick around a few weeks. He says you're a little shorthanded around here."

"Yeah," Nick said, and his smile faded. "I'm sure Martin told you that my dad left us with some unexpected debt we're trying to dig out from under. We had to let some of the hands go." He winced. "Even Rick."

"Rick? No way." Rafe was shocked—Rick had cowboyed at Three Rivers Ranch longer than he or Nick had been alive. No wonder his dad was so worried.

"He offered to go," Nick clarified. "He said he could see the handwriting on the wall. He was looking at retirement anyway. He was seventy-four."

Rick, long and lanky, with a face like creased leather after a life spent outdoors, had taught Nick and Rafe how to ride and cut cattle back when they'd been strapping teens and free labor. There was no such thing as a cowboy school around here—you learned it on the job. At Three Rivers, you learned it from the best. "I am really sorry to hear it," Rafe said genuinely.

"Last I saw him, he was heading up to Colorado to fish. Hey, you need a job?" Nick asked, smiling again. "I can hook you up. Pay sucks, but there's work."

Rafe laughed. "I'm good, thanks. I told Dad I'd help out until the end of the year. I've got one more final, and then I'll have my degree, and then I'm out of here."

"Dude," Nick said with a shake of his head. "I can't believe you're getting a degree in social work. Who would have guessed it?"

Rafe thought Nick might have guessed it if he'd thought about it. Rafe's longest part-time job in high school had been working with underprivileged kids. And then, in the army, he'd been lucky enough to meet a couple of like-minded buddies who were also into martial arts. Buddies who, like him, had watched more young adults wash out of the army than should have. It seemed like so many of the young guys coming into the service were ill prepared. They'd been brought up on video games. Rafe and his best friends Jason and Chaco wanted to give back. They wanted to start a program for underprivileged kids, to give them alternatives to gangs, to drugs, to poor choices in general. To make them strong.

"I always thought you'd go into martial arts," Nick said. "I still have a headache from that kick to the teeth you gave me," he said, rubbing his jaw. "Hurt like hell."

"I don't remember why I kicked you, but I'm sure you deserved it," Rafe said with a grin. "And I am going into martial arts. But with a degree."

"Chicago, right?" Nick asked.

Rafe nodded. Their plan was to open a gym on

the south side of Chicago. They'd consulted with one of Rafe's professors and designed a program that would teach boxing and martial arts. They would partner with organizations to provide life-skills training. Rafe was a firm believer in the practice of martial arts, and he credited it with keeping him away from bad influences when he was a teen. His younger brother, Rico, had not been so lucky. Rico had run with the wrong crowd and had worked for a time as a petty thug. He'd matured out of that scene, but was left with what had all the markings of a lifelong battle with alcoholism if he didn't get it together.

Rafe's buddy Jason Corona was from Chicago. His dad was some muckety-muck in construction there, and he and Jason had secured grant funding from the city's parks and recreation department to get their program up and running. Jason, Rafe, and Chaco Jones, the third Army Ranger, were all putting in their savings to renovate an old office space that Jason and his dad had found. Rafe had lived lean the last few years and had saved everything he'd made from the army, and then, after he retired from the service, he'd saved what he'd made from his work at an organization for the intellectually and developmentally disabled. The GI Bill had paid for his schooling. When it was all said and done, the three of them managed to scrape together what they needed to get started. But it was apparent to Rafe that fundraising would have to be a top priority for them, and that was not something any of them had any experience with.

"That's awesome, Rafe," Nick said. "I have to admit, I'm a little envious that you're leaving the ranch to pursue something you like. This place can turn into a millstone around your neck if you're not careful," he said, and smiled as if that were a joke. But Rafe knew it wasn't. "I'd like to see more of the world than this seventy thousand acres, but it's not looking good," Nick added with a rueful smile.

Nick had wanted to be a pilot since they were kids. The ranch had a private airstrip for Nick's two private planes. Well, one now. Rafe's dad said Nick had sold one recently.

Nick glanced down at Rafe's clothes. He still had on the jeans he'd worn to herd those cows back through the fence. They were dirty, and his shirt was rumpled from where Hallie had been sleeping on him. "What did you say you were doing here so early?"

"Oh," Rafe said, and jerked a thumb over his shoulder. "I thought I'd check in on Hallie." It was a small lie, but a necessary one.

"Why?" Nick said.

"Last night, Dad and I rode out to round up the Creedy cows—"

"They got out again?" Nick asked, and sighed wearily.

"Yep. When I came back, your sister was trying to get in her car. I say 'trying' because she'd been at the bottle and had in mind she was going to drive to Houston."

"*What?*" Nick looked confused. "Hallie doesn't drink," he said, as if Rafe were very wrong about this, as if Rafe had completely misunderstood.

Rafe shrugged. "She did last night."

Nick groaned heavenward. "She's been a wreck since her engagement was called off. She was totally in love with that asshole." He paused a moment. "I guess you heard about that."

"I hadn't until last night." But then he'd heard about it, all right. Hallie announced that she'd walked in on her doctor fiancé pumping away into one of her bridesmaids. She told him that the doctor had begged her not to call it off, apparently sans pants and with his limp penis on display.

Admittedly, Hallie's recounting of it was half sloppy drunk and half jilted bride, but Rafe gathered that the doctor had tried to convince Hallie that his infidelity was a one-off, that he'd been stressed, that she'd been away at the ranch for long periods of time, and what was he supposed to do? It was a dick move for the guy to try to tie his cheating to Hallie's absence in some way. Rafe had never even laid eyes on this man and hated him.

"She'll be all right," Nick said. "Hey, we should grab a beer and catch up."

34

"That would be great," Rafe said.

"I'll call you." Nick clapped his shoulder again, and then walked on.

Rafe watched him disappear into the shaded path to the house before turning toward the stables, where he'd left his truck.

He and Nick used to be close, but they'd drifted apart when Rafe joined the army, and Rafe hadn't felt the need to repeat everything Hallie said last night. He recalled her pretty face, red and splotchy from all her crying. "I'm going to Houston right now, and I'm going to tell him how he's ruined my life while it's all clear in my mind," she'd said, jabbing a finger into her temple, in case Rafe was uncertain where her mind was.

He'd had to put his hand on her elbow to steady her. "I don't think anything is clear to you right now," he'd said. "Why don't we get something to eat? You'll need all your energy to tell him off, right?"

"You don't get it, Rafe!" Hallie had shouted angrily, and grabbed his shirt with both fists, shaking him. *Luca is getting married before me! Luca!*

Rafe had not understood the significance of that. "Okay," he'd said cautiously, holding his arms wide, because he'd had no idea which way she was going to sway next. "How about that sandwich?"

"No," she'd shouted, and shoved him hard, stumbling backward when she did, then swaying toward him again. "What kind of sandwich? Not peanut butter."

"Ham?"

She'd glared at him as if she'd suspected some sort of trickery. "Okay," she'd said at last, and pointed at him. "But *then* I'm going to Houston."

"Got it." He'd steered her inside—no small feat given her shoe situation and her general inability to navigate at that point—and poured her into one of the high-backed chairs at the kitchen island with the gleaming marble top. He'd called out to her mother twice before Hallie told him to stop yelling. "She's not here. No one is here. They are all out living their fabulous lives while mine is *crumbling.*" And then she'd put her head down on the bar.

She'd continued to mumble while Rafe opened the fridge and rummaged around until he found some turkey. He'd made her a sandwich, one guaranteed to soak up some of the alcohol, but he'd ended up eating that sandwich, because by the time he'd finished making it, Hallie was melting off the barstool, dissolving into tears.

So he'd picked her up in one arm, had the sandwich in the other hand, and he'd taken her up to her room and laid her on her bed. He'd put the sandwich on the nightstand beside her. He'd turned to leave, but her hand had shot out and she'd gripped his thigh. "Don't go," she'd said, her hazel eyes pleading with him. "Please don't go."

Rafe had stood there, his pulse ratcheting up. He'd stared at her hand on his thigh. He shouldn't have been there in her room, and yet, he hadn't had the heart to leave her like that. "You know I can't stay here with you, Hallie."

"I don't want to be alone right now," she'd pleaded with him. "I think too much when I'm alone. Look what happens when I think too much," she'd said, waving a hand at herself.

He'd studied her a moment. "You raise a valid point," he'd agreed. And he'd stayed.

Rafe reached his truck, got in the driver's seat, and started the engine. But he didn't drive on— he stared into space, thinking about last night. Thinking about how he'd sat up in bed beside her, and she'd snuggled in next to him like he was a stuffed animal. It was nothing. They were friends. They'd been friends a very long time.

But also, they were *not* friends.

Frankly, it had been very uncomfortable for Rafe, but only for him, because he hadn't known what to do. He didn't like that feeling. He *always* knew what to do. Until it came to Hallie, and in that respect, he was always going blind. She was passed out on him, her head on his chest, her strawberry blond hair spilling over his arm, a tear or two still leaking from her eyes as she slept off her drunk.

For years, it had been like this with the two of them. Hallie turning to him for help.

And him quietly, privately, and desperately in love with her.

Chapter Three

"What in the Sam Hill are you still doing in bed, Hallie?"

Hallie forced her eyes open and met her grandmother's blue-eyed gaze through the frames of her red and purple eyeglasses. Those glasses were a little jarring next to the pink and blue hair. "Grandma, I told you—one color at a time," Hallie croaked.

"It's almost eleven, girl! You need to get *up*. And what are you doing in that dress?"

Hallie blinked the sleep from her eyes. Her grandmother was wearing a T-shirt that said "Make love, not war." Also jarring. "It's a long story," she said, and managed to push up to sitting.

"Dolly!"

Hallie froze. That bellowing voice belonged to her mother.

"Oh boy, here we go," Grandma muttered.

A moment later, Hallie's mother appeared at the threshold of her room, wearing a pinched expression that clearly telegraphed her displeasure with something.

Cordelia Applewhite Prince presented a stark contrast to Hallie's grandmother. She had collar-length blond hair that she wore slicked back in a very stylish manner. She wore slim capris that showcased her very trim ankles, and a crisp white shirt tucked artfully into only one side of her capris. It was supposed to be a casual sort of look, but on her mother, it looked like she'd been done up by fashion editors.

Her mother looked at Hallie, then at her grandmother. Then at Hallie again. "Why are you still in bed, and *why* are you sleeping in your wedding dress?"

"It's not my wedding dress, it's one of the *reception* dresses, obviously," Hallie protested.

"You smell like whiskey," Grandma offered. "Not that I'm judging. I like a two-finger pour now and again."

"I smell like tequila," Hallie corrected her as she rubbed her eyes. They felt so *sticky*. Oh, right—she still had on makeup.

"I don't understand," her mother said, and walked into her room, tripping over something on the floor and quickly righting herself. She gracefully folded her arms over her middle and glared at Hallie.

Hallie wondered briefly what she'd done in a previous life to deserve this family at this moment. "There's nothing to understand, Mother, other than I accidentally drank too much."

"I didn't think you drank at all," her mother said. "And certainly not in formal wear."

"Well, Mom, what *is* the appropriate attire for tying one on?" Hallie asked weakly. "I *don't* drink. Hence the bed," she said, gesturing around her. "Hence the massive headache," she added, pointing to her head.

Her mother frowned. And then she turned her attention to Hallie's grandmother. "Dolly? May I please ask what is the meaning of the two potted cedars that you forced Martin to drag up to the family cemetery?"

"You may," Hallie's grandmother said graciously. "After Thanksgiving, I'm going to decorate them for Christmas."

Hallie's mother gasped loudly. "Over my dead body."

"People decorate roadside cedars all the time," Grandma responded.

"My husband's grave is not a roadside attraction."

"Well, my *son's* grave is," Grandma countered.

"Guys? My head is throbbing," Hallie reminded them.

They were talking about a grave in a small family cemetery, a short walk up the hill from the house, where generations of Princes had been buried on a grassy little mesa beneath a copse of live oak and pecan trees competing for space. For reasons no one understood, Hallie's mother had taken to going up there after they'd buried the ashes of Hallie's father earlier this year. She sat next to his grave for long periods and talked to him, as if he were sitting right there. She'd gone up there so often that she'd installed a couple of lawn chairs, a patio umbrella, and an old cooler that Martin kept stocked with water and wine coolers. It was bizarre, especially because Hallie's parents had been separated at the time of his passing.

It was even more bizarre now that Grandma was tagging along and making it a really weird threesome.

"I will not allow it, Dolly!" her mother said, her voice rising with indignation.

"Who made you queen of Christmas?" Hallie's grandmother snapped.

"Not the queen of *Christmas,* the queen of the cemetery!" her mother declared, and, as far as Hallie could tell, was quite serious.

"Could you please stop arguing?" Hallie put her hands to her ears.

"What's going on in here?"

Well, call the drum major, because the marching band was assembled in her room. Hallie's twin, Luca, sauntered in like the sheriff at the OK Corral arriving to break up a bar fight. He paused, wrinkled his nose, and looked around. "What's that smell?" When no one answered him, he looked at Hallie and asked, "Why do you look like that?"

Hallie loved her twin more than most anyone, but sometimes he could be a little obtuse. "Why do you think?" she asked darkly.

He studied her. Then he shook his head. "I don't . . . I'm not getting it."

"She's hungover, Lucas," Hallie's grandmother said with great exasperation. She had long insisted on calling him Lucas, despite that not being his name. She liked the name Lucas better, she said, but they all knew that the only reason she called him that was to annoy Hallie's mother, who had never gotten over a cousin naming her baby Lucas a month or two before Hallie and Luca were born.

"Hungover?" Luca snorted. "Hallie doesn't drink."

"But I did, and now I look and apparently smell like this," Hallie said. "So now that we've established what is wrong with me, could everyone please leave and let me die in peace?"

"It's not the Prince way to let people die in peace," Grandma said matter-of-factly.

"I'm worried about you, Hallie," her mother said. "This drinking is troublesome."

Hallie's indignation came out half bark, half laugh. "Are you kidding me right now, Mom? I drink too much *one* night, and you're going to lecture me when we all know your happy hour generally starts at noon?"

"That is a gross exaggeration," her mother said defensively.

"Mom, give her a break," Luca said. "She's going through some stuff."

"If you ask me, Christopher Davenport is just winning this thing left and right," Grandma offered, referring to Hallie's ex-fiancé. "If Hallie drinks herself near to death in her wedding gown, that bastard is winning."

"I'm not . . . it's not—why are you all in my room right now?" Hallie cried.

Not one person moved.

There was no getting through to these people. "I think I'm going to be sick," she announced. Still, no one moved. So she gave them a couple of good preludes to a full-blown dry heave.

"Oh no," her grandmother said, and hurried to the door, pushing Hallie's mother out before her. "Luca, get her a bowl or something. Let us know if you need anything, sweetie!"

"I'm going to heat up some soup for you!" Hallie's mother said as she hurried out with Grandma.

Luca looked at Hallie. She looked at him. His eyes narrowed. She made an exaggerated gagging sound. "Yeah, okay," he said, throwing up a hand. "I know when I'm not wanted." He walked out.

When they'd gone, Hallie rolled over to the edge of her bed. Something thudded to the floor, and when she leaned over to see what, she spotted the book *Sideways*. She'd read the book a long time ago. Rafe must have taken it down to read last night. She leaned over and picked it up and laid it on the bed. Then she gingerly moved her legs over the side and stood up, testing her stability. Okay, she could stand without the room spinning.

That's when she realized she was standing on something soft and looked down again—this time, she spotted a pair of leather work gloves peeking out from beneath her toes. She moved one foot and stared down at them. They weren't hers—those gloves were very large and well-worn. She picked them up and put them on top of the book. And then she slowly, carefully, made her way into the bathroom and ran a hot bath.

An hour later, Hallie emerged, feeling much better and suddenly ravenous. She pulled on a pair of yoga pants and a cashmere hoodie over a T-shirt, and piled her hair on top of her head in a loose bun.

She went downstairs to the kitchen, where, much to her unmitigated vexation, she found her entire family assembled for Sunday lunch. The only person missing was Ella, Luca's fiancée. Even Nick had come out of the woodwork and was at the kitchen island with Luca, munching on a sandwich and drinking a beer. Her grandmother and mother were seated in the upholstered chairs near the fireplace.

"Wow," Nick said as Hallie walked in. She tried to skirt past him, but he caught her in a bear hug. "You're so *pale*."

"Shut up," she said, but she was smiling when she pushed him away. She looked at Luca. "Where's Ella?"

"Work. Jesus, Hallie," Luca said as he looked her up and down. "Are you, like, *okay?*"

Hallie sighed heavenward. This family made having a personal crisis impossible. "I'm fine," she said with a flick of her wrist. "This is all much ado about nothing. It so happens that I discovered, in the worst way, that the thing with tequila is you don't know you're getting drunk until you're completely blotto." She opened the fridge and examined the contents, hoping for a cheeseburger to magically appear. When none did, she pushed aside a head of lettuce and discovered a pie dish containing a half-eaten quiche. She pulled it out, grabbed a plate, and cut a piece of it to warm.

"So, hey, while we're all gathered, I have some news," Luca said.

Hallie stuck her dish in the microwave and prayed to the wedding gods that he would not reveal some new detail about his wedding next spring. *We're releasing biosustainable balloons!*

"Ella and I have successfully integrated some prairie chickens near the spring behind her house." He followed his announcement with a proud smile, and looked from one family member to the next.

"Some what?" Nick asked when Luca's gaze settled on him.

"Prairie chickens," Luca said, still beaming. "They're all but extinct, you know. But we've got a flock of them thriving at Blue Dove."

Blue Dove was the name Luca had given his conservation and ecological restoration project, named after some Indian petroglyphs they'd found on a cave wall near the spring. Luca had worked tirelessly to secure funding for the project, and last month, they'd started clearing invasive, nonnative plant species from the two thousand acres that would make up his natural-state paradise.

"That *is* good news," his mother said. "Now I know what to serve for Thanksgiving."

"You're hilarious, Mom," Luca said.

"Speaking of Thanksgiving, it's in a couple of weeks," Hallie's mother continued. "Chet and his family are coming," she said, referring to her brother. "That means your cousins. Hallie, honey? Will you be able pull yourself together before I plan a big day?"

The microwave dinged. "What's that supposed to mean?" Hallie asked.

"Just that you've been moping around, and I'd like to know you won't be mopey Thanksgiving Day while we have guests."

47

Hallie glared at her mother, uncertain if that beating in her chest was indignation or rage. Did her mother really think a light switch drove her grief?

"I'm just asking," her mother said.

"Mother, I swear—"

"Leave the poor girl alone, Delia," her grandmother interrupted, and tossed aside her magazine. "Worry about my cemetery Christmas trees."

"Hallie," Nick said. "You know what you should do? Get out of the house. See a movie, go shopping. But stop wandering around here with nothing to do but think."

Hallie yanked open the door of the microwave. "I'm so glad everyone feels free to tell me what I need to do. No one ever tells *you* what to do, Nick."

"I'm just saying," Nick said. "Don't you *want* to get out of the house?" he asked, and shot a meaningful look in the direction of their mother and grandmother.

"Yes, she does," her mother piped in. "Because if she doesn't get out of the house, she can help me chop down some unauthorized Christmas trees."

"Oh, for heaven's sake, Delia!" Hallie's grandmother said with much exasperation. "If you don't want them up there, I'll help you move them."

"By 'help,' do you mean instruct me from your chair?"

"Well, why would I change the way we've learned to coexist after all these years? But I'll bring the wine coolers. Speaking of wine coolers," she said, and stood up. "I'm going to Walmart." Grandma walked out of the kitchen.

Hallie was fuming. It only had been a little over a month since she had walked in on Chris's ass riding high in the air. She was furious that her family thought they had the right to impose an arbitrary time limit on mourning the end of her engagement and the plan she'd made for the rest of her life. It was all "pull yourself up by the bootstraps" around here, and never "you deserve all the cake." Not one of them seemed to realize that it wasn't just the gross humiliation of it all, but that everything she'd thought she'd be doing from now to eternity had flittered away, too. She didn't know what she was supposed to do with herself. It wasn't like she had a job. She'd never even really had a job. Not a *real* job, like a career.

Hallie sliced off some quiche and slapped it onto a plate, then slid onto a barstool next to Nick. "Are *you* on my side?" she murmured.

"Always," he said. "But this is not the place to host the meltdowns, if you know what I'm saying."

She knew what he was saying, but where was she supposed to go? She'd sold her condo in

Houston in anticipation of being married. She *had* no other place to go. She had nothing to fall back on. She had no real skills other than asking rich friends to donate money to worthy causes.

"Wanna come see the wild chickens?" Luca asked, sliding his arm around her shoulders.

"No, " Hallie said firmly.

"I'll bite," Nick said. "Let's go have a look."

"Fantastic," Luca said, and looked like a kid who'd just gotten what he wanted for Christmas. He stood up, took his plate around to the sink. "You're going to love this, Nick."

"Don't oversell it," Nick said with a grin, and slid his plate across to Luca as he stood. Hallie's brothers walked out of the kitchen together and left Hallie alone with her mother.

She didn't dare look in her mother's direction, because if she made eye contact, there'd be a conversation. She would rather gouge her eyes out than have another conversation. *Don't look. Don't look. Don't look.*

She looked.

She couldn't help herself—the silence was more than she could bear, and in a moment of weakness, Hallie shot her mother a sidelong glance.

Her mother was clearly waiting for her moment to pounce and said immediately, "Did you think I'd disappear if you didn't acknowledge me?"

Hallie groaned. She could kick herself. "Mom?

Can we please not do this again today?" she asked sincerely. "You've made it very clear how you feel."

Her mother rose gracefully from her chair and walked to the sink. She turned on the faucet and ran water over Nick and Luca's plates. She turned the water off, braced her hands against the edge of the countertop, and leaned slightly forward, studying Hallie. "How I *feel* is that my daughter is disintegrating before my eyes. Two days ago, I found you in that chair eating half of a blueberry pie. The day before that, I finally convinced you to take off the sweats you'd worn for a week. I put them in the burn pile."

"What? I love those sweats!"

"I'm particularly grateful you decided to bless us all with a bath after last night—"

Hallie threw up a hand before her mother could say more. "Look, I know you care, I do, but I've been through a *really* rough patch, and it's not like I want to be depressed, you know? I can't help it. I don't expect you to understand."

"Oh, I understand better than you can know," her mother said.

Hallie laughed bitterly. "No, you don't."

"You don't think so? You know your father's history."

"Mother," Hallie said firmly, and put down her fork. She didn't want to hear again about her father's infidelity. Seeing Chris's was bad

51

enough. She didn't want to be coaxed into hating her dad, too. "Please don't review all the marital woes you had with Dad, okay? It's hard enough to deal with him being gone, much less knowing every horrible thing he ever did. Anyway, Chris isn't Dad."

Her mother winced, as if she found that remark painful. "Except that he is, Hallie, he's exactly like your father was, and if there is anyone who understands, it's me. That's what I am trying to tell you. And I know that the best remedy for a shattered heart, the best *revenge* for a shattered heart, is to live well. Do you think Christopher is happy right now? I can promise you he's not. I can promise you he is kicking himself."

Hallie snorted. He was probably fucking Dani right now, and probably all of Houston knew it. Hallie had discovered that Dani was a very vocal lover. She'd never heard such cries of ecstasy.

"And you know what is going to make him even more unhappy? If he knows that you have moved on, and are living your best life. He would cut his wrists."

"Mom!"

"But the problem is, you're *not* living your best life. You're letting that man eat away at you. You've taken up drinking—"

"It was *one* night—"

"And you're crying to whoever will listen to your sad tale—"

"I am not! I don't *see* anyone, because I don't dare go to town and face all the hideous expressions of pity!" Hallie shot back. "I am entitled to be depressed! I have earned this right. Has it occurred to you that maybe what is wrong with me is bigger than Chris? That maybe I am so depressed because everything I touch turns to shit?" She was very angry now, and shoved her plate across the kitchen bar and stood up, intending to storm from the room as she had done so often in the last few weeks, even though the storming never brought her any satisfaction. Nothing did.

"You were engaged to a man who treated you horribly, and you're in shock, honey. That's all this is."

"Oh, really?" Hallie asked with a snideness she generally could not summon. Her mother drove her crazy, and had for thirty years—but Hallie loved her mother. It was just that in the last few weeks, her mother had become so unbearable, always looking in on her, always trying to offer some pithy bit of advice. "You know what's *really* hard? To take advice from you, a woman who sits by her husband's grave for hours on end. You're not living so well, either, are you, Mom?"

Her mother's mouth twitched. She looked almost hurt by that remark, and Hallie almost apologized for it. "I'll clean that up later," she muttered, gesturing to her plate, and turned to walk out of the kitchen.

"My God, you are determined to be miserable, aren't you?" her mother said sharply. "You've always been so happy, Hallie. The happiest of all my children, finding joy in the world wherever you went!"

"Nope. Not true!" Hallie shot back.

"And now you *look* for misery!"

She *looked* for misery? Was that true? Hallie had to pause to think about it—it seemed to her that misery was the one seeking her. When was the last time she'd felt truly happy?

"I'm sorry, honey, I didn't mean that," her mother said quickly. "Look, if you won't talk to me, will you at least find someone you can talk to?" her mother asked, her voice softer and plaintive.

Hallie didn't answer. She was never going to talk about it, not to her mother, not to anyone. She didn't need to talk about it because she'd obsessed over it for weeks and she'd come to the conclusion that what had happened with Christopher Davenport was just another chapter in the story of her life. Every time she put her mind to something—ballet, college, marrying well, being a society wife, whatever—it never ended like she thought it would. It never worked out. She didn't know what it was about her that turned everything into such an unmitigated disaster, but here she was, thirty years old, and she didn't know what the hell she was doing, she was living at home, and she had no earthly idea what was supposed to come next. What direction she was supposed to go? Who was she supposed to *be?* How did she get out of this cycle of always falling back on her family or a man instead of making her own way? She had never lived truly on her own. There was the summer she'd gone to Dallas and interned at a charitable foundation. But she'd stayed with her cousin in the Preston Hollow neighborhood, which had included maid service and a family chef, and the work at the foundation had been hard with very little thanks, and in the end, the foundation couldn't afford to keep her on full-time. So she'd come home. Again.

Hallie went back to her room, closed the door behind her, and looked around.

It *did* smell in there.

Hallie pushed Rafe's gloves and the book aside, and lay down on her bed. *This is ridiculous. Get a grip.*

But grip what, exactly?

Hallie picked up her phone. She did feel a little like talking to someone. Not to family—they were too close to her, and wanted too desperately for her to get over her hurt. She called Charlotte. Charlotte was the office manager at the Saddlebush Land and Cattle Company, the primary Prince holding. Hallie and Charlotte were friends. But the call to Charlotte rolled to voice mail.

Hallie put the phone down and shifted, and when she did, her fingers brushed against Rafe's gloves.

Rafe. Now there was a good listener. He'd listened to her whine about any number of things through the years.

She sat up and found her shoes. When she had them on, she picked up his gloves and the book and went outside. There was a slight chill in the air, and in the north, she could see the gray hue on the horizon, the slow creep of clouds toward the ranch.

She started walking. Past the brick patio strung with small white lights, edged by a bar on one end, a dining area on the other. Past the zero-edge pool, and the rose garden and the maze her father installed when she was seven. Past the garage, the paddock, the stables.

She went out an iron gate and into a pasture, walked a quarter of a mile, and skirted around the hangar and the edge of the airstrip Nick used for his plane. She took that path down to the river, then up again, walking through cactus and cedar and wild lantana.

She knew this path so well she could traverse it blindfolded.

Roughly a mile from her house, she ended up in front of the Fontana house.

How long had it been since she was here? A very long time. Years, maybe. She couldn't remember any longer why she and Nick and Luca had stopped walking down here on summer days. Probably had to do with being teenagers with friends and interests that took them away from the ranch. Or the fact that Mrs. Fontana was sick a lot of the time.

She owed Rafe a big thank-you for saving her last night. Who knew? Maybe the two of them could hang out. They hadn't done that in a while, not since she'd been engaged to the lagoon creature from Houston.

Maybe they could talk about books. Or life. Maybe both. She needed to get out of her own head for at least a little while.

She walked up to the door and knocked. The moment she did, her pulse ratcheted up, and she began to second-guess what the hell she was doing. Why would Rafe want to hang out with her? Like he needed her woebegone life messing with his.

The door suddenly swung open, and two little girls with big brown eyes stared up at her. A woman with short, dark curly hair stood behind them. She was pretty and a few years younger than Hallie.

Hallie suddenly smiled. "*Hola*, Angie," she

said with a salute. "I haven't seen you in ages! How are you?"

Angie, Rafe's little sister, stared at Hallie as if she couldn't quite place her.

"Oh. Don't you remember me? I'm—"

"Hallie?" Angie said with great surprise. She stepped halfway out the door and looked down the drive, as if she thought more people were coming. "Is something wrong?"

"No! I just . . . it's just me. I was hoping to catch Rafe at home. Is he here?"

Before Angie could answer, Mrs. Fontana crowded into the open door. "Hallie!" she said, smiling, and spread her arms wide. She was thinner than the last time Hallie had seen her, and her skin had a sallow tint to it. Her hair was much grayer, too. "Come in, come in! Girls, move out of the way and let Miss Hallie inside."

"I hope I'm not interrupting," Hallie said, and stepped into Mrs. Fontana's thin embrace. But she gave Hallie a surprisingly tight squeeze. "Is Rafe here?" she asked when Mrs. Fontana let her go.

"Yes, he's here," Mrs. Fontana said, and put her arm around Hallie's shoulders, pulling her inside. "You're a sight for sore eyes, Hallie. It's so good to see you. Come in."

Chapter Four

The afternoon had started off like so many other Sunday afternoons at the Fontana residence. Rafe's dad was watching football. His mother was making a stew for dinner. Angie had brought her three young children, all under the age of six—Isabella, Abigail, and the toddler, Silas.

Rafe, who had been studying, was on the floor with the kids, wrestling a wildly laughing Silas, and taking turns lifting the girls up on his feet. He loved the kids, and when he was around them, their pure view of the world made him want his own kids in a way that sank talons into his core.

Two people were missing from the family tableau. Angie's husband, David, worked the oil fields, two weeks on, two weeks off. And, of course, Rico. But in fairness, Rico currently was in a last-ditch rehabilitation program to persuade him to adopt what they all hoped would be lifelong sobriety. Nevertheless, he was so often in their thoughts that it almost felt as if he were present. Particularly because Angie had arrived today with news about him. "He's getting out in three weeks. He'll be home for Christmas, Mom!"

"That is an answer to my prayers," Rafe's mother said, beaming with delight.

Rico had struggled with addiction most of his adult life. As every family with an alcoholic knew, addiction could bankrupt a family spiritually and financially. Rafe didn't know exactly what Rico had done that had prompted his father, who was notoriously tightfisted, to send him to a ninety-day program, but he knew that it was probably Rico's last shot on the family dime. He'd skated on the edge of real legal trouble for years—if he kept drinking, he'd end up dead or in jail.

"He's coming out clean and sober, and he swears he's going to make it work this time," Angie said as she opened a Tupperware container and spread some Cheerios onto the dining table for her children to nibble. "Come on, kids, before you destroy Uncle Rafe."

"He better make it work," Rafe's father muttered. "He's been given enough chances."

Martin Fontana loved his children, but he was not a man who suffered failings in them. Or back talk. Or silliness. Rico's program was just outside of Austin. Twice a month, no matter what, Rafe's parents went to visit him. No more, no less. Angie managed to get by at least once a month, but with three young children and a husband gone half the time, it was difficult for her. It was the same for

Rafe. Between school and flying back and forth to Chicago on weekends, he had very little time to drive up to see Rico.

Rafe loved his brother, and he wanted more than anything in this world for his brother to remain sober. But he wasn't as optimistic as the rest of his family that this time would be different. He'd known soldiers who'd turned to drugs and drinking, who never could shake the need to numb. Rico seemed to have the same obsessive need, as if he was numbing himself from the expectations his parents and life had put on him. Rafe felt compassion for his brother, but he'd never understood what it was his brother couldn't seem to face. They'd grown up in the same environment, under the same roof, with the same parents, had had the same education. They'd been taught the value of hard work.

And yet, Rafe could look back and see that even as a little kid, Rico had always wanted something more. Something different.

"What's he planning to do?" Rafe asked Angie as he got up and returned to his seat at the table.

"He's going to work for me," his father answered. "For free at first, but if he stays clean and works hard, I'll talk to Nick about the possibility of a part-time job. He can live at home and save some money. Who knows, maybe by then, Nick will have worked things out with the cash flow and Rico can stay on at Three Rivers.

And if he hasn't worked it out, well, we'll all be looking for a new place to go."

"What?" Rafe asked, surprised by his dad's declaration.

"I'm just saying that the money situation is bad up there at the main house, and Mrs. Prince, well, she's got ideas of things to cut we just can't do without. I keep butting heads with her. Maybe she thinks her majordomo could be cut, who knows? Nick could run that place wearing a blindfold."

"Stop butting heads," Rafe's mother scolded him. "What are we going to do if you get laid off? We live here rent free, and where are you going to get a job at sixty-two?"

Rafe's father sighed and rubbed his face. "I'm just saying, we need the help around this place, and Rico owes us that much. His family needs his help."

Rafe was fairly certain Rico would not be interested in a long-term position at Three Rivers. Rico needed to be in the middle of things, and Three Rivers Ranch was so vast and so removed from the middle of things as to be a whole other universe.

And was his dad really worried about being laid off?

"What do you think Rico ought to do, Rafe?" his mother asked.

Rafe never had to answer that question because they were interrupted by a knock at the door. The kids shrieked with excitement, and Angie went after them before they could answer the door and send anyone running.

At first, there was so much chatter that Rafe didn't hear who was at the door. But then he heard Angie say *Hallie,* and he'd been so startled that he'd gone blank for a moment, lurching to his feet and upsetting the salt and pepper shakers in his haste, as well as the stack of books and papers he was studying that afternoon. His clumsiness drew a look from his mother before she went off to greet Hallie.

And then Hallie was inside his house. Hallie Prince was standing by a paneled wall beneath the shrine his mother had created to her children, a collage of framed photos capturing the three of them in every conceivable activity from grade school all the way through high school.

Hallie couldn't get past that shrine because his nieces and nephew were blocking her path, staring up at her as if she were an exotic peacock.

She was carrying a book and something else in her hand. She looked much better than she had earlier today, but that wasn't saying much. She still seemed a little wan.

"Hi," she said, smiling at them all. "Remember me?"

Of course they remembered her—presumably not with the crystal clarity with which he remembered every little thing about her, but of *course* his family remembered the daughter of the famed Prince family.

It was so odd to see her in his parents' living room, with its Saltillo-tile floor and the big-box furniture-store set of two chairs and a complementing couch. It had been years since she'd been in this house. These days, it was odd to see her anywhere outside the rarefied air of the mansion at Three Rivers, which was swathed in marble and silk and hand-scraped hickory floors. Instead of a shrine to the Prince kids, valuable pieces of artwork hung on the walls.

"Hallie," his dad said, coming to his feet. "Well, this is a surprise." He did not sound like it was a happy surprise.

"Right?" she said cheerfully, because Hallie generally lived life undaunted. "I debated if I should knock on the door, but I was out getting some air, and I found these gloves, and I'm pretty sure they belong to Rafe." She held them up.

Angie stared curiously at the gloves. "Where'd you find them?"

"Umm . . . by the stables."

"Why do you think they are his?"

"Why?" Her cheeks turned slightly pinker. "I saw him there last night, and there they were this morning."

"The book, too?" Angie asked curiously, her brows dipping as if she were trying to work out a puzzle.

Rafe felt compelled to say something because his sister was too nosy by half, but before he could think of something innocuous, Hallie said, "Nope. This is just a book." She nervously tucked a bit of hair behind her ear.

"Can I see?" little Izzy asked.

Hallie handed the book to Izzy.

Rafe knew the book. He'd read half of it last night while Hallie slept beside him.

"Does it have pictures?" Izzy asked, opening it.

"Just words. So here's a fun fact—when your uncle and I were a little bit older than you, we used to trade books to read. I thought he'd like this one."

"Which uncle?" Izzy asked, her brows dipping into a *V*. "I have two. I have Uncle Rico and Uncle Rafe."

"Uncle Rafe."

Izzy eyed Rafe with suspicion, looked at the book, and wrinkled her nose, probably because there were no pictures. She pushed it back toward Hallie.

"I think the concept of sharing books is a little foreign to them," Rafe said.

"Sharing anything," Angie agreed. "Well, Rafe? *Are* those your gloves?" She fixed her dark-eyed gaze on him, as if she expected to catch him in some sort of coded, nefarious exchange with Hallie.

Or maybe he was reading too much into this.

He wasn't the type of guy to wear his feelings on his sleeve, but he felt like his were displayed in flashing neon lights right now. "They look like mine. I didn't realize I'd lost them." He walked around the end of the table and held out his hand for them. "Thanks," he said to Hallie.

She smiled and dropped them into his hand.

He turned around, ostensibly to put the gloves on the table, but really so that he could give Angie a warning look before she started grilling Hallie.

"Something smells so good," Hallie said brightly.

"Mexican beef stew," his mother replied. "An old family recipe."

"Well it smells delicious," Hallie said. She looked around, her gaze landing on Rafe's dad. "Cowboys game, huh?"

"Ah . . . yeah," he said, and exchanged a glance of uncertainty with Rafe's mom.

His parents didn't know what to do with Hallie Prince. None of them did. That was always the way with the Prince family. They were neighbors, they were playmates. But the Fontanas never forgot that they were first and foremost the employees.

Rafe was stumped by her appearance here, too. Why would she walk down here when she could leave those things in his dad's office at the mansion? In all the years Rafe had known Hallie, he'd never known her to take long walks by herself—she was deathly afraid of snakes.

"Can I offer you something to drink, Hallie?" his mother asked.

Rafe's pulse ticked up. Surely his mother wasn't going to ask Hallie to hang out. Surely he wouldn't have to sit here and make small talk, all the while pretending his stomach wasn't doing little loop-de-loops. Surely he wouldn't have to face the very real fact that he could be both an Army Ranger and a lovesick cowboy with a raging case of nerves. That was not exactly the image of himself he wanted living in his head.

"Oh no," she said. "I just meant to drop those things off and then, you know . . . carry on." She gave that a jaunty little fist pump.

Thank God.

But in the next breath, Hallie said, "But if you have some tea already made, I'd really appreciate it. I'm kind of parched."

No, no, no. You just said . . .

"I've always got tea," his mother said cheerfully, already moving toward the refrigerator. She limped now—she'd had a benign tumor removed from her liver, and inexplicably, the limp had developed.

"When my kids were at home, we probably went through a gallon of it every day. Sit down, Hallie, make yourself at home."

Don't sit. Don't sit. Don't—

67

"Thank you," she said, and glanced uncertainly at the dining room table.

"Here," Angie said, and pulled out a chair. "Ignore Rafe's mess."

Ignore Rafe. Please.

He slowly resumed his seat and began to stack his papers.

"Do you know my mom?" Izzy asked. She was a chip off the old block, just as suspicious as her mother of Hallie's unexpected call.

"I do. I haven't seen her in a long time, but we all grew up together on this ranch."

"You lived *here?*" Izzy asked, jamming her finger against the table.

"Another house," Hallie said. "But very close by."

"She lived in the mansion, Izzy," Angie said. "You know, the one behind the gates where Papá works."

Izzy stared at Hallie. "Are you a princess?"

"No," Angie said, perhaps a little too forcefully.

"Did you play with my mom?"

"Izzy," Angie said. "I didn't know Miss Hallie that well. She was a big kid when I was a little kid."

Hallie smiled at Angie. "You weren't quite old enough to explore the ranch with us. Remember, Rafe?"

"Ah . . . yes," he said. He remembered everything. Like the first time he'd felt pangs of love for her, although at the time he hadn't known that's what it was. He'd been what, twelve? Hallie had been ten or so. He and Nick and Luca and Rico had been playing on the saddle stands in the stables, pretending to ride. Hallie wanted on one of the saddle stands, too, but four rambunctious boys outnumbered her. He remembered her strawberry blond hair, long and braided, her cutoff jeans, and the white T-shirt she wore with a glittery picture of a cat. She'd tried to muscle her way onto one of the saddle stands, but they kept pushing her off, telling her to get lost. And then, suddenly—he still didn't know how she'd done it—she was on his saddle stand, and he was on the ground. She'd knocked him off with a strength that had surprised him, and jumped into the saddle. He'd fallen hard enough that the breath was knocked out of him, and as he'd tried to drag the air into his lungs, Hallie had leaned over the saddle stand, the tip of her braid swinging over his face.

"I *told* you to let me ride," she'd said, and then had laughed gaily, clearly quite pleased with her victory.

To this day, Rafe could recall how strange and fluttery he'd felt when he looked up at her pretty face looming over him, with the big hazel eyes and the freckled cheeks.

His mother returned with a glass of iced tea.

"Thank you so much," Hallie said, and sipped.

"I'm going to drink this and get out of your way. Just going to take a walk, you know." She waved her hand in the direction of the road and the Creedy property.

His mother nodded.

"Need some air in my lungs," Hallie added, and took another drink. "You know, clear my head, that sort of thing."

She sounded a little nutty. Since when did Hallie feel compelled to convince others of the benefits of walking?

She realized that no one else was talking, and looked at all of them, staring curiously at her. Okay, all right, someone needed to move her along, because this was getting too weird for Rafe. He shifted forward, prepared to ask her if she needed a ride, because he didn't buy the walking thing for a minute.

"I didn't know you were, like, a *walker*," Angie said, not unkindly, but as if she was curious about this sudden and apparently new side of Hallie. "I don't remember you doing anything but dancing. Weren't you a ballerina?"

Hallie blinked. "Well. I *was* a ballerina, but I'm not anymore. Except in my head." She laughed self-consciously. Then quickly sobered.

Izzy and Abigail looked at Angie. Angie stared at Hallie.

"And you're right," Hallie hastened to add, "I'm not really a walker. But I'm going to be. Actually,

I'm thinking of becoming a runner." She paused, swallowed another gulp of tea. "I guess you could say I'm all new leaves these days."

"What?" Angie asked.

"If you're going to walk, you'd better take a jacket," Rafe's father said. "There's a norther supposed to come in tonight."

Rafe glanced at Hallie, and they both tried to hide a smile. They used to joke about how obsessed their fathers were with the weather. Every day, the two of them began with a full accounting of all possible weather situations and then discussed it for what seemed like hours. *Might get a little rain. Maybe thirty percent chance. It's coming up from the Gulf, so you can count on some moisture.*

"Oh, hey!" Angie said as Hallie picked up a very curious Silas to sit in her lap. "I hear congratulations are in order! You must be so excited about your wedding, Hallie."

Hallie started. She put down the glass of tea with a dull thud onto the table.

"The big day is, what, New Year's Eve? Isn't that right?"

Jesus, Angie didn't know the wedding wasn't happening. Rafe inwardly groaned—he tried to think of something to say as both of his parents turned toward Hallie, clearly uncomfortable. He stood up, prepared to rescue her from this quagmire.

"Actually, no," Hallie said before he could find words, and began to rock side to side with Silas. "We've postponed the wedding." This she said to Silas.

Postponed. Interesting choice of words. Last night she'd wanted to drive to Houston and strangle her fiancé. Today her wedding was postponed?

"Oh. Sometime next year?" Angie asked.

"Angie, could you please help me in the kitchen?" his mother asked tightly.

Angie looked at her mother. Whatever she saw in her mother's expression was enough to move her, and she said, "Sure." She stood up and turned slightly, shooting a dark look at her father— presumably because he'd failed to enlighten her about what was going on at the ranch.

Silas wiggled out of Hallie's lap, and she watched him toddle after his mother.

"So Dad says Luca has quite the setup going on over by that old spring," Rafe blurted, trying desperately to change the subject. "Lots of bulldozing."

"Oh!" Hallie said, and sat up a little straighter. "Guess what? Luca has chickens."

"He's got what?" Rafe's dad asked.

"Chickens."

"Chickens? I don't understand," Rafe's mother said as she came back into the dining room with a bowl of chips. Angie was right behind her with salsa.

"I don't either," Hallie admitted. "All I know is that they are supposedly feral, and there used to be millions of them around here, but now they're almost extinct. So Luca has stepped in to save the day." She laughed. Then thought better of it. "I mean that sincerely. Sometimes what he does sounds a little crazy, but he's really making a difference."

Rafe's mother didn't seem to buy it, and looked at him quizzically, as if she hoped he would translate.

"It's part of his effort to return the land to its natural state," Rafe explained. "He wants to restore the wildlife that flourished here before land development."

"Hey, you know what, Rafe? We could ride out and see the chickens," Hallie suggested with enough enthusiasm to startle him. "I haven't been riding in a *long* time."

"I'd say about ten years," his father said.

Hallie laughed. "Has it really been that long? Even more reason to get back in the saddle, right? Remember how we all used to ride? We were all cowboys then. Even me."

"I remember," Rafe's dad said.

"So?" she said to Rafe. "Want to go look at some chickens?"

Rafe's mother and sister turned to look at him, Angie with that look of suspicion again.

Why did he feel so clammy all of a sudden?

"I'd love to, Hallie, but I've got to study for my last final," he said, gesturing to his stack of papers and smiling apologetically.

"Oh. Sure. I understand."

Dammit if she didn't look a little crestfallen, even while managing a weak smile for his sister. "You want to ride, Angie?" she asked.

Angie laughed and gestured to the three children clustered around her. "I don't think so."

"Rafe can go," his mother said. "He could use some air, too. He's had his nose in a book all day."

"I sat down an hour ago," Rafe said.

"You need some air," she said again, and gave him a pointed look. "You *do*."

"Oh no, that's okay," Hallie said with a wave of her hand. "I mean, I busted in here and interrupted everyone's day." She abruptly stood. "I'm going to go so Rafe can get back to studying."

"You didn't interrupt us, Hallie," his mother said firmly. "We're family."

Well, that was a stretch, and judging by the look on his father's face, he thought so, too.

His mother turned her back to Hallie, and with her eyes and brows, she gave Rafe a look for which there was no other interpretation—she wanted him to go.

Four-year-old Abigail chose that moment to shove a doll up at Hallie's face, distracting her from her good-byes. "Oh, how pretty!" Hallie exclaimed, and squatted down to discuss the doll with Abbi.

Rafe's mother took the opportunity to lean over him under the pretense of picking up the salt and pepper shakers. "She just had her wedding called off. She's lonely. Go ride with her," she whispered hotly.

Rafe was not the son who would say no to his mother's few wishes, but he did not want to ride with Hallie. He didn't want to be near her. He needed to keep a distance between them, an ocean if he could, because that was the only way he could keep old yearnings from bubbling up and making a mush of his brain.

But his mother was glaring at him, and he rolled his eyes at her, but he stood. "Yeah, Hallie, let's take a ride." And then he instantly wanted to punch himself in the mouth, because her face lit with delight. He didn't want her to be delighted.

"Really? Are you sure?"

"You bet," he said, and ignored his mother's overly pleased smile at having made one of her children bend to her will.

"I should warn you that I'm not really sure what we're looking for."

"Chickens!" Izzy said.

"Chickens," Hallie agreed with a smile for Izzy. "But for all I know, they may look like sparrows."

"Sparrows?" Rafe repeated.

Hallie shrugged. "I don't know, I've never seen a feral chicken. Thank you so much for the tea, Mrs. Fontana," she said to his mother. "Good to see you, Angie."

"You too, Hallie."

"Good-bye, Martin! See you at the house!"

"Take care," his father mumbled, his attention on the game.

Hallie smiled happily at Rafe in the way that sent little sparklers shimmering down his spine. "Meet you at the stables in an hour?"

"For chicken hunting," he said disbelievingly.

"Exactly," she said.

His mother saw Hallie out. When they heard the door close, Angie whipped around to him. "What just happened? Since when does Hallie Prince come off her throne and pay us a visit?"

"Watch your mouth, Angie," his dad said. "The Princes have made it possible for you to have the life that you've lived."

Angie snorted. "I'm just saying, since when does one of them deign to come around us? It's always about how we can serve them."

"She brought my gloves," Rafe said, and walked back to his old room to get a few things. He understood where Angie was coming from— the Prince family had always been held out as gods among mortals, either by themselves or by others.

But Hallie wasn't like that. Hallie didn't have an arrogant bone in her body. She was definitely one of a kind.

She was everything.

Chapter Five

Hallie dressed in jeans and western boots—the cute black ones with the big splashy yellow flowers—and made her way to the stables. She was surprised to see Rafe already in the paddock with two saddled horses. He was leaning against a post, his arms crossed, waiting for her. He watched her walk through the gate and make her way across the sand and loam. "How'd you get here so quick?" she asked.

He glanced at his watch. "You said an hour. It's been an hour and a half."

"It *has?*" Well, that was the fastest hour and a half she'd spent in some weeks. She'd been trying to decide what to wear. This was her first foray out of the house in something other than yoga pants, and after last night, she'd wanted to look nice. She wanted to remind Rafe that she didn't always look like she'd been living behind a fast-food restaurant near the highway.

"Nice boots," he said.

"Thank you. I got them at Allen's," she said, referring to a boot shop in Austin. She turned her ankle and dipped into a little curtsy so he could see them.

"I didn't realize I was supposed to put on my fancy boots to look at chickens." He eyed the flowers on her boots. "Quite the garden."

"It's always important to look your best," she said with a bat of her eyes.

He smiled down at her, his expression indulgent. Much the way her brothers often looked at her. *Whatever, Hallie, you're a dork,* they'd say.

"That one is yours," Rafe said, using his chin to indicate the taller horse of the two.

That horse checked her out with one enormous brown eye. He looked less than thrilled that she'd been assigned to him. "Why that one?"

"Because you haven't been on a horse in a long time, and he's pretty forgiving." He pushed away from the post and walked to the horse.

Hallie put her hands on her hips. "I think I ought to be insulted by your presumption that I will need to be forgiven, but I am feeling magnanimous at the moment and I will ignore it. Your caution is duly noted, but I will point out that it hasn't been *that* long." She bowed majestically, then straightened and walked over to stroke the horse's nose.

The horse tossed his mane.

"I guess we'll find out soon enough, won't we?" Rafe put his hand on the small of her back to usher her forward. "Just try not to get thrown, okay? I don't want to have to pick up the pieces."

The way he was smiling down at her all sparkly-eyed and dimple-cheeked beneath that shadow of a beard made Hallie think she wouldn't mind at all if Rafe picked up her pieces. "*You* try not to get thrown," she said, sounding like a six-year-old. When had he gotten so dreamy, anyway? While she was off planning a Big Society Wedding, Rafe had turned into a drool-worthy rock of a man in his jeans, long-sleeved tee, and flannel shirt.

He chuckled as he cinched the saddle belt on the horse. "You going to mount this bad boy, or are you going to stand around staring at me all day?"

Was she staring? Oh, she *was* staring a little. She could feel a blush creeping into her cheeks and pushed past him. "Move aside, cowboy, I've got this."

Except that she didn't have it. She could hardly bend her leg enough to fit her foot into the stirrup. This is what happened when one stopped dancing—one lost all flexibility and turned oneself into a two-by-four piece of wood.

"Don't hurt yourself," Rafe said as he watched her.

"Shut up," she said through a huff of breath at the exertion.

"I'll get a stool," he suggested.

A stool is what they used for children who were just learning to ride, and Hallie was appalled that he thought she was *that* raw. "I've got this. I don't need a stool." She stubbornly tried to hop up with one leg and pull up with her arms at the same time. She managed to get halfway up the horse before promptly sliding down.

Rafe tried to hide a laugh, but when she glared at him, it busted out of him.

"It's not funny!" Hallie insisted.

"It's hilarious."

"It's not my fault I lack upper-arm strength."

"It's *totally* your fault. Anyone can improve their strength if they are so inclined. Stay right there and I'll get a stool—"

"Forget the stool! Give me a hand," she said, gesturing for him to help her. Her foot was still in the stirrup, for Chrissakes, and there was no way she was going to dislodge it without some intervention. The horse shifted to one side, and she feared she would be rent in two. "Rafe, help me!"

"I don't know if I—"

"Just push me up," she insisted.

"Why are you so *stubborn?*" he demanded, and planted his hands on her bottom so firmly that Hallie gasped. His fingers dug into her flesh, and with a grunt of effort, he vaulted her up onto the saddle with such force that she almost went off the other side. She quickly righted herself and turned a beaming, breathless smile down to him. "You didn't have to *throw* me."

He put his hands on his hips and looked at her as if she wasn't speaking English. "Yes, I did," he said. "You can't willy-nilly disregard the physics that an assist like this requires."

Hallie's mouth gaped. "Okay, so I've gained a few pounds!" Actually, it felt like a lot. She really had to stop planting her face and her misery in buckets of ice cream.

"You don't look like you've gained an ounce, but that is not the point. The point is, you should use a stool," he said, not unreasonably.

"Whatever." She leaned over the horse's neck and patted him. "You remember me, don't you, Billie? He didn't have to throw me, did he?"

"That's Brutus," Rafe said, and turned to the second horse.

"No way," Hallie said, and sat up, staring at the ears of the horse. "Billie has a star between his eyes."

"Billie is a mare and she has socks. Brutus has the star." He easily tossed himself up onto the back of the second horse without any apparent regard for physics.

"Billie and Brutus," Hallie said. "Sounds like a rom-com."

"A what?" Rafe asked as he gathered the reins. He made a clicking sound to the horse and spurred him forward.

Brutus obediently followed. "A rom-com," Hallie repeated.

"Not following you," Rafe said as they rode out of the paddock.

"Are you serious right now?" Hallie said. "*Romantic comedy*. Like *Crazy, Stupid, Love*."

Rafe shook his head. "Feeling good in the saddle? Can you handle it?" He turned a studious eye to her form and frowned when he looked at her feet.

"What do you mean, *'can I handle it.'* Riding a horse is like riding a bike, Rafe—you never forgot how to do it. Once a cowgirl, always a cowgirl—"

"Okay," he said, holding up a hand. "But for the sake of accuracy, you were never a cowgirl. More of a sidekick."

He had a point. "Details," she said flippantly. "So come on, seriously, you've never seen *Crazy, Stupid, Love*?"

"Is that a movie?"

Hallie stared at him, unable to comprehend how he could be so woefully uninformed. "What about *Bridget Jones's Diary*, or *You've Got Mail*?"

He looked at her blankly. "Movies?"

"You've got to be kidding me, Rafael Fontana!" Hallie said. "How can you be so cool and know *nothing* about pop culture? We need to change that. You can't go through life with no knowledge of rom-coms. You're only hurting yourself with that nonsense."

He laughed. "For starters, I'm not cool. How do you propose we improve my knowledge of pop culture?"

"Well, obviously, I'm going to have to host a movie night." The idea popped out of her mouth without thought, but the moment it did, Hallie instantly liked the idea of it. She could picture the two of them in the media room with the classic *When Harry Met Sally.* She could watch that movie a dozen times. It was quite possible she already had. Frederica could make popcorn—well, Frederica was a part-timer now, so Hallie would have to do it. She could figure out popcorn, couldn't she? It couldn't be that hard. "You could come to the house," she said breezily. "I'm going to learn to make popcorn. Not the microwave kind, of course, but the way the pioneers made it."

Rafe squinted straight ahead. "I don't think pioneers made popcorn."

Hallie laughed. "Of course they did! What, you think popcorn just showed up one day?"

"My guess is they had enough on their hands just trying to feed themselves."

Hallie reached for her back pocket to grab her phone and Google this important fact, but discovered she hadn't brought it with her. Interesting. She'd been stalking Christopher's

Instagram account, but today, she hadn't thought about it.

"Okay, nevertheless, you could use some popcorn and romantic comedy in your life, Rafe."

"I could also use some study time for my final," he said, and glanced away from her. "It's my last one."

Hallie deflated. Was she so down in the dumps that she'd conveniently forgotten that Rafe had his own life and was not actually responsible for her RFC (Recovery from Christopher), no matter how badly she wished it were so?

She was a bad friend. She hadn't asked him much about what was going on in his life recently. They hadn't had much contact in the last couple of years, because she'd been so caught up in trying to be the perfect fiancée who would become the perfect wife. How had she let that happen? She'd been friends with Rafe longer than almost anyone else.

Unfortunately, Rafe wasn't the only friend she'd neglected in her constant back-and-forth between the ranch and Houston. She hadn't talked to Kara or Melissa in ages. But it was very obvious to her, in examining the evidence presented just today, that her friendship with Hot Army Guy Slash Cowboy Rafe was a powerful antidote to her stupid ex. She'd hardly thought about Chris at all since Rafe had stood in front of her car with a saddle on his shoulder.

The image of Rafe in front of her car sent a strange little shiver down her spine. She didn't want to dwell too long on the notion that she had so little to fall back on she was having to rely on her old friend so nakedly. A guy who was probably too respectful to think of an excuse to send her away.

Jesus, he wasn't hanging out with her out of pity, was he? Was this a *pity* outing? Oh, she didn't like that at all. It made her feel a little nauseated, because there was nothing worse than a pity friend. Hallie liked to think she was not a needy person. Or *was* she? The very idea sent her mood plummeting, and she reacted by giving her horse a press of the knees and a heel to the flank to send him to a canter.

Rafe watched her bounce by, then smoothly caught up.

"Hey, let's take the shortcut," she suggested.

"Not a good idea," he said. "We had a heavy rain last week. The river might be too high for the horses."

Killjoy. "When did you become so mature?"

He laughed. "When was I not?"

Hallie responded by suddenly yanking the reins and sending Brutus veering off through the dormant oil field, leaving the road to cut across to the river. It felt good to feel the horse gallop, and Hallie bent over his neck, spurred him to stretch his legs beneath her. Brutus thought this was a good idea and obliged her, letting loose for an all-out run.

She realized how out of shape she was as the horse barreled toward the river. Her legs were beginning to shake, and her arms felt like noodles. And then, from the corner of her eye, she saw Rafe shoot past her on the mare. He was riding with perfect form, and she swore as he passed her that he tossed a smirk in her direction.

Brutus took this as a challenge and did not intend to be left behind. He picked up more speed, his hooves churning up the grass beneath them. Hallie cried out with alarm when she thought she might bounce right off his back, but at the river's edge, Brutus brought himself to an abrupt halt.

With a gasp, she sat up and looked at Rafe. Something clicked between them, and they simultaneously burst into laughter after the shared exhilaration of the ride.

"I told you I've still got it!" she announced gaily.

"If by 'got it' you mean you're still crazy as a bat, then yeah, you've still got it, baby," Rafe said, his eyes shining with laughter.

Her heart was skipping wildly in her chest. Good Lord, but he was handsome. Was this *new?* Had she been so intent on Chris that she'd failed to notice? Or had he been this way for all the years she'd known him and, inexplicably, she hadn't noticed? Because he seemed unusually hot to her just now, with his windswept hair and square jaw and the delight shining in his caramel eyes. And as she grinned at him like a loon, she noticed he was looking at her in the very same way.

And then she realized, with a tiny intake of breath, that he was looking at her the way Chris used to look at her—with desire. But Rafe's look was so potent it could have knocked her off that horse if she hadn't been holding on. It was *so* potent that she had to look away before it burned her up. She shifted her gaze to the river. Had she really just seen that? Surely not. Of course there were times in the many years they'd known each other that she'd felt a little sizzle between them, but that was natural—they were male and female. And then it would float away as soon as he cuffed her on the shoulder or told her he had to go, that he had to get ready for a date.

"See? It's low," she heard herself say. "I knew it would be low. Don't ask me how I know these things—it's a gift." She risked a look at him.

Whatever she thought she'd seen was gone from his eyes, just like the other times she'd felt that crazy electricity between them. Okay, so she'd imagined it, good to know. Because Rafe would never look at her like . . . *that.*

The bigger question rattling around her heart was if maybe she'd wanted him to look at her like that.

Oh Lord, get a grip, Hallie. Talk about rebound. Her thoughts suddenly annoyed her. She nudged Brutus with her knees. "Let's go!" she said gaily, and sent him splashing into the shallow river.

Rafe followed, and they rode on to the spring.

When they could just make out the roof of the little house that belonged to Luca's fiancée, Ella Kendall, in the distance, Rafe pulled up. "Let's walk from here," he said. "We can go up on the cliff, remember?"

There was a point above the natural springs that was a bit of a cliff. When they were kids, it was about six feet above the water—a great jumping-off place. But then the springs had gotten clogged with sediment and runoff, and the water had dropped, and it had become a dangerous jump.

Luca was going to bring the springs back to life.

Rafe easily dismounted and then helped Hallie down by grabbing her by the waist as she braced her hands against his shoulder. The moment her feet hit the ground, he dropped his hands and turned away. "The path is muddy," he said as he tethered the horses to the low branches of a cedar tree. "Watch your step."

He led the way through the thicket and up the path through cedars that choked out any other vegetation, grabbing her elbow once to help her over a particularly tough spot.

They emerged onto the cliff overhang, a limestone shelf that was big enough for maybe three people to sit.

Hallie used to stand on the edge of the cliff, but today, she was unnerved by the drop she'd once thought nothing of. She sat. Rafe sat beside her in companionable silence, scanning the area around the spring. Luca had begun clearing the land. He said the first step to restoring the ecology was to remove the invasive species from his dedicated acreage. Hallie didn't know what all that entailed—Luca had definitely explained it at some length, but her eyes tended to glaze over when he talked in such detail—but nevertheless, just by his clearing out what he had so far, she could tell this old spring and the land around it would be beautiful when he finished. A pristine piece of land that looked nearly as it had when God created it—grasslands and native trees and a healthy spring.

But no chickens.

"Where are the chickens?" Hallie asked, craning her neck. She was actually disappointed—she'd never seen a prairie chicken. "Do you think maybe the coyotes got them?"

"Maybe," Rafe said. "Are you sure we're in the right place?"

"No," Hallie admitted. "I'm not sure about anything."

Rafe glanced at her. "You don't think Luca was pulling your leg, do you?"

Hallie considered that a moment. "I would say that under any other circumstance that would be a distinct possibility. But he was so damn excited about the chickens."

Rafe laughed. "The man's got a vision, all right."

"He does." Hallie sighed. "My talented twin."

Rafe leaned back, stretched his legs long, and propped himself on an elbow. "He's got a big heart, too."

That remark made Hallie think of Chris. A heart surgeon. She'd always been a little intimidated by that. Christopher saved lives and she . . . well, she was a failed ballerina with nothing going for her but some serious social connections.

"Have you ever known someone with a talent so far beyond you that it makes you feel inadequate?" she asked.

Rafe gave her a sidelong look. "I think we're not talking about Luca anymore, are we?"

Hallie flushed at her transparency. "How do you *do* that?"

"I just know you, Hal, and I know that you've always been pretty determined to be on equal footing with Luca, so that's how I do that."

"Do you blame me? Grandma has always treated Luca like a king."

Rafe laughed. "And your dad treated you like a

princess, so I'm guessing in the grand scheme of things, you two are even."

Hallie couldn't help her smile. "So true. It used to make Nick and Luca so mad. 'How come *she* gets to do whatever?' " she said, mimicking her brothers.

"So who are you comparing yourself to?"

She sighed, annoyed that she'd brought it up. "My ex-fiancé. He's a heart surgeon. You know that, right?"

"Yeah, I know. And?"

"And . . . ?" Hallie made a whirring motion with her wrist to indicate he needed to come along on the thought path. "He's a *heart* surgeon."

Rafe shrugged. "Okay, so he learned some complicated stuff. You could have, too, if you could stand the sight of guts."

"I can't."

"Exactly. But is that his true talent? Learning about hearts?"

"That's more talent than I'll ever possess," Hallie said. "I never said this to anyone, but honestly, I never knew what he saw in me. I mean, you'd think he'd want someone more like . . . him," she said.

"An ass?"

Hallie laughed. Rafe winked at her and she got that warm, glittery feeling she sometimes experienced around him. He always had her back.

"I meant smart and accomplished."

"Okay," Rafe said. "We're not doing that today. You're smart and accomplished, too. Give yourself a break, Hallie."

"You know what I mean," she said, and drew her knees up to her chest and wrapped her arms around her legs. "I have average intelligence, and I'm not particularly accomplished at anything other than being privileged. I haven't done anything. Nothing! I've flitted from one charity event to the other, either giving away our foundation money or asking for money for a cause." She shivered. She didn't know if it was because it was getting colder or if the truth about herself made her feel weak.

"Not true. You were a camp counselor."

She and Rafe were both camp counselors one year when they were teens, and they'd had a blast with the boy-versus-girl competitions. The kids liked it—but she and Rafe were obsessed with beating each other.

Rafe sat up, shrugged out of his flannel shirt, and draped it around her shoulders without a word. She likewise accepted it without a word and pulled it tightly around her. It was so typical of their friendship—he was the all-around good guy, always looking out for her. Not as exciting as his brother, Rico, maybe, who was always looking for a good time. But solid and dependable. An Army Ranger. A real mensch, as her dad would have said.

His shirt smelled like him. A faint hint of orange and nutmeg. Spicy. Male.

"Do you remember what I said when I called to tell you I was engaged?" she asked.

"Ah . . ." Rafe squinted into the distance, as if trying to recall. "I think you said you'd found someone who was too good for you."

"Exactly," she said. "I knew from the beginning that it was improbable."

"My God, you're hard on yourself," Rafe said. "Are you the same woman who told me you were going to mop up San Antonio with my face when I suggested you couldn't sing?"

Hallie arched a brow. "When did I say that?"

"You were sixteen or seventeen. You were at the pool with your friends. Remember? Someone had a karaoke machine, and you asked me what I thought of your performance of a Maroon 5 song. I told you to stick to dancing."

Hallie tilted her head back and laughed heartily. "I had forgotten about that! You were obviously deaf to my talent—no one rocks Maroon 5 better than me or Adam Levine."

"No one destroys Maroon 5 quite like you."

Hallie could remember the sticky summer night. Rafe had come in from working cattle with the other cowboys. She and Lindsey and Kara watched them riding across a field toward the stables. They were wearing their skimpy bikinis, eating the hot dogs her dad had made them, and when they weren't performing with the family's latest gadget—the karaoke machine—they were talking about boys.

Rafe's brother, Rico, was there, too, now that she thought about it, and when he and Rafe came up from the stables, Rico was all smiles and winks, sneaking sips of beer from behind the barbecue pit. Back then, Hallie didn't know he had a problem with alcohol—he was like all the teenage boys they knew. But looking back on it, she could see the signs. He was always one of the ones who drank a lot.

But they were all so brazen then, so full of themselves. Such teenagers.

She thought she'd been pretty darn good at singing. She started humming the Maroon 5 tune.

"Don't," Rafe warned her.

"Beauty queen of only eighteen, she had some trouble with herself," she warbled, horribly off-key. But it wasn't her fault—she didn't have a karaoke machine out here to help her. "That's the song 'She Will Be Loved,' " she informed Rafe.

"I know. And you're butchering it."

"He was always there to help her, she always belonged to someone else," she sang, even louder.

Rafe suddenly swung around and tackled her, pressing his hand lightly against her mouth. "Make it stop," he said, grinning down at her. Hallie shrieked with laughter. And it happened again—a moment so brief, yet so pyrotechnic, sizzling in her groin. Rafe's gaze was intense and full of heat.

He abruptly moved his hand and sat up. Hallie did, too, feeling a little light-headed. What was *that?* What had just happened? That had felt so ... sexual.

"So anyway," she said, and gave her head a shake, trying to rid herself of the insane idea that there was an honest spark between them. "Talent. I don't know if I ever really told you that I flunked out of ballet school," she blurted. Her admission startled her. She never talked about her experience at the School of American Ballet in New York to anyone—even after twelve years, her humiliation still burned. But it had been so long ago, it hardly seemed worth mentioning. This was the one thing she'd never really told him.

"Flunked out," he repeated. "How do you flunk out of ballet school?"

Excellent question, sir. "You flunk out if you're not good enough. They gave me chances because of who my dad was. Chances they never would have given anyone else, trust me." She shook her head, recalling with vivid clarity when she'd not been invited back after the winter session at the School of American Ballet. The school fed its best dancers into the New York City Ballet, and Hallie had dreamed all her life of being a ballerina with a prestigious company like that.

When she found out she was not invited back, she'd tracked down the director, certain there had been some mistake. But the director very carefully told Hallie that she didn't have what it took.

"What do you mean?" Hallie had demanded. "I have never missed a class. I practice after hours. I'm so dedicated—"

"Unfortunately, Miss Prince, dedication is not a substitute for raw talent," the director had said. "I know you're disappointed, but I need to be honest with you—you simply do not exhibit the level of talent that we can nurture. Perhaps a ballet in your hometown?" she'd suggested.

The worst part of it, Hallie would later discover, was that her parents already knew. The director had taken pains to explain it to the school's generous benefactor before anyone bothered to explain it to Hallie.

"I'm sorry, Hal," Rafe said. "I know that's what you always wanted."

"It was. It took a long time to face the truth, that I didn't have the talent to be a prima ballerina, and all the training in the world wasn't going to miraculously give me that talent either. The best I could ever hope for was the corps. Turns out, I'm a pretty good journeyman."

"Nothing wrong with that," he said. "But,

Hallie, do you have any idea how much courage it takes for a person to face up to the idea that certain things they believed about themselves may not be true? Most people can't face it, let alone admit it. And so many people, if they can face the truth, try and numb their feelings. You didn't do that. You faced it head-on. That's courage. That's a big deal."

"But did I face it? I came home and quit ballet. After high school, I went to college to the dance program there, but I never got the good roles. I quit that, too." She gave him a crooked, sheepish smile. "And it's not like I didn't cry buckets for two years. I had to be dragged kicking and screaming to the truth about my talent. Maybe choreography, maybe teaching, an instructor told me, and she seemed iffy about that. No, I never really faced it, Rafe. I just quit. I quit, and then I bounced around." Hallie sighed. She fixed her gaze on his caramel-colored eyes. "Here I go again, dumping all my woes on you. I don't mean to, it just keeps happening."

He shook his head.

"I need to say I'm sorry, Rafe. I shouldn't have subjected you to that last night."

"It's really not neces—"

"Don't say it's not necessary, because it is," she said, and caught his wrist. "I mean, come on—I tried to bean you with a shoe."

"You were way off."

"I turned into a caricature of a drunk sorority girl when I took a swing at you."

"Again, not even close."

"And then to add insult to injury, I almost threw up on you."

"Don't mention it," he said, and held up his palm with a grimace. "Seriously. Don't mention it."

"I'm just trying to say that I've had a moment to reflect . . ." She looked skyward. "Really it's been more like an entire day of reflection, which may not seem like a lot to you, but trust me, that's a lot more than I normally allot to self-reflection, and *anyway,* I really feel awful that you had to babysit me last night. I want to make it up to you."

He viewed her speculatively for a long moment. "Okay," he said, and turned the arm that she was holding so that he could hold her wrist, too. "I think I've got just the way you can make it up to me."

Her heart should not have skipped fourteen beats, but it did. "Really?"

"Really. Here's how: Stop running yourself down. Stop apologizing for being human. Now here comes the tricky part. Stand up."

"Why?" she asked as he sprang to his feet. He was still holding her arm, and she was still holding his.

"Just do it."

Hallie pulled herself up with his arm. He put his hands on her shoulders and turned her around so that she was facing the wind. "Now scream."

"Scream?"

"Yes, scream. Let it out. Get it out of your system. Let all the frustrations and disappointments and hurt go."

Hallie laughed nervously. "I don't know . . . what about the chickens?"

"What chickens?" he asked, sweeping his hand to the area below them. "Come on. Trust me."

She did trust him. One thousand percent. She took a breath and screamed. Sort of. It felt weird to scream without any terror being present.

"Come on," Rafe scoffed. "You can do better than that. Remember when Nick fell into that culvert and broke his arm? Now *that* was a scream."

"Ooh," Hallie said with a wince, remembering it all too well. She took a deep breath, and then she screamed as loud as she could. She screamed so hard her eyes felt like they would pop out of her head.

After a minute of her screaming, Rafe stepped up beside her and joined her, although his scream was more of a bellow. He grabbed her hand, and the two of them screamed and bellowed their frustrations until a flock of birds lifted out of the trees.

"Oh, shit!" Hallie cried, and fell back against Rafe as if she'd been startled. "Was that the chickens?"

He caught her by her shoulders. "Hope not for your sake," he said, and set her upright on her feet. "So?" He grinned. "Do you feel better?"

"Loads." She smiled. "Do you?"

"I do. Now promise me you won't let this dick fiancé of yours assign your worth to you. Promise me only *you* will do that."

Hallie groaned.

"I'm sorry, did you say something?" He cupped his ear with his hand. "*Promise* me, Hallie. Stop letting him get under your skin. I don't care if he is texting you or sliding into your DMs—"

"He is."

"Stop wasting precious brain cells on him and start thinking about what you're going to do with your life."

"Okay," she said, nodding. He was right. He was absolutely right. "I promise."

"You said it today—you're turning over a new leaf. Look forward, not backward."

It was way past time to do exactly that. "Okay. I promise."

He smiled, pleased with himself.

Hallie cocked her head to one side and looked him over. "Why are you such a good friend to me, Rafe?" she asked. "I don't deserve you."

"Are you kidding? After all you've done for me?"

"For you?" she asked, confused. "Almost throwing up on you?"

"Remember the care packages you used to send me when I was in Afghanistan?"

"What, you mean the pillow and the socks and the deodorant?" She flicked her wrist. "Hardly the same category."

"Oh yeah? What about the pictures?"

"Oh," she said, and looked off a moment, remembering.

"You sent me pictures of home. This ranch. My dad. Rico and Angie. Do you know how much that meant to me?"

She smiled, then laughed softly. "What about the cowboy stress relief doll whose hat came off when you squeezed him?"

He laughed, too. "And the 401(k) coin purse. And the bacon dental floss, and the disposable undies. And my personal favorite, the 'Fight like a girl' socks you sent to the whole company."

Hallie laughed. "Yeah, I've got a slight problem always thinking I'm much funnier than anyone else does."

"I think you're hilarious, Hallie. And that is my point—friends give each other what they need. You sent me a reminder of home in so many ways when I needed it most. And now, I'm going to return the favor and kick you out of the doldrums. Simple." He slipped his hands into his back pockets and smiled down at her in a way that made the sparks go off in her again.

"Thanks, Rafe." Hallie stepped forward, put her arms around him to hug him, and pressed her cheek to his chest.

But Rafe felt stiff, and his hands remained in his pockets.

He was not returning her hug.

He was probably done with her for the day. Okay, she got that—it had been a roller coaster. So Hallie lifted her head and rose up on her toes. She meant to kiss his cheek, but Rafe suddenly turned his head as if to look at her, and her mouth caught the corner of his mouth.

Hallie froze, her lips on his.

Her lips were on his soft, warm lips. Rafe put his hand on her arm, and Hallie turned her head a little more. Not so much as to suggest she was actually *kissing* him, but maybe a little like she was kissing him, because it felt good.

It felt very good.

It felt sort of serious, too.

But Rafe pulled himself free of her. He stepped backward and gaped at her, his hands on his waist, his eyes locked on hers. "What was *that?*" he demanded.

"That?" She was looking at his mouth. She wanted to go back there, just for a moment, anyway. She brushed her hair from her face. "I meant to kiss you on the cheek, but then you moved." She shrugged. "I didn't mean to."

He stared at her. Hard. Like he didn't understand what had just happened or who she was.

Well, neither did she. "It was an accident."

He took a minute to consider that. He didn't look convinced, but at last he nodded. "Okay," he said. "Okay." He dragged his fingers through his hair and stared at the ground, then slowly lifted his head. "Okay."

Hallie tried not to smile, but she couldn't help herself. She felt strangely giddy. Anticipation waved in her chest. She felt . . . turned on.

Rafe pointed at her. "Don't make it weird."

"*You're* weird."

"We need to head in. *I* need to get back to studying." He started walking. Or maybe he was sprinting. Whatever he was doing, he was moving fast. So she'd made a tiny kissing mistake—he didn't have to act like he'd contracted Ebola from her and had to get to the doctor right away.

Hallie followed him up the path and allowed him to help her onto her horse.

They chatted on the way home—well, *she* chatted—as they rode through prairie grass and oaks, past clumps of prickly pear cactus and limestone rocks that seemed to erupt from the surface of the earth. Rafe seemed tense . . . until she mentioned the book *Sideways*. Then the tension seeped out of him, and they talked about it like two friends. Their own private book club. Maybe, he said, she was a little like the main character in *Sideways*—maybe she needed to get away and reevaluate where she was in life, just like Miles in the book had done. "But without the wine tour," he added with a wink.

"Are you kidding? *Totally* with the wine tour," she countered.

Everything slid and molded back into place between them. No sparks, just two old friends who had known each other since childhood. Two booklovers, two Texans, two ranch kids.

It looked and felt and smelled and tasted like the friendship they'd always had—and yet, something was bothering Hallie.

Something she couldn't quite put her finger on.

She had this confused sense that Rafe liked her, but in a way, he didn't like her. That he wanted to be her friend . . . but he didn't want her to be his friend.

It was weird.

Chapter Six

Cordelia Applewhite Prince put on a jacket and walked up the hill to the family cemetery. Hallie was right—it was a curious thing that she came up here as often as she did. Cordelia couldn't explain it, other than she knew that it somehow made her feel closer to Charlie.

Next to Charlie's grave, she'd installed two lawn chairs—one for her, obviously. The other for Dolly, her mother-in-law, who had horned her way into this little piece of paradise. Cordelia also had a cooler and, up until a month ago, a sun umbrella. Martin had taken the sun umbrella down last month because he said it would get ruined with the winter rains.

So for the winter months, Cordelia wore a wide-brimmed straw hat that she'd picked up from the end-of-season clearance aisle at Walmart.

Until her Charlie died, Cordelia had never been inside a Walmart. It had never even occurred to her—she had people to do her shopping, and honestly, if she was buying for herself, she was going to do that in Houston or New York or Los

Angeles. But in the endless hours after Charlie's death, when the days and weeks had spilled into months, Cordelia discovered that she desperately needed something to do with herself. Because if she didn't have an activity, she was tortured by the many, many thoughts of what might have been had she and Charlie not separated.

He might still be alive. She might have noticed something in his health, might have made him go to a doctor before it was too late. Even if she'd just checked on him once in a while, made sure he was eating right and taking his blood pressure medicine, he could still be here. She hadn't done any of those things, and then he was dead. Flat on his back on the putting green with the cigar clamped between his teeth.

To say she felt a lot of guilt was a gross understatement. Somehow, she'd managed to pin his enchilada-clogged arteries on herself.

But on the other hand, there were lucid moments when she didn't blame herself entirely. If Charlie had managed to keep his pants zipped, they would not have separated. That was his fault. Perhaps Cordelia could have been more forgiving. But when it had happened again and again, she couldn't take it. She couldn't abide being disrespected like that.

Looking back on it, as she had done so often since he died, she had to wonder, was it really so awful that he cheated? It wasn't as if they were burning up the bedsheets. It was a strange question for a woman to ask herself, but Cordelia truly didn't know the answer anymore. All she knew was that she would rather have him around than not.

In the beginning, Cordelia had walked around her house with his ghost haunting her in every room. But after a month or two, she had to get away from the ranch and the memories. So she'd started driving every day, going wherever her car took her. And it took her, more often than not, to the new, shiny Walmart on the San Antonio highway. Who knew it was such an amazing store? Who knew you could find anything a person could possibly want in one of the aisles of that enormous store? Aisle after aisle of things she'd never known she wanted or needed.

That's where she found these chairs and the little wicker side table. And the sun umbrella. Her hat. And more.

Cordelia plopped into a chair and propped her feet on the cooler and surveyed her little kingdom of graves. There were about two dozen, give or take, surrounded by a tidy little wrought iron fence. There was Odell Martha Prince, who had died in 1846, and the tiny headstones of the four infants who had preceded her in death. There was Leroy Prince, who'd departed this earth in 1948. He was the artist of the family, according to Dolly. And Omar Prince, who had died at the age of thirteen in 1892 from what family lore would have you believe was a bad case of constipation.

Cordelia glanced to her left, to Charlie's gaudy headstone with the cherubs and trumpets carved into it, standing proudly at the feet of his grandparents. His ashes were buried beneath it.

An oak leaf scudded across the top of his grave, and Cordelia announced, "Your daughter thinks I'm a head case. She might be right." With the heel of her shoe, she nudged an acorn off the cooler. "I certainly never pictured myself as the crazy old lady in the hat hanging out at her cheating husband's grave. Did you?"

No sound but the breeze rustling the leaves of the live oak that stretched over her head and his grave. Dozens of little brown leaves rained down on her.

"Martin's annoyed with me. He won't come out and just say it, but I can tell. He's about as stubborn as you were. He and I don't see eye to eye on running this ranch. I'm sure he thinks I ought to stay in the kitchen."

She thought about that a minute.

"Well, maybe he doesn't think that, but I'm telling you, he doesn't think I know what I'm doing."

Another rustle of wind through the tree showered another round of leaves on her.

"I miss you, Charlie. I can't seem to help myself, you rotten lying bastard, but I do. And

I damn sure don't want to spend the rest of my life missing you like this." She looked up. She often wondered if he was looking down at all of them like the family pastor said. She didn't know what she really believed about an afterlife, but she liked to think he was looking over them. "Reverend Bristol told me to take comfort in the idea that you are always near me." Cordelia snorted. "I told him I figured you were nearer to Missy Gutierrez at the title company, because you always had an eye for a good ass and I know you were sniffing around her before you died." She sighed. "The reverend was not amused. Frankly, neither was I."

She leaned back, propping her head against the lawn chair. This thing was as sturdy as the old retired longhorn steer that lived in a pasture behind the house. That was aluminum and plastic fabric for you—indestructible. And to think of all the money she'd spent over the years buying quality wood furniture. Those pieces wouldn't last a month up here on the hill. Cordelia decided she was like this chair—sturdy. A little nutty, maybe, but she would outlast all the fine citizens of Three Rivers, that was for sure.

"Well, anyway, Charlie, our girl is having a rough time. You know, I get it—I know what it's like, no thanks to you. Which I tried to tell her. And you know what she said? She told me to take a hike in so many words." She lifted her head and glared at the headstone. "It's a good thing I never caught you in the actual act. I can't even imagine. But you would have met your ultimate demise a whole lot sooner if I had."

She lowered her head again. "Hope that makes you feel bad. I hope you know what your daughter is going through right now and you feel really awful."

She closed her eyes, thinking of Hallie. They didn't communicate well, never had, really, and Cordelia didn't know if that was because she was truly as offensive as Hallie seemed to believe, or if Hallie wore too many feelings on her sleeve.

"What I really wish is that you were here to help me. I don't know what to say to our girl. She got drunk last night. *Hallie!* The one who is always lecturing me about how much I drink. She mopes around, she doesn't want to see her friends, she's eating anything that's not nailed down. She feels worthless, I know she does, because that's the only way you can feel after the fury dies off."

Silence. Even the wind stilled.

"Seriously, Charlie, why are men such pigs?" Cordelia asked softly.

A crow soared overhead and cackled at her. "I wish to God I hadn't loved you so damn much," she muttered, and sat up, annoyed with her maudlin self.

A movement down by the airstrip caught

Cordelia's attention, and she spotted two riders. "Who the hell is that?" she asked aloud. Nick and Luca had already come back from checking in on the prairie chickens. Apparently the chickens were already hunkering down and getting ready for winter, so there wasn't much to see.

Cordelia considered waving at the riders. A friendly wave, a welcome wave. But then again, she didn't want anyone to get the wrong idea and actually walk up this hill to talk to her. She shuddered at the idea of small talk.

She watched them a little longer and realized that one of them was Hallie. Maybe she'd gone out with Luca. He was a good twin—he'd probably gone along to cheer her up.

"We need to put a better path up here! A good rain, and this will be dangerous, Delia!"

Cordelia didn't even turn her head to acknowledge Dolly as the older woman hauled herself up the hill. Cordelia had given up trying to dissuade Dolly from coming up here—it was beyond Dolly's ability to allow Cordelia this space for herself.

Dolly fell into the lawn chair beside Cordelia with a grunt. Cordelia glanced at her from the corner of her eye. She was wearing a cheap woven poncho, undoubtedly bought at one of those touristy places in Mexico. She'd rolled up her distressed jeans and was wearing red Converse high-top sneakers. Ridiculous.

"I thought you were going to Walmart," Cordelia said.

"I did, and *oooh boy,* don't go to Walmart on a Sunday afternoon. Talk about crowded—it was nut to butt in there."

"Well, thanks for that visual," Cordelia drawled.

"You've been spitting at Martin again, I see."

Cordelia shot her a look. "Did he say that?"

"Nope. That's how I know. He's moping around like someone punched him, and I know only one person who can make a man feel like that."

"He's stubborn! He thinks he has all the answers."

"All men do, Delia. Look what I got us." Dolly pulled a box of donut holes from beneath her god-awful poncho.

Cordelia shook her head. "I don't eat that crap, you know that."

"Suit yourself," Dolly said with a shrug, and opened the box. "You're gonna get to my age one day and realize that life is too short to deny yourself a donut hole now and then." She popped one in her mouth and squinted down the hill as she chewed. "Who's that?"

"Hallie."

"Hallie! I'm surprised she remembers how to ride a horse anymore. Who's she with?"

"Probably Luca."

"I don't think so," Dolly said. "I saw Luca and Nick at Jo's Java."

Cordelia looked at Dolly. "You were at Jo's Java? I thought you didn't like driving in town."

"I can manage on a Sunday when there's not so many people whipping around me and driving too fast and looking at their damn phones. So if that's not Nick or Luca, who is it?"

That was a good question. Cordelia looked again, squinting, trying to make the riders out as they drew closer.

Something hard slid in Cordelia's belly. "That's not *Christopher,* is it?" He'd been texting and messaging Hallie, wanting to talk. As far as Cordelia knew, Hallie had ignored him.

"No," Dolly said. "Least, I don't think so." She munched her way through another donut hole as she considered the rider. "Christopher's scrawnier than that man. Fact, I can think of only one man who's built like that."

"Who?" Cordelia asked curiously.

"Rafe Fontana," Dolly said. "I always did think that boy was a hunk-a-hunk of burning love."

Martin's son? Cordelia felt suddenly hot. "But I . . . they don't . . ." Good Lord, she couldn't even think. Cordelia liked Rafe, she always had. But she didn't like the idea of him hanging out with Hallie when she was so vulnerable. Hallie didn't handle rejection well and tended to throw her lot in with anyone she could lean on.

114

Dolly didn't say a word, but extended the box of donut holes to her.

Cordelia took two. "I mean, you don't think Rafe is getting any ideas, do you?"

"Well, if you're worried about that, you ought to get her out of the house," Dolly said.

Cordelia looked at Dolly. "Do you know something?"

"No," Dolly said, waving her hand at Cordelia. "What I know is that he's a man and Hallie is a very attractive woman. Rafe is respectful. He's a good kid. But Hallie is who she is."

Cordelia knew precisely what Dolly meant. Her daughter was charming. She could attract men without even knowing she'd done it, and then hitch a ride on their star without looking to see where that star was going. "She doesn't ever leave! She doesn't want to see her friends, she wants to mope."

"Maybe Ella could help," Dolly suggested.

Ella. Luca's fiancée. Ella had a calming influence on Cordelia's twins. "I'm going to call her right now," she said, and reached for her phone.

But first, she took another donut hole. Dolly was right—life was too short.

Chapter Seven

Creedy's cows got out again on Tuesday, and this time, they ambled over to Mrs. Bachman's place and ate half her kitchen garden. Toting a rifle, Mrs. Bachman met the sheriff and threatened "to shoot those damn cows if Creedy can't keep them on his land."

Once again, the sheriff called on Rafe and his dad to help move them back to the Creedy ranch. "Problem is, Creedy's so old he probably don't remember his cows keep getting out," the sheriff said. "He's got to be ninety if he's a day."

"I'll get that fence fixed," Rafe promised, and drove down to the Creedy house to have a word.

Mr. Creedy's old ranch house was desperately in need of paint. But he had a very neat garden out front. He walked out to meet Rafe. His torso slanted east when he walked, and he moved about as slow as it took autumn to show up around here after a long hot summer. Rafe explained the problem with his cows. "Tell you what. I'll fix that fence for fifty bucks plus materials. It's going to need some new barbed wire and a post. I'd say that's a bargain."

Creedy had agreed, but not before he offered his opinion that it wasn't any big deal if the cows wandered a little bit, and what else were the Princes going to do with all that land?

"Well, sir, it's their land, and they don't want your cows," Rafe said. "But today, your cows were on Bachman land."

Creedy screwed up his face. "That woman would complain about the second coming of Christ," he said, and spat out a wad of tobacco juice. But he shook hands on Rafe's deal.

The next day, with a new fence post and yards of shiny barbed wire, Rafe worked on taking down the damaged section of the fence and putting up the new. He was happy to have something to do—he hadn't been able to concentrate on studying for his last exam, not since he'd gone out to the springs with Hallie. Hell, he hadn't been able to do much of anything but wander around sort of dumbfounded about that afternoon.

Had Hallie *kissed* him? Really kissed him? Or was it an accident, like she'd said? It had happened so quickly—a lifetime or a moment, he wasn't really sure—but he was positive that there had been something real in that kiss.

He was annoyed with himself for obsessing over it like a lovesick kid. He was happy to have something to pound in the meantime.

117

He had an audience for his work—a line of bovines had gathered, hoping with their tiny bovine brains that Rafe had some hay with him. They stood like a jury, shoulder roast to shoulder roast, chewing their cud as he measured and cut barbed wire to be strung. Every now and then one or two of them would dip their heads to the grass that grew high along the fence line and chew for a while.

Rafe had been at work for about an hour when he paused to wipe his brow. When he did, he noticed someone lurching down the road, arms swinging out at odd angles. A jogger. As the person neared him, he realized it was Hallie. She stopped a few feet from him, wheezing for air. She put her hands to her back, then bent over, hands to knees, and wheezed more.

"I guess you started running," Rafe said, amused and surprised by it.

"Had to," she said breathlessly, still bent over. "My family is so sure I'm going to walk up to Granite Bluffs and dive headfirst over the side that I've got to at least give them the illusion that I'm trying to buck up."

"That's ridiculous," Rafe said. "You would never dive off Granite Bluffs. Too messy."

"Exactly," she said, lifting up. "Maybe you could go around and explain to my mother that I'm going to be okay."

He snorted. "Hard pass."

Hallie laughed.

Damn. That smile. That heart-teasing smile. And those lips. *Damn Hallie.* Damn her for kissing him, for sparking that tiny flame of hope in him. It was going to take a tsunami to douse it.

"I may need to rethink this running thing," she said, still breathing hard. "I'm so out of shape. And *sore!* I could hardly walk after we rode out to see the chickens. And may I just add," she said, holding up a finger, "running is *so* much sweatier than I thought it would be."

"You're exerting more energy than you need to," Rafe pointed out. "You should work on your form. A lot. Like, maybe go back and start over. No one should look like they're running from the walking dead when out for a jog."

"Oh, *really?* And who are you, José Bolt?"

"I think you mean *Usain* Bolt, and I'm just saying, maybe learn the correct form before you give it up altogether. It will make it easier."

She rolled her eyes, and then ran the back of her hand under her chin. "Okay, like what?" she asked, gesturing for him to speak.

"Like, for starters, you were running hunched over. Can't get air in your lungs that way. Tighten your transverse and stay erect."

"My what?"

"Your transverse."

She screwed up her face in a *huh* fashion.

119

Rafe whirled his hand in the general direction of her abdomen. She looked down and examined her clothes as if she thought she had splattered them with mud. Rafe couldn't help himself—he put his hand on the flat of her belly just below her navel.

Hallie stared at his hand. "Oh, hey, I remember that now. I used it when I danced ballet."

He dropped his hand and looked away from her. "I could teach you to run if you want." The minute the words left his fool mouth, he immediately, instantly, wanted to kick himself. To offer to spend time with her was almost as stupid as touching her. He thought a kiss-not-a-kiss would cause him to obsess? That was just the tip of the iceberg.

"Are you implying my running is so bad I need lessons?" she asked with mock injury.

He made himself look at her. "I sure am."

Hallie laughed with surprise. "You're on, cowboy stud. Teach me how to run. I need to get my butt in shape. No more buckets of ice cream. Well, I don't mean *never,* but you understand."

He'd always appreciated that about Hallie—she didn't get her feelings hurt very easily. Add that to the list of things he really liked about her.

Rafe picked up the barbed wire he'd just cut. "If you really want to do it, we can start this weekend." Except that he was supposed to be in Chicago this weekend. *Yeah, go ahead, Rafe—*

pour some gasoline on your little fire. "I mean, if you think you can handle it."

She blew him a raspberry. "I can handle it. I'm up for anything you can show me because I am determined to get in shape, and who knows, maybe I'll even dance again." She suddenly rose up on her toes and twirled around.

A snake of heat ran down his spine. When he was a teen with a raging case of hormones, he used to spy on Hallie practicing her ballet. Once, he'd been working with the cowboys, storing hay at the top of the barn for winter. From his perch there he could see Hallie on the east lawn patio. From a distance, her dance was silent to him, but what he remembered was how elegant she was. Her graceful arms, her slender legs stretched long. Her torso remarkably flexible. She lifted one leg high overhead, her toes pointed, her arms curling up the leg. And then she let go, twirled around, and landed with her arms outstretched, one leg long behind her, and her back bent to such a degree that she was looking at the sky. "Why did you quit, anyway?" he asked curiously.

"Oh, you know," she said, with a flick of her wrist. "Life."

Rafe arched a brow. That was not an answer. "Are you going to dance again?"

Her cheeks turned pink. She rubbed her nape. "Maybe. I don't know. *You're* nosy. What are you doing, anyway?" she asked, in a clear attempt to change the subject.

Rafe silently gestured to the fence.

One of the cows mooed.

"They got out again?"

"They got out again."

She walked over to the fence and reached for the nose of one of the cows. That cow tried to lick her hand. A few of the other cows would have rolled their eyes if they could have, and sauntered away, moving down the fence in search of better grass.

"So guess what, I think I've figured a few things out. Want to hear?" she asked when the last cow ambled away from her to join the others.

"Sure," Rafe said.

"I was thinking about Chris."

Rafe almost groaned. *Way to ruin a perfectly pleasant morning, Hallie.* The last thing he wanted to hear about was *that* guy.

She kept her gaze on the cows as they moved away in a lazy line. "I figured out what Chris saw in me. And before you say anything, I am looking forward. I am just figuring out a few details first."

Rafe said nothing, but he could easily name a dozen things the doc saw in her off the top of his head. Her ability to laugh at herself. Because she was so damn pretty. She was funny, she ran like an emu—

She turned around. "It was the money. Duh! And the Prince name. Get it? I was someone whose family could possibly build a wing of a hospital just for him someday. What he saw in me was opportunity."

"Look, I don't know the man," Rafe said. Although he felt like he did. Hallie had talked enough about him that there were times Rafe felt like he was almost in the same room with them. "But I know you, and I'm sure he fell in love with *you*." He said it emphatically, like a guy totally infatuated with her would say it. Or her mother. He instantly feared he'd said too much.

But Hallie hadn't seemed to notice. She was already shaking her head. "Nope. He started losing interest right after Dad died. The day George told us there wasn't as much money as we'd thought," she said, referring to the Prince family attorney, George Lowe. "Chris was there when George said we were going to have to tighten our belts, and that my wedding needed to be scaled back. And that, my friend, is when things began to change."

This talk of her fiancé was agitating him. Rafe began to wrestle the rotted fence post that had to come out of the ground. "You think he cheated on you because he wanted a big wedding?"

"It wasn't the wedding, it was what it represented. That's when he stopped coming to Three Rivers. That's when he said he was *sooo* busy with work. That morphed into maybe I shouldn't come to Houston, because he would probably be working all weekend. He was working, all right, but not at the hospital. I think when he figured out the family fortune wasn't quite the fortune he thought it was, he started to change."

"Hallie—"

"I know what you're going to say," she said. "But I'm not complaining. I'm just saying. I honestly don't care anymore, Rafe. I really, truly don't. He broke my heart and I'm done with him. I just want to understand why he did, that's all." She traced her finger along a stretch of barbed wire, resting the pad of her finger on a barb.

Rafe couldn't begin to guess what reason her fiancé had for cheating on her, other than he'd lost his mind. "Maybe that's it, and maybe it's not. All I know is that time has a way of making us see things in the way we need to see them in order to cope and move on."

She glanced at him over her shoulder. "You really believe that?"

He didn't know if he believed that or not. He thought about Casey, his buddy in the army. Casey had died in a freak accident in Afghanistan when his Humvee rolled over on a pitted dirt road. Rafe had been shocked and heartbroken. But he'd told himself that at least Casey hadn't died in a hail of bullets, or been blown to bits by a bomb. "Yeah, maybe. Look at your dad. In the beginning, you could hardly breathe. But now you can look back and appreciate the sort of man he was. You can breathe again."

"True," she admitted.

"Look, all I know is that I don't care if this dude is the preeminent heart surgeon in America. I think he's a fucking idiot."

Hallie's eyes widened. She grinned. "I need you to follow me around all day and say things like that."

In a heartbeat.

"You really are the best, Rafe." Her smile was full of gratitude. "Thank you."

"Just trying to help," he muttered, and looked away. Because when he looked in Hallie's eyes, his body thrummed with want and old desires, and he thought about that kiss, and he wanted to kiss her so bad that he ached.

He picked up the posthole digger and rammed it into the ground. He was startled by Hallie's hand on his arm.

"Hey," she said. "Are you all right?"

His gaze fell to her lips. "Fine."

"Okay. Well, thanks for listening. *Again,"* she said with a playful roll of her eyes.

He could feel himself tensing. It was a natural instinct, preparing to fight or flee. He should flee, but for the second time that day, Rafe touched her. He brushed her hair back over her shoulder and said, "Will you stop thanking me, already? I'm starting to feel like your pastor."

"Friends thank each other."

"Friends just do for each other," he said. "Here's some friendly advice, which you've heard before because I've said it about a dozen times this week alone. Stop thinking about the doc. Start thinking about what you need and where you're going from here." He touched her cheek. "Find the thing that makes you want to get up every day, and forget the thing that wants to make you stay in bed. The earth's going to keep turning, Hallie. You're not going to be in the same place as you were yesterday or where you are today."

"You are *so good* at the supportive-friend-after-a-breakup thing. But you must think I'm a hopeless case."

"Not for a minute," he said. "I just think you're going to have to dig a little deeper to figure out what your passion is, because it's not going to miraculously show up on your doorstep."

"Right," she said, nodding. "You're so *right*. It's starting to get annoying." She smiled. She poked him in the chest. "You're pretty damn smart, Rafe."

"That's right, I'm a freaking genius," he said, and put the digger between them. "That's why I'm out here digging postholes."

"I know how you must *love* that, so I'll leave

you alone." She started backing away from him. "I still have your shirt from Sunday. I'll run it over to you sometime this week."

"Not until I teach you how to run. I'll text you. I mean, if you're serious about taking it up."

"Of course I am. How hard can it be?" She turned and began to lope back down the road.

Rafe shook his head as he watched her. That emu had no idea how hard it was going to be. "Straighten up!" he yelled after her. "Shorten your stride!"

He heard her laughter float up, and she responded with a girlie fist pump as she carried on that he found utterly goofy and charming.

Well, he'd done it. He'd figured out a way to put himself in her orbit. Part of him screamed *idiot*—he wasn't getting away from that kiss. He'd just put hope into a situation where hope had no business being.

Another, entirely masculine part of him was stoked. He wanted to be with her and near her, and if being a coach was how he had to do it, so be it. At least it was something to do other than stare longingly at her.

He would have to text Jason and let him know he couldn't make it this weekend, because that's how pathetic this thing inside him was—he was going to blow off the future he was trying to build under the pretense of teaching Hallie how to hold herself while she ran.

For the second time in a matter of days, he considered what a chump he was, pining after the one girl he'd never get. He struck the digger into the ground with such force that it reverberated through him.

Chapter Eight

Hallie did not take Rafe's advice about her running form or the actual "moving on" with her life. At least not initially.

She wanted to move on. But it wasn't as easy as it sounded. So that evening she made herself predictably miserable by scrolling through her Instagram account. Through all those pictures of a happy bride-to-be, basking in the glow of affection from Chris, all of it manufactured for her page. She was one of *those* people, who had spent the last two or three years constructing her high-society life in pictures, carefully choosing the perfect photos that showcased her perfect, enviable life. Pictures of her and Chris and craft cocktails on the beach. With her bridesmaids in the bridal salon, where she coyly pressed a finger to her mouth, as if to suggest that she shared a secret with everyone who saw the photo of one of the many gowns she considered. Pictures of gourmet dining and sunsets and engagement rings and shoes.

Hallie had over twenty thousand followers,

thanks to the announcement of her engagement in *Bridal Guide* magazine last year.

When she realized what a following she'd developed, she began to reach beyond the pretty life she'd constructed, where there was no mention of her father's death, no hint of a scaled-back wedding, not a whisper of trouble with Chris. She'd combed the internet for pictures of what she'd like to have at her wedding, like the floral arrangements suspended over a dining table with a two-word caption: *Should I?* That one had earned over a thousand likes and half as much in comments.

She was not a narcissist—or at least she didn't think so. She had been playing the part that she was supposed to play in Chris's view of the world. *Starring Hallie Prince as the fiancée, the soon-to-be wife, the girl who has it all together! The girl who has taste and class and time to post on Instagram!*

She couldn't believe she'd fallen for his stupid platitudes, the ones that lured her into agreeing to marry him. *You're the woman of my dreams, Hallie. I never knew I could feel this way before I met you, Hallie. I've been waiting for you all my life, Hallie.*

"Barf," she muttered. He'd said those things, but he hadn't acted those things, he had *not* acted his part, and she should have questioned it a lot sooner than she did. The signs that should have raised doubts had been everywhere. She couldn't count how many times she'd felt in the way of his busy life. But she'd excused him because he was a *surgeon,* and she was a *failed dancer.* She'd wanted him to come to Three Rivers, particularly after her father had died and they needed to rally around the home base, but Chris always had an excuse. "I'm covered up at work," he'd say. "Come to Houston." Of course he was covered up with work. His services were in demand. He had lives to save!

But when she arrived in Houston, how many times had she found a note in his condo that said he was working a late shift, or he'd meet her and hurry her off to dinner because he had to get up at the crack of dawn? And yet, he could find time during the week to play golf or take his boat out on the Gulf.

Hallie couldn't blame Chris. She blamed herself for falling for it. She'd allowed herself to be swallowed whole by his expectations and, she had to admit, her family's expectations. She had lost herself in that, but then again, she'd never really found herself. After she'd washed out of ballet in such a humiliating fashion, she'd gone along with what everyone thought she ought to do. She was supposed to be a society wife, so she'd prepared for it, because what else was there for her? She was supposed to be the person to show up at charity functions and award dinners, to make sure the doorman was tipped at the end of the year, to schedule Chris's vacations, host his dinner parties, wash his dirty underwear. That was all anyone had expected of her.

That's all she'd expected of herself.

Hallie closed her eyes. Why couldn't men be more like Rafe? Solid, trustworthy men who didn't need women to take care of them?

She opened her eyes and looked at her iPad again, and went to her email.

There was the usual glut of sale notices, daily news bulletins and the like. She scrolled through them, scanning the subjects, seeing nothing she wanted to open until she came to one received two days ago. *We Want You Back.* It had been sent by the Comeback Center at the University of Texas, her alma mater. Or rather, what her alma mater would have been had she graduated. What the heck was a comeback center?

She opened the email.

Dear HALLIE JANE PRINCE,

Did you know it's never too late to return to college? Many college students leave school without finishing a degree plan because the demands of work and study can be difficult to juggle, financial obligations may require tough choices, or health issues necessitate taking a

132

break. Whatever your reason for leaving before degree completion, we want to help you finish.

At the Comeback Center, we will work with you to design a course of study that meets the adult student's needs and satisfies the requirements for your chosen degree program. Our records indicate you lack eighteen hours toward obtaining a bachelor of fine arts in dance. Call us today to learn how to finish what you started!

Was this for real?

Hallie read the email again. She clicked on the link provided, which took her to a page on the University of Texas website. But why were they sending this to her? She hadn't quit school because of a job or lack of money or health issues. She'd quit because she couldn't dance her way into an occupation. She was never a principal dancer in all her time there. She never got on with a company. So what was the point of a bachelor of fine arts in dance when she couldn't use it to dance?

Out of curiosity, she went back to the UT website and looked at the dance program. As she scrolled through the slated performances for the semester, and information about the degree, something caught her eye. It was buried in a paragraph, but there was a link to UTeach Dance. When she followed the link, she discovered that a person could get a BFA degree that included certification in children's dance instruction.

She snorted and closed the link. "Who would I teach? I don't know any kids."

She flipped back to Instagram once more and looked at her languishing account. She hadn't posted on Instagram in over a month, because she didn't know how to transition from pictures of a happy bride planning for her wedding to the sad sack she was now—the one who hung out in her room on an unmade bed with empty candy bar wrappers everywhere. The person who prepared dinner for two and then ate both portions. The person who knew just how many times Mr. Creedy's cows had walked through a hole in the fence.

Yeah, there was no mystery as to her weight gain and general myopic feeling. And when she looked at her Instagram, she felt only one thing: what a fool she'd been.

If she were honest—God knew it hurt, but okay, she'd be honest—she'd known for a few months that this thing with Chris wasn't great. Maybe, if her dad hadn't died, Hallie would have finally pulled the plug. But her dad *did* die, and she couldn't think after his death, not really, and another two or so months had passed before she realized that nothing had really changed. She and Chris were not ideal. But then, it felt like too much to face the fact that maybe they shouldn't get married. Her grief over her father's death had made her turn a blind eye to what she knew was true with Chris.

Rafe said that grief had a way of making people see what they needed to see. Maybe she had needed *not* to see, and didn't, until Chris put his business right in front of her, on the bedsheets she'd bought at fucking Saks, thank you.

Hallie tossed aside her iPad with the happy-not-happy pictures.

She was sick of the moping around. She was sick of eating to numb herself, of feeling sorry for herself, of the whole damn thing. She wished she could move on to something else, but that was the problem with her life. She'd never really been on her own. She'd never learned how to cope without someone to help her. She was easily persuaded into relationships, and had a bad habit of turning the relationship into her job, her purpose. Where was *she* in that? How could she possibly know what she was capable of if she never got out and lived life on her own terms?

Getting out on her own suddenly sounded like a great idea. But how?

She got up and went into her walk-in closet. It was the size of a study, with double racks for clothes, a center island with drawers for her lingerie. The racks were stuffed full, coordinated by color. Floor-to-ceiling shelves on the back wall were devoted entirely to shoes and purses.

She had been steadily filling her closet with the clothes she'd bought in preparation for a life as an important surgeon's wife and a big-money fundraiser on the charity circuit. Chris had once told her she needed to stop looking like she was always on her way to a nightclub, and more like a River Oaks wife. Hallie had been offended by that remark, but Christopher just laughed it off. "You know what I mean."

Oh, she'd understood what he'd meant, all right. He'd wanted her to look like a trophy wife, and instead, she was disappointing him by looking like what he must have imagined was a floozy. It wasn't as if she was dressing provocatively. But neither was she dressing primly. She wasn't wearing Chanel, she was wearing cute Alice + Olivia. Nevertheless, instead of shoving a foot up his ass like she ought to have done, she'd gone shopping.

Hallie cringed now as she stared at all the designer togs and frippery in her closet. She imagined it all in one big pile on the floor. *Instagram* that, *bitch*.

Which . . . was not a totally bad idea, come to think of it. She didn't really have a firm plan, but it seemed entirely reasonable that change needed to start with her view of herself. She needed to get in shape, and she didn't need these designer clothes.

She started yanking clothes off the hangers until she had an armful. She marched out of the closet and threw the first item on the floor. And then quickly swooped down to pick it up. She wasn't a heathen.

She marched the armload to her bed and dropped it, then returned to the closet for the next armload. And again and again and again, until she'd taken out every bit of clothing that even remotely reminded her of being Chris's wife. Boating clothes, golf clothes, sparkly dresses for fundraisers, sensible suits for business meetings. By the time she was done, she had an impressive pile of clothing.

She went back into the closet for a pair of wool pants she'd bought in London the time Chris had insisted she come along to a conference he had to attend. With the exception of the cocktail party to welcome participants and speakers, she'd hardly seen him at all. So she'd amused herself in the only way she really knew how—a trip to the Royal Ballet.

And lots and lots of shopping in Knightsbridge.

When she took the pants from the hanger, she noticed a vaguely familiar-looking cardboard box on a shelf behind the clothes. The shelf was supposed to be for shoes, but this box was too small for that. She rehung the pants, picked up the box, and saw a copy of her wedding invitation pasted on the outside. Her wedding invitations? She hadn't remembered putting them in here.

She carried the box into her room and collapsed, cross-legged, onto the floor. She removed the lid and took out one of four hundred invitations to her wedding.

Mrs. Cordelia Applewhite Prince
requests the honor of your presence
at the wedding of her daughter

Miss Hallie Jane Prince
to
Dr. Christopher Drew Davenport

son of Mr. and Mrs. David Davenport

on December 31 at seven o'clock in the evening.

Dinner and dancing to follow.

Four hundred invitations that were never sent because Christopher had been fucking Dani.

Surprisingly, Hallie felt nothing but disgust as she stared at the crème-colored paper and gold script. How had the box ended up in her closet, anyway? She didn't remember putting it there, although anything was possible. She hadn't exactly been herself these last few weeks.

Was it Mayrose, the housekeeper? Maybe she thought Hallie would want to reminisce one day. Or maybe she had it in for Hallie because of the candy wrappers.

Hallie ripped the invitation in half and tossed it onto the floor beside her. But something about the torn invitation caught her eye. That was what Instagram *should* be about—real life. The day after the party. The hours of heartache, the tedium of existence—regular life. But no, people wanted to see the girl with the perfect life have the perfect wedding. What she wouldn't give to deconstruct that life now on Instagram. Just tear it all down—

"Hold the phone," Hallie said aloud.

Why *not* deconstruct it on Instagram? What if she deconstructed a high-society wedding and the illusion of a perfect life? She was a very visual person, a visual learner. What if she showed the real her to the world and to herself, and not the carefully manufactured princess?

She popped up from the floor and went back into her closet to search through her built-in chest of drawers until she found what she was looking for: a camera. It was left over from the days before phone cameras were really good, a gift she and Luca had gotten for their birthday one year. Luca didn't care much for his after a couple of weeks of taking funny pictures, but Hallie loved hers. Luca said she had a good eye. She took pictures of everything—people, animals, landscapes. What had happened to *that* Hallie?

She spent several minutes checking out the camera, making sure it still worked. When she was convinced it was good to go, she looked around her room for a place to start, and her gaze landed on her reception dress. She'd left it on the chaise since last Sunday when she'd wrangled it off her body, leaving it mangled there, ignoring it and thereby ignoring the horrible drunk evening in which she'd humiliated herself.

The dress was wrinkled, and there was dirt at the knee area and along the hem. She'd even managed to tear one of the spaghetti straps. It was an ignominious end to a very expensive reception dress. She lifted the camera and took a picture of the dress lying haphazardly on the chaise, then looked at the screen. She liked what she saw.

Hallie picked up the dress and the camera and went outside, walking along a flagstone path that wended through palms and loquat trees, through azalea and bougainvillea, past shaped hedges, and through a stone archway into the pool area.

The sun was just going down, the light sort of golden. The Saltillo-tile patio wrapped around the back of the entire house, beneath a lanai, and bled into a vine-covered pergola over more patio. Ceiling fans turned lazily on a gentle breeze. Giant pots of chrysanthemums added color.

Beyond the patio, down a few steps, was a

zero-edge pool, and beyond that, miles and miles of ranchland, as far as the eye could see. It was a beautiful vista, often photographed for publications. When she was a child, a movie crew had filmed here.

Beneath the pergola, Hallie dragged a chair over from the dining table, climbed on top of it, and pushed half of the dress through the wooden slats and vines above. The dress hung down crookedly.

She reached up on her tiptoes and rearranged some of the vines of the climbing hydrangea to hang out the sleeves so that it appeared as if the dress had grown into the arbor. She added a garden hose to hang beside it, and a pair of gloves peeking out from the bodice. She climbed down from the chair, then took several pictures from different angles of what looked like an abandoned dress hanging there.

She returned to her room and uploaded the pictures to her laptop and edited them, added some filters, trying black and white, then a sepia tone. When she was ready, she created a new Instagram page: the Deconstruction of a High-Society Wedding.

She posted two pictures of her dress and invited her followers to view them.

Fifteen minutes later, no one had viewed her photos. Not a single heart was clicked, not a single comment was made.

"Okay, well, you're not doing this for the glory, remember?" she muttered to herself. She paused, shrugged a little. "Maybe for a little revenge though."

She shut her laptop, picked up the box of invitations, and took them outside. This time, she walked around the edge of the patio to the fire pit, and upended the box of invitations into the pit. She arranged them so they were clearly legible, then grabbed a fire starter. It was dark now, and it was only in the glow from the round, solar flower bed lights that she could see the invitations. Through the video lens on her camera, it made a very eerie scene. She zoomed in, slowly walked around the fire pit, then zoomed out, and with her fire starter, set the pile on fire. She videoed the edges of the invitations curling black before the entire invitation disappeared into blue flame.

She posted the video on her new Instagram page.

And then she boxed up all the clothes she'd taken out of her closet, destined for Dress for Success. She'd helped raise funds for the nonprofit once—its goal was to help women gain economic independence in a variety of ways, including giving them clothing for job interviews and work. She looked around at the boxes and felt good about what she was doing. The last few hours had been cathartic. She was looking forward, and not backward. Rafe had told her to think about what she needed and go for it. For the first time in a long time, she actually had some budding ideas.

And she couldn't wait to tell Rafe. She texted him a couple of pictures of the dress and typed, See? New leaf—photographer.

A few seconds later, the three little dots popped up.

He posted a thinking emoji. That wasn't exactly what I meant.

But still, pretty cool, right?

The three dots came up again. Thought the dress was a whole lot prettier on you, but I like what you've done with it. Pretty cool, leaving it to die up there all alone.

A tiny little trickle of warmth ran through Hallie. It was never going to hurt her feelings one bit for someone to say she looked good in her reception dress, even it was good ol' Rafe, and not a new husband.

She typed: Starting an Instagram page— Deconstruction of a High-Society Wedding. Check it out. Tomorrow, you will discover some new uses for wedding shoes and pumpkins.

☺. Now that is something I've been waiting for, for a very long time. I've got a pumpkin and a shoe over here and I don't know what to do with them.

Hallie laughed. She sent back a GIF of the emoji blowing a kiss.

She did not get a response.

She put down her phone and looked at her nearly empty closet. She thought about Rafe, stretched out on her bed, reading a book. Was she crazy to wish he was here right now so she could blow that kiss directly at him?

Was she crazy to think of kissing him again?

Crazy, all right. Talk about rebound—the first guy to be nice to her after Chris, and all she wanted to do was curl up beside him and hide from the world. That was so like her, and that was part of her problem. Besides, she was pretty sure Rafe Fontana had better things to do than comfort her.

Chapter Nine

At six on Saturday morning, Rafe texted Hallie. Get up and get ready to run. I'll pick you up at 6:30.

He was not surprised to get her response: WTF?!?!

He chuckled to himself and texted, Get up. He hit send, then whistled as he got ready to go.

Hallie was out on the drive when he arrived in his truck. He leaned across the seat and opened the passenger door. She didn't move, but glared at him with her arms crossed tightly across her body.

"You ready?" he asked.

"This is insane. Plus, it's freezing out here. There is actual frost on the actual pumpkin, Rafe."

"You'll warm up."

"Where are we going? I thought this was a running lesson."

"It is. But we're going someplace where we won't disturb the cows or your family. I anticipate a lot of moaning and groaning from you."

She did not disappoint—she groaned, dropped her arms like a child who'd run out of options, and got in his truck. He turned up the drive.

"When I said I was going to take up running, I didn't mean in the middle of the night," she complained.

"The sun is shining, Hallie," he said, and pointed at the thin line of light beginning to appear on the horizon.

"The point is, it's *too early*."

"You need to train yourself to run before the heat of the day."

"I need to *train* myself to never open my big fat mouth again."

He laughed. "I think the odds are stacked against you."

"Shut *up,* Mr. Perfect Army Ranger guy."

He tapped her thigh with his fist. "Are you always so grumpy in the morning?"

"What do you think?" She slumped in her seat and looked out the window.

"I think you're definitely a morning grouch." He was enjoying this. "What if I told you there are donuts at the end of a run?"

Hallie slowly turned her head to give him an appraising look. "Donuts from Jo's Java?"

He snorted and shook his head. "Do I look like an idiot? Of course Jo's Java."

"Okay," she said. "All right then. Maybe you're not as annoying as I was thinking."

Rafe laughed.

He drove to the high school and parked outside the stadium.

"Edna Colley High School," Hallie said, peering up at the stadium. "My dad paid for that stadium, did you know?"

"I heard that around town," he said, and opened the truck door. "Come on. We're going to the track."

She was moving a little slow, and had to jog a little to keep up with him, which Rafe thought was good for her—it would at least get her sluggish, not-a-morning-person blood moving. He walked through a gate and out onto the track and shrugged out of his jacket. Underneath, he was wearing a T-shirt.

"Look at you!" Hallie said, and put her hands on his biceps and tried to squeeze them. "You're a *beast!* Did they do this to you in the army? Or did you always have these giant arms?"

"Okay," he said, smiling wryly as he caught her arms and forced her hands from his biceps. "I want to show you a couple of things before we start. Is it okay if I touch you?"

She sighed as if he was taxing her. "Do you think I'll melt? Of course you can touch me, Rafe. We're friends. We've known each other all our lives, remember?"

He didn't think she was going to melt. She was sexy as hell, and she looked very sturdy. She looked like she could give as good as she got. His mind tried to detour into giving her what he wanted to give her. He reined it back in. He turned her around so that her back was to him. "Stand up straight."

"I am standing up straight."

"You've got your weight on one hip and your hands on your waist like you're about to tell me off. Stand up straight."

She muttered something unintelligible under her breath, but dropped her arms and stood up straight.

He put his hands on the sides of her hips. Lightly. Hardly touching her at all. But Hallie made a little jump as if he'd startled her. He felt a little jump in him, too. He was acutely aware of every place his hands and fingers touched her body. He drew a shallow breath and pressed lightly against her, then pushed her pelvis forward just a bit. "Feel that?"

"I feel your hands on my butt," Hallie said.

"I meant the position of your pelvis."

"Don't try and talk sexy to me."

"That's where you want your pelvis to be," he said. And then he stepped away before he did something crazy, like slip his arms around her waist and draw her into his chest and nuzzle her neck.

"Suck in that core, girl," he said. "Arms waist level." He bent his elbows, demonstrating. "Don't look at your feet, look forward. Ready?"

"Why are you making this so complicated?"

"Let's go," he said, and started off in a jog. After a moment's hesitation, Hallie did, too. She ran slowly, probably because he was telling her to keep her feet beneath her and to stop hunching her shoulders.

"Too many instructions!" she shouted at him. Rafe dropped out and watched her run around the track. She had a weird swing of her arms that made him want to laugh. When she made it one length around the track, she stopped. She sounded asthmatic.

"Had enough for today?" he asked.

She straightened up and punched his chest. "I'm not a quitter!" she said breathlessly. "Not yet, anyway."

"Then let's go again." He ran with her this time, chatting easily as she labored in her breathing. "You're running too fast," he advised her. "You want to go at a pace where you can still talk."

"Talk!" she wheezed. "Don't be stupid—I can't even *breathe.*"

They made another lap, and when they came back to the start, she folded over and gasped for breath like she was having a panic attack. "How far was that?" she asked breathlessly. "About a mile or so?"

"You've gone a half mile."

She glared at him. "You are lying, Rafael Fontana!"

"Each lap is four hundred meters," he said, pointing to the four hundred mark on the track. "Sixteen hundred meters makes a mile."

"I hate you," she said curtly, and took off again.

They continued like this, Hallie near to collapsing at the end of every lap, but getting up to go again, and Rafe jogging alongside her, encouraging her. When she'd gone two miles, she collapsed onto the track flat on her back and sprawled out. "I'm dying. I'm *hot.* I have on too many clothes. How long is a marathon?"

With his legs braced and his arms folded, Rafe stared down at her. "Laps or miles?"

"*Laps,* meanie."

"One hundred and four. You've done eight so far." He squatted down beside her. "It was hard, wasn't it?" he asked sympathetically.

"*So* hard."

"I know what could make it better."

Her face filled with hope. "A donut?"

"Not a donut. Glutes. If you work on strengthening your butt, this won't be so hard."

Hallie slowly pushed herself up to her elbows. "I really, honestly, want to punch you in the mouth so bad right now," she said. "What I'm ready for is a damn donut, Rafe. Shut up about strong butts."

"Fair enough," he said, and stood up, offering his hand to help her up. "Let's get a donut."

She slipped her hand into his and allowed him to haul her up. She came up with a bounce and a suspicious glare. She was standing close enough that he could see flecks of gold in her hazel eyes, and the tiny line of perspiration that ran down her temple. "Tell me the truth," she said. "Were you trying to kill me?"

"I would never try and kill you on a track, Hallie. Too easy. I like a challenge in all that I do." He slipped his hand under her elbow.

"Oh yeah?" Her gaze flicked to his mouth, and Rafe's blood immediately began to flow a little quicker in his veins. She wasn't going to kiss him again, was she? One time was an accident. Two times was definitely—

"What sort of challenge?" she asked.

So many thoughts rambled through his head, so many images, that he was struck silent for a moment. The challenge of wooing her, for a start. Of seducing her. The challenge of making love to her in a way she would never forget and would compare every other man to for the rest of her life. Yeah, that kind of challenge.

"Cat got your tongue?" she asked, and lifted her gaze to his.

Was he just deranged, or was he feeling something flow between them? Something sharp and tingly, a thousand bursts of laser light in his head. He had the fleeting idea that he should kiss her. Turn the tables. Take her beneath the bleachers and ruin years of a friendship that he truly valued. It sounded ridiculous in his head, but in that very heated moment, it seemed almost worth the risk.

"Or are you feeling guilty for torturing me?" she asked, her eyes narrowing.

"Nope," he murmured. "There are other ways I'd like to torture you—"

Divine intervention saved him from saying something he would definitely regret—two people walked out onto the track and waved cheerfully at them. He caught sight of them from the corner of his eye, and like he'd trained himself to do over the years, he faded away from Hallie. "Like some squats, here and now, baby," he said cavalierly, and grinned. "But I guess it's donut time." He put his hand on her nape and squeezed like he used to do to Angie, and started them walking in the direction of the truck.

Hallie picked out the largest jelly donut Jo Carol had in the bakery display. Rafe opted for a breakfast sandwich and carefully avoided Jo Carol's inquisitive look that was darting back and forth between him and Hallie beneath her towering hive of platinum hair.

"It's good to see you, Hallie," Jo Carol said as she made their coffees. "You look good in spite of everything."

Leave it to Jo Carol to subtly slide into gossip.

Hallie looked up. "Thank you," she said uncertainly.

"Are you going to be sticking around Three Rivers?" Jo Carol asked, and fixed her gaze on Hallie, watching her closely. "I know your mom must really love having you at home."

Rafe could see the color rising in Hallie's cheeks. Jo Carol kept her finger firmly pressed against the town's pulse, and every little thing about the Prince family was fodder. Rafe had no doubt Jo Carol would be sharing Hallie's answer with whoever came in the door today.

But Hallie was a pro at this. She suddenly smiled prettily and shrugged. "You know, I'm not really sure," she said, as if thinking about it for the first time. "I have *so many* options, and I haven't quite decided."

"Oh, you do?"

"I do."

"Anything you want to share?"

"Nope." Hallie smiled, and took her jelly donut.

That was all Jo Carol would get today, and Rafe could tell from Jo Carol's sly smile that she knew it. So she turned her large bosom and her attention toward Rafe, because she was not one to give up without a fight.

"Rumor had it you were in town," she said as she poured coffee into their cups. "Rumor has it you're going to be a college graduate soon."

"Rumor's been busy," Rafe said. "I've got one last final and I'll have my degree."

"Well, that's great, Rafe," Jo Carol said. "We're

all so proud of you. I've always said to the young men around here they ought to consider the armed services. It's great they can help people go to college who otherwise probably couldn't afford it."

Rafe felt a sharp prick of self-consciousness with that remark. Not because what she said wasn't true—his parents maybe could have afforded to send one of them to college, but not all three—but because it was a blatant and pointed reminder of how vastly different his life was from Hallie's. She had options, *so many* options, as she'd said. She could have gone to any college she'd wanted. She could have gone to any college in the world. Charlie Prince would have sent her to Russia to study ballet if she wanted.

He was lucky because the government had paid for his college.

Jo Carol handed him the coffees. "I'm sure Hallie will miss you when you're gone. Won't you, Hallie?" she asked slyly.

"Of course I will," Hallie said. "I *always* miss Rafe—we've been friends since we were kids. But we'll text. Won't we," she said, elbowing him playfully.

"Sure," he said.

"Mm-hmm," Jo Carol said, and arched a brow in Rafe's direction. "And your poor parents. I know your dad needs you right now. How is your mother, by the way? I haven't seen her in a while and I hope she's okay."

Rafe could feel a prickling on the back of his neck. He wanted away from Jo Carol and her prying ways. "Mom's doing great. Thanks for this." He held up the coffee.

"You bet. Anyway, I'm sure both of your parents are relieved Rico will be home by the time you leave town."

Hallie gasped with surprise. "Rico's coming home?" she asked with great delight. "I haven't seen him in ages!"

"Rumor has it," Jo Carol said with a sly little shrug. "You two enjoy this beautiful morning, now."

Too late for that, courtesy of one Jo Carol.

The sun had come up and warmed the day, so Rafe suggested they go outside where Jo Carol couldn't hear a damn thing they said. They walked out to a sidewalk bench near the town square. Occasionally, a car would slowly rumble by, the tires bouncing along the cobblestones of Main Street. At one end of the thoroughfare was the courthouse. At the other, the shiny new Saddlebush Land and Cattle Company, the Three Rivers Ranch business headquarters. They'd recently installed a bronzed statue of a bronc rider in front of it.

The bench they chose was beneath a live oak tree, and there was a dark stain at one end Hallie

155

did not like. So she sat next to him, so close that she was touching him. He could feel the warmth of her, and as he ate his sandwich, he imagined that it was her skin touching him. And then he took it from there, torturing himself by imagining skin on skin, because apparently he liked choosing the worst time and place for sexual fantasies. Hallie in a bath. Hallie in a bed. Hallie on top . . .

"I'm so excited Rico is coming home," she said. "Why didn't you tell me?"

The sexy images self-destructed into tiny little bits. Rafe made himself look at her. "Must have slipped my mind."

"No one can make me laugh harder than Rico. Sometimes, the image of us as the twins from *The Shining* pops into my head, and I can't help laughing."

Something turned a little sour in Rafe's belly. "What?"

Hallie looked at him with surprise. "I never told you? Where were you? Oh, that's right, you'd gone off to the army. It was the year Rico and I graduated from high school. We were hanging out and Rico had the idea for Halloween. He found these cheap blue dresses and bought wigs." She laughed. "It was hilarious."

Rafe couldn't imagine how they'd been invited to the same party. Rico had always run with a very different crowd—a boozy, pot-smoking crowd, mostly cowboys and oil field workers. "I didn't know you two were getting invited to the same parties."

"It wasn't a party. It was an event at the Galaxy," she said, referring to an avant-garde theater in town. "They were screening *The Shining* and everyone was supposed to come in costume." She ate more of her donut.

Rafe put half his sandwich back in a little bag, his appetite gone. This long-ago Halloween event didn't sit well with him, and he wasn't entirely sure why. "Was it a date?" he asked, careful not to meet her gaze.

"What?" Hallie laughed. "Oh my God, Rafe! Of course not. We were hanging out as friends, just like you and I are hanging out as friends. It's just that Rico and I have both been kind of aimless at times and available for things like that." She shrugged. "It was fun."

Rafe swallowed down a lump of something bitter. It wasn't as if it mattered—it had been ten or so years ago. So why did it feel like it mattered?

Because he'd always been a little jealous of Rico's easy, breezy way.

"Hey, when *are* you leaving?" she asked.

"Hmm?" He was still thinking of his charming, fun-loving, troublemaking little brother.

"When you finish school. You're moving to Chicago, right?" She looked up at him and smiled. "Rumor has it you're going," she said, mimicking Jo Carol.

Yes, he was going. His plan had always been to be out of here before she got married, to be long gone so he wouldn't have to see the happy bride with her new, wealthy doctor husband. Or worse—with a happy family. "First of the year."

"You haven't said much about it. Is that perhaps because I've been sucking up all the available air with my woes?" She turned her head and looked him directly in the eye.

She had a bit of jelly in the corner of her mouth. Rafe impulsively scraped it off with the tip of his little finger. "You haven't sucked up *all* the available air."

"Bullshit," she said cheerfully. "No one gets down in the weeds of self-pity like I do, trust me. Tell me about Chicago."

Rafe wanted desperately to tuck the loose strand of strawberry blond hair behind her ear. He wanted desperately to tell her everything about the program. To lay down on a blanket in the hills somewhere and just talk about life and plans and hopes for the future.

"With two close friends, I'm starting a program for teens," he said. "The goal is to get them off the street and away from drugs, and teach them how to use their minds and bodies productively."

"By teaching them martial arts."

"Among other things," he said. "We're

158

designing the program so it tackles everything—tutoring, physical training, peer support. You name it. All three of us have some connection to troubled youth. For me, it was Rico. Jason's sister died of a heroin overdose while we were in Afghanistan. And Chaco is a recovering alcoholic."

"But why Chicago?" she asked. "Why not here?"

Because you are here. Because I can't spend my life mourning you.

"Jason's from Chicago and lives on the South Side. His family has a lot of connections. It's really the perfect location, near some low-income schools and neighborhoods that have high dropout rates. We found a space and we're starting to outfit it. I get up there as often as I can to help, but until I finish school, I can't be there as much as I'd like."

"You're amazing, you know that?"

He snorted.

"No, you really are. You were born wanting to do good."

Rafe chuckled. "Isn't everyone born wanting to do good?"

"No. And even if they are, it seems like most people turn that around by the time they are adults and want to do good for themselves and not others. I'm just saying, you're one in a million, and you deserve the best of everything."

159

She was one in a million, and oh, how he wanted to kiss the tiny bit of jelly that remained on the corner of her mouth.

Her eyes were on his mouth again, and maybe he was imagining things, or hoping things, but Rafe could feel the heat begin to swirl around them, wrapping them in a cocoon.

They both jumped when her phone suddenly started playing trumpets.

"Shit," Hallie said, and slapped a hand to her heart. "Why do I choose these ringtones?" She dug her phone from her pocket and looked at the screen. "Christ Almighty."

"Something wrong?"

"It's Chris." She turned the screen to Rafe so that he could read the text.

> Hallie, please talk to me. I saw your Insta page and I am so, so sorry I've caused you so much pain. I made a huge mistake. Please talk to me.

Rafe's gaze locked with Hallie's. A smile slowly moved across her lips, and in the next minute, they were both laughing. "What should I say?" she asked, giggling. " 'Just wait till you see what I do with the shoes'?"

"What do you really want to say?" Rafe asked, ignoring the pinch in his chest, afraid to hear the answer.

"I want to say, 'Get lost. Don't text me.' Or how about this—'Today I learned how to run from assholes like you, Chris.'" She laughed, then looked at her phone again. A frown creased her brow. She abruptly typed in a text, then read aloud, "I've moved on, Chris, exclamation mark, exclamation mark. Please don't text me." She hit send.

She was putting the phone back in her pocket when it trumpeted again. Hallie and Rafe bent over the phone together.

> What do I need to do to get you to talk to me?

"I don't want to talk to him," she said flatly.

"Don't respond," Rafe advised. "Block his number." Wishful thinking.

Hallie suddenly brightened. "I've got it." She typed something into her phone, hit send, then laughed and showed Rafe the text she'd sent. Give me a puppy and I'll consider it.

Rafe was confused.

"Chris is afraid of dogs," she said. "Like, really hates them."

"*What?* Just when I think I can't dislike this guy any more."

"Right?" she said, giggling. "That will do it, trust me. The subtext is in his face." She laughed. But Rafe's doubt must have been obvious

161

because she said, "Why are you looking at me like that? He'll never do it. He seriously does not like dogs. He will definitely get the message."

If it were Rafe, he'd crawl over broken glass to make amends. A dog seemed a whole lot easier. "Were you honestly prepared to live your life without dogs?" he asked in disbelief. "You love animals. You once had a pair of gerbils and a huge rabbit."

"I was willing to compromise," she said. "I was thinking of giving cats a try." She hopped up from the bench. "Oh, man, I'm sore," she said, bending backward.

"Next time, we hit the gym," he said, and stood, too, depositing their coffee cups in the trash receptacle.

They began to make their way down the sidewalk, Hallie with her arm looped through his. Rafe imagined they looked like an old couple that had lived their entire life together. In a way, they were—they had lived many years in this friendship, him pining for her, her cheerfully coming along on a ride with him she didn't even know she was on.

They strolled past the bank and a bulletin board where several community notices were posted, and paused to look. Hallie pointed to a very colorful poster in the corner. Join friends and family Thanksgiving Day for Kidz Korner performances of The Nutcracker. There was a picture of a ballerina below it, and below that, the time and place.

"A kid ballet!" Hallie said. "Isn't Kidz Korner that organization that works with disabled kids?"

"And developmentally challenged," he said. "The summer I graduated from high school, I worked there part-time."

She smiled up at him. "See? This is what I'm saying, Rafe. You're too good. You're Mother Teresa good."

"Trust me, I'm not. I happen to like kids, that's all," he said as they continued on. "So do you."

"I do. But when I graduated from high school, all I could think of was boys. Anyway, why has no one snatched you up? It was always a mystery to me and my friends why you didn't have a girlfriend."

"I had girlfriends," he scoffed.

"Yeah, like a new one every week," she said with a laugh as they reached his truck. "Everyone said Luca was the player, but you were giving him a run for his money."

Rafe opened the door of his truck for her. "You think I was a player?"

She slipped past him and turned around before climbing into his truck. They were standing too close again, and that electric thrum sparked again, but this time, it was a sharper jolt to his system. This closeness kept happening. Was he doing it subconsciously? Was she?

"I really don't know," she said. She tilted her head curiously to one side, and touched her fingers to his chin. "You need a shave."

A second, two seconds, three, passed before either of them spoke or moved. He couldn't shift his head from her touch. His gaze slid to her mouth, and he drew a long, slow breath. He had that feeling once again that he was going to kiss her. Just take her in his arms and kiss the breath out of her. And that was just the start of what he'd do.

Her hand skated down his chest. "Is something happening right now?" she murmured. "Asking for a friend."

"I don't know . . . is it?"

"I don't know . . . is it?" she echoed.

Something was happening all right. The world was collapsing around them, and his heart was exploding in his chest. But the warning bells went off, and red flags began to wave. He thought of all the tricks he'd taught himself to keep his hands off her. Of all the things his father had said to him when he'd wanted to ask Hallie to his prom. *People like the Princes don't mix with people like us.* And now the money issues at the ranch, the layoffs. What if he kissed her? What if he did more than kiss her? And what if, after all that, she backed off and things got weird, and holy hell, he'd never forgive himself if he got tangled up in something that broke his heart and cost his dad his job somehow on top of that.

So Rafe tamped down his feelings once again, smothered his desires, and leaned forward. He kissed her forehead. "Nope. Nothing is happening."

She bit her bottom lip as she peered up at him. She looked like she was considering debating him. He wished she would. He wished she would tell him that something was damn sure happening, and she wanted it as bad as he wanted it. But she said, "Okay."

He suppressed a sigh of disappointment. "Ready to go?"

Her eyes searched his face. She was clearly unsatisfied with that response, but she didn't push him. She said instead, quite seriously, "Did I ever tell you I danced in *The Nutcracker* once?" And she fell away from him, into the seat in the truck. "I was eight and I was a sugarplum fairy. A defining role."

The stunningly abrupt transition from sizzling heat to cold air was too much for Rafe. "You don't say," he said, and closed the door. He walked slowly around the back of his truck. It felt like his nerves were frying up like bacon beneath his skin.

When he got in the truck, she said, "In the middle of the dance, I stumbled out of my pirouette and slammed into a cardboard tree."

She gave him a sidelong look. "I crash into things a lot."

He didn't know what that meant. All he knew was that his mind was still wrapped around the taut sensations of restraining himself. His longing for her still reverberated in him, was still devouring him from the inside out.

As Hallie continued her blithe chatter about a childhood ballet, Rafe suffered in silence all the way back to the ranch.

Chapter Ten

Hallie stood in the drive at the ranch and watched Rafe pull away.

What the hell had happened in town? Because *something* had happened. One minute they were laughing at the text from Chris, and the next, he was kissing her on the forehead when she knew, she *knew,* he wanted to kiss her.

She'd definitely wanted to kiss him.

Or was it a case of her wishing too hard and imagining heat all over again?

But could she really invent that kind of moment? Because it felt a lot more intense than the day of the prairie chickens. Today, the way he'd looked at her—like he was starving, like he was desperate for a drink of water, that look of wanting—was something she'd seen before. Not just in the last week. Maybe not as potent and blistering, or so deeply seated in his eyes that her blood had begun to rush, but she'd seen various shades of that look before.

Actually, many times before.

But it always disappeared. Like a switch,

like something he could turn on and off. Those moments always ended in the same way, too—he'd laugh at something she'd said and send her away, like she was a kid and he was kissing her on the forehead and sending her off to bed.

She didn't want to be like a kid to him. She had wanted him to kiss her. *Really* wanted it.

And still, Hallie was confused about how she felt about that. She wasn't certain of her motives. She didn't trust herself to kiss Rafe for the right reasons, and not because this was some sort of weird rebound thing she was going through. She would die if she did that to him. She cared too much for Rafe. She truly loved him. He'd been one of her best friends forever, and she couldn't think of a better way to mess it all up than to have some sort of rebound crush and act on it.

But again, was it a rebound? It didn't feel that way. It felt weirdly genuine.

This was so confusing! The only thing she knew for certain was that she and Rafe were in a sort-of-cool space, but at the same time, a not-so-cool space.

With a small shake of her head, she walked into the house. She was suddenly feeling so tightly strung that she needed to stuff something into her mouth and into that tension. That jelly donut hadn't come close to touching the confusion she was feeling now.

In the kitchen, Hallie dug through the fridge—

where was a plate of nachos when you needed it—and finding nothing appetizing, she grabbed the milk and closed the fridge door. She shrieked—Luca was standing right there, frowning down at her. The milk slipped from her hand, but Luca dipped and caught it against her leg.

"What the hell, Luca?" she said irritably as she reached for the milk carton and slid it onto the counter. "You scared the crap out of me. You should announce yourself!"

"How could you not hear me?"

Good question. She gave him a good once-over as she opened a drawer in search of a cereal bowl. He was wearing work clothes—dirty jeans and a canvas jacket. "What are you doing here, anyway?" she asked. "I thought you were living your best life at Ella's house."

"First of all, you've seen Ella's house, and so you have to know that the only being that can live its best life out there is Priscilla the pig, and second, we are staying at my loft in San Antonio. And *third*—" He thrust his arm at her. He was holding her reception dress, which Hallie had failed to notice in the middle of her near heart attack. "What about *you*, Hallie? What kind of life are you living? Because I found this hanging from the arbor like a slain soldier."

"I forgot to take it down," she said. "I'm surprised the groundskeepers didn't take it down."

"The groundskeepers? The grounds*keeper*. We're down to one guy. Come on, Hal, what is going on?"

"Nothing! I was messing around. Where is the cereal, anyway?"

"I haven't seen you eat cereal since we were ten," Luca said, and opened up the pantry, walked inside, and returned with a box of Cheerios. "And what do you mean you were messing around? With your wedding dress?"

"For like the thousandth time, that is *not* a wedding dress, it is a *reception* dress."

"Same thing."

"*So* not the same thing."

"Whatever it is," he said, holding it up, "I'm pretty sure it doesn't belong hanging from an arbor with vines growing out of it."

"I was taking pictures of it for my Instagram page."

"Your what?"

How could she live among so many people with such limited knowledge of social media? "I've started a new Instagram page. It's a ruined wedding account."

Luca sighed. He draped the dress over the back of the barstool and pressed his hands against the bar. "Hallie. I've always had your back. But it's been six weeks or so since the big bombshell, and you're still wallowing—"

"Luca, *stop,*" Hallie said. "I am not wallowing.

It's an art project, that's all. It's something to do." She poured Cheerios into her bowl. "It's not like I have *anything* to do right now, so indulge me. Let me take a few pictures." Luca didn't speak. Hallie shrugged. "Well? Am I right or am I right?"

He sighed. "So how long are you going to hang out here with nothing to do? How long before you have a lawn chair in the cemetery?"

She gasped. "That is never going to happen," she said firmly. "Actually, I have plans. First, I'm going to get in shape. I've started running."

Luca snorted. "Okay," he said, as if he thought that was some setup to a joke.

"And I'm maybe thinking of going back to school." She watched her brother to gauge his reaction. The email she'd received had taken up residence in her head. What if she finished her bachelor of fine arts? What if she learned how to teach kids what she could never truly master herself? What if she struck out, all on her own, and accomplished something with no one's help? What if she did all those things? Wouldn't she be happy? Wouldn't she be proud?

"Really?" Luca perked up. "*This* is interesting. Go on."

"I got an email from the Comeback Center."

"The what?"

"The Comeback Center at UT Austin. Apparently it's this program that entices people who

171

didn't finish their degrees to come back and finish them."

"I thought you had given up on dance."

When he said it like that, it sounded so lame. It sounded like she was a quitter. "I gave up on being a professional dancer. But maybe I could teach it."

Luca stared at her a moment, thinking it through. "I think," he said slowly, as if he was choosing his words, "that this is a great idea."

Hallie immediately brightened. "You do?"

"Absolutely."

She grinned. "I'm just thinking about it. There's a lot to consider."

"Keep thinking," he said with a wink. "Okay." He pushed away from the bar. "Let's see this Instagram page or whatever."

Hallie fished her phone out of her pocket and pulled up her Instagram page to show him. But when she looked at the account, she gasped.

"What?"

"I don't believe it! Yesterday, I had one hundred and ten followers. Today, I have twenty-seven hundred!" She twirled around on her barstool with a grin. "It's taking off. It's going viral."

"That does not sound good." Luca came around the bar and looked over her shoulder at her phone. He peered at the photos of her dress, at the invitations burning in the fire pit. And another

172

one she'd added last night of a garter. Not *her* garter, because she'd never gotten around to getting one. But a party favor garter she'd picked up at some bridal event somewhere through the years—she'd found it in her closet. She'd wrapped it around the neck of an old stuffed bear she had stuck in her closet. She'd arranged the bear's legs and arms to appear to be a flailing so it looked like it was choking.

Luca leaned over her shoulder. "You took these?"

"I did," she said. "I used the camera we got for our birthdays, what, ten years ago, remember?"

"Yeah," he said. "I always thought you were a really good photographer. You have an artistic eye. These are really good, Hal. I find myself curious about the lunatic behind the photos, and I already know how crazy she is."

Hallie grinned with pleasure. "I have to text Rafe," she said, switching over to her texts.

"Rafe. Rafe Fontana?"

"He's the only Rafe I know," Hallie said as she began to text him the news.

"Why are you texting Rafe?"

"You wouldn't understand," she said. "Rafe and I have this thing—"

"A *thing*?"

"Not like that," she said, frowning at him. "We're really good friends, you know that. And I told him about my page. I just want to tell him

173

how many people are following it now because he'll get it. He gets *me*."

She paused there. She never held anything back from Luca, but something whispered that this was different. There was a lot in her head she still needed to make sense of. Her friendship with Rafe had developed many different faces—he was a good soul, a balm to the wound in her heart—but there was more to the story and she was only just beginning to realize it.

Whatever the story, it all came back to Rafe—his soul was pure light. He was the sort of man anyone would want in his or her corner. He had an innate ability to understand things that were too hard to put into words. He *listened*. He was kind, he was considerate, he was smart . . . all the things that made him perfect. Add the heat that had been stirring between them, and wow, Hallie felt like she was walking around with a powder keg in her head. Yes, her feelings about Rafe were complicated, and Luca would not understand.

Speaking of Luca, she suddenly noticed that he was studying her a little too closely. His scrutiny made her squirm, so she stood up from her stool. "He's teaching me to run," she said.

"Come again?"

Luca looked suspicious. *Damn it.* He knew her too well. If she wasn't careful, he'd pin her down and make her talk. "You heard me." She stood up and tried to move around him, but Luca threw out his arm like a crossing guard so that she couldn't pass. "You didn't eat your cereal."

"Too many carbs."

Luca gave her a withering look. "I saw you put down half a cake two days ago. Don't act like carbs are suddenly your nemesis."

"I'm a new leaf," she said, and pushed his arm aside. "I'm a runner now. Move."

"Well, that's just crazy talk," Luca said flatly. "And FYI, people don't need lessons to run."

She thought about Rafe's hands on her hips, and a tiny little shiver swept down her spine. "I happen to be very bad at it, so there." She tried again to push him aside, but Luca wasn't having it. Hallie was suddenly reminded of the summer Luca shot up, growing a good six inches taller than her. That had ended their occasional fistfights. Hallie had won them all up until that point.

"You can't be *that* bad at running."

"Be supportive! I'm really trying to change, Luca. I'm getting out of my head. I'm shedding my old skin."

"Gross," he said.

"Truth."

"And Rafe is helping you get out of your head, et cetera?" he asked, the suspicion back.

"Why not? You know how he is—he's fit and he's a teacher and he's always helped me."

Luca studied her a long moment. He pressed

175

his lips together, like he was thinking, and then he said, "Actually, I do know how he is."

He said that in such a strange way that Hallie wondered what exactly he meant, but before she could ask, Luca pulled her, against her will, into a tight embrace.

"Noo," she said into his chest. "Stop *hugging* me all the time."

"Can't. You're my twin sister and I love you and I want to help you and I don't like to see you hurt. It kills me."

"I'm not a big fan of being hurt, either, but I'm over it," she said into his stinky canvas coat. "Now I'm just filled with rage and a very strong desire to be different. Plus, my Instagram page is going viral, and I need to add some stuff before I lose my audience. By the way—" She tried to lean back, but Luca slapped his hand on her head and held her in place. "Do you still have the china dish samples I gave to you and Ella?"

"Probably."

"Great. Can I have them back? I want to smash them."

Luca squeezed tighter. "Aw, Hallie, bless your heart. I see you, you know. I get you. I know what you're thinking before you even know it."

"Then you must know I'm thinking I want you to let me go," she said, her voice muffled by his coat.

Luca kissed the top of her head.

"Why does everyone keep kissing my head like I'm a kid?" she said, rubbing the top of her head. At Luca's quizzical look, she said, "Never mind," and stepped around him. She picked up a banana on her way out.

"That's a big fat carb stick!" he called out, and pulled her uneaten bowl of cereal over to his place and poured milk into it.

Hallie's Instagram page had gained more followers before noon, along with some inspirational comments, most of them along the lines of *You go, girl.*

She texted Rafe: Up to 3,000 followers on my wedding deconstruction page! My rage is contagious.

He texted back: Congratulations on single-handedly starting a new cottage industry for bitter brides.

Hallie laughed.

By early afternoon she was in the garden shed. She'd cleared a space on one of the wooden benches, pushing aside the spades and terra-cotta pots, the bags of fertilizer and potting soil. She was hard at work hammering the heel of one of her wedding shoes into the pumpkin when she heard someone come into the shed and glanced over her shoulder. "Hey! Hi, Charlotte."

The family business office manager smiled. She shoved her hands into the pockets of her jeans. She glanced at the pumpkin, then looked uneasily at Hallie, as if she expected Hallie might be thinking of hammering her. Hallie had been getting that look around here a lot lately. Well, pardon her already—how was a person supposed to act when her wedding had blown up just as she was getting ready to send out invitations?

"Love your hair," Hallie said, gesturing lazily with the hammer. Charlotte had cut her curly blond hair to shoulder length and given herself bangs. She looked pretty and outdoorsy and determined in everything that she did. No wonder she was so successful with the family business—she was really so much more than her title of office manager implied. Charlotte was the one who knew where the bodies were buried and why.

"What's up?" Hallie asked as she turned back to her work. "Need a spade? A pumpkin? An unused wedding shoe?"

"No thanks," Charlotte said carefully. "Just reading the tea leaves here, but are you really nailing that shoe into the pumpkin?"

"I really am," Hallie said, and gave it one last whack to make sure it was secure. The next phase was the pumpkin guts, which she planned to arrange so that it looked like the pulp was billowing out of her shoe.

"That's so *weird*," Charlotte said. "I love it."

"It's art," Hallie said. "What brings you down

to the potting shed, otherwise known as the least visited building in our happy little compound?"

"This is not a happy compound," Charlotte corrected her. "And anyway, I was just wandering around."

Hallie laughed. "Liar," she said cheerfully, and put down her hammer, standing back to admire her work. "You are the busiest person I know besides Ella. I don't believe for a second that you're just wandering around, especially here. So who sent you out here to check on me? Was it my brother?"

Charlotte didn't answer right away. When Hallie pinned her with a look, she immediately threw up her hands in surrender. "Okay, but don't blame me. I didn't want to come out here at *all,* trust me. I was the one who said, 'Let the girl have her meltdown already.' "

"I would never blame you, Charlotte. I know my family. And I already had my meltdown. Was it Nick?"

"Nick! He'd have to pull his head out of his ass first. I can say no to Nick. But your mom, on the other hand, is scary, and I really, *really* don't know how to say no to her." She winced.

"Of course you can't!" Hallie agreed. "That takes a lifetime of training and continuing education credits, trust me. So I'll bite—*why* did Mom send you out here?"

"She thinks you should get out of the house

more. You know, to speed along the process of getting you back to normal. She said I should take you shopping."

Hallie stared at Charlotte. And then she burst into laughter.

"Okay, it's not *that* funny," Charlotte said, pouting a little.

"It's *hilarious*. Leave it to my mother to come up with something so out of character for you." Charlotte was not a shopper. Charlotte was about as far from a shopper as a girl could possibly be. Hallie had dragged her along to a bridal salon a few weeks back when Ella was looking for a gown. But Ella had insisted the gowns were too expensive, and Charlotte had loudly suggested they leave and go to a thrift store instead.

Ella was all over that idea. "I can't see paying that kind of money for a dress you'll wear only once," she'd scoffed. But the minute the words had left her mouth, her face filled with horror. "But that's just me," she'd hastened to add, because everyone in the family knew that Hallie had *three* dresses for her wedding.

"I tried to tell your mom you wouldn't believe it," Charlotte said. "But she wouldn't listen, and then she told me I overthink everything. Do I overthink everything?" she asked quasi-rhetorically.

"No," Hallie said firmly. "Well, sometimes."

"Anyway, she said you're ignoring your friends, and you're not leaving your room."

"I'm not in my room right now," Hallie said. "And I am not ignoring my friends. My friends are ignoring me. It's awkward."

"And then Luca mentioned that you'd taken up running, and, well, your mother was *really* concerned then," Charlotte added.

"Why does everyone say that like it is so wildly out of the realm of possibility?" Hallie demanded. "I'm trying it on for size, that's all."

"Listen, I get it," Charlotte said. "But I also know you can slowly cut yourself off from the world if you're not careful. I know because I've done it."

Hallie had to concede there was some truth to that. She was, after all, in a potting shed hammering her shoe into a pumpkin. But that did not mean she needed her mother directing her life. "So my mother told you to come out here and tell me that I'm ignoring all my friends, which would basically include you, and I need to get out of the house?"

"Actually, she was pretty specific that I *not* say that, and that I should pretend this shopping thing was all my idea. I told her that you and I don't really have a shopping relationship, and also, I'm a horrible liar."

"Very true on both counts," Hallie agreed. "Let me guess—she told you to stop complaining or something along those lines and get on out here."

"Almost verbatim," Charlotte agreed. *"But,"* she added, "it so happens that Mariah is having a sale. We could check that out, and then swing by the Magnolia. Ella is working tonight. We could get our drink on." With a snap of her fingers, she did a weird swivel dance with her hips.

Mariah Frame was a mutual friend who owned a clothing boutique and hair salon in Three Rivers. And Ella was a part-time hostess at the Magnolia Bar and Grill, which was Three Rivers' version of an upscale restaurant. They did make great cocktails.

"So here I am, asking you to help me catch two birds with one net. One, make my boss's mother happy," Charlotte said, holding up a finger, "and two, spend time with my very good friend over a cocktail, and my other very good friend can serve us. Win-win-win."

"Okay, Charlotte," Hallie said. "But the minute I see a look of pity from *anyone* in town because my wedding imploded, and that includes Mariah, I'm going to punch you in the face."

"Deal," Charlotte said easily. She added softly, "I can't imagine how hard it must be."

Hallie hoped Charlotte never found out. She'd seen those looks of pity in town since the debacle with Chris. She'd seen it on Jo Carol's face. Probably everyone knew the truth by now.

She'd also seen those looks when she came back from the ballet school in New York, mainly because she'd told everyone she was going to New York to become a famous ballerina.

How many times in her life was she going to have to come back to Three Rivers with her tail between her legs? Just when she thought she was over it, another swell of angry grief would rise up out of nowhere. "It *is* hard. But probably not for the reasons you think." It wasn't the loss of Chris, it was the feeling that she wasn't worth the effort of remaining faithful. She glanced at her pumpkin art. "But things are looking up. Especially with my new art project," she said, pointing to the shoe in the pumpkin. "I'm channeling my rage into a new Instagram page. It's called the Deconstruction of a High-Society Wedding."

"That is a *fantastic* title. But you're going to ruin those beautiful shoes," Charlotte pointed out.

"Nope. I covered the heel with plastic and stuffed the shoe with newspaper. And the pumpkin guts are on plastic."

Charlotte moved closer to have a look.

"Here are the pumpkin guts," Hallie said, and uncovered the seeds and pulp from the pumpkin. "I'm putting it here."

"That is the craziest, coolest thing I ever saw," Charlotte said, her voice full of awe. "You do you, Hallie." She started for the door. But she paused and said, "Just so you know, your mother is in the great room waiting on my full report."

Hallie groaned to the ceiling. "Why can't a person be miserable in peace around here?"

"Because it's Three Rivers," Charlotte said, and grinned. "Everyone wants in on the party."

Chapter Eleven

Charlotte drove them into town, puttering like a grandma up the long drive and unabashedly ignoring Hallie's tips for driving. She drove through the tall wrought iron gates that heralded An Important Estate, then slow-poked along the county road all the way into Three Rivers, parking safely in front of Mariah's shop on the square.

Hallie could hear Mariah's bubbly chatter before they even opened the glass door. As they stepped inside, the little bell above the door tinkled, announcing their arrival. Mariah was in the middle of regaling three women with a story.

"So the next time the UPS guy showed up, I stood on the other side of the glass door and watched him toss that box, and I'm like, can you not see me standing right here? Can you not see me writing down your truck number?"

The women laughed uproariously.

"Oh, hey, Charlotte," Mariah said. "*Heeeeey,* Hallie," she added, in a tone that was both sympathetic and dying of curiosity.

The three women glanced at Hallie and Charlotte, but one of them turned to another and obviously whispered something, which Hallie had to assume was about her. *There's that Prince girl. You heard what happened to her, right?*

"Hallie, you look *great!*" Mariah said with far too much enthusiasm.

"Thanks, I think."

"It's *great* to see you," Mariah added. "I'm *so glad* you're feeling better."

"You are just way too happy to see me," Hallie observed.

"I'm *super* happy to see you out and about," Mariah said, and called out to the women, "I've got some great pieces on sale, ladies! But you better hurry up and have a look. I close in thirty."

When the women had moved to the back of the store, Mariah turned to Hallie, pulled a sad face, and said, "How are you *really?*"

"Cut the crap, Mariah," Hallie insisted, and Charlotte laughed. "Did my mother call you, too?"

"What? No!"

"Well, here's the good news—you don't have to ask how I am because I'm fine." Mariah looked at Charlotte as if seeking confirmation that Hallie was indeed fine. "I saw that," Hallie said. "I'm standing right here. Wait a minute—have you two been talking about me? You've been talking about me!"

"Who *isn't* talking about you?" Mariah blithely

agreed. "You burned your invitations. You grew vines out of your wedding dress."

"She's hammering wedding shoes into a pumpkins," Charlotte added matter-of-factly.

"I had vines growing out of my *reception* dress," Hallie said. "And it's called revenge art."

"Oh, really?" Charlotte said, sounding enlightened. "I thought it was called crazy-pants art. But don't worry, Hallie, we're your friends. We're not going to try and cheer you up because that's no fun. We're going to have a look around, and then Mariah and I will take you out for a drink for old time's sake. Deal?"

"Deal," Hallie agreed.

They shopped a little, and an hour later, with their sale items tucked in the hatch of Charlotte's car, Mariah, Charlotte, and Hallie were seated in a booth in the bar area of the Magnolia Bar and Grill, waiting for Ella to get off the clock in five minutes.

When Ella did appear, it was with a tray of pink drinks. "It's a new cocktail Mateo is trying out," she said, and pointed at the bartender. Mateo waved.

Mariah clapped her hands with delight. "What is it?"

"He hasn't named it yet. He said we are allowed to make suggestions, but he will not accept girlie names." She put a glass in front of each of them, got rid of the tray, and sat down with them.

They agreed the drink was good. Mariah asked Ella about her wedding, but Ella demurred, said there wasn't much yet to tell. Hallie knew that wasn't true, but Ella was always very careful not to talk about her wedding in front of her. It wasn't necessary really, because in spite of what had happened to her, Hallie was genuinely happy for Ella and Luca. She was grateful that her twin had found his person. A tiny bit jealous, yes, but quite happy for them all the same.

They hadn't finished half the first drink when another round arrived. The new drinks were gold in color. The four of them waved at Mateo.

"He wants to change the menu," Ella said apologetically. "When he tries new things, he gets the whole bar liquored up." She abruptly sat up and looked toward the entrance. "Well, *hello,*" she muttered.

They all turned to look at the entrance, and Hallie felt a jolt—Rafe had just walked in. Or, more accurately, he'd arrived on a cloud of sexy. He was wearing jeans that fit him very well, a T-shirt beneath a denim jacket, and a knit cap on his head. He was also wearing glasses, which he rarely wore, and was sporting the scruff of a late-afternoon beard.

"Am I crazy, or does he get better looking every year?" Charlotte mused.

"You're not crazy," Hallie muttered.

He said something to the hostess, and they watched him follow her across the bar.

Hallie was suddenly thinking about a kiss that was not a kiss but was almost a kiss.

"Seriously, how has he remained single?" Mariah asked curiously as he slid onto a barstool.

"He's moving to Chicago," Hallie said. She wondered if she sounded as disappointed as she felt.

Mateo stopped in front of Rafe and tossed down a bar napkin.

"That's too bad. I'm going to miss that eye candy around here," Charlotte said. "Hell, *I* should have snatched him up."

Hallie shifted in her seat. The mere suggestion, even said in jest, was jarring. She didn't like being jarred on girls' night out. And this was another new development—being jarred about anything to do with Rafe.

Rafe turned in his seat, scanning the room, and his gaze landed on them. He smiled. And then he stood up and sauntered toward them like he knew how hot he was. When he reached their table, Charlotte said, "Hi, handsome."

"Charlotte." He looked around at the four of them. "Am I wrong to feel a little fear? Seems like an awful lot of woman gathered in one place."

They all tittered. They were such girls.

"We've been shopping," Charlotte announced.

"Mariah is having a big sale. What are you doing here?"

Rafe's gaze slipped over Hallie. "I'm meeting a friend."

They were ogling him, Hallie realized. Well, who could blame them? He looked so deliciously rugged, so . . . *manly.* She thought she might have licked her lips.

Rafe looked from one of them to the next. "Why are you all looking at me like that? You're kind of freaking me out."

"I don't know why *they're* staring, but I am because you are really *hot,*" Charlotte said cheerfully. "I mean, who knew you cleaned up so well?"

Hallie gasped and gave Charlotte a look of disbelief.

Rafe chuckled. "I will admit to putting on a clean shirt. May I assume from this declaration that you're still in the market for a sperm donor, Miss Bailey?"

"Well?" Charlotte grinned. "Are you interested?"

"Charlotte!" Mariah said. "Jesus!"

"What? It might come down to a sperm donor, and no one teaches you the proper way to ask that question, just so you know."

"I'm pretty sure they would advise you not to bring it up in a crowded bar while your friends are watching," Mariah said.

"Well, excuse *me,*" Charlotte said, and sank a little in her seat, as if she were disappointed she couldn't discuss it right now.

Rafe grinned affectionately at Charlotte. "You wouldn't want my donation anyway, Charlotte. Have you forgotten how mad you got at me at Christmas a few years back?"

"Oh," Charlotte said, and wrinkled her nose. "I almost forgot about you and that damn fruitcake. Never mind."

"That's what I thought." He suddenly turned his head toward the entrance. "Ah. My date is here. Ladies, it's been a pleasure." He smiled and bowed, and his gaze slid over Hallie again— quickly, briefly, hardly anything at all.

She couldn't even summon a smile, she was so stunned. His *date* was here? *Rafe was on a date?*

"I guess he's just a regular cowboy now, huh?" Mariah said as she watched him walk away to greet a petite brunette at the door. Of *course* she was petite and brunette. And probably very wholesome and grounded and lacking all categories of major drama. The perfect girl for him and the exact opposite of Hallie. The woman smiled up at Rafe. She put her arm around his waist and hugged him, then followed him across the room to the two bar seats.

"Cowboy? I thought he was into martial arts," Ella said. "Isn't that why he's moving to Chicago?"

"He's probably moving to Chicago to get out of this two-bit town," Mariah said.

Hallie slowly sipped her too-fruity drink, her eyes glued to Rafe and the woman he was with. They were merrily chatting it up, the two of them all smiles and laughter. Hallie was surprisingly envious of the easy rapport they appeared to have. Rafe was generally the quiet one, but as she surreptitiously watched the way he smiled at the cute little pixie, she couldn't help noticing the tiny creases around his eyes, and the way he tipped his head back to laugh.

Was he actually dating a woman and hadn't mentioned it to her?

More important, did Rafe ever look at her like that? Or was she always such a sad-sack friend that his face was frozen into concern and understanding?

A tiny little shudder ran down her spine. Was it possible that she was the one in a group who always needed support? Good God, she hoped not—nothing was worse than being *that* friend. She wanted to be the brunette. She wanted to be the person he desired. But wait—was *that* what she wanted? The idea had popped into her head so fast and flew over all her natural barriers that she had to stop and think about it.

Did she really want to be with him? *Kiss* him, yes. But date him? That was a whole other level.

"I don't think I can drink another one," Ella

192

said, nodding at the four new cocktails staring at them.

"Me either. Hey, I've got an idea. Let me out, Charlotte," Hallie said, and nudged Charlotte.

"Why?"

"I'm going to give two of them to Rafe."

Her three friends looked at her.

She looked back. "Well? Do you want them to go to waste?"

Mariah's eyes narrowed. "Who cares? They're free. It's not like we're saving the whales by drinking them."

"Okay," Hallie said, lifting her hand. "Fair enough. I want to know who she is. Don't you?"

"Yes," Mariah said instantly. "Let her out, Charlotte!"

Hallie stepped out, gathered two of the gold drinks. "I'm on it," she said, and then strolled across the room to the bar. *"Heeeyyy,"* she said as she neared Rafe and his date.

The young woman glanced up, startled.

Rafe glanced up, too, and shook his head as if he'd expected some shenanigans. "Hi, Hallie."

"Hi there," she said, and turned her bright smile to the brunette. "Sorry to interrupt, but we have more craft cocktails than we can possibly get down. Mateo is experimenting. Can we pass some off on you?"

"I don't know," Rafe said, eying the drinks. "Did you spit in them?"

Hallie laughed as if that was the funniest thing she'd ever heard. "No, silly." She pushed her way in between the two of them to deposit the drinks on the bar. And then she very casually slipped back, but not all the way, leaning against the back of Rafe's stool so that he had to shift forward to see around her. "Sooo," she said, smiling. "I'm Hallie Prince."

"Hi. I'm Brittney. No *A*."

Maybe she thought Hallie was going to write her name down. Brittney-no-A looked at least ten years younger than Rafe, which—and she intended to mention this later—was a little too young for an old guy like him. "So . . . how do you two know each other?" Hallie asked, and slid a look at Rafe.

"We're in a sociology class together," Brittney-no-A said. "We've been studying for our final."

"Oh. *Study* partners." Hallie smiled and shot Rafe a look.

He returned a look that was supposed to be withering, and tried to force her back a step with his arm. But Hallie held firm. "So, Hallie here," he said, reaching for Hallie's wrist and wrapping his fingers around it, "Is an old, *old* friend of mine." He squeezed her wrist.

"That's right. We go *way* back."

"Oh, really? Like, how far?" Brittney-no-A asked.

"Oh, *years*. Let me think." Hallie tried to pull her wrist free, but Rafe was gripping it. "I can remember him when I was seven or eight. Funny story, but he was a little shrimp then, even though he is years older than me—"

"Two years older."

"I actually beat him up once, can you believe it?"

"No you didn't," Rafe said with a snort.

"Why?" Brittney-no-A asked, puzzled.

"We were playing war, my brother and me against him and my other brother. I captured him."

"I *let* you capture me," Rafe said.

"Oh, I *captured* you," Hallie argued.

"Actually, you tackled me from behind, which was against the rules, and then I confiscated your gun."

"Well, I agree to disagree," she said magnanimously.

"You can't agree to disagree if I'm not part of the agreement," Rafe pointed out.

"Anyway," Hallie said, ignoring him, "that's how far back we go. So far back that he can't remember what actually happened the day I tackled him and he stole my gun." She smiled at Rafe.

"You have a very faulty memory."

Brittney-no-A looked back and forth between them. "Did you two guys, like, used to date?" she asked.

"No," Rafe said instantly and forcefully.

"God no," Hallie said just as forcefully. "That would be, like, *gross.* He's like a brother to me."

Rafe turned his brown eyes to her, narrowed and probing. "I'm like a *brother* to you?"

"Aren't you?" Hallie smiled in a way that dared him to deny it. She was going to say something. She could feel it on the tip of her tongue, ready to spring to freedom. Something totally inappropriate, like *You have a great ass for a brother,* or *Did we really almost kiss? Because if we did, why are you here with her?* Or even, *Do you feel this electricity between us, or is it really just me, because I might need to get my hormones checked?* Or any number of thoughts and questions pinging in her brain—

Ella suddenly and stealthily appeared at her side. "Hi, Rafe."

"Hello, Ella. Meet Brittney. No *A.*"

"Hello, Brittney," Ella said calmly and politely, because she was a very calm and polite woman. "Hey, Hallie, I have to take off. And Mariah is complaining she needs to get home. Plus, your phone keeps chiming." She handed Hallie's phone to her. She glanced down and saw three text messages from Chris. She knew what had happened—her phone went off, Mariah tried to see who was texting her, and because Ella was a decent person and her future sister-in-law, she'd grabbed the phone to give to Hallie before her friends could snoop.

She smiled gratefully at Ella. "Thanks." But she wanted to stay right here, comfortably wedged between Rafe and his date with a woodland fairy.

Rafe wasn't having it. "You better go, Hal," he said, and gave her a slap on the back hearty enough to make her take a step forward. "I'm sure you have something you want to blow up."

"As a matter of fact, I do," she said. "But it's not presently convenient. It was nice to meet you, Brittney. You kids don't stay out too late."

Brittney laughed. "She's funny," she said to Rafe.

"Oh, she's a riot," he agreed, and waggled his fingers at Hallie in the universal signal that she needed to go.

So off Hallie toddled, feeling strangely discombobulated about Rafe's date.

By the time they'd gathered their things and left a tip, Rafe and Brittney-no-A had moved to the dining room. Rafe was leaning over, his eyes on her face, talking earnestly about something.

On their way to Charlotte's car, they passed Rafe's muddied truck with a bed full of hay. When they climbed in the car, Charlotte hit the button to start the engine, but she was looking at Rafe's truck, massive beside her small SUV. "I'm not kidding—he's way too hot to be hanging around Three Rivers. Such a great guy."

"Maybe he's taking the girl with him to

197

Chicago," Mariah said as she applied lipstick in the passenger mirror. "She's pretty."

"She wasn't *that* pretty," Hallie said.

"I thought she was *really* pretty," Mariah said.

"Whoever she is, she won't be long for his world. He's going to have all the women he wants in Chicago," said Charlotte. "Am I right?"

"*So* right," Mariah agreed. "Right, Hallie?"

"Umm . . ." Hallie thought about the way Rafe had smiled and laughed with the brunette. "He's been one of my best friends for, like, a thousand years. It's hard for me to look at him like that." Except that it wasn't hard at all. She was doing it right now in her head. She was doing more than just look. She was imagining things, very salacious things, like what he was hiding in those jeans, and what he was going to do with the woman after dinner.

What the hell is the matter with you?

"Can men and women really be just friends?" Charlotte waxed reflectively as she put her car in gear.

"Why not?" Hallie asked.

"Because, you know, the laws of attraction and all that."

"No way," Mariah said confidently.

"Of course you can. Look at Ella and Mateo. They're just friends," Hallie said.

"But that's different. He used to be her boyfriend. They decided to be friends *afterward,*"

Charlotte said. "And she's told me that there is still a weird tension between them because they did sleep together. It's not the same as just a friend."

"I have a guy friend, but he's gay," Mariah said. "He works for a clothing line."

"Come on," Hallie said. "Are we really going to go with the theory that women can only have male friends if they're gay? That's so nineteen seventies! You *do* have other guy friends, Charlotte. You're friends with Nick."

Charlotte laughed roundly at that. "I am *not* friends with Nick. I tolerate him, that's all. He's actually pretty lucky I stick around."

"He is very lucky," Hallie agreed. "Don't ever leave."

"He'd probably burn the place to the ground if I did, that grump."

"Seriously, Hallie, I don't know how you can be just friends with Rafe," Mariah said as they pulled out of the parking lot. "He is *so* good-looking."

"He really is," Charlotte agreed. "He's *much* better looking than—" She suddenly stopped talking. "I mean . . ."

"You can say it," Hallie said with a sigh of weariness. "He *is* so much better looking than Chris. He is. But we've been friends for a really long time." Why did she keep saying that? Well, she had the entire back seat to herself to obsess about why she did. What *would* it be like to be with Rafe? As a lover? As a couple?

"You know what's interesting? When Rico is around, no one really notices Rafe," Charlotte opined as they drove through town. "But then again, Rico is the life of the party. Rafe is a lot quieter."

Rico was a lot of fun. But Rafe? He exuded strength. And he was always, *always* there for her. Even if she butted in on his dates.

She glanced at the back of Charlotte's blond head as they pulled onto the highway. "Were you *seriously* asking for Rafe's sperm?"

"Why not?" Charlotte asked, shooting her a look in the rearview mirror. "Jealous?" She grinned. Mariah laughed. Hallie clucked her tongue at her friend.

She wasn't jealous. She was something, but it wasn't jealous. But the thing with Rafe just kept getting stranger and stranger, turning down roads she'd never been on before. They were starting to make her a little carsick. She felt crazy with confusion. Crazy with desire. *Crazy, crazy, crazy.*

Chapter Twelve

Thanksgiving was a disaster.

It was especially upsetting because Thanksgiving had always been Cordelia's favorite holiday. She and Charlie enjoyed hosting, inviting scores of guests to the ranch throughout their marriage. The weather was generally beautiful this time of year, so they'd set up tables for dining on the expansive patio and have the buffet catered.

Some years, they'd hire musicians. Other years, depending on how their favorite football teams were performing, they'd set up giant screens to watch the games. It was always a feast, always a house party, always a very memorable event.

That was because Cordelia took great care to make it memorable. It was during occasions like this that she shone—she was, after all, the premiere hostess in this part of Texas. Everyone would say so. She was not being smug, she was making an objective observation. Invitations to her events were coveted, from Austin to the border.

This was her job, it was what she did. Her mother had trained her to be the best, and Cordelia had honed her hostessing skill for years as the wife of a powerful man. "Nothing reflects on a woman quite like her figure, her children, and her ability to host a dinner," her mother would say.

But this year, Thanksgiving turned out to be another in a long line of raging disappointments. For one thing, Charlie was not here. He'd gone off to the great putting green in the sky and left her to fend for herself. Like she didn't need him, like his children didn't need him.

Since then, they'd had to cope with so much— his death, the shaky family cash flow, staff layoffs, and now, embarking on the holiday season without his boisterous presence. Even though she and Charlie had been separated at the time of his death, he would have been here for Thanksgiving. She and Charlie saw eye to eye on that—family holidays were important and sacrosanct. They required a show of unity even when there was no unity between them. Looks were important. Optics mattered.

For another thing, invitations sent to family had been declined. Cordelia hadn't figured out quite what to make of that. Her cousin Walter was in Dallas and said he had a house full and couldn't get away. Charlie's sister, Cindy, was off with her husband in France, but Cordelia thought

202

she might have put off her trip a week or so and come to the ranch instead. Wasn't it obvious the family needed to be together? Wasn't it obvious that Cordelia and her kids were hurting?

So her only guests were her brother, Chet; his wife, Sandy; and two of their four sons— Rex, who was graduating from Harvard in the spring, and Jonah, who owned an Applewhite car dealership in Austin.

Oh, and George Lowe, a constant in her life for as long as she'd been married. He'd been trying to help her navigate the mind-numbing bureaucratic tasks that follow the death of a spouse. Mounds of paperwork had to be filed. Death certificates had to be obtained. Deeds and leases and old contracts had to be rounded up. George was a widower, and his only daughter lived in Seattle. She had not come home for Thanksgiving, so Cordelia had invited him. He was like family anyway.

Nick was here, too, slinking about and brooding as if the weight of the world rested on his shoulders. He ran the family business now, and Cordelia knew he hated it. She hated it for him, but unfortunately, someone had to take charge, and he was the heir apparent.

Luca and Ella were home, too, but Luca had announced yesterday to one and all that they would be leaving early.

"Why?" Cordelia had demanded.

"We're going over to the Hurst place," Luca said. "Brandon invited us."

Hallie, who was arranging champagne flutes in a line like so many dominoes for that ridiculous Instagram page, gasped. *"Brandon?* You mean he's speaking to you?"

Cordelia was curious to know the answer, too. Brandon Hurst had been Luca's lifelong best friend. They'd had a falling out, but apparently, the two of them had patched things up.

"Yep," Luca said cheerfully.

Cordelia supposed she ought to be grateful that Luca and Brandon were mending fences, but she wished they could do it on some day other than Thanksgiving. This was *her* holiday.

"That's fantastic, Luca!" Hallie had said. "I kind of miss the lug."

Hallie sounded enthused and happy, and Cordelia had to admit, her daughter had picked herself up out of the doldrums and was making her best effort to return to normal. With the exception of this strange notion that it was somehow fun to ruin things intended to be used in her wedding and then take pictures of them. It made no sense to Cordelia.

Hallie was returning to some type of normal, but she wasn't exactly the same woman she'd been before the fiasco with Christopher. She was obviously rudderless. She'd gained a little weight. She was wearing a very cute blue and white paisley dress with flounced sleeves. Cordelia remembered that dress—Hallie had bought it in New York on a weekend shopping trip, and it had fit her perfectly. But today, it looked really tight. Funny how she used to worry about Hallie being rail thin when she danced ballet. Now she worried Hallie was going to get fat.

It was that paisley dress that ruined Thanksgiving, if anyone was interested in Cordelia's opinion.

No one was interested in her opinion.

The brouhaha had started in the middle of a meal that was mediocre at best. They'd been seated around the dinner table and, Cordelia would admit, she'd had too much wine. But no one had told her how she was supposed to numb herself to the emptiness she felt when she looked at Charlie's place at their hand-carved dining table. If it wasn't wine, what was it?

The dress was the thing that made Cordelia snap, but it had really begun with the fact that the meal was just awful. Frederica had not come to cook. For the first time in Cordelia's memory, the longtime family cook had politely declined to prepare a meal for the Prince family. Yes, they usually had Thanksgiving catered, but Cordelia assumed that Frederica would know that *this* year, of all years, they would not do that. And when Frederica had claimed "other plans," Cordelia panicked—it had been an age since she had prepared a meal herself. She'd begged Frederica. She'd even offered a bonus. But Frederica had said, in that very quiet way of hers, that she had other plans and could not come to the ranch.

When Luca had gamely tried to suggest the turkey was "pretty good after all," Cordelia had waved her wineglass at him and said, "It's retaliation for cutting her hours, you know."

"What are you talking about?" George asked. He was seated to her right.

"Oh, come on, we all know the turkey is dry, the cranberries are bitter, and the dressing is bland. That's on me. Frederica blames me for cutting her hours, but honestly? She can thank Charlie Prince and those high-roller tables in Vegas. Am I right?"

Everyone looked at their plates.

"She never struck me as vindictive," George offered. "Maybe she just had other plans."

"Whatever," Cordelia muttered, and poured more wine into her glass.

"For heaven's sake, Delia. She has a new job," Dolly said, and lifted her gin and tonic.

That sentence had not computed. "A new *job,*" Cordelia had repeated, as if she didn't even know what the word meant. Really, who in Three Rivers could afford a full-time cook? Mrs. Hurst, maybe, but she lived at that ranch by herself, and Cordelia was pretty sure Big Barb the mail lady had told her that Mrs. Hurst had her meals delivered. "I think you misunderstood something, Dolly."

And yes, if anyone asked, that opinion had sounded dismissive even to Cordelia, because again, she'd had too much to drink, and who could take anything seriously from an old woman whose gray hair was tipped with orange and brown in homage to the Thanksgiving season?

"Well, I didn't misunderstand a bloomin' thing, Delia," Dolly had snapped back, predictably annoyed. "All I know is that Debbie Wainwright likes having a cook."

Cordelia put down her wineglass and stared at her mother-in-law, irrationally incensed by this news. George pointed out later—much later—that Cordelia ought to be grateful Frederica had managed to make up the hours she'd lost at Three Rivers Ranch, because she had a family, and her mother was in a senior home.

"Are we speaking of *Debbie Wainwright?* The same woman who prides herself on practically masticating her children's food for them has hired a *cook?*"

"Gross," Jonah said.

"Debbie's very nice," George opined, as if that meant she ought to have Cordelia's cook. "I like her." He popped an olive into his mouth.

Debbie Wainwright was fifteen years younger than Cordelia and a whole lot prettier. She didn't want George to like Debbie. She didn't want Debbie to hire her cook away. She wanted Charlie back, she wanted Frederica back, and she wanted her old Thanksgivings back, and *she* wanted to be queen bee around here. Not Debbie Wainwright.

"You don't need Frederica, not really," Sandy said. "I think the meal is great."

"Well, thanks to *you*, hon," Dolly had said, because Dolly was always eager to heap praise on anyone but Cordelia. "Your green bean casserole pretty much saved the day."

Cordelia couldn't argue with that. Sandy, tall and big-boned with a mop of short brunette hair, was a practical woman. She'd never let the Applewhite wealth affect her. She'd never had a cook, although they were richer than Midas. No, Sandy had prepared meals for her four sons, had gone to all their games with a cooler full of drinks and snacks. She'd made her own Christmas decorations, she'd done all the laundry, and she'd probably cleaned that massive house in the Dominion by herself. The maddening thing was, Cordelia should have called Sandy and asked her how to cook a damn turkey, but she hadn't thought of it.

"It was nothing," Sandy said about the casserole. "Hallie asked if I could whip it up, and I said sure. It's so easy, Delia. All you need is some green beans, some cream of mushroom soup—"

"Hallie asked you to make the casserole?" Cordelia had asked, interrupting her sister-in-law before she could cook another batch. The idea that Hallie had gone behind her back and called her aunt Sandy had made Cordelia irrationally—read drunkenly—angry. She'd turned a cold look to her traitorous daughter. "I didn't know you liked it so much, sweetie."

Hallie looked up from her plate. "I like Aunt Sandy's casserole. And you were complaining about having to make dinner, so . . . I asked her."

"I was not *complaining*," Cordelia said quickly, although she *had* complained about it, and her whole family knew she had, and if they'd forgotten, Dolly was there to remind them all with a snort and roll of her eyes.

"Well, it doesn't matter who asked," Sandy quickly interjected. "I was going to make it anyway, so there you go." She picked up her fork and speared some turkey.

Of course she was going to make it, because they were all sitting around this table thinking that Cordelia Prince was nothing without Charlie. And for some reason that she would never understand, she took out her frustration on her daughter. Maybe because she didn't want Hallie to make the same mistakes she'd made in her life—to be nothing without Chris or another husband. Maybe because her daughter was an easy target. Cordelia didn't like to look too

209

closely at her motives because she knew she was not going to like what she saw.

But that didn't stop her from taking a big swig of wine and saying, "Well, it is awfully good, Sandy. But Hallie, honey, you should avoid so many carbs. You don't want to put on any more weight than you already have."

Someone gasped. Maybe Ella? And then Hallie turned her hazel eyes to her and said, "I'm sorry, Mother. I'll excuse myself from the table so you don't have to look at me."

"No, Hallie," Luca said, but it was too late. Hallie was on her feet, marching from the dining room, and even though Cordelia knew she was terribly, terribly wrong to say what she had, she worried that Hallie's zipper might bust open with all her arm swinging.

Dolly watched her go, then shot a look of disgust at Cordelia. "Well, Delia, you sure know how to go and put a fork in something, don't you? Reminds me of the time my mother announced to the mayor's wife at Sunday brunch that the mayor had been spending an awful lot of time after hours with the county auditor. Who was a *man*. Now *that* was a perfectly good meal gone to ruin, just like this one."

A cacophony of voices exploded around the table, and everything had gone to shit.

Cordelia was now sitting on the patio with a cup of coffee at her elbow. When she heard footsteps behind her, she closed her eyes and prayed that whatever her punishment, it would be quick.

"Are you all right?"

Cordelia opened her eyes and looked at George. "No. I'm a horrible person."

George sighed. He took a seat beside her at the table. "You're not a horrible person, Delia. But that was not nice."

"I know." Cordelia groaned. "I don't know why I said it. I don't know what's wrong with me sometimes. I'm just so out of sorts, and everything is changing, and I don't want her to end up like me, so I just . . . popped off."

George patted her hand.

"Do you hate me?"

"Never, Delia. I actually feel bad for you in a way."

"You do?"

"Sure. Must be hard to live in your skin sometimes."

"You have no idea," she muttered. "I'm going to chase everyone off. Martin walks around on eggshells, Frederica probably won't come back, and I heard Mayrose on the phone asking a friend if she had any work for her. Am I mean to Mayrose, too?"

George's response was to smile sympathetically. Cordelia took that as a yes.

"Delia."

Chet's deep voice rumbled over her. Cordelia

211

braced herself as her brother marched around the table where she could see him and glared at her in disbelief. "What is *wrong* with you?"

"That is the million-dollar question."

"I swear, you've got the meanest mouth this side of the Red River, you know that?"

She winced. Her fears were confirmed. "I sort of do."

"There's just no excuse for that." He talked like he was spitting out nails.

"I *know*."

He folded his arms across his chest and glared at her. "Well? Are you going to fix it?"

"What do you want me to do, Chet? Have you seen what she's doing?" Cordelia could just imagine what her brother thought of a sparkly shoe full of pumpkin. Or the slow-motion crash of the china plates. Or the upside-down flowers fed to Ella's pig. "She's destroying things she was going to use in her wedding and posting pictures of it. She's sleeping until ten or eleven. She's eating *mashed potatoes*."

"So what," he said sharply. "*She* says her pictures are an art project. Rex says she has forty thousand followers."

"I don't care!" Cordelia said loudly. "She's obviously lost, don't you see that? She's lost her father and her fiancé. What does she have?"

"She has her beauty and her brains, and she will figure it out," Chet said.

Cordelia snorted.

"I knew you'd see it that way. That's why I just offered her the chance to get unlost, away from here and *you*."

Cordelia looked at George, then at Chet. "Excuse me?"

"I offered to send her to our place in Aspen."

"Aspen? Why?" Cordelia asked, confused.

"So she can think without someone telling her what she needs to do."

"What did she say?" Cordelia asked weakly.

"She's interested," he said. "I told her everything upended on her, and it's no wonder she needs a little time to sort everything out, but that maybe she can't do that here with such a watchful eye."

Chet meant well, but Cordelia already knew Hallie was not going to listen to her uncle. She didn't listen to anyone. And Chet hadn't seen her moping around since the breakup.

Breakup. That seemed too soft for what had happened to her girl. *Betrayal* was better. Or, as Dolly would say, *That was some bullshit.*

"I think that sounds like a great idea," George said.

"Are you both insane? She is not going to go off to Aspen and *find* herself."

"Why not?" Chet asked. "She likes the outdoors. It's a great place to think. She could do some shopping if she wants—"

"Nope. No shopping," George said. "There isn't the money for the kind of shopping Hallie likes to do."

"Then it will be my gift," Chet said. "Never knew a girl who didn't like a little retail therapy to get the creative juices flowing. Anyway, that's beside the point. The point is that she needs to take a couple of weeks and get in touch with herself. None of this," he said, gesturing to the house and land around them. "None of your opinions either."

"She's my daughter, Chet. I am allowed to have opinions. And is she supposed to go off on this self discovery by herself?"

"She's thirty, Delia. She's a big girl now. She *should* go by herself, if she really wants to think things through. This is the one time in her life she can focus solely on what she needs."

"He's right," George said.

Cordelia shot a look at him.

"He is," George said. "You two are like oil and water. You could both use some time for self-reflection."

Cordelia could feel her hackles rising. "Are you serious right now, George? You're going to analyze me?"

"Seems to me that everything you say about Hallie could be said about you. Except maybe the mashed potatoes. But you have your own vice," he said. "How much wine have you had today?"

So much that she felt indignantly ashamed. "I am not going to sit here and listen to this. I lost my *husband,*" she said. "My world has fallen apart."

"Maybe you ought to start one of those photo pages like Hallie," Chet offered.

George laughed.

"Not funny," Cordelia muttered.

"Well, you're going to do whatever you're going to do, Delia," Chet said as he started for the door. "I can't save you from yourself. But I can damn sure try and save my niece from you."

"Oh, sure, ride in here with your shining armor and white steed, Chet. Pretend that all she needs is a week or two in Aspen! Stop acting so superior. I'll go and talk to her right now."

"She's gone," he said.

"Where?"

"I don't know. I guess she needed some air." He walked into the house.

"I guess I'll take off," George said.

"What? You're going, too?"

George smiled sadly at her. "I'll see you soon, Delia," he said, and put his hand on her shoulder and squeezed. Not affectionately. But in a manner that made her think George pitied her.

Was she so wrong about her daughter's aimlessness? Was she wrong to be worried about her? It's like the poor thing had no idea who she was without Chris.

Just like her mother didn't know who she was without Charlie.

The last thing Cordelia wanted was for Hallie to feel the way she felt. She wanted Hallie to be happy. She wanted her to fill her life with love. She did not want Hallie to know the bitterness of corrosive disappointment like she'd known the last few years.

Maybe Chet was right.

Chapter Thirteen

Rafe was feeling pretty miserable, and he had no one to blame but himself. His mother's cooking had always been his undoing. They'd dined on turkey and cranberry sauce, tamales and *ensalada Navideña*, and Angie's pumpkin pie, which she'd self-declared was famous. "*Everyone* loves my pumpkin pie," she said.

"Who is everyone?" her husband David asked as he helped himself to a second slice.

"*Everyone,*" Angie said, and playfully thumped the back of his head.

It was a good day. The kids were on their best behavior, spending most of their time on the trampoline in the backyard while Rafe and David tossed things to them. Angie and his mother were going over some family photos for some craft project they had in mind.

When the meal was over, Rafe, David, and his father watched football. David asked Rafe's dad about his work.

He shook his head. "Don't know if I'm going to be around much longer," he said. "The Princes have some big problems," he said, jabbing a finger in the direction of the main compound. "Miss Delia wants me to get rid of half the horses. You can't do ranch work without horses, I told her. She said there wasn't going to be anyone to ride them anyway, which I take to mean there is another round of layoffs coming. I'm down to three hands as it is. That's not enough to work a ranch this size."

"She can't run that place without you," David said.

"Sure she can. She's got Nick. My gut tells me she's looking for an excuse to get rid of me."

He continued on with his theories of successful ranch management, which included selling off some useless acreage that the Princes were dead set against.

Full and drowsy, Rafe was stretched out on the couch, fighting off a nap as his dad and David talked. He'd almost succumbed when his phone pinged. He dug it out from between the cushions and was greeted with a very pregnant woman holding her belly. Her head was cropped out of the meme. I ate too much, Hallie texted.

Rafe smiled. He sent a text back, a GIF of a balloon exploding into purple goo. Me too.

Hallie texted back with several laughing emojis, and followed that with, What are you doing?

218

Thinking about a nap. You?

Too many men. Too much football. Luca and Ella found an excuse to leave. She punctuated that with an emoji of a skeptical face, followed by a mad face. I need to get out of here. Do you have an animal that I should come and feed? Rafe texted back, Nope.

Are you on a DATE?

It's Thanksgiving. I am not on a date.

Then let's go for a run!

Rafe almost laughed out loud. Who are you and what have you done with Hallie? Two days ago when I asked you to go run, you told me to go fly a kite.

Go fly a kite! Lololol. I'm sorry, was it 1950 two days ago? That is not what I said. ☺

I'm trying to protect your princess image. Unfortunately, the sailor image keeps making an appearance, and no, that's not what you said. Smiley face with symbols typed over its mouth to indicate swearing. A line of laughing faces. Come on, let's go.

He thought about it. He didn't think he could run even ten yards as full as he was, but as usual, his desire to see Hallie outweighed all of his common sense.

He pushed himself up to his elbow and looked at the TV screen. The Cowboys were up by fourteen, which rarely happened these days. He texted, Okay.

> Great!! I'll pick you up in thirty. Let's drive down to the Magnolia and run the river path.

> I don't like the way you drive.

> I don't like the way you complain about my driving. Need to make a quiet getaway from here, which will involve sneaking out the side door like I'm thirteen all over again. Fun times.

Rafe pushed himself up off the couch. David barely spared him a glance.

"I think I'm going to go get a run in," he announced.

"Cowboys are up by fourteen, man!" David said without taking his eyes off the screen.

"I can't handle the bitter disappointment when they blow that lead." No one argued or objected.

He changed into sweatpants and a hoodie, and

walked out with a cheery, "Back later." He jogged down the road that separated the mansion from the real world. He saw Hallie's SUV coming down the road at a speed that was too fast, and had to put himself in the bar ditch to avoid being hit.

She rolled down the passenger window. "What are you doing in the ditch?"

He gave her an exasperated look, then climbed into her SUV.

She looked so pretty this afternoon—running tights, a down vest over a black tee, her hair in a high ponytail.

"You don't look as full as me." She poked his stomach, then goosed the car and shot it down the road and stopped just past a cattle crossing. "Didn't you eat?"

"Trust me, I ate my weight in tamales." He glanced at the seat behind them and noticed boxes of champagne glasses. "Having a party?"

"Party for one, actually. I'm setting them up in the warehouse, and I'm going to domino them."

"You're going to what?"

She hit the gas, and the SUV rocketed backward onto the crossing so she could turn around. "You know, like dominoes."

"They'll break."

"Exactly." She flashed a sunny smile.

"How was your Thanksgiving?"

She turned the wheel and pulled out onto the road. "Pretty shitty, if you want to know the truth. But don't ask—it's not worth the breath to explain how dysfunctional my family can be, and besides, I've decided I'm done complaining to you all the time."

"You are?"

"One hundred percent," she said cheerfully. "I told you! I'm a new leaf."

"You mean you're turning over a new leaf—"

"I'm making changes, and I'm waking up to possibilities." She rocked the Range Rover down the road and past the ornate gates of the Three Rivers Ranch. She was driving like a maniac, and Rafe grabbed the handle over the door.

She gave him a sidelong look. "Scared?"

"Yes, I am. You drive like a madwoman."

"It is just so weird that you're this brave Army Ranger and it's the little things that scare you."

"Our definition of 'little thing' is not the same," he said. "Every time you turn the wheel, I see my life flash before my eyes."

"Rafael Miguel Fontana, are you actually implying that women are bad drivers right now?" She laughed.

"Not at all. I'm implying that Hallie Jane the Princess is a bad driver. You drive almost as bad as you sing." He braced himself as she hurtled around a corner.

"Chicken," she said, and barreled onto the main road through town.

She slowed down to the speed limit and coasted

along Main Street. It looked like they'd just entered the ghost town formerly known as Three Rivers—Prince Tool and Die was silent, the restaurants were closed up and shuttered for the holiday. Even Jo's Java House, which was usually a hive of activity, was dark. The only exception was the cars parked on the town square.

Hallie suddenly gasped and braked the car so hard that Rafe nearly pitched through the windshield.

"What the hell was that?"

"It's the ballet! Remember? Kidz Korner? They're performing in the Galaxy Theatre!"

Rafe looked toward the old movie theater that had been renovated into a community stage, and recalled the flyer posted to the community bulletin board.

"This is fantastic!" Hallie said, and suddenly hit the gas, pulling into a municipal parking lot.

"Hallie, what—"

"We have to see it," she said, as if that were a foregone conclusion.

Rafe looked at the people walking toward the theater, entire families, some of them holding the hands of children dressed as ballerinas or toy soldiers. "What is that?" Rafe asked when a little girl wandered by wearing a pair of pink tights and a big pink puffy thing around her torso.

Hallie gave it a discerning look. "If I had to guess? A sugarplum. Or maybe bubblegum.

Could go either way." She reached behind Rafe's seat and pulled out a camera.

"Wait—what are you doing?"

"I'm going to take some pictures!" She flung open the driver's door and got out.

Rafe got out, too, and joined her in front of her vehicle. They surveyed the theater across the street, the families streaming in. Someone had set up a food trailer selling hot dogs, popcorn, and cotton candy. A banner proclaimed that this was the third and final performance of the ballet, following two at locations in San Antonio.

"Can we go in?" he asked. "Isn't there a ticket or something?"

"I bet they take donations at the door," Hallie said, then patted her pockets. "But I don't have a dime on me. Come to think of it, I didn't bring anything but a key."

"More safe driving tips, courtesy of Hallie Prince," Rafe said, and shoved his hand into his pocket and pulled out a twenty.

"Great," she said.

"Sure—it's my twenty."

She tried to snatch it from his hand, but he jerked it away. "Excuse me, what do you say?"

Her hand landed on his chest, and she smiled up at him with a pair of happy dimples. "*Thank* you, Rafe," she said in a singsong voice, and while he was distracted by her smile, she snagged the twenty. "Come on, we want to get a good seat."

She took his hand as if that were the most natural thing to do.

Rafe let her, because it was beginning to feel to him like it was the most natural thing to do. He'd held her hand more times in the last two weeks than he had during their entire friendship.

The last two weeks had been a bit of a fever dream for him. He'd been thinking a lot about her. Fantasizing about her, really, wondering what she was doing. Checking her Instagram account for revelations. Mulling over what the hell was happening between them.

He'd even thought about her while he was in bed with Brittney.

Yeah, that.

Rafe glanced at Hallie as they jogged across the street, and felt a twinge of guilt.

He hadn't intended for things to go so far with Brittney. He hadn't intended for anything to happen at all. They'd struck up a friendship during the semester, had gone out a couple of times, and when she'd texted him, he'd been more than happy to meet up. Not because he had any particularly strong feelings about Brittney, other than she was cute and fun to hang out with—but because he'd needed something to distract him from the thoughts he was having about Hallie. Distractions that were increasingly hard to conjure up.

That night with Brittney, in his desire to put

Hallie out of his mind, he'd let one thing lead to another, and yes, he'd released a little tension that had more to do with Hallie than with Brittney.

That disturbed him more than anything. He was not that kind of guy. But lately, it felt as if he'd been skating closer and closer to the middle of a frozen lake, and the ice was getting thinner, and he was trying desperately to hang on to anything, even those things he knew would not hold him. Sooner rather than later, he was going to go under and not be able to get out. And yet, he just kept skating.

"Is it weird we don't have a kid in the show?" he asked when they reached the entrance.

"Only if we don't stick that twenty in the bucket. That makes us good community partners. If we didn't stick a twenty in the bucket, we could be counted in the pervert column."

He chuckled.

"Don't you sort of wish you had a kid in the show?" she asked as she surveyed the crowd. "I do. I think that would be awesome to have a mini me onstage."

"You do?"

"Sure," she said, and glanced up at him. "I want kids. I want to go to their performances and clap louder than anyone. Don't you?"

"I do," he said. "Someday."

"Well, if you have them with Brittney, they are going to be little pixie children. Just saying."

He smiled wryly. "Are you implying there is something wrong with pixie children?"

"Not at all," Hallie said breezily, and dipped inside the theater.

The entry was crowded with parents and siblings and grandparents and, just as Hallie said there would be, a conveniently located bucket for donations.

On one side of the theater, children wearing costumes that had been created with varying skill were huddled around one of the dance instructors. A few of them, Rafe noticed, were intellectually or developmentally disabled. One was in a wheelchair.

"Hey," Hallie said, and surprised him with a soft punch to his side. "Is *that* who I think it is?" She pointed to a woman wearing a green pantsuit. She had sleek brown hair that was knotted behind her head and a pair of very high heels.

"I have no idea who that is."

"You don't know *Genevieve Bertram?*" she whispered.

The woman turned. She saw Hallie looking at her. She smiled. She waved. And she started in their direction

"Oh no. *No,*" Hallie whispered, and at first tried to slide in behind Rafe, then suddenly stepped forward and said very brightly, "Hi, Genevieve!" and held out her arms. "It's been such a long time!"

The two women gave each other a half-hearted hug. "I'm surprised to see you!" Genevieve said. "I didn't think you had anything to do with dance anymore. I didn't think you were even in Three Rivers anymore. Oh, that's right, didn't you get married recently?" she asked, smiling at Rafe.

"Nope, didn't get married, still a fan of dance," Hallie said stiffly. "And still in Three Rivers." She groped for Rafe's arm. "This is my friend, Rafe Fontana."

"Oh. A pleasure to meet you, Rafe," Genevieve said politely, and took his hand in both of hers to shake it. "Are you a fan of the arts, as well?"

"I am," Rafe said.

"So are you still dancing?" Hallie asked Genevieve. Rafe noted she was gripping his arm as if she thought he intended to escape.

"Here and there. I'm more of a patron of the ballet now," Genevieve said. "I had a knee injury a few years ago, and I've been slowly working my way back."

"I'm sorry to hear that," Hallie said.

"Surprisingly, that injury led to some rewarding work," Genevieve said. "I'm on the board of Kidz Korner. I helped choreograph the performance today. So I guess I'm dancing again in a way."

"That's fantastic."

"What I'm really hoping to do is take this pilot program citywide and perhaps discover a true talent. You remember, Hallie, there wasn't anything like that when we were dancing. It was whoever could afford to put their kid in ballet classes. But I would dearly love to find the next prima ballerina, no matter where he or she comes from."

"What a great idea," Hallie said.

Genevieve glanced over her shoulder. They were ushering the kids through a backstage door. "I should go." She smiled at Hallie. "It was really good to see you. I hope you enjoy the show. Nice to meet you, Rafe." She smiled and glided away with the grace of a ballerina.

"She seems nice."

Hallie released her death grip of his arm. "She is. She was my archrival in the San Antonio corps de ballet when we were teenagers. She always got the good roles. They said she had good lines."

"Excuse me, the show is about to start," a man in a blue vest said. "Please take your seats."

Hallie and Rafe followed everyone else into the theater.

The auditorium was already filled. As several families were still looking for places to sit, Hallie and Rafe decided to stand in the back. Or, rather, Hallie decided Rafe should stand in the back. "Wait here," she whispered, and started to walk away.

"Hey," he whispered loudly, and caught the back of her jacket before she could get away. "Where are you going?"

She held up her camera and then disappeared into the darkness down the aisle.

Rafe shifted uncomfortably. The aisle was so narrow that he had to squeeze against the wall in order to let people pass. The lights started to dim, and Rafe twisted around, peering into the darkened theater, searching for Hallie. He spotted her on the other side of the theater, her camera to her eye.

The curtains suddenly opened. A set, crudely painted onto plywood, revealed a bedroom. Six kids sort of shuffled onto the stage in party clothes, including the kid in the wheelchair. The music began, and a teacher appeared below the stage, shadowing the moves the kids were supposed to make.

Rafe had never seen a ballet. He'd at least heard of *The Nutcracker*, but he had no idea what was happening, who or where the dancers were supposed to be, other than clearly in someone's bedroom.

The kids danced, including the one in the wheelchair. Not one of them seemed to want to crawl off the stage like he had in the second grade when he was forced to be a singing tree in the school play. Every one of them seemed to want to be up on that stage.

The dance ended, and the theater went dark. There were a lot of scraping sounds and whispers from the stage, a lot of feet scrambling to get in place. When the lights came on again, another group of about seven kids, dressed like toy soldiers and ballerinas, were arranged on the stage. When the music started, the soldiers paired with the ballerinas. One girl, however, didn't have a toy soldier to pair with.

The music began. The pair work between soldier and ballerina seemed more difficult than the first dance, and there seemed to be some disagreements as to who was supposed to do what between two of the couples. But like the first group, the children were determined to finish their dance.

It was the girl dancing solo who caught Rafe's attention. She had Down syndrome. She was not intimidated by the lack of a partner, but quite the opposite—she was dancing as if she had a partner, and with great enthusiasm that put her a beat or two ahead of the rest. She danced with an earnestness he doubted he'd ever applied to any job. She never once looked at the teacher below the stage—she didn't have to. She knew this dance, and he found himself wondering how many hours she'd devoted to learning and practicing it.

Rafe's vision began to blur slightly, and his nose felt a little stuffy as he watched the girl. He was alarmed by his reaction—he was supposed to be a man's man, an Army Ranger who taught martial arts to tough street kids. But what was that bit of wetness beneath his eyes? A fucking *tear.* All he knew was that he felt that fervent little dancer in his heart. Right in the middle of his big fat heart.

A touch to his hand startled him, and he glanced to his right. Through a sheen of tears, he saw Hallie smiling up at him. "Softy," she whispered, and slipped her arm around his waist, hugging him into her side.

"*You* are," he muttered, and put his arm around her shoulders. He needed someone to hold on to while he watched the girl dance.

When the number ended, and the girl bowed, and Rafe clapped loudest of all, Hallie looked up at him with so much tenderness swimming in her hazel eyes that he feared he would crumble into sticky bits right there in front of God and all the parents in Three Rivers.

She reached up and brushed the lone tear from the corner of his eye.

"Allergies," he said gruffly.

"There is a *lot* of dust in here," she agreed.

They watched two more performances, then slipped out into the silence on the street. It had begun to rain, and they jogged to her car. Once inside, she showed him the pictures she'd taken of the kids. "These are damn good," Rafe said, flicking through the shots. She'd managed to capture the kids as artists, and not curiosities, or even awkward preteens. Even his little ballerina.

"I'm glad we stopped," she said as she viewed the pictures. "I haven't seen a ballet in a long time. Although technically, it wasn't a ballet. Other than the costumes and the music, it really wasn't a ballet at all. More of a performance."

Rafe laughed. "You're going to critique a group of kids?"

"I'm critiquing the *choreography*. Those kids could do real ballet, you know? They can do more than hop around. Genevieve is not going to find her prodigy if they don't actually perform ballet."

"Maybe you should offer your services and teach them," he said with a wink. "You can be a part-time photographer-slash-choreographer-slash-dance-instructor."

"You laugh, but maybe I will. I've been thinking about it. I mean maybe. I don't know if I could even plié."

"I don't know what that is, but you should try it. It's like a bike, right? No one forgets how to ride one."

She gave him a curious smile. "Don't you know *anything* about ballet?"

What he knew about ballet was that there was a time in his life he lived for glimpses of her thighs and her breasts in the tights and leotards she wore on the east lawn. "Today was my first time."

Hallie gasped with delight, her eyes as big as fried eggs. "That is *ridiculous*. How have we been together so long if you've never seen ballet?"

Rafe stumbled over what she'd just said, knocked off balance by the word *together*. That meant something to him, and it didn't mean friends.

Apparently, it meant something to Hallie, too— he could tell by the way her cheeks bloomed. "I'm just saying that we should fix your total ignorance of ballet. You can't be a big softy and not even know what you're being soft about."

"Well, *you* can't critique a performance if you don't know if you can do whatever you said."

"*Plié!*"

"My point is, you loved ballet. You should try it again."

She didn't say anything for a moment. She looked out the windshield at the rivulets curving down the glass. "I really did love it," she agreed, her voice gone soft. "But sometimes, you have to own up to what is. I wasn't as good as I needed to be. Genevieve was good. She was really good. I was always so envious of her."

"You were good, too, Hallie. You went to New York—"

"But not good enough," she interrupted. "That was the final verdict. I was not good enough. They told me so. They told me in New York, and not so directly, they told me in college."

He was going to say something, but she put

her hand up. "Look, I've accepted it. I'm over it. What I'm not over is how I utterly lacked a plan B. That was my biggest mistake. And I feel like I've been looking for that plan ever since."

The rain started falling harder. They both stared out the window. People were coming out of the theater, running to their cars.

Rafe understood what she meant. He hadn't had a plan B when he fell in love with Hallie all those years ago. He'd joined the army to get away. It had seemed the only way to move on, because like Hallie, he couldn't carry the tune of loving her. Thank God for the army—at least he'd figured out his plan B there. He had a vision, but the goal was the same—escape Three Rivers.

"I guess we're not running," she said, and slumped in the driver's seat. "Probably just as well. My core is currently engaged with a Thanksgiving dinner."

People were hurrying to their cars, dragging along little sugarplums. Cars began to pull out of the parking lot.

"We'll give it a few minutes," Rafe said. He adjusted his seat, leaning back.

"So, speaking of plan B," Hallie said, and began to trace her finger around the steering wheel. "Uncle Chet suggested I go to Aspen for a couple of weeks and think about things." She glanced at him from the corner of her eye. "He thinks I should get out of the house. And by getting out of the house, he means away from my mom."

"Oh." Rafe could feel his heart deflate a little. There seemed like so little time left with her as it was. He would be off to Chicago, and she would be taking pictures of dresses, and they would text, but it wouldn't be the same as these few weeks had been. "When?"

"Now. Early next week."

Rafe had never been to Aspen. He'd probably never go to Aspen. People like the Fontanas went to Red River in New Mexico if they wanted to ski. Rent was cheap, ski passes were cheap. He imagined Aspen was full of jet-setters and glittering Michelin-starred restaurants and perfect powder. It was amazing to him that, at times, it would seem as if there were no differences between him and Hallie, nothing to stop them from being, as she'd said, *together*, and then, in the space of a breath, something would pop up that might as well have put the Gulf of Mexico between them.

"I think I might do it," Hallie said. "What do you think of that? Do you think I should go to Aspen?"

"That sounds great," he said, and forced himself to smile. "I'm envious. I've never been."

"Hmm," she said, and folded her arms, twisting about in her seat to look at him. "Maybe I should just stay here. I'm feeling much better about things. More optimistic and all that. I have some ideas of what comes next. So maybe my plan B is right here."

"Maybe," he said.

"What do you think, Rafe? Should I stay at the ranch and learn how to run? Or should I go to Aspen for a couple of weeks and think?"

He didn't understand this conversation. "I think you need to do what your gut tells you to do."

Why that would cause her to look as annoyed as she did, he had no idea. He didn't know what he was supposed to say. "Your uncle is very generous."

"Rafe!" she said, as if he were being intentionally obtuse.

He laughed with confusion. *"What?"*

She groaned. She twisted forward in her seat, bounced her head back, and closed her eyes as she gripped the steering wheel. And then she opened her eyes and twisted again, and this time, she planted her elbows on the console between them. "You know what *I* think? I think it sounds kind of lonely."

"Then don't go."

She stared at him. "Are you kidding me right now?"

He dragged his fingers through his hair, perturbed by the mystery of the female brain. "I don't know what you want me to say."

She was glaring at him now. "We've had a great time the last couple of weeks, haven't we?"

"We have."

"Do I need to spell it out for you?"

"Obviously, because I have no idea why you are annoyed right now."

"I have always done what is expected of me. But I've been talking about being a new leaf—"

"Turning one over."

"I'm a new leaf, and I'm reaching for the brass ring. Are you with me so far?"

"No," he admitted. He didn't think it was wise to point out her mix of metaphors at this particular juncture. "So . . . the brass ring is, what? Aspen? If that's your brass ring, you should go for it."

"Really? You think I should just take off for a couple of weeks," she said, shrugging as if it were no big deal.

But it was clearly *some* sort of deal, even if the deal escaped him. Selfishly, he didn't want her to leave. He was already counting the days before he had to go. He wanted her to stay as long as he was here, give him this magic bit of time for as long as she could before their lives inevitably diverged. "Okay, Hallie. What do *you* think you ought to do?"

"You didn't answer the question," she said, and poked him in the chest. "Maybe *you're* the one who needs to stop doing what is expected of you, did you ever think about that?"

"What are you talking about?" he demanded. "I'm trying to be supportive here."

"I know!" she shouted, and banged her hand on the console. "You're always very supportive! You are the *one person* in my life who thinks everything I do is amazing! But this is not a plea for a pep talk, Rafe. Like, I *know* I ask that from you a lot, and I am trying to be better about it, but I would really, sincerely, like to know if you *really* have nothing to say about me going away for two weeks, other than encouraging me to go and be my best self. Does that mean I imagined everything?"

He suddenly understood. She wanted him to tell her not to go. And Rafe did what every self-respecting male with a long-burning torch for a woman would do: he panicked. "I don't . . . I think that . . . I mean, maybe you do need some space."

"From you?" she asked, and shoved him in the chest. "Why are you so . . . *determined?*"

"Determined about what?"

"Is it that girl? Is it Brittney-no-A? Are you seriously dating her?"

He blinked. He had a sudden image of Brittney's bright smile, her delicate, small hands.

"You *are*."

"Sometimes," he admitted.

Her eyes widened. She slowly sank back. "Do you love her?"

He laughed. "*No,* Hallie. She's someone to hang out with."

She bit her lip as she studied him. "You're sleeping with her?"

He didn't like where this was going. It was too intrusive, even for her. "You don't get to ask that."

"Why not? Aren't we friends?"

"It's none of your business who I sleep with."

"I told you I was sleeping with Chris after I met him."

"That's your choice—it's not mine."

"What are you afraid of? Why the hell are you so determined to *fight* it?"

Myriad emotions began to churn in his gut. He wasn't entirely sure what she meant. Had he given himself away? Had he stayed too long in her company, was it clear he'd wanted too much? "Fight *what?* Will you just say what you're trying to say?"

Hallie suddenly climbed halfway up the console and worked to get one leg over it.

"What are you doing?"

"Coming over there," she said, and freed the leg, sliding it over his lap until her knee was on his door's armrest. She caught his face with one hand and turned it toward her. She leaned awkwardly and managed to graze his temple with her mouth.

"*Wait* a minute," Rafe said, and put his hands on her waist, pushing her back a little. "Are you *kissing* me?"

"No, Rafe, there's a smudge on the window I want to wipe off. *Yes,* I am trying to kiss you! Could you just work with me here? Because this is already a lot more awkward than I thought when I pictured it in my head!"

"Come on, Hallie," he said reprovingly.

She did not move away. Quite the contrary—she slid onto his lap and pressed her palms to his cheeks.

"I don't . . . I don't understand what you want me to do," he said, and removed his hands from her, holding his arms back, his hands gripping the leather interior to keep from touching her.

"Are you blind? Look," she said, as if she were about to propose a Faustian bargain—one that he feared he might take. "You've always been such a good friend, Rafe. You always know exactly the right things to say. But I think you've been saying them so long that you've convinced yourself there is nothing more here, nothing bigger between us. I think the reason you never told me about that girl is because there *is* more to us, and you don't want to admit it. And I don't want to go to Aspen wondering if there is something more."

Rafe swallowed down the lump in his throat. This was the moment he had worked so hard to avoid. So many images raced through his head. His dad. The view of the Chicago skyline when he flew into Midway airport. The days, the weeks, the months and years of denying himself

241

his true desire for her, and yet never being able to let go of the idea of her. "Listen," he said, and his voice, he realized with some mortification, was shaking.

"Don't lie to me, Rafe," she said. "Don't you dare lie to me."

His thoughts were so jumbled he didn't know how to even think through such a highly charged moment as this. It felt like right before combat—that buzz of anticipation, that rush of adrenaline.

Hallie's eyes were locked on his, her gaze piercing, and he knew she could see right through him. She saw past his facade. His heart began to hammer in his chest. He had no plan B for this. He had no idea how he was going to get out of this. He had reached the middle of the lake, and the ice had broken, and he was sinking.

"Why do you think we keep pretending this isn't happening?" she whispered. "Because we both know it is. I mean, I'm sitting on your lap, and you're hard, and you haven't thrown me off."

"Jesus, *Hallie*," he said, and his voice was rough and full of need, and he would have been ashamed if he hadn't ached so much with the truth. "You are so fucking outrageous."

He didn't know who reached first, but the rush of adrenaline turned to desire, and she was in his arms, and her body was pressed against his, and she felt so good, curves and softness, just like he'd imagined she would feel.

It was pure electricity, pure adrenaline. Her lips were butter soft, her skin smooth and pliant. It was just a kiss, but the thrum of something deeper was there, and his body was responding rapidly. Too rapidly. He felt himself tumbling hard and fast down the cliff.

He caught her head in his hands to look at her. He wanted to groan—she looked so alluring with her tousled hair and wet lips. "I wasn't done," she said, and grabbed the collar of his shirt, pulling him up, so she could continue kissing him.

They fell back again into the reclined seat, and Rafe caught her, ran his hand against her cheek and temple. The fire between them was dangerously hot, arousing him to the point of bursting. He slipped his hand under her shirt and moved to her breast, slipping his fingers beneath her bra and cupping the mound of flesh.

She made a soft little moaning sound into his mouth, and that was it. Rafe sat up, still anchored to her, and with a Herculean move, twisted her around and pushed her onto the back seat.

Boxes of champagne flutes fell to the floorboard. He was on top of her, their legs tangled and half off the seat bench. Hidden behind tinted windows, they were rolling around like teenagers, and Rafe didn't care. This woman, with the irresistible smile and glittering hazel eyes, this woman who had captivated him and had made him yearn and ache in ways no one else had ever come close to matching, was at last in his arms, and he was kissing her, and his tongue was dancing with hers, and his hand was riding her body, seeking warm flesh wherever he could find it.

The kiss went from arousing to molten, incinerating him from the inside out, turning his thoughts to ash. He was a puddle of desperate desire, a man formerly known as Rafe. This was everything he'd wanted, and it wasn't nearly enough. He wanted all of her. He wanted to feel every bit of her skin against his, wanted to run his hands over every line, every curve. He wanted to be inside her. *Inside her.*

Those prurient thoughts were pushing him down, beneath the surface of rational thought, sinking him deeper and deeper away from his reserve.

Hallie arched her back, pressed her leg in between his, against his erection. She swept her hands up his chest and into his hair, her fingers grazing his ears, then his neck. Her kiss was full of promise and anticipation, and if it had been any other time, any other place, Rafe was certain he would have abandoned all his principles and lived in the moment. He would have fulfilled the single most pressing desire he'd ever had; he would have put her on her back and taken them both to a place that neither of them would ever forget.

His body was hard with anticipation, but when

she reached for the drawstring of his sweatpants and slid her hands into the waistband, something awful happened—his damn head overruled his groin.

His traitorous head began to whisper that she was a friend, not a lover. She was a Prince, not a girl he could sleep with. She was not some one-night stand, some temporary infatuation. What they were doing would complicate things.

What they were doing would ruin the most important friendship he had.

She nipped his lips, and he lifted his head. She wiped the pad of her thumb across his lower lip. "Sorry," she said breathlessly. "But not sorry." She looked like a woman who wanted to rip his clothes off of him then and there. He felt like a man who wanted that to happen. It all felt so strong and real and maybe even a little inevitable. But it also felt incautious. Dangerous.

"We have to stop, Hallie. Right now."

"What? Why?" she asked, and shifted up onto her elbows. "We're having a good time. A *very* good time." She slipped her hand around his neck and tried to pull his head back to hers.

Rafe winced, but he resisted her. His desire was so potent it sliced through him like a blade. He had fantasized about this for so long, and it was happening, and he, the good son, the one everyone could depend on to do the right thing, was putting on the brakes.

He leaned down and kissed her cheek.

And then he pushed up, moved her legs from the seat bench, and raked both hands through his hair.

Hallie pushed up, too. "What's the matter?"

"We can't do this." The words stuck in his throat—it felt like he needed to cough them out.

"We just did this."

"But we can't go any further. You know that."

Her small laugh sounded strangled. "Last time I checked, I'm a grown woman and I can do what I want. What are you talking about?"

"We are friends. You just got out of a relationship," he said. "An *engagement*. This is some sort of rebound for you."

"No, it's not."

"And I'm leaving for Chicago—"

"So what?"

"My family—my father, *me*—we work for your family, Hallie. We are your employees."

Hallie stared at him. "What are you doing right now? Why are you ruining this?"

"Because we don't want to ruin a lifelong friendship—"

"Hey!" she snapped. "You can't deny there is something more here, Rafe. It's been simmering for the last two weeks for sure, and I think maybe it's been there even longer. Am I wrong? Tell me I'm wrong, and I will apologize profusely and go away."

She was more perceptive than he knew, and he still couldn't bring himself to admit it. Admitting it would be the first step in confessing the truth about his feelings for her. "Even so, it doesn't change our reality."

The fight seemed to go out of her. She drew her legs up and wrapped her arms around them and buried her face in her knees. "I think I could die right now."

"Hallie," he said, and put his hand on her leg. "I'm trying to spare us both. This could never go any further, so why even start? Why risk our friendship?"

"Is *that* what you were thinking of while I was kissing you?" she asked, raising her head. "That I was ruining our friendship? Man, I was somewhere else completely. I can't believe I was so off the mark."

"Come on, you know I'm right," he said.

"I *don't* know that," she said. "I don't think we have to declare our intentions here and forevermore at this very minute, Rafe. It's entirely possible to just enjoy the moment, and we were off to a pretty great start, or at least I thought so, while you were being so fucking responsible or honorable or whatever it is you're being right now."

He didn't know what he was being. He thought about how Hallie was still reeling from a broken engagement. This wasn't about him. He thought about his dad telling him that Mrs. Prince was looking for a reason to let him go. He thought about their friendship and tried to imagine what it would be like if he and Hallie ruined it—could he live with no more text messages? Would he have to avoid the main compound forever?

This was going to torture him forever, he knew, but he'd thought about this moment for so long that he already knew the answer—this could not be.

Hallie was staring at him, anger and desire flaring in her eyes as they moved over his face. What was worse was that she was so damn beautiful, her hair spilling over her brow, her lips slightly swollen, the color in her cheeks high.

Rafe thought of his family. Of Mrs. Prince. Of Jason and Chaco. He thought of all the reasons that this would never work. His feelings were rising in the back of his throat, making him feel slightly nauseated. "I'm flying out to Chicago in the morning," he said. "When I come back, I have my last final. Then it's Christmas, and then I'm moving."

"I know. You've told me like five thousand times. What is your point?"

"My point is that we shouldn't start something here, in the back seat of a car, that we both know we would never finish. It's only going to hurt us, and there is no reason to risk what we've meant to each other for many years."

"Maybe the reason is that things change. People change. Maybe the reason is that we need to know. You keep talking like I asked you to marry me, and I didn't. I wanted to make out, Rafe, so pardon me. What harm is there in enjoying each other while we can? I can handle it."

A fling? That's what she'd settle for? That was not what he wanted. It was so far from what he wanted that Rafe felt sick. "*I* can't handle it," he said, more sharply than he intended. "*I* can't."

Hallie suddenly scrambled up onto her haunches. "Got it." She awkwardly tried to climb over the console and the reclined passenger seat, falling onto her butt, and then slinking back to the driver's seat.

Rafe started to do the same, but she turned on the car. "You can stay back there. I'm dropping you off."

Rafe eased back. "Great," he said. "It's already gone south—you're pissed."

"I'm not pissed," she said as she backed out of the parking spot. "I'm just . . . embarrassed."

He crossed his arms over his chest, holding himself tight from the disappointment billowing over him.

They drove in silence to his house. She kept looking at him in the rearview mirror. Rafe kept racking his brain for what to say, but he knew Hallie, and she was furious right now. He was pretty furious with himself.

At the end of his drive, she turned a sunny smile to him. "Thanks for getting me out of the house." She looked strangely serene.

"Anytime."

"*Ooh,* I don't think you mean *any*time, but okay. Have a great trip to Chicago!" she said cheerily, and faced forward.

Rafe slowly got out of her car, then watched her barrel away. If he could, he'd kick his own ass.

He walked into the house and shrugged out of his jacket in the entry.

"Hey, bro."

Rafe's head came up with a start. "Rico!" Rico wasn't supposed to be home yet, and Rafe wasn't ready for Rico. But somehow, he managed to plaster a smile on his face. "I didn't know you were going to be here today."

"Neither did I. They cut me loose a couple of weeks early." Rico embraced his brother. His dark curly hair was a little long, but his dark brown eyes were shining with delight, and he looked healthy. "Man, come in, come in. I gotta hear what's going on around town. Pop says I'm stuck here until I pay him back for everything." He laughed. "That shouldn't take more than about twenty years. Got any get-rich-quick schemes for me?"

Rafe laughed wryly. If he had one, he'd be tapping into it and getting as far from town as he could right about now.

Chapter Fourteen

Hallie talked Grandma and Luca into helping her with her next shoot—that's what she called her photography sessions now, because she considered herself a professional wedding deconstructor—and while her grandmother made it clear she wasn't doing any work, she was happy to ride along.

Luca groused about it, but he went up to the cemetery and grabbed Grandma's lawn chair all the same, then marched down to Hallie's car and flung it into the back while ranting about how stupid this was and how he didn't care how many followers she had.

"You don't have to go," Hallie said sweetly as Luca fitted his tall frame into her front seat.

"What, and leave you two wandering around looking for a way out of the warehouse like the Israelites in the desert?" He snorted his opinion of their ability to find their way out.

It turned out Luca was right—Hallie couldn't even find the light switch in the warehouse. "Move," he said with exasperation, and walked into that dark warehouse with no fear. After a minute or so of listening to Luca cuss, the warehouse was suddenly flooded with fluorescent light. Hallie and her grandmother were standing in a large reception area, demarcated by glass walls that separated them from the rest of the warehouse. In the middle, offices were boxed together in windowed cubes.

"Behold, Hallie, your warehouses," Luca said, and swept his arm grandly at the cavernous space.

They were her warehouses, all right. Three of them, side by side, left to her by her father. Three giant, empty warehouses that she had absolutely no use for.

She stepped out of the reception area and into the empty space, recalling the day she'd learned about this gift from her father, on the same day they'd buried his ashes. Or, rather, had tried to bury his ashes—a family brawl had broken out, thanks to all of them trying to drown their sorrows in alcohol. Hallie was not sure who had actually thrown the first punch, but her designer dress had been torn, and Nick had to break it up, and then George had ushered them into the study and told them that they needed to stop acting like heathens and adjust to a new reality. When pressed, he'd said, "I don't know how to sugarcoat it, so I'll just say it. Charlie had a gambling problem."

This was not news to any of them. It wasn't as

if her father's frequent trips to Las Vegas or his reckless betting was a big secret—everyone in town talked about it.

But then George had said, "Now, don't misunderstand. It's not like you're *poor*. But you're not as rich as you think."

That's when the emotional roller coaster she'd been on since the day she found out her father had died suddenly took a downward turn. "Rich" was the only way the Princes knew to be. Hallie certainly didn't know how to be anything but privileged. She was very much aware of it, and she knew she had more than others dared to dream of having. But that didn't mean she knew how *not* to be like that. The Prince family had made an art of living high on the hog.

"You're going to have to start doing things differently," George had continued.

"How differently?" Nick had asked.

"Don't spend as much," George had said.

That's when Hallie had really lost it. All her grief came pouring out of her, in ways big and small. Her father had died, things were not great with Chris, and she was now being told that she might not have the big society wedding she'd been planning for a *year*.

"Listen, all of you," George had said, when everyone started talking and shouting at once. "Charlie was a good man at heart, but he had his demons. Nevertheless, he loved his family, and

253

the last time we updated his will, he made sure there was something in there for each of you."

What her father had made certain was in that will for Hallie were three empty, aging warehouses on the highway.

She would never understand it. It felt like an afterthought, frankly. She could imagine him making certain there were important things left to his sons—Nick was handed the reins to the family business. Luca was given land. Her dad had even left land for the never-before-seen bastard son, her half brother, Tanner Sutton. But for his only daughter, his little princess? The girl who was never supposed to be anything but pretty? Charlie Prince had left three empty warehouses.

Hallie had loved her father so much. But he'd never expected more for her than to be taken care of by him or another man. In his mind, Hallie was a girl, and girls married and had babies. Even when she'd come back from New York, devastated, hurting, humiliated by being asked not to return to her ballet school, her father—who had gotten her that spot with a sizable donation—was very cheerful about it. "Don't worry about it, sweetheart. One of these days you'll be chasing toddlers around, and you won't even think of it."

Her father had not understood that she would think about it every day for the rest of her life. She had really wanted to be a ballerina, from the earliest time she could remember. As a little girl, she'd worn tutus with everything. It may have sounded frivolous to him, but it had meant something to her. It was in her blood. And at that point in her life, she hadn't thought of toddlers. She'd thought of dancing in big productions, of dedicating herself to her craft. She hadn't really thought of marriage and babies until all of that went away.

"Smells like rotten food in here," Grandma said, wrinkling her nose.

"What are you going to do with this place, anyway, Hallie?" Luca asked as he flipped on the lights in the office cubes.

"I don't know. What could I possibly do? Sell the property, I guess."

"Good luck with that," her grandmother said. "I know Charlie tried to sell it a few years ago and couldn't get any takers. Where's my chair, Luca?"

"Right here, Grandma," he said, and with one hand, popped open the chair and set it down for her.

"This place gives me the creeps," Hallie said, and rubbed her hands on her arms. "Another selling point."

"Have you never seen the warehouses before?" Luca asked.

"Once. I came with George to see what they were." She didn't add that she'd been so distraught she hardly gave the place a look at all.

She was looking at it now. It was nothing but a big empty room. It had enormous fans on either end of the space, the blades turning absently with each lift of a breeze. There were industrial lights overhead, hanging about six feet apart. The concrete floor looked as if there had been some sort of structure attached to it once—shelving, maybe?—but whatever it had been was long gone.

Her grandmother was right about the smell— it was awfully musty, as if it hadn't been opened in years. She could hear a drip coming from somewhere, and parts of the concrete floor were wet. She wondered just how long these warehouses had been sitting empty. She wondered why the Princes had ever come to own warehouses anyway. For what purpose?

"What are those things?" she asked, pointing to some giant machinelike contraptions stacked along one wall.

"Look like HVAC units," Luca said. He was walking across the warehouse floor to the back wall.

"What am I supposed to do with HVAC units?" she demanded.

"Maybe you could sell 'em for scrap," Grandma opined. "I doubt they're any use to anyone now."

Hallie slowly turned a circle, taking it all in. "Can you believe this is what Dad left me? *This.*"

"Maybe you should stop thinking of them as warehouses," Luca called over his shoulder. "Maybe you could do something with them."

"Like what?"

"You'll have to figure that out." He opened a metal box on the wall and rummaged around inside. Suddenly, the bay door rumbled to life and, with a loud squeak of metal, slowly began to lift. "That's better," he said.

Natural light flooded the space, and a surprisingly lovely view appeared of a pasture and pond, some oak trees, and a few cows grazing. If that bay door were a window instead of a door, this space wouldn't be nearly as ugly.

Hallie walked to the open door and looked out. "I think I know why he left this to me."

"Why?" Luca asked.

"Because he couldn't leave me out. He had to leave me *something* after he took care of you and Nick and Tanner. This is what he had left. Which worked out perfectly, because he wouldn't have trusted me with anything but empty space."

"Hallie, that is not true. Your father adored you," her grandmother said.

"I know he did, Grandma. But he had a very traditional way of viewing the world, and I am a girl, and he had strong ideas about girls."

"Maybe," Luca said. He shoved his hands in his pockets. "And maybe he left them to you because he trusted you to know exactly what to do with them. Did you ever think of that?"

Hallie laughed. "Right. Because I know so much about warehouses."

"You don't right now. But you could learn it. I think the bigger issue is that you don't trust yourself enough to figure it out."

That remark annoyed her, mostly because it resonated with her. She *didn't* trust herself. She didn't trust anything about her life right now. If she stuck her finger into any pie, she would fully expect it to go bad. "Have you been reading self-help books again?" she asked her brother.

"Yep. How to get along with difficult people."

"Well, how long are we going to sit around here?" Grandma complained.

"Right. Let's get the boxes," she said to Luca.

She and Luca hauled the boxes of champagne glasses and various other bags of props. In the mix was an H-E-B grocery bag, which Luca deposited at their grandmother's feet. She leaned over, unzipped the bag, and pulled out a wine cooler.

"Grandma!" Hallie said.

"Don't worry, I brought enough to share." She reached into her bag and pulled out two more.

Luca took one without so much as an arched brow.

"You know I'm skating onto thin ice here,

given the last time I drank," Hallie said, and took the other bottle her grandmother offered.

"You just need a little practice, that's all," her grandmother said with a grin.

Hallie twisted the cap and took a sip—and instantly coughed the sip onto the floor. "Oh my *God,* what is this?" she said, holding the bottle up. "A *pineapple* wine cooler?"

"Why not? They were on sale."

"That statement is definitely a sign of just how much this family has changed. Since when did a Prince ever worry about anything being on sale, much less cheap wine coolers?"

"That was because we hadn't discovered Walmart, and sales are a big part of the Walmart culture," Grandma said. "When in Rome!" She lifted her bottle in pretend toast and drank.

Hallie had a sip or two of hers, then handed the sickly sweet wine cooler to Luca. She began to set out her champagne glasses while her grandmother and Luca watched. What she loved about them was that they didn't ask *why* Hallie was doing what she was doing. Especially her grandmother—unlike Hallie's mother, Grandma apparently had no compulsion to explain to Hallie why this could be considered bizarre behavior, or how it suggested she wasn't moving on with her life.

That's what her mom had said yesterday, when she'd attempted to apologize to Hallie for her remarks at Thanksgiving dinner. The so-called apology had somehow veered off into a discussion of what her mother perceived as Hallie's lethargy. What her mother failed to realize was that Hallie *was* moving on with her life—she just wasn't doing it like her mother wanted her to.

When Hallie got the glasses set up, she arranged some lovely silk flowers around them. Her phone dinged. She scrambled for it, digging it out of the bottom of one of her bags, hoping it was Rafe.

She was very disappointed to see that it was not Rafe. It was Chris, damn him. **Please, Hallie, can we talk?**

She scrolled through her texts to make sure she hadn't missed one from Rafe, because she hadn't heard from him since she'd crawled onto his lap and kissed him, and then had gotten mad when he said it wasn't a good idea. Maybe he was right about ruining a friendship, because frankly, she was a little panicked that she hadn't heard from him. She'd checked her phone a thousand times, and nope, he'd just flown off to Chicago and left her to stew in her juices.

She could be such an idiot sometimes. She kept thinking he'd call and smooth it over with a careful consideration of what had happened between them, but he didn't. He was going to make her do the careful consideration this time.

He was right. Of course he was right. She *had* just gotten out of a relationship, and she'd already decided that, for once in her life, she needed to figure out how to stand on her own two feet. And he was right that they had a fantastic friendship. Not to mention he was going to Chicago, and she was very seriously thinking of moving back to Austin to go to school. What did she think would come of it then? Was she going to start some holiday fling and then take off? No. She would never do that to Rafe.

But what had he meant, anyway, that *he* couldn't handle it? He couldn't handle what? Her? Was she so off the chain? Was the prospect of being with her so repugnant that he couldn't handle it?

But that made no sense—he handled her better than anyone and had for a long time. Was she just not his type? Was she too needy? How could she be too needy for Rafe? He helped *everyone*. How could she, of all people, be the one that tipped him over the edge?

What was his type, anyway? Little dark-headed, petite pixie women?

"Are we going to do this, or are you going to stare at your phone?" Luca asked.

"Oh, honey, did you get a message from him?" Grandma asked.

Both questions startled Hallie, and she looked up from her phone. "What?"

"I know you two haven't been talking, and I was just wondering if he sent you a message." She waggled her brows as she sipped from the bottle.

Hallie's eye widened. Grandma knew about Rafe? "You know . . . *how* do you know?"

"Your mother told me. She said he's been calling and texting you."

"Wait . . . *Chris?*"

Her grandmother laughed. "Who else would I be talking about?"

Hallie blinked. She'd almost said it. She'd almost said *Rafe*. She glanced at Luca. Her twin was silent, his look thoughtful. Appraising. Like he knew something. "Yep," she said, and tossed the phone into the bag. "But I'm over him. I mean, okay, I'm still pissed about the wedding that I planned for more than a year. But Chris?" She fluttered her fingers. "So done." She began to arrange the flowers next to the glasses.

"I had a broken engagement before your grandfather came along," Grandma announced.

"You did?" Luca asked. "I never knew that. Who was he?"

"Oh, he was just some old boy from Tennessee who came through here with big plans to run cattle. He sure was easy on the eyes. He didn't have a lick of sense, mind you, but he was so cute I said I'd marry him anyway."

Hallie laughed. "So what happened?"

"Well, I got to thinking about it, and I decided I didn't want to marry a pretty face. The pretty wears off after a while, and then you're stuck with a dimwit."

Luca chuckled. "Thank God you called it off, because we wouldn't be here otherwise. Is that when you met Grandpa?"

Hallie knew this story, but she never tired of hearing it.

"Maybe a year later I met Grandpa at the annual Battle of the Flowers dance," she said. The Battle of the Flowers was a signature event during the period of Fiesta each spring in San Antonio and surrounding areas, when the battle for the Alamo was commemorated. "He was so handsome." She sighed dreamily. "Tall, like you, Luca. Rugged, like Nick. Nick looks a lot like your grandfather when he was young."

Hallie laughed out loud. "Grumpy?"

Her grandmother smiled. "Your grandfather was just as smitten as I was, although he wouldn't admit it. We danced all night, then we went outside and had a little smooch."

"Just a little one?" Luca teased her.

"Goodness, don't make me blush," Grandma said. "Oh, I knew he was the one for me after that kiss, let me tell you. Sometimes, you just know. *I* knew."

"Yep. I knew it was Ella, too," Luca agreed.

Hallie felt an unwelcome swell of jealousy. She had never felt so certain of anyone.

"But your grandfather was too stubborn by half. He didn't think it was a good idea to marry a girl from the country."

"What?" Hallie asked as she set the aperture on her camera. "But he was from the country."

"Well, sure, but he lived at the ranch with his family. I lived on a little farmstead, like Ella's. And he had big plans. He wanted to get into oil, and he thought if he did, he'd join the ranks of oilmen and rub elbows with the fancy people, and he didn't want to be saddled with a country girl."

Hallie hadn't heard the story quite like this and paused in what she was doing. "So what changed his mind?"

"Me!" Grandma said brightly. "But I made him think it was his idea." She chuckled, and sipped from her bottle. "That's what you have to do sometimes, you know. I pretended like he didn't mean that much to me and made sure he saw me with other boys. Whoo-boy, that settled things right then and there."

"That sounds a little manipulative, Grandma," Luca said.

"Well, sure it was," Grandma agreed. "Do you know a better way?"

Hallie laughed as she got down on her knees and started taking pictures.

"Now, y'all don't need to tell Delia I told you that, especially you, Hallie. She'd have a stroke. If you're going to reconcile with Chris, she wants you to do it on your own terms."

Hallie's head snapped up. "She wants me to reconcile with Chris?"

"Well, I wouldn't say she *wants* you to," Grandma said with a shrug. "But if you do, is all I'm saying. She wouldn't want you to manipulate him, because that's what Margaret Sutton Rhodes did to your father, and she's never gotten over it."

"Oh my God," Hallie breathed. "He *cheated* on me, Grandma. He betrayed me completely."

"I know, honey," she said, and smiled sadly. "But your mother, well—she reconciled with your father twice, remember. Sometimes, you have to put up with the bad to get to the good."

That statement nauseated Hallie. It made her feel sorrowful and angry—furious with the sentiment, of course. But there was something about her mother's grief that resonated with Hallie. In a weird, sick way, she could understand it.

Luca, however, was not amused. "Hallie is not Mom. She doesn't want to be with a cheater. *We* don't want her to be with a cheater."

"Well, okay," Grandma said cheerfully. "I'm just saying that if you change your mind, no one is going to judge you. When you get a little older, you'll understand that things that seemed do or die when you're young tend to lose their punch with a little time."

Hallie shook her head. "I can't believe I'm actually having this conversation."

"I can't either," Luca said fiercely. "You deserve so much better than him, Hallie."

"Really? I don't know," she mused. "Maybe I got exactly what I deserved."

"*What?*" Luca snapped.

"I don't know, I'm just talking," she said vaguely, but the thought had crossed her mind. Had she *really* loved Chris? Ever? Sure, she remembered all those giddy feelings of excitement and lust when they'd first started dating. And she'd had some good times with him. But had she really *loved* him? Or had she been going along with the life plan that had been set for her? Had she ever even taken a moment to really *think* about what path she was on? Or had she abdicated all the thinking after her shot at ballet hadn't worked out? Hallie wasn't so sure she'd thought much about anything with Chris other than what she was going to wear and what china pattern she ought to pick out. So maybe she had totally deserved that very rude awakening.

She looked at the photos she had and was satisfied. It was time for the main event. "Okay, Grandma, are you ready to do the honors?"

"I am indeed," she said, and stood from her lawn chair.

"Hope this works," Hallie said.

"It's not going to work," Luca said. He stood at the other end of the line, his arms folded across his chest. "They're top heavy. They aren't going to domino."

Hallie ignored him, pulled a box from a corner,

and positioned herself on top of it with her camera. "Okay, on the count of three. One, two, three!"

Her grandmother tipped the first champagne glass into the next one with her espadrille. Both glasses fell, but only one of them broke. The second one completely missed the third.

"Yet another opportunity in which I get to say, 'I told you so, Hal,' " Luca said smugly.

Hallie and her grandmother looked at each other and burst into laughter. Luca shook his head.

They never did get it to work, but after Luca's intervention, Hallie had several broken champagne flutes lying on a bed of flowers. She took pictures, and then she and Luca cleaned everything up.

"Biggest waste of my time since high school," Luca groused.

Luca had Hallie drop him at Ella's when they were done. Hallie drove Grandma home. When they pulled into the long drive down to the ranch house, Hallie's heart did a little bit of a jump— Rafe's truck was parked in the drive of the storage shed. She could see Rafe, too, wearing a canvas jacket and cowboy hat, loading things into the back of the truck. Was he home from Chicago so soon? Was she supposed to be pleasantly surprised, or mad that he hadn't told her?

She was going to go with pleasantly surprised.

"I guess he's going to put up that porch swing I got at Walmart after all," her grandmother said. "I think it will look nice over on the east lawn. Sometimes Mary Gruber gets a little dizzy when we're doing our tai chi and needs to sit down for a bit."

Hallie coasted to a halt behind Rafe and rolled down her window, prepared to show him she wasn't mad, that in fact she was sorry. "Hey!" she said, perhaps a little too brightly.

Rafe whipped around. And then he grinned, ear to ear. But it wasn't Rafe grinning at her. It was Rico.

Hallie squealed, threw the gear into park, and hopped out. "Rico! You're home!"

"Hey, girl, you're looking hot as ever," Rico said, and grabbed her up in a hug, kissing her cheek. He stepped back and let his dark brown eyes travel over her. "Mm-mmm, you just get better looking all the time."

"Oh stop," she said, batting her eyes at him. "In a minute, I mean. At least go on for a minute. Hey, when did you get home?"

"Thanksgiving. I've been instructed to help Dad around the ranch. He says you've lost a couple of hands."

"Yep. Are you putting up Grandma's porch swing?"

He looked past her to the car. "Is that Miss Dolly? Oh, I've got to get a kiss from my favorite grandma," he said, and very theatrically slinked around the front of the truck. By the time he reached the passenger window, Hallie's grandmother had rolled down the window, and Rico reached in to hug her, nearly pulling her out.

"You're a sight for sore eyes," Grandma said happily.

Everyone loved Rico—he was the life of the party. Which was what had gotten him into trouble, apparently, but still, everyone was always very happy to see him.

"You gonna be around, Hallie?" Rico asked when he finished chatting with her grandmother. "If you need me to, I could do a little ass kicking for you. I hear you might have someone in mind." He grinned.

She had to appreciate someone who could speak about her dumpster fire without wearing a woeful look. "If there is any ass kicking, I'll do it," she said. "But you can watch. Sure, I'm going to be around."

"That makes two of us," he said. "But between you and me, I gotta get out of here. Dad is already breathing down my neck about paying him back for everything I've ever done by working it off. The only problem is, I don't think his idea and my idea of a solid day's work are going to match up."

"Knowing Martin and knowing you, I'd say probably not." Hallie grinned. "Great! I'll see you around."

"Awesome." He smiled with genuine affection.

Hallie was still smiling when she got in the car. "That boy is such a player," she said to her grandmother.

"But he's a darn cute one," Grandma said. "If I was sixty years younger, I'd be doing a double take."

Her grandmother was right—Rico was a very handsome man, just like his brother. Only Rico was a lot flashier. In high school, on those days he'd deigned to attend, he always wore mirrored sunglasses and a studded belt. He had a nice physique, but he wasn't as thick with muscle as Rafe was. He sported tattoos, where Rafe sported none, at least none that could be seen. Rico let his hair go long and shaggy, where Rafe kept his neatly cut. Rafe was a choirboy, her father had once said of him.

Hallie remembered the evening her father said it. The two of them were on the patio, watching the sun slide west. Rafe had come riding in from the pastures, and the two of them watched him trot up to the stables and the paddock, and come down off his horse. He was wearing boots and jeans and a white T-shirt that fitted him close, and was drenched with his sweat.

"See that kid?" her father had said, and pointed a cigar in Rafe's direction. "That's the kind of kid you hope your own kid turns out to be. He's more concerned about others than he is himself."

"He is?" Hallie had asked. She was sixteen, and all she thought about was ballet and boys and clothes.

"Damn sure is. You know what Martin told me? After school, Rafe volunteers his time to teach martial arts to these mentally challenged kids from the south side of San Antonio. Now that's a calling," he'd said, and hoisted a beer bottle to his lips. "Let me tell you something, Hal," he'd said, and pointed his cigar at her. "It takes a special person to see the world by looking outward. Most of us stand in the world and look inward. Always helping others. You know his mom is sick, and he looks after the other two kids and even makes dinner some nights. Martin told me," her father had said, and gave that remark a shake of his head. "Don't see too many people like that. That's a different sort of heart than what any of us have," he'd said.

"What do you mean?" Hallie had asked.

"Bigger. Expansive." Her father drank more beer, then said, "Can't say that about any Prince I know. Just not how we're wired."

Hallie had laughed.

She hadn't really understood her father's regard for Rafe that day or why he was making Rafe sound like Mother Teresa. But her father had been right about Rafe.

She probably shouldn't have tried to kiss

Mother Teresa. She'd wanted to, and she still did, but she needed to respect his wishes.

And he did not wish her to kiss him.

They reached the house, and Hallie helped Grandma with her lawn chair. When they walked into the house, Hallie's mother was waiting for her, one arm crossed over her middle, the other hand holding a martini. She looked annoyed. "Hi, Mom," Hallie said as she hauled a box into the mudroom and set it on a counter.

"I thought you'd never get home."

Hallie laughed. "Why?"

Her mother stepped to her right. Behind her, a very chubby black and brown puppy with speckled fur, one floppy and one pointed ear, and an enormous red bow tied around its neck was lying on the floor with a massive bone. Its back legs were splayed behind it, and its front paws, which were the size of tea saucers, were holding the bone as the puppy gnawed on one end.

"Who is that?" Hallie asked.

"Your new puppy," her mother said, and sipped from her glass. "And there's not enough gin in the world."

"Mine! What are you talking about?"

"This puppy is a gift from your ex, Hallie. Chris came by today. Actually showed up at this door. He said you told him if he gave you a puppy, you would talk to him. Well, here's your puppy, so now I guess you have to talk to him."

Hallie's fury was instantaneous. She was going to kill him. She was going to use her bare hands and strangle the life from him. "I didn't mean it! He knows I didn't mean it!"

"I don't care if you meant it, what are we going to do with this dog?" her mother demanded.

"We should name her first," Grandma offered.

"It is a he, and if we name that dog, we keep him. You know how this works, Dolly."

"We're not naming him," Hallie said. "He's going back."

At that, the puppy's head came up from the bone. He seemed to realize that there were others in the room, and sort of flopped around until he gained his feet and trotted over to have a good sniff of Hallie's shoes.

"You'll need to house-train him," her grandmother said.

"I'm not keeping him! Chris is an idiot! I said that because he is afraid of dogs."

"He's afraid of *dogs?*" her mother asked incredulously, and drained her martini glass. "What is the matter with people?"

"Oh, look, that little cutie just peed on your boot," Grandma said with delight.

"Shit," Hallie said, and shook it off.

She was going to *kill* Chris.

Chapter Fifteen

There was nothing that could force a man to face his demons quite like an uncomfortable couch in a freezing basement in Chicago. That couch, which Rafe surfed for two nights, had become his sounding board. In the middle of the night, with one arm slung over his eyes, he thought about what had happened with Hallie on Thanksgiving. He thought about all of it—how aroused he'd been, how stunned he'd been, and how goddamn practical he'd been.

Why was he like that? What possible childhood trauma could have made him so responsible? Why could he never be the guy to cross a line from time to time?

But he wasn't. Maybe because Rico was the line crosser. Growing up, it had seemed like having two line crossers in one family was a lot. Someone had to clean up the mess.

All that regret made for some miserable nights in Jason Corona's house.

Jason lived with his family in a cramped bungalow in the Ashburn neighborhood of

Chicago. In addition to him, there were five younger brothers and sisters, an *abuela*, and his parents, all under one roof. Rafe had once asked Jason why he lived at home—he made pretty good money working in security for the Chicago Bears football team.

Jason had seemed surprised by the question. "Where else am I going to live?"

Rafe would have thought anywhere else. Some place he might at least have his own bathroom— there were only two in this house. Rafe had been living in his family's home for a few weeks, having given up his apartment when his dad said he needed help. But for him, it was a temporary gig, a stop on his way to Chicago, and even knowing that, he couldn't wait to get out of there. Nothing against his family—but he was a grown man, and he didn't need his mom asking when he'd be home for dinner.

Jason's family was a big, fun-loving group, and not one of them seemed to mind living like sardines. They spoke mostly Spanish, and while Rafe himself was Hispanic, he didn't know much Spanish, other than some schoolyard Spanglish. His parents had been raised at a time when many Hispanic Texans tried to erase their ethnicity and appear to be white. They spoke English, and some had adopted English names. Fortunately, things had changed a lot since then, but Rafe and his siblings had never learned the language.

He and Jason and Chaco worked all day at the new gym, bolting suspension straps to the walls and putting in a wood floor for the martial arts training. They'd go home for showers and meet up for dinner. Tomorrow, Rafe was returning to Texas.

He was returning to the mess of his emotions he'd left behind. He'd tried like a soldier to churn those emotions out of him as they worked, but that tactic wasn't as effective as it used to be. There were too many questions rumbling around in his head.

His emotions were also jumbled up with the news that the project had hit a small road bump. The former retail space he and his friends had taken was in an old building, in a run-down part of the neighborhood that worked by its own set of rules. Jason's dad had greased the wheels, but there were some holdups to getting the permits they needed to finish the work. The biggest obstacle was the permit for the overhaul of the ancient plumbing. "It'll come through," Jason had told Rafe and Chaco. "Just going to take some time. That's the way it works around here—you grease one palm at a time."

Chaco had moved to Chicago from Pittsburgh. He was short, muscular, and dark brown, and he constantly complained about the cold of Chicago. "Dude," Rafe said. "You're from *Pittsburgh*. If anyone should be complaining right now, it's me."

"You'll see what I mean when you move up

here," Chaco said. "With that air coming off the lake? You can't get that kind of cold out of your bones." He'd paused to adjust his tool belt. "When *are* you moving up here, anyway?"

"End of the year," Rafe said. "I may be bunking with you until I can get my social work license."

"Maybe you ought to hold off," Jason said. "Me and Chaco, we've got jobs. But that permit might take another month or two."

"Nah," Rafe had said, and had picked up a table saw. "I need to get a job so I can get licensed as a social worker."

What he really had to get was out of Three Rivers in the worst way. It was hard enough to be in Chicago and think of Hallie clear across the country. But it was ridiculously hard being a mile away from her and pretending like he wasn't about to bust out of his own skin. It was absurdly hard to give nothing away, to let his family think that he saw the Princes and their wealth with the same cynical view his family shared. It was impossible to live with the daily ache of loving her from a distance. He was Cyrano without the muse or the nose, but just as hopeless.

But he was feeling a little unsteady about Chicago. This had seemed like such a great idea when they were sitting around Afghanistan, trying to kill time. The implementation wasn't what he'd thought it would be. He thought it would be easier. And cheaper.

His brooding did not go unnoticed by his longtime buddies. "What the hell is wrong with you?" Jason asked as he finished dressing for dinner their last night.

Rafe was sitting on Jason's bed, lost in his thoughts. "Me? Nothing."

"Are you worried about the permit? Dude, don't be—Dad says it's no big thing," Jason tried to assure him.

"Sure," Rafe said. He hadn't thought about it since Jason had explained it to them. He was thinking how he'd fly home in the morning, study for his final, and then . . . *and then* . . .

"It's like, you have to pay these bribes. That's just the way you do business here. Nothing I can do about it."

"I'm not worried," Rafe assured him.

"Good," Jason said, and clapped him on the shoulder. "I'm not either."

Chaco was waiting at a corner bar and pizzeria popular with ex-military. US flags, service flags, and large, blown-up military insignia covered the walls. The poolroom in back was always crowded when Rafe and the guys came here. Tonight, the place was packed because of a Chicago Bears game.

They were a couple of beers in, Chaco with a soda, discussing John Horowitz from their last deployment. "I talked to him today," Chaco said. "Dude, he's in San Antonio, at the hospital there."

"No way," Rafe said. "Brooke Army Medical?"

"Yep. They had to take the rest of his leg—it got infected."

None of them spoke for a few moments. Any soldier who came back from a tour without physical injury felt relief. Felt *lucky*. Felt maybe a little survivor guilt mixed in there. John had taken a hit and lost half a leg and half an arm when the armored personnel carrier he was in had driven over an IED.

They had transitioned from talking about their last deployment to football when Rafe's phone pinged. He picked it up, expecting his dad, but was surprised to see it was a FaceTime call from Hallie. He didn't know quite what to do—she hadn't texted him once since the big fiasco of their very hot kiss. "I should take this," he said to Jason and Chaco, who were currently arguing about the Bears' prospects for the playoffs, and ignoring him completely.

Rafe punched the answer button. The screen filled with what looked like moving shag carpet, and he thought it was a mistake, that she hadn't meant to FaceTime him at all. But then the bottom of a large paw covered the screen. "What the hell?" he muttered.

The shag moved and Hallie's face appeared. "Hey," she said. "Remember me?"

His heart did a little leap and spin like an Irish dancer. "Couldn't forget you if I tried."

One of her brows rose up. "Have you tried?"

"Nope."

"So I'm calling to tell you that you were right," she announced, then squeezed her eyes shut as the dog began to lick her face.

"I was right about what, and whose dog is that?"

"It's not a dog, it's a puppy, and it's from You Know Who, and that's what you were right about."

"Hey, who's that?" Chaco grabbed Rafe's shoulder and pulled him to one side, trying to see the screen. Hallie used the puppy's paw to wave at Chaco.

"A friend." Rafe did not miss the slight roll of Hallie's eyes.

"The cute girl? Or the cute puppy?" Chaco asked.

"The cute girl!" Hallie confirmed. "He doesn't know the puppy yet."

"Hey, friend," Chaco said, and winked at Hallie before fading away to continue his argument with Jason.

"So he brought me a puppy," Hallie said.

Brought. He'd brought it to her? She saw him? Were they talking? Did Rafe have any right at all to ask after the things he'd said? "Brought you?"

"*Brought.* You were right, I never should have

said what I did, because apparently, some people can't read the sarcastic subtext after all."

"Being right is a particular gift of mine," Rafe said.

"Show-off." She smiled.

The puppy suddenly lunged for Hallie, and with a laugh, she toppled backward, the phone went dark for a moment, and he could hear her fumbling around for it. But it wasn't Hallie who filled his screen again. It was Rico.

"Hey, bro!"

His heart did another little leap, but this time, it felt uncomfortable. "Hi, Rico. What's going on?"

"Just chilling at the big house," Rico said. "Man, did you get a look at this canine? Blue heeler. He's pretty stinkin' cute." Rico faded back. He and Hallie were sitting in the same chaise on the east lawn of the mansion, the puppy crawling over their laps.

So many questions and cusswords raced through Rafe's head.

Hallie suddenly dipped to one side, out of view. "He's chewing my sneaker!"

It felt to Rafe like this scene was playing out in slow motion. Hallie and Rico, *just chilling*. A lump the size of Chicago formed in his throat. He cleared it and asked, "So, ah . . . what are you two up to?"

He hoped he didn't sound accusatory. Or pathetic.

"Not a damn thing," Rico said cheerfully. "I'm trying to get her to go into town with me, but she won't go. She helped me hang a porch swing today. Got some muscle on her," he said, and reached for Hallie's bicep and squeezed.

"Ouch," Hallie said.

Miss Dolly's porch swing. Great—that was Rafe's project after his last final.

"She's a beast, man," Rico said, and smiled fondly at Hallie.

"No, I'm not!" She laughed, and she was beautiful.

She was beautiful.

She was everything.

Hallie held the puppy to her. Its tongue slid out of the side of its mouth, and its tail beat steadily against her arm. "*What* am I going to do with this puppy?"

"Name him?" Rico suggested.

"You are no help! I'm not naming him. I'm giving him back."

She was going to see the doctor again? So many questions about where she'd been and what she'd been doing slid into Rafe's thoughts at the same time that his disgust at his own hypocrisy went skipping through. You couldn't tell a woman they were only friends and then have an opinion about her love life.

Unfortunately for him, he had a very strong opinion about her love life.

"Okay, Rafe, I just wanted to show you that you were right. *Again.*" She pushed the dog into Rico's chest. "You're always right about everything."

He was? News to him. He didn't think he was right about anything at all. "See you soon?" he asked hopefully.

"Who knows," she said. "Say bye, Rico!" She held the phone up, over her head. Rico was on the grass now, holding the squirming puppy. "Bye, Rafe!" he said obediently.

The screen went dark.

So did Rafe's mood.

It took him a moment to realize Jason and Chaco were looking at him. "Who's the girl?" Chaco asked.

"I told you," Rafe said. "Just a friend." *Just a lie.*

"Sure," Chaco said, and he and Jason laughed.

Rafe was up and out of the house at dawn. Mrs. Corona was the only one awake when he left. She kissed him on both cheeks and sent him off with what he thought was a Spanish blessing. The flight was uneventful, but when he arrived in San Antonio, he took a slight detour on his way home and swung by the Brooke Army Medical Center.

"Hey!" John said when Rafe walked into his room. He was surrounded by get-well balloons and pots of flowers. Someone had hung a US flag with the badge of the 75th Ranger Regiment superimposed over the stars on his wall. "Man, so good to see you," John said, and reached out his hand for Rafe's. "Chaco said you might stop by."

Rafe leaned over John's bed to greet him, and when he did, he noticed the mound of John under the covers, the unmistakably missing leg. "How are you?" The question seemed ridiculously stupid. How could a man be when he was missing half his limbs?

John grinned, unfazed. "Can't complain. I'm going to get fitted for prostheses, and then, dude, there's no stopping me. Hey, maybe you can retrain me in martial arts."

Rafe laughed.

"I'm serious, man," John said, still grinning. "If you can run on fake legs, surely you can fight on them, too. Remember that class you taught?" he asked, referring to a martial arts training course Rafe had delivered to his company over a long, hot summer in Afghanistan.

"You were the *worst,* Horowitz. You fight like you dance."

John howled with laughter. "If it wasn't for you, I wouldn't have passed that course. I always appreciated how you took the extra time, you know?"

Rafe had forgotten about grabbing John during downtime and working with him one-on-one. The training was something his superiors had asked him to do. It wasn't mandatory, but in the army, everything was noticed. If John Horowitz wasn't getting the martial arts, people noticed. People judged. It was just the way a bunch of guys full of testosterone viewed the world. "It was no big deal, Horowitz."

"Not to you," John said. "But it was to me. Think you could train me once I get my legs under me?"

Rafe laughed. "I could hardly train you *with* your legs. But I'll sure as hell try if you're up for it."

"I'm definitely up for it," John said.

They talked about the gym, with John lamenting he would love to do something like that. They talked about Chaco and Jason, gossiped about other guys in the company, most of whom were still in the service.

When Rafe finally left to get home so he could study, John waved to him with the stump of his arm. "Come back, Rafe. Promise you'll come back."

"I promise." He walked down the long corridor toward the exit, swallowing down the swell of weird tears, not unlike those he'd experienced at that kids' ballet. There was something about John's spirit and his fierce determination that got to Rafe. It was like the girl's determination—she wasn't going to let a little Down syndrome get in the way of her dancing. John wasn't going to let the lack of limbs get in the way of his training in martial arts.

His vision was so blurry when Rafe stepped onto the elevator that he thought he was going to have to turn and face the wall before tears started sliding down his cheeks. It was like he was walking around with marshmallows for guts.

Chapter Sixteen

Chris was thoroughly unapologetic when Hallie finally broke down and called him and demanded he take the puppy back. "If you want me to take him, you'll have to bring him to me."

"I don't want to bring him, Chris!" she'd said angrily. "I don't want to see you! That's what I have been telling you!"

"Well, actually, you haven't been telling me anything, because you won't talk to me. I know you hate me right now, Hallie," he'd said patiently, as if he were talking to a hysterical patient. "I don't know how else to get through to you. Do you realize this is the first time I've spoken to you since everything happened?"

Since everything happened, as if there were a series of unfortunate events instead of one singularly unforgiveable one.

Hallie had hung up on Chris, and then she'd looked at Sulley—she'd named the blue heeler after the big blue monster in *Monsters, Inc.,* because it was impossible to have a cute puppy and not name it—and she had to smile. Sulley was adorable. But he was a puppy. She could hardly take care of herself right now, much less a puppy. And besides, she felt completely manipulated by that dog and Chris, and was determined not to stand for it.

So here she was in Houston, standing outside of Chris's condo with Sulley on a leash. He was trying to eat the flowers in the gardens instead of peeing like he was supposed to do.

She'd texted Chris, had told him she was bringing the dog back, and that she wanted no drama, but that she would like the sparkly Jimmy Choo clutch he'd given her for her thirtieth birthday. She needed the clutch for an art project.

Hallie was particularly proud of herself because she hadn't even bothered to dress for Chris like she'd always done. No heels, no skirt with a modest length. No blazer, no neat tail of hair. She hated thinking of herself that way—it was like she was constantly auditioning to be the perfect society wife. Forget it. Today, she was wearing running tights and a hoodie. Her hair was piled on top of her head in a knot she hadn't even bothered to look at. She had on her new running shoes that she had tested *just this morning* without any help from Rafe Fontana. He probably thought she couldn't do it without him.

"Time to get this over with," she said to Sulley. She adjusted the tote bag she carried on her shoulder that contained Sulley's toys, and tugged on his leash to move him along. The puppy had no idea how to walk on a leash, and was a bundle of splayed legs and teeth nipping at everything within reach.

Hallie was a little nervous. She didn't trust herself not to punch Chris in the mouth. She'd fantasized about it, because that was the one thing she wished she'd done before she'd walked out of his condo that night.

She was ready—but then Chris surprised her. When he opened the door, he was clearly the nervous one. He didn't know what to do with his hands and kept rubbing them on his jeans. "Hello, Hallie." His gaze flicked over her. "You look great."

Liar. "Hello, Chris. Here's your dog." She scooped Sulley up and thrust him at Chris so that he had no choice but to take him.

Chris slowly put the puppy down. Hallie thought she ought to tell him that wasn't a good idea because Sulley wasn't house-trained, but then decided Chris could discover that on his own. Sulley trotted into the condo with his leash trailing behind. "I got him for you. You love dogs, Hal."

"I don't give a damn about the dog. Give him to Dani for all I care. I don't appreciate you trying to manipulate me that way, Chris—it was a cheap move."

"I'm not manipulating you, I swear it. I'm *desperate*. Hallie, please listen—"

"No, see, that's what you don't seem to get," she said. "I don't *want* to listen to you. There is nothing you can say that will ever erase the sight of your ass pumping into Dani's va-jay-jay."

Chris blanched. And then he did something that Hallie had predicted she would never, ever see. He fell to his knees and clasped his hands before him, begging her. She stared down at him in shock. He really was desperate. For the first time, she noticed the dark circles under his eyes, and the way his jeans hung loosely on him. Christopher Davenport, surgeon, looked like shit.

Maybe she'd meant something to him after all.

"I know I fucked up, Hallie," he said, almost tearfully. "I don't know why I did it. It was just . . . living apart is hard, and I'm not saying that it happened because you weren't here, I'm saying I'm a weak man, and I get that, and I don't deserve you. But I will do anything to get you back. You can check my phone as often as you want. You can drive me back and forth to work. Whatever it takes," he said, clasping his hands, imploring her. "Just give me the chance to make it up to you. *Please.*"

"By making me responsible for monitoring your behavior?" she asked incredulously. "That's not how this works, pal."

"However you want to do it. I just love you so much, Hallie. I love you more than anything, and I am lost without you. Please forgive me," he said. "*Please,* Hallie. Tell me what I have to do to earn your trust."

She stared at him, trying to work this out. This was the überconfident Christopher Davenport on his knees before her. She was the one who was always begging him to forgive her for something she'd done that he didn't approve of. Hallie probably should have been more gleeful about his apology on bended knee, but she felt strangely sorry for him. She reached out, grabbed his hands, and pulled on them, forcing him to stand. "You know what? I forgive you, Chris," she said, surprised by her admission. "But we are not getting back together. I would never be able to trust you."

That was true, but she realized it was more than that. Since she'd broken things off, she felt like she could breathe. She felt totally free of expectation. Well, not counting her mother, but that was a yoke she was destined to bear all her life. But Chris? Society? Looking and behaving in ways others expected her to look and behave? She was done with that phase of her life. She was deciding her own path now.

"Don't say that," he said pleadingly, and his eyes brimmed with tears.

"May I have my Jimmy Choo clutch?"

He seemed uncertain, but turned and walked to the dining room table and picked up a box. He handed it to her. "Will you at least think about it?

Will you at least consider giving me a chance? How about this," he said, sounding even more desperate. "I take you out on a date. *One date.* We start over. You know, we got a little lost there after your dad died. You were grieving, and I was working so much."

"Uh-huh. That's when I needed you the most," she reminded him.

"I know. I know you did, and I failed you." He shoved his fingers through his blond hair. "It was so overwhelming, you know? I wanted to be there for you, and I couldn't, and I just needed a release, and Dani, well, I warned you about Dani."

That was true. He'd warned her that Dani had a reputation for betraying her friends. Maybe he'd warned her because he knew that Dani was already betraying her. With him.

"That doesn't excuse it," he was quick to add. "But I'm just trying to explain that she caught me when I was at my most vulnerable, and I was so concerned about you and my workload, and things sort of snowballed."

"Oh," Hallie said. "They *snowballed.*"

"I'm not kidding around here," he said adamantly. "Why would I beg you if I didn't truly love you? It was a bad time, and I wanted to keep my problems from you because you were dealing with so much."

"Interesting," she said, and tucked the Jimmy

Choo box under her arm. "I don't know how you could have possibly known what I was dealing with because you were too busy to see me or talk to me."

"That's not true, Hallie. I know you don't believe it is true because you are here. You've come to see me."

"Because you wouldn't come get your dog!"

"Isn't it more than that?" he said, and took a step closer. "Do you honestly expect me to believe that you just stopped loving me because of the one mistake I made?"

"I honestly expect you to believe it. It's called conditional love, Chris. I promise to love you until you betray me, and then I don't."

"Love doesn't work like that." Chris slowly reached for her elbow. He drew her a step or two closer. "You and I have been together for three years, baby," he said softly, his voice sexy. "You don't throw away *three years* because of one mistake. You don't erase three years of love because you're pissed."

Hallie suddenly thought of her mother and that strange feeling of sorrow she'd had in the warehouse with Luca and her grandmother. She imagined her father saying these very things to her mother. When she looked into Chris's eyes, she remembered a trip to Tahiti they'd taken in the spring. Tahiti was beautiful, a true paradise. The waters were crystal blue, like his eyes, and

293

they'd gone snorkeling, and they'd made love in a hammock, which, for the curious, was not as easy or as sexy as one might expect. "Sulley just peed on your floor," she said.

Chris whipped around as the puppy trotted over to Hallie, his leash trailing.

"Goddammit," Chris said, and strode into the kitchen for paper towels.

Hallie waited until he was down on one knee, cleaning up the mess.

"Thanks for the clutch. And, oh, by the way, I'm taking Sulley," she said, and bent down to scoop him up. "Of *course* I give a damn about the dog," she said, and turned around and walked out of his condo.

"Hallie!" he shouted after her, but she let the door slam on his shouting.

She hadn't even made it to her car when she received a text.

I won't stop until you listen to me and believe me. I know you're furious right now but there is so much we should talk about. I'm patient. I can wait as long as it takes and I will never stop loving you. And I think you still love me, too, because you came to Houston. You came to see me.

"Is he serious right now?" Hallie asked. She

slowly turned and looked up. Chris's condo was on the fifteenth floor, but there he was, on his balcony, his arms braced on the railing, watching her.

"That is, like, super creepy," she said to Sulley. She put him in the back seat dog harness and tossed the Jimmy Choo clutch onto the passenger seat.

As she pulled out of the parking lot, she allowed herself to think of that trip to Tahiti again. One night, after a day in the sun, Hallie had been too tired to go to dinner. So Chris had gone down to the bar to have a drink. He returned in the middle of the night, smelling like flowers. Everything smelled like flowers in Tahiti.

But she also remembered another night, when she was a teen. A family trip to Cabo San Lucas, where they had—or used to have—a beach house in a fancy resort. She and Luca had snuck out one night, down to the beach. And through a window to the resort lounge, she'd seen her father and a woman she didn't recognize. They were sitting on barstools, facing each other, her legs between Dad's, and Dad wearing a loopy grin. Hallie had been only fourteen, but she instinctively knew what that was.

She didn't think about that grin until she was grown and her mother had kicked her father out of the house for cheating again.

Chris had been naked with Dani, and yeah . . .

that night in Tahiti felt a lot like that night in Cabo.

Hallie was not her mother. She would not overlook infidelity just to be a Davenport. She would not put up with indiscretion just to have all the Jimmy Choo clutches she wanted. She'd rather live in sweats and hoodies and eat cheap tacos and work for a living.

If she was going to work for a living, she needed to figure out how and when and where. She wished Rafe were here; she wished she could talk to him about all of this. But he was in Chicago, chasing his dreams, and besides, she'd probably blown it with him. She glanced at the puppy in the back seat. Maybe she was going to be one of those women who lived alone with an entire coterie of animals. "What do you think, Sulley? How does Taco Bell sound to you?" She pulled onto the highway.

Chapter Seventeen

It was Rico's idea to do the Jimmy Choo shoot on the east lawn. And when he said "shoot," he meant with firework rockets.

Hallie was skeptical about his plan. "What if it goes wrong and we catch the house on fire? My mother will never forgive me."

"It's not going to go wrong, Hallie. Do you think I haven't experimented with Roman candles and rockets all my life?"

"That sounds about right," she agreed.

Rico had found a section of PVC pipe onto which he had affixed the rocket. On top of the rocket was her Jimmy Choo clutch. Hallie had told him about her trip to Houston to confront Chris about the puppy.

"So you told him off, huh?" Rico asked as he worked on the setup.

"I didn't tell him off, exactly. But I let him know I'm not getting back with him."

"Stick to your guns, kid," he said. "So what are you going to do now?"

She put the puppy down and watched him

bound off toward the bushes. "I think I'm going to Aspen."

"Awesome," Rico said. "You're doing the right thing."

She'd told him about her uncle's offer last night when the two of them had decided to go into town for hot chocolate and wandered around the square looking at Christmas lights. Rico was enthusiastic about the prospect. "You'll have that whole place to yourself. Do you ski?"

"Do I ski," she scoffed. "Okay, not very well. I like a good snowplow on the harder slopes."

"I could teach you how to ski, you know."

Hallie looked at him as she picked up the rocket packaging from where he'd tossed it on the grass. "Really? You're a skier?"

"You don't remember? My family used to go to New Mexico every Christmas."

She didn't remember that. But then again, her family had generally gone to places like Aspen or Zurich.

"I could drive up," Rico said. "Bring the pup, because you don't want to leave him with Mrs. Prince. I could bring a few groceries—"

Hallie's phone suddenly rang. She pulled it out of her pocket, looked at the screen, and hit the mute button. Chris again.

"So what do you say?" Rico asked.

He was asking about Aspen, but Hallie looked

at the contraption he'd made. "I say let's do this," she said, pointing at it.

Rico grinned. "Stand back. Where's Sulley?"

She glanced around for the puppy. He was busy digging up a bush. "He's okay," she said, and started the video on her camera.

"Okay, here goes nothing." Rico crouched down, lit the fuse, then ran back, laughing like a kid. The rocket exploded. But it did not shoot the clutch into the pasture as Rico had predicted. The clutch exploded along with the rocket, and pieces of rocket and clutch went flying.

"Rico!" Hallie shouted, and pointed at a small flare of fire in the grass. Rico was quick to stomp it out, then walked around the lawn to make sure no other hot spots had flared up. When he was certain there were no more, he picked up a piece of her clutch and held it up. They both burst out laughing.

"What in the hell is going on here?"

Rico and Hallie jerked around toward the sound of Rafe's voice. Hallie didn't know he was back, but here he was, striding into their midst, dressed in jeans and chaps, and holding Sulley, who was struggling to get out of Rafe's grip. Rafe looked at the debris, then at Rico.

Hallie felt instantly contrite. "It's my fault," she said quickly, raising her hand like a naughty kid at school. "I wanted it for my Instagram page. I'm up to forty-four thousand followers."

"Congratulations," Rafe said coolly, and put

down her dog. "You almost lost your puppy. I caught him before he ran up the road."

"Oh. Thank you."

"Do you realize you could have started a fire?" Rafe said to Rico. "That pasture is as dry as kindling."

Rico glanced guiltily over his shoulder.

Rafe's gaze raked over Hallie. He walked to where the PVC pipe was still jammed into the ground. "Get this cleaned up before Dad sees it," he said in a low voice to Rico, then turned and walked away.

Hallie and Rico watched him go. Hallie glanced at Rico, who shrugged. She ran after Rafe's departing back. "Rafe!"

He did not slow as he rounded the corner of the garage. "Rafe, *wait!*"

He slowed. He looked skyward. Then down. And then slowly turned to face her.

"I'm sorry," she said. "Really, I'm so sorry. Go ahead, tell me what a fool I am."

Rafe sighed. "You've done some crazy things, Hallie, but that was dangerous. Do you really need to be told that you could have burned down the ranch?"

"No," she said sheepishly. "You're right. I thought it would work. Rico said—"

"Here's a tip—don't go with what Rico says. He doesn't have the best track record for making good decisions."

"Right." As if she needed to be told that. She was a fool, all right. She was a fool for having made things weird between her and Rafe, for listening to Rico, for trusting Chris. A fool in general.

The sound of her mother's raised voice floated out an open window from the house, and both Hallie and Rafe glanced curiously in its direction. A moment passed before they heard Martin's softer voice in response.

Hallie looked at Rafe. "Did you take your test?"

"Tomorrow."

"Are you ready for it?"

"I think."

Was she misreading the tension between them? Was he really mad about the rocket, or was it still that damn kiss? That stupid, dangerous, and foolish kiss bouncing back and forth between them, a giant pair of lips that neither of them could see around? "I want to wish you all the luck."

"Thanks."

Her mother's voice, even louder, reached them again, and this time, Martin's was raised, too. "What are they going on about?" she asked.

"Don't know." Rafe was staring at the house. He looked worried.

Hallie wasn't worried. She'd heard her mom and dad fight plenty of times. Whatever it was would blow over. But whatever the problem, her mother and Martin were having a full-blown row about it.

"Rafe . . . I need to tell you something."

Rafe reluctantly turned his attention from the house. "Okay."

"I'll make it quick," she said, wincing a little when she heard her mother shout something that sounded like *horse's ass.* "You were right. I shouldn't have kissed you like that."

Rafe looked startled by the mention of it. "I don't think that . . . I don't think that we—"

She put up her hand. "I really need to get this off my chest. I can be an idiot sometimes, I know that about myself. And with you, well, you've always been there for me, and you're so important to me, and maybe I felt like my feelings were changing, but the bottom line is that I totally misread the situation."

"Wait, Hallie," he said. "I wouldn't say that you *misread*—"

She couldn't wait for him to smooth it over, she had to get this out. "Don't try and make it better. I understand how awkward it must have been for you. I totally get it. You are right, your dad works for my mom, and besides, you're going to Chicago, and I may be in Austin soon—"

"Austin—?"

"And the bottom line is that I took advantage of your kindness and the situation, and I was wrong to do it. So. I'm sorry I got pissy about it, but I was way out of line. I would hate to lose you over something like that. Because we both know nothing could ever really work between us . . . right?" How funny that she should wait so hopefully for him to correct her when she knew what she said was absolutely true.

Rafe wasn't going to correct her, no matter how much she wanted him to. Because Rafe, good ol' dependable Rafe, was too responsible. He shook his head. He gave her a sad smile, almost as if she'd told him her dog had died. "No," he said quietly. "Nothing could ever really work between us."

There it was, a definitive rejection. And now that *that* was out in the open, now that she knew how he really felt, maybe those giant lips would disappear from her mind's eye. It was a hot air balloon, hovering over her and ruining everything.

"I don't mean that to sound harsh. But I don't think you really understand. It's not that I don't—"

Hallie's mother suddenly shouted so loudly that it felt as if her voice rattled the windows. *"Don't you dare tell me what to do, Martin Fontana!"*

"Oh my God," Hallie breathed. "What is the *matter* with her?"

"I think I should go find out," Rafe said, and was striding away without finishing his thought.

Hallie would have to settle for his affirmation

that there could never be anything between them. But she hadn't had a chance to ask her last question. Could they still be friends?

Honestly, she was glad she hadn't asked that, because she wouldn't be able to bear it if he was weird about it. As it was, her heart was hammering in her chest, and she felt like she wanted to throw up. She didn't get it. She'd done the right thing, she'd apologized, and she ought to feel relieved. But she felt almost frantic. She felt humiliated. She felt incredibly sad, like she'd already lost her best friend.

Why in God's name hadn't she left well enough alone?

Hallie made her way around the edge of the house. Rico had cleaned the lawn and was playing with Sulley. "Hey," he said as she walked over to him to get her dog.

"Hey," she said.

He peered at her. "You all right?"

"Yes!" She smiled. "I am *so* all right." Because she was going to Aspen.

Chapter Eighteen

When Rafe walked out of the building where he'd taken the last final test of his last college course, he paused to look around him. Funny how the sun looked the same. The school, too. The grass, the trees, the cars in the parking lot—everything was exactly the same.

Everything looked and smelled the same, but really nothing was the same. Because Rafe was a college graduate.

He couldn't believe that was true, that he'd actually accomplished that goal. He was the first in his family to have a college degree. He felt elated and capable and . . . and strangely empty. As if everything he'd been holding in his tank had been released. All the hopes, the dreams, the long nights—all of it was gone.

"Oh my God, we did it!" Arms slapped around him from behind and squeezed hard, and then Brittney popped in front of him, beaming. "A bunch of us are going to get a drink to celebrate. Want to go?"

He smiled at her, caressed her arm. "Can't make it. My family is waiting."

"Okay. Call me later?" She started to bounce away, to catch up with her friends, but when Rafe didn't answer right away, she paused. She was smiling. Happy to be done with college, just like him. And she was smiling when she said, "You're not going to call me later, are you?"

"What?"

She shrugged. "I always thought it was a semester thing. I mean, you're moving to Chicago, I'm getting a job here."

It was weird, reaching a milestone like this at his age without anyone to really share it with. Sure, his family was waiting for him to celebrate. But it wasn't the same. He gave Brittney a sympathetic smile. He might have had someone like Brittney to share this moment if he'd allowed himself to think past Hallie Prince for a single moment.

But he never had.

"Probably not," he admitted.

Brittney put her sunglasses on. "One more time for old time's sake?"

He was tempted. Sorely tempted. But it didn't feel right. He had no real interest in Brittney, and he didn't think she had any in him. He reached out for her hand and squeezed it. "I don't think so." He leaned forward and kissed her cheek.

"Yeah, okay," she said with a laugh. "When a

guy starts kissing you like a grandpa, it's over. Good luck, Rafe!" she said cheerily, and started walking backward, away from him. "Maybe I'll see you at graduation! Or after! I'm going to call you and see how it's going!"

"I hope you do," he said, and waved. Brittney turned around and jogged to catch up with a group of classmates.

Rafe watched her go, but he wasn't thinking of Brittney. He was thinking it was long past time that he got over Hallie and started thinking about his future. He'd go to Chicago, set up shop. Maybe meet a woman there—this time, for real. But one thing was certain—the next time he had sex, he wanted it to mean something. No more Brittneys.

Rafe looked around the campus once more. Nope. Nothing was different. Just him. He was embarking on a whole new life. But there was one last thing he had to do first.

Yesterday, standing in the drive at Three Rivers Ranch, listening to his dad and Mrs. Prince argue as Hallie had apologized to him, he had realized something. He had to let it go, this thing he had for her. Because he'd meant what he'd said— it was not going to work. But he needed her to understand why. He needed her to understand how important she was to him, too, and how he needed to preserve that, because the alternative was too grim. He didn't want this secret between them anymore. He wanted to come clean and clear the air, so she'd understand and maybe, just maybe, he could get on with his life.

Yeah, he had a few things he needed to say, but he'd chosen instead to walk into the ranch house and break up the fight between Mrs. Prince and his dad about the horses.

His family was waiting for him at home. They'd decorated the house with streamers and shiny letter placards that spelled out *Congratulations*. His nieces and nephew were bouncing off the walls with excitement, even if they didn't understand the occasion. "Grandma made a cake!" Izzy shouted at him.

"Fantastic," Rafe said, and swung Izzy up on his shoulders before they went inside.

His mother greeted him with tears in her eyes. "First an Army Ranger, now a college graduate. My son is a college graduate!" She hugged him tight.

His father, usually a very stoic man, greeted him with emotion. "I'm so proud of you, son," he said, shaking his hand. "Now you go to Chicago and get that place up and running. You might need to support your mother and me." He laughed, but Rafe could see the worry around his father's eyes. The row he'd had with Mrs. Prince, he'd said, was "a doozy."

The kids and Angie had made a homemade

mortarboard for Rafe to wear. He wore it to join David out back for a beer while Rico sipped a soda. The three of them laughed about Mr. Creedy and his cows, and talked about the playoff prospects for the Cowboys.

His family had made this party just for him. They were all so proud. *So* proud. And all Rafe could think of was Hallie. He wanted to text her, he wanted the funny little GIFs she would send about his last final. But he didn't see the point. The careful cocoon of friendship he'd spent years spinning around them had unraveled.

He looked at Rico, who was swinging his nephew around like an airplane. His nieces were bouncing around him, begging for a turn. The truth, which Rafe would never admit to anyone, was that he'd been so pissed when he saw Rico and Hallie together on the lawn. What they'd done was stupid as hell—but that's not what made him so irrationally angry. What had made him angry was how incomprehensibly jealous he'd been at their laughter. It had reminded him of all the times in his life he'd seen Hallie with another man—a boyfriend, a friend, a fiancé— laughing while he stood on the sidelines, forcing down his envy.

That afternoon he'd been full of resentment at how fun loving and carefree Rico could be, how easy it was for him to make friends or to make a girl laugh. And there Rafe stood, always the guy in the background, the nice guy, the respectful guy, the guy who always, *always* did the right thing.

He didn't text Hallie even when a bottle of champagne was delivered from the big house, the card signed by Mrs. Prince on behalf of all the Prince family. "She'll probably take that out of my paycheck," his dad had said, and everyone laughed.

Rafe appreciated the gesture, but he'd thought something would come from Hallie. It didn't. He didn't know if he should be offended—after all, he was the one who had firmly closed the door he'd fought for years to keep open.

He'd done the right thing. Why, then, did he feel so miserable?

He heard nothing the next day, either, and spent the day out on the ranch with a couple of hands on a range check, out in places where people, cars, and phones didn't work. When he rode back into cell range, there were no messages.

The day after that, he stopped in at Jo's Java on his way into San Antonio to see John Horowitz.

"I hear we have a new college graduate in town," Jo Carol said. She poured him a cup of coffee and put a donut the size of a dinner plate in front of him. "That's on the house. We're proud of you, Rafe."

"Thanks," Rafe said, grinning. It was a little cold today, so he took a seat inside and looked at the Christmas lights strung over Main Street while he worked on that donut. A figure appeared on the street, striding toward the coffee shop, and as the person came closer, Rafe realized it was Nick Prince. Nick was walking past the window when he spotted Rafe sitting inside. He lifted his hand and walked in the door.

"Hello, Nick, you handsome devil, you," Jo Carol called cheerfully. "Want a coffee?"

"Thanks, Jo. I take it black," Nick said.

"You like it as plain as your father. He did not like the fancy drinks I make now. Complained how long it took to get a cup of coffee." She laughed jovially.

"He had his quirks, that's for sure." Nick threw a couple of bills on the counter and walked to where Rafe was sitting.

"Hey, Nick."

"Mind if I sit?"

"Not at all," Rafe said, and gestured to the chair across from him.

Nick sat. He grinned. "I hear congratulations are in order."

"Yep."

"Dude, that is awesome," Nick said, and reached across the bistro table and squeezed his arm. "I always knew you'd be the one to get out of this town."

"Oh yeah?"

"You had that thing, you know?"

"No," Rafe said, grinning.

"I don't know how to explain it. But you could always tell which guys were going to stay in Three Rivers forever, and which guys were going to go on and do something with their lives. I honestly thought you'd stay in the army and be a general. But I should have known you'd want to get into social work. You always had a knack with kids."

Rafe smiled, pleased that Nick remembered.

"You're lucky, man." Nick tapped his cup to Rafe's. "Here's to seeing the world."

"Well. Chicago, anyway," Rafe said. "What about you?"

"Me?" He shrugged. "My dad left us in a bind. Looks like I'm not going anywhere any time soon. We can't even keep our payroll up." He sighed, glanced out the window a long moment.

Rafe inwardly winced. It was hard to imagine Three Rivers without their majordomo, but he was beginning to suspect his dad was right—he was working on borrowed time. "Are you still flying?" he asked Nick.

"When I can. I flew Hallie up to Aspen yesterday, but that's about as much flying as I've done in a couple of months." He sighed and leaned back in his chair.

Rafe took a sip of his coffee to hide the fact that his heart had abruptly stopped working. What an idiot he was. Here he'd been waiting for a text, hoping for it. But she was in Aspen. Moving on with her life. Working things out. He was such a chump.

"When are you leaving?" Nick asked.

Rafe looked up. "Ah . . . after the first of the year. We ran into a little permitting problem, so things are behind schedule. I hope to be there sometime in January."

"Gonna keep helping us out until then?" Nick asked, referring to the ranch. "We need all the help we can get." He smiled ruefully.

"As long as I can."

"I appreciate it. You're a great help. So is Rico." He glanced at his watch. "I've got a meeting in ten minutes at the bank. Ought to be lots of fun." He looked up. "Congratulations again."

"Thanks, Nick."

Nick stood and put his hand on Rafe's shoulder and gave it a squeeze, then walked away. Rafe heard him speak to Jo Carol on his way out. He watched him walk down the street to the fancy offices of the Saddlebush Land and Cattle Company as he thought about what Nick had said. And Hallie being in Aspen.

Everything around him looked the same again today, but really, nothing was the same.

When Rafe finally made it home that day, he was exhausted. His mother insisted on heating up some leftovers for him, and after he ate, he went into his room to surf the internet.

He was looking at Aspen when Rico popped his head in. "Hey, got a minute?"

"Sure," Rafe said. He closed his laptop and pushed it aside. "What's up?"

"I need to borrow some money," Rico said, and glanced over his shoulder, almost as if he feared someone was listening.

"For . . . ?"

"A little road trip," Rico said with a wink.

"Trip," Rafe repeated suspiciously. "I thought you were working for Dad."

"I am. I'm just taking a few days off, that's all. A week. Ten days, tops."

"Why?" Rafe asked. "Where are you going?"

Rico stepped into his room and closed the door. His eyes were shining, and Rafe immediately wondered if he'd been drinking. "Aspen," Rico said.

The air swept out of Rafe's room. He had to swallow to make himself breathe. "What?"

"Yeah, man, I'm going to Aspen. Going to do a little skiing." He mimed skiing.

Rafe's tongue felt as if it was stuck to the roof of his mouth. He swallowed again and closed his laptop. "With Hallie?"

Rico grinned. He sank down on the end of Rafe's bed. "I don't know about that. But she offered me a place to stay if I brought her dog."

Rafe stared at him. "She honestly asked you to bring her dog?"

Rico laughed. "No, man, that was my idea. I called her up and told her I was headed that way and would bring him if she liked."

"What do you mean, you're headed that way?"

"I might have said I was checking out a job in Wyoming." He grinned, like he thought that was clever.

"And she offered you a place to stay?"

"For a couple of days."

He felt nauseated. Light-headed. He forced himself to ask the question burning a brand in his brain. "Are you two . . . together?"

"What? *No,* dude," Rico scoffed. "Come on, Rafe, it's *Aspen.* And she's staying at her uncle's house. He owns all those car dealerships. You know that's got to be a *house,* right?"

Rafe slowly released the breath he'd been holding. There was a shift in him—a tectonic shift. He put aside his laptop and stood up. "You're not going anywhere, Rico."

Rico rolled his eyes. "Come on, Rafe, don't drag me down. When in my life am I gonna get to do something like this?"

"I don't know, but it won't be this time either. For fuck's sake, you just got out of rehab! The last place you need to be is on the slopes in a party town. You owe Dad a lot of money. You owe him more than that—he keeps bailing you out, and he needs you to help him out right now."

"I'm going to Aspen," Rico said. "I told Hallie

315

I'd drive that dog up there, and she is expecting me. It's a two-day drive, so I'm leaving in the morning."

"Call her and tell her you'll look out for the dog while she's gone." He picked up his phone and tossed it at his brother. "Call her. Tell her you're not coming."

Rico looked at the phone. Then at Rafe. "Not doing it."

"If you don't call her right now, we'll walk out of this room, and I'll tell Dad what you're up to. He'll kick you out, Rico, and then what are you going to do? You've got no place to go."

Rico stared at Rafe. After a moment, he muttered under his breath and snatched Rafe's phone from his hand. He dialed Hallie's number and listened to it ring. It rolled to voice mail. "She didn't pick up. I'm not going to leave her hanging, Rafe. Besides, it's boring around here. Dad won't even let me drive into town."

"So how exactly are you going to drive to Aspen? Dad is trying to keep you sober, Rico, don't you get that? He's trying to save your damn life."

Rico's face mottled with anger. He glared at Rafe, and for a moment, Rafe thought he would hit him. He even squared off like this was going to be a fight. "Go ahead," Rafe said calmly. "Take a swing. But before you do, think about how much grief you've caused our parents the last few years. And now you're going to just take off and drive up to Aspen, just forget the job Dad gave you when he *needs* you, and ski? And you're going to borrow more money to do it. Yeah, Rico, sounds like a brilliant plan."

"Try and stop me," Rico sneered.

Rafe laughed. "If that's what you want, little brother, I'm happy to oblige."

Chapter Nineteen

Hallie had been in Aspen for four days now, and while clear thought had been slow in coming, she was beginning to see her way forward.

She'd come with a load of books, her running shoes, and a laptop to research the possibility of teaching ballet.

On the day Nick flew her up, they had lunch, and he flew back to Texas. She'd cooked for herself that night and watched a light snowfall and read from her stack of books, starting with *Woman Last Seen in Her Thirties*, about a woman much older than Hallie who had to start her life over when her husband of fifty-three years left her. But it resonated with Hallie—the book was essentially about the hurt of having the rug yanked out from beneath your feet, and the inevitable spring of hope and healing that comes from hard luck.

She needed this sort of inspiration if she was going to hope and heal.

Yesterday, she'd wandered around this huge mountain house, debating what to do with her life. She had reached out to the Comeback Center. A woman named Tasha had responded right away with an offer for Hallie to come in and talk about what she needed to do to finish her degree. Hallie had made an appointment for a couple of weeks away.

Late in the day, Hallie stood in the middle of the enormous living room, with soaring beams overhead and a view of the mountains beyond.

And her reflection in the windows staring back at her.

She had a memory of being here one Christmas. How old was she then, maybe fifteen? She'd stood in this very spot and had gone through a series of ballet poses, watching her reflection.

Hallie put down her teacup and moved into first position—heels together, feet at an angle, arms curved, and hands meeting at her pelvic bone. From there she moved into fifth position—attitude forward, attitude back, relevé, fifth position.

"Good God," she whispered. She'd lost so much flexibility, could not put her leg up as high as it should be. It had been so long since she'd tried—her disappointment with her talent had left her without any desire to even try a few poses.

Why *had* she quit, anyway? Yes, she'd been bitterly disappointed and had felt like a failure. But why hadn't she been courageous enough to think beyond what she thought she had to be to what she could be? She'd taken the candy-ass way out of her disappointment and had moped around about it. *Ugh.* She hated that about herself. "Coward," she muttered.

Arabesque, arabesque, relevé, attitude devant, croisé devant.

Could Genevieve still do these poses? Probably—she had certainly moved with the grace of a ballerina when Hallie had seen her on Thanksgiving Day. Genevieve did not seem like the sort of person who would just . . . quit.

Arabesque. Hold.

Hallie studied her reflection. She was wobbly, and God knew if she could get up en pointe. But she decided then and there that she wasn't quitting. She was going back to ballet. It was her first love, it was still her love, and ten years of mourning was enough. She would never be a principal ballerina. She was past the age she could successfully join a corps de ballet. But she could teach it. Not to potential prima ballerinas like Genevieve wanted to find. No, she was thinking more of boys and girls like her, who were never going to be the star, but who would love ballet like she did and want to learn. She was thinking of the girl with Down syndrome, who obviously appreciated ballet.

She lowered her leg and gave her reflection a critical once-over. She thought of the kids on Thanksgiving, moving awkwardly around the stage in their version of *The Nutcracker*. She thought of all the kids out there who would never be anything but also-rans. But she could help them discover the joy of it.

It was an idea, anyway, and she hadn't had any great ideas in a while.

Well, except her Instagram account. That had worked out to be a surprisingly good idea. Hallie had spent this morning in a coffee shop going over it. She was at forty-eight thousand followers, but the revenge art had lost its luster for her. She'd done what she'd set out to do with that page, to mentally deconstruct her engagement to Chris. To tear down the symbols of that failed engagement, one by one. There was nothing more to be said for it.

It was time to build her aftermath. Her path forward. Her new leaf.

She revised the title of her page and the description: *After the Deconstruction of a High-Society Wedding: The Aftermath.* She posted the pictures she'd taken at the kids' ballet.

And a picture of the mountains and a gentle fall of snow, taken from Uncle Chet's window.

And a shot of a steaming cup of hot chocolate.

She decided Uncle Chet was right—she *did* need this time alone to sort through her thoughts. His house was perfect for it—in spite of its opulence, there were few amenities. They had never bothered to install a television, because anyone in Aspen was outdoors until it was time to sleep. The house was so high up in the mountains that there was no cell service. The evenings were supposed to be for cooking good food, drinking excellent wine, and having lively conversations. That was the hard part—she appreciated the solitude and the lack of distractions, and she loved having the opportunity to read uninterrupted . . . but she was also glad Rico had suggested bringing her dog to her on his way to Wyoming. She wouldn't mind having another warm body around for a couple of days. She'd never been the type to be comfortable alone for long periods of time. Maybe because she was a twin, who knew, but she liked having someone around at the end of the day to talk to.

Nick hadn't liked the idea of her being in Aspen by herself.

"Why not?" Hallie had asked him.

"I don't know. You're my sister. I worry about you."

"I'll be fine," she'd said. "I'm thirty years old. It's well past time I took care of myself so people don't have to worry about me. Someone has always been looking out for me, and as a result, I've never gotten anywhere on my own. I need to figure things out by myself."

"Why? What are you trying to prove?" he'd asked her. "What's wrong with having people to care about you?"

"Nothing! I don't know. I think it's held me back, that's all."

"No, Hallie, people caring about you hasn't held you back. *You've* held you back."

There could be a lot of truth to that, she supposed.

Nick didn't say more about it. But when they had landed in Aspen, had lunch at the Ajax Tavern, and he'd dropped her off at Uncle Chet's and made sure the heat was working, he said, "Okay. Do whatever it is you have to do here, and call me when you're ready to come home." He'd hugged her, and added, "And don't spend all our money."

"I'll try really hard not to," she promised.

Nick had laughed. Which, Hallie realized, was a rare sound since Dad had died. "Love you, Nick," she said.

"Love you more."

And he was gone. And Hallie was left alone with her thoughts.

The next day was sunny and still, the calm before the heavy snow that was predicted for overnight. Hallie was lucky—the caretaker, Mr. Collin, had stocked the fridge and the woodpile before she arrived, so she had what she needed.

She expected Rico at any time, but decided to squeeze in a run while she waited. Rafe would be proud of her—she'd started being serious about getting fit and had been running every day. He was right about running, too—when she ran at the correct speed and with the correct posture, it wasn't so hard. Every day she managed to go a little farther.

She ran a trail that went into the forest at the end of the drive. She paused along the way to take a photo of herself in mittens and a knit cap on the trail to post to Instagram when she was next in town. She started out at a slow pace, having discovered that running in the thin mountain air was a lot harder than running near the coastline. Her legs felt especially heavy, and she ran out of steam pretty quickly. She ended up walking the last mile back to Uncle Chet's house, and by the time she turned up the steep drive, snow had begun to fall, she was freezing, and she really needed a bathroom.

A bark brought her head up from her trudge. Sulley was both running and sliding down the steep driveway to her. "Sulley!" she cried, and caught the wiggling puppy, lifting him up off the ground and then getting tangled in his leash. "When did you get here?" she asked, and buried her face in his fur.

Sulley was not content to be carried, and squirmed until she let him down, darting alongside her up the drive, his snout to the ground. About halfway up, Hallie saw the Fontana truck and wondered what Rico had to promise Martin to borrow it for his trip.

Near the top of the drive, Sulley broke away from her and ran as fast as his thick little legs would carry him up the hill. Hallie saw Rico slide off the tailgate of the truck, and she waved. But then her heart did that flippety-floppety thing because that wasn't Rico, that was *Rafe*. She stopped in her tracks, confused. Then concerned. And elated at the same time. It wasn't Rico, it was *Rafe*. Stubborn, recalcitrant, decent-guy Rafe.

He stood at the top of the drive in a knit cap and quilted jacket. His hands were shoved into his pockets, and he looked serious. He didn't move other than to put one hand down to calm the puppy.

Hallie walked up and stopped a few feet away to catch her breath. "Hi."

"Hi," he said.

"Where's Rico?"

"Grounded."

"Huh?"

"He's not ready for a road trip."

"Oh." She was confused. Rico had made it sound like everyone was on board with his plan to go to Wyoming and look for work. "So why didn't he call me?"

"He did. So did I. You don't answer your phone."

"I didn't—oh," she said, and winced. "No cell service up here. You have to go into town."

"Well, that would explain it." He smiled thinly.

Hallie eyed him curiously. "So does this mean you're—"

"I'm dropping off Sulley," he said, and rubbed his chin. He was watching her closely. "And I'm heading back."

"What, *tonight?* You're crazy if you think you can start back with a winter storm on its way. And second, you drove for two days to bring Sulley, and now you're going to drive two days back?"

"Not tonight. I thought I'd get a room in town."

Why was he being so weird? Hallie snorted as she wrapped her arms around her body. "You can't find a room in Aspen this time of year. Unless you want to stay at some flea-bitten place."

He shoved his hands deeper into his pockets. Sulley started barking at a ground squirrel. "I'm sure I'll find something."

"No, you won't. Can we talk about this inside? I'm freezing."

He glanced at the house as if he wasn't certain he wanted to go inside.

"Rafe," she said impatiently. "I also have to pee. Come in." She walked past him, scooping down to grab Sulley's leash, and went inside.

When she emerged from the bathroom, she found Rafe standing just inside the door, taking in the mountain house. "Nice," he said. He looked out the enormous picture windows at the view of the mountains. It was a beautiful vista with the snow starting to fall over the peaks.

Hallie tried to gauge his mood. "I've got some stew if you're hungry."

He turned his gaze from the window. He shoved his hands in his pockets again and looked at the floor. "I should probably find a place to stay."

"Don't be ridiculous. Stay here. There's five hundred bedrooms."

"I'm not sure that's a good idea."

"Oh, for heaven's sake, Rafe. This house is so big you could wander around for two days and never see me. Besides, the snow is starting to really come down."

He turned around to look. The snow, which had started just moments ago, was already heavy.

"I can't get stuck here."

Hallie laughed at the panic in his expression. "Don't worry—they clear the drive when it snows. I won't have to eat you to survive—you can make a clean escape in the morning."

He lifted a finger. "Minor point, but I'm the Army Ranger. I'd be doing the surviving on you."

"Don't be so sure about that," Hallie said pertly. "Seriously, Rafe, please don't drive in this. You can lock yourself in one of the bedrooms if you're worried about me attacking you."

"I'm not— That's not what I'm thinking—"

"What are you thinking, then?"

He chewed on his bottom lip. "I just . . .

327

His obstinacy was exhausting her. "Look, whatever. There are six bedrooms, but be the Army Ranger and plow out of here if you have to. You're being surprisingly stupid, but you do you. I'm going to heat the stew." She turned her back to him and opened the fridge.

A moment later, she heard him walk across the room. She heard the door open and Rafe walk through and the door shut behind him.

He left.

Hallie braced her hands against the kitchen counter and looked heavenward, blinking back a few unshed tears. Rafe had been her oldest and closest friend, and now she'd lost him, too.

Chapter Twenty

This was nuts.

Hallie was right—he was being stupid. He was going to risk his neck going down mountain roads to maybe find a room so he wouldn't be tempted by her. How could he have survived two tours in Afghanistan and yet couldn't survive one hot kiss with Hallie Prince?

He hated himself and his lack of panache right now. He'd come here for a reason. He'd come to say what he'd been holding close in his heart all these years. But he had to man up and *talk* to her. Tell her the goddam truth for once. So he grabbed his things, Sulley's box of food and toys, and headed back to that enormous mountain house with its sweeping views and six bedrooms.

When he entered the mudroom, he had to step over Sulley, who was racked out at the door, his head on a pair of Hallie's boots. The puppy was a trooper—he'd ridden shotgun for two days without a whimper, his nose pressed to the window.

When Rafe stepped into the main room, Hallie

jerked around. She was holding a tissue, and quickly tossed it into the trash. "I thought you left."

He frowned. "I wouldn't leave without saying good-bye, Hallie."

She looked relieved. She took a breath. "No, you wouldn't, would you? I mean, I didn't think you would, but I wondered if . . . are we still friends, Rafe?"

"What? Of course we're still friends."

Hallie suddenly flashed that dimple-inducing smile of hers, dipped her knees, and said, "Thank God! I thought you were still mad at me for that damn kiss."

"No—"

"You are more than welcome to stay here. Far on the other side of the house. I mean, I don't want to find out if you snore. That would, like, ruin everything for me."

"Same," he said. "Thanks, Hallie."

"No need to thank me. It's what friends do for friends," she said, repeating what he'd once said to her. "Would you like a drink? Uncle Chet left all the stuff for gin and tonics. He even left some limes. Before you say anything," she said quickly, throwing up her hand, "I hid it when I thought Rico was coming."

"I wasn't going to say anything. And yes, I would love a drink."

Hallie turned around to the fridge.

"I'll be out of here tomorrow," he announced unnecessarily.

"Good for you, Army Ranger."

He slid onto a barstool and looked out the window again. It was turning to dusk, and the snow was beautiful. It was quiet here. Serene. Sort of like Three Rivers in the early morning hours. He could see why her uncle had suggested this to her—a person could practically hear their thoughts up here.

"What about Rico's job?" she asked.

"His job?"

"He said he was getting a job in Wyoming." She put two glasses on the kitchen bar.

Rafe shook his head. "He had no plan other than to ski. He wasn't honest with you."

"Ooh," she said, nodding. "I get it now."

"He's not a bad guy," Rafe said. "But he doesn't do well with confinement." A gross understatement.

"Yeah," she said thoughtfully. "You know he's going to bolt sooner or later, right?" she asked as she bent down to the freezer drawer for ice. "I mean, he's not cut out for ranch life. Not like you and me."

Were he and Hallie cut out for ranch life? He'd never thought about it that way. "I know," he said. He didn't know what Rico was cut out for, really.

She made his drink, squeezed a wedge of lime

into it, and slid it across the bar to him. She looked up. Her eyes were shining. She smiled. "I'm glad it was you, Rafe."

She didn't have to explain. He wanted to be glad it was him, too.

A soft smile appeared on her lush mouth. "Hey, do you still play checkers?"

"Checkers?"

"There's not a lot to do here," she said as she returned to the pot on the stove. "No TV. I brought a bunch of books," she said, and with the wooden spatula, pointed at a box. "When Uncle Chet and the crew come up here, they sleep, they ski, they eat; rinse and repeat."

He got up and went to the box of books to have a look. She had brought some fiction, a book about the fundamentals of dance, a guide to Austin.

"So if you're not a big skier, you have to make do with a book or a game or get creative." She glanced over her shoulder at him, smiling a little.

Oh, he could get creative. He could think of a million and one ways to pass the time with her, and not one of them involved a book or a puzzle. He sipped the drink. He was feeling less weird about this. Everything felt like it was settling back into place—him quietly, privately pining. Her chatting and talking as if nothing was between them. Maybe he didn't have to confess. Maybe he could go on loving her in secret. "I've got news for you—I'm pretty damn good at checkers."

Her smile broadened. "You always step up to the plate. The stew should be ready in about ten minutes. Could you build a fire?"

"I knew that Army Ranger training would come in handy someday," he said, and stood up from the stool.

This felt natural. Like the old Hallie and Rafe. It was easy between them, the tension of their attraction sufficiently shoved under stew and snow and a lot of years of knowing each other. It was crazy, but the snow was quietly, but decisively, closing the world off, and this was beginning to feel unbelievably perfect.

They ate stew at the kitchen bar while Rafe's fire roared in the hearth. He polished off the gin and tonic, then joined her in drinking the wine she'd opened. By the end of the meal, he was feeling mellow and even more comfortable.

He did the dishes while she showered, then set up the checkers. Hallie returned to the living area in sweats and an oversized hoodie, her hair piled on top of her head. He thought about Brittney—he'd never seen her without heavy eyelashes and lipstick, not even when they'd slept together.

He'd put the checkerboard on an ottoman, and she sat cross-legged on one side, while he sat with his back to the couch and his legs stretched before him.

Hallie was a smack talker. "Prepare to be humiliated," she said. "I don't take prisoners, I *annihilate* them. Every checker of yours I conquer, I will throw into the flames of checker *hell*," she said very dramatically, and swept her arm toward the fire.

He laughed. "You've played too many video games."

As they played, she tossed her captured chips into a pile. It reminded Rafe of a rainy weekend many, many years ago, when he and Rico had gone to the mansion with his dad. The Prince kids had pulled out a Monopoly game, and the battle had begun. Hallie had behaved just like she did tonight— with threats and a lot of *ho ho ho*s when she made a good move, and ridiculed him for stacking his chips neatly. The only difference between the thirteen-year-old Hallie and the thirty-year-old Hallie was that the thirteen-year-old Hallie had been sent to her room for unsportsmanlike conduct. She'd beaned Luca with a shoe.

Rafe beat her the first game, and Hallie shrieked with playful dismay. She said she couldn't believe she'd been beaten by someone who scratched his head so much as he tried to figure out where to move.

Toward the end of the second game, she thought she had it won, and in her best video game voice, she shouted, *"Finish him!"* so loud that an exhausted Sulley got up from his place in front of the fire and hurried to her side to make sure she was all right.

Hallie thought she had Rafe blocked, but she missed one part of the board where she'd left herself vulnerable. Rafe kinged her.

"No way!" she cried, and pushed his hand away from the board to study it. "Okay," she said, nodding in concession. "But now you've asked for it. I've been holding back." She came up on her knees and began to arrange the board again. "It's a strategy. You let your guest win a round or two before you start polishing the floor with their fat losing face."

"I don't think you really know how to play."

She gasped with pretend outrage and grabbed his hand, lacing her fingers through his and squeezing tight. "How *dare* you? Now I must seek revenge."

Rafe was smiling. He liked the warmth of her hand and the chill air around them. He was looking at her, thinking of all the times he'd watched her from a distance, always hiding from his feelings.

"Why are you looking at me like that?" she asked.

"Like what?"

"Like *that.*" She made a whirring motion at his face.

Because I love you. I always have. I always will. He slowly withdrew his hand from hers. "That's just my face."

"No," she said, and caught his hand before he could pull it away. "Will you stop being so careful? I'm not going to screw up again." She gave his hand a squeeze and let go.

Rafe wanted to kick himself all over again "Hallie . . . I'm sorry I am so careful around you. But I have my reasons."

"Apology accepted," she said, and solemnly bowed her head over her hands in prayer pose. "I understand. I am a master at pushing buttons without even realizing it."

"No, that's not what I mean," he said. "Honestly, I love how impetuous you are. I mean, short of getting blotto and trying to drive to Houston. I love that you can just be you."

Hallie burst into laughter. She laughed so hard that she tumbled over backward, and Sulley was there in an instant to lick her face. She pushed the dog away with a belly rub and sat up, brushing loose strands of her hair from her face. "Oh, Rafe. I haven't been just me since, like, 2008." She suddenly stopped laughing and stared across the checkerboard at him. The firelight made her skin look as soft as butter, and he was thinking of the feel of her skin beneath his lips—

"But if you love that about me, then why did you say you couldn't handle it?"

He stilled.

"Remember? You said you couldn't handle it."

"I remember," he said quietly. "I've tried to explain it—there are too many issues with . . . us," he said, gesturing awkwardly between the two of them.

"I know. Your dad works for my mom."

"That's one," he said. "But there is more to it. I don't know if I can ever make you understand."

Hallie rolled her eyes. "I understand every word you've said, Rafe. I get it. You're my friend, and I . . . I had a moment. Well, it was more than a moment for me, but sometimes I am not good at reading the room. The thing is, you really have no idea how much you mean to me, and I get it."

Her eyes were glittering in the low light of the fire. Her skin was flushed. Rafe thought he'd never seen a more beautiful woman in a pair of sweats in all his life. "I just wonder if maybe you see what you *want* me to mean to you at this point in your life," he said.

Hallie sighed irritably. "Don't do that, Rafe. Don't try and explain to me what I'm feeling. You want to know what you mean to me? *Everything.* How's that? Your friendship—*you*—mean everything to me. And maybe I'm wearing crazy pants, but I think I mean something to you, too."

So here it was, the moment he would come clean or slink off to Chicago like the coward he was. "You're right. You mean more to me than I have ever said, Hallie. Frankly, there aren't adequate words to describe how I feel about you." He sat up. He looked her directly in the eye. "I've been living with a secret for a very long time."

She blinked. "*What?* Are you all right?"

"I'm fine. But if you haven't already figured it out, I have been in love with you since we were kids."

Hallie's eyes widened, and she went very, very still.

He plunged ahead. "I love you, Hallie Prince, and I get to stay close to you by being your friend. But my greatest fear," he said, pressing his hand over his heart, "is that I will do something to fuck that up and I won't get to be near you, and I will spend the rest of my life regretting it."

Hallie's mouth gaped open. She stared at him so hard that he wondered if he'd been a fool to admit it. "Why have you never said anything?" she asked, her voice shaking.

"Are you kidding?"

"No! Why have you never told me?"

"When, Hallie? When you were dating that banker's kid after high school? When you were engaged to the doctor?" He dragged his fingers over the crown of his head. "You have lived your life on a pedestal. You're a woman who has everything. You can have whatever you want, whoever you want. You have no idea what it's like to come from a family entirely dependent on another."

"I don't understand—I haven't asked you for anything—"

"No, but think about it, Hallie. What if I'd told you, five, ten years ago? What if, for a period of time, you were into it? Like now, after you've just ended an engagement, and you are searching for the next thing in your life. What if things were great between us for a while, but then I couldn't give you the sort of life you deserved, and something bigger and better came along? We'd break up. I'd lose you forever. Well, I can't lose you forever. So I've kept it to myself."

Her brows dipped into a frown. "Then why are you telling me now?"

"Because things changed between us in the last few weeks. You were right, there was something there, something beating like a heart between us. It used to be easy to keep this secret from you, but to keep it now feels like I'm lying to you, and I don't want to lie to you. I needed you to know the truth before I left for Chicago."

She was silent. Her hazel eyes were locked on his, and he was desperate to know what she was thinking. It seemed like several moments passed before she slowly rose up onto her knees. She leaned forward on the ottoman, and checkers cascaded off the side. "I *knew* it," she said softly. "I love you, too, Rafe. Maybe not as long as you have, or in exactly the same way, but I love you, too. Don't you know that? You are the closest thing to a best friend I've ever had. And now you've told me the truth, and you've thrown me for a gigantic loop, and I feel upside down and sideways and giddy and excited, and I want to know, what are you going to do about it? What *now?* And God help you if you make it weird, because I will kick you in the balls."

Rafe smiled. She could not have been more beautiful. Her eyes were on his mouth, her gaze intense, her expression determined. He knew what now. The answer was swirling and crackling around them. This was a very bad idea. A *very* bad idea. He knew it in his gut, and yet he felt powerless to stop the wheels he'd set into motion with his confession. He lifted his hand and stroked her face. "I have one pretty solid idea what to do about it."

She grabbed his hand, laced her fingers through his, and pulled him closer. "Then do it."

It felt like his chest cracked open, and years and years of emotions that had been locked down were suddenly set free. It seemed as if a lifetime of desire was scorching the earth between them. He reached for her.

Or maybe she reached for him.

All he knew was that the board toppled off the

ottoman, and he was dragging Hallie onto his lap, and Sulley was barking with glee.

The cork had blown, and there was no returning the genie to the bottle. Rafe had no hope that she would ever return his desire and regard in the same depth and breadth that he'd come to feel them, and he knew this would end badly for him. But he was tired of fighting it. "I can't pretend anymore," he said to her, and kissed her, and when he did, a deep shiver ran through him. A streak of lightning.

He cupped her face with his hand, and she gripped his wrist with amazing strength, sinking into him as he touched his mouth to her forehead, breathing in the floral scent of her freshly washed hair, then moving his mouth across her smooth skin. He tightened his grip on her as he lifted her face to his, and splayed his fingers across her cheek. He could not remember ever having felt sexual desire as urgently as he did on that bear rug. He could not recall a moment of ever having wanted to be inside a woman as desperately as this. "I've wanted you for so long," he said roughly. "I can't stand to be near you and not touch you."

"Really?" she asked, sounding surprised, and put her arms around his neck to kiss him. Rafe grunted with all that want and fell backward, sliding down to the floor with her on top of him. He was kissing her like he'd always wanted to kiss her, holding nothing back, and with all the longing he'd felt for *years*.

He caressed her body, his hand sliding up under her T-shirt and hoodie, landing on warm, butter-soft skin. Moving up to her breast, around and down her back, and then slipping into the waist of her sweatpants, moving to her hips.

The feel of her in his arms at last was intoxicating. He'd fantasized about this so often that it seemed like a dream to hold her now, touching and tasting her skin.

He rolled over, flipping them around so that she was on her back beneath him.

"I knew it," she said, and closed her eyes as she kissed his neck, then the line of his jaw.

"Knew what?" he muttered against the hollow of her throat.

"Just this," she said vaguely, and closed her eyes as her hands wandered his body, caressing his shoulders, his arms, pulling his shirt free of his pants, and sliding her hands onto his rib cage.

Rafe no longer cared about any consequences for this. The only thing he cared about was making love to her, at long last. Every stroke of her hands sent him a little closer to the edge of his control. Every touch of his lips to her skin sent him even that much deeper. The hunger in him raged. The desire to feel her, touch her, taste her, to be inside of her, resurrected old impossible hopes in him. As his hands and mouth covered her body, she gripped his head. "Wait, Rafe—this is crazy!" she said breathlessly.

No, no, no, don't stop now.

"What are we doing on the floor? We should find a bed."

He stared down at her with surprise. Yes, a bed. A big bed so they could roll all over it. He stood up, then reached down and picked her up off the ground, swinging her up into his arms.

Hallie laughed. "What are you doing?"

"You said bed. I'm taking you to bed." He marched in the direction of what looked like might be bedrooms.

"I'm a princess!" she said with delight. "No, not this one. Too cold," she said when he used his foot to push open the first door they came to.

He moved on, to the second door.

"Nope," she said, and pointed catty-corner across the hall. "That one. It has a beautiful view—"

"So do I," he said, and swung through that door, depositing her on a bed. Her things were scattered about that room, he realized as he shrugged out of his shirt. Hallie things—a camera. A pair of jeans and boots on the floor. A lacy bra on the end of the bed. Running shoes.

She bounced up to her knees and took off her hoodie. She was grinning like a Cheshire cat. "You're not going to have second thoughts, are you?"

"I can't even think right now, so no." He could safely say, in that room, feeling as hard and as determined as he did then, that he would never have second thoughts about this. And especially not when Hallie pulled her T-shirt off and sank down onto her heels on the bed.

"Do you have a condom?"

"No."

"No?"

He paused in his delightful review of her breasts. "I don't carry them around on the off chance I might get lucky, Hallie. Do you have one?"

She plunged half her body over the side of the bed, reaching for her purse. She dug maniacally through it, yanked out her wallet, dug through that, and somehow, miracle of miracles, pulled a pair of attached condom packages from it. "Ta-da!"

He kicked off his shoes, then leapt—literally leapt—across the room to that bed, tackling her and smothering her in kisses. Her hands were quickly on him, caressing him, tweaking him, arousing him even more. She slid his jeans down his hips and wrapped her fingers around his erection.

Everything disappeared for Rafe. He was aware of his body pulsing in her hand, aware that he was perilously close to losing his control. He pushed her back, removed her sweatpants, reminding himself to take his time. She was wearing thong panties, and those, he decided, could stay for the moment. He rolled on the condom, then moved between her legs and began to rub against that little strip of fabric as he took the hills of her breasts into his mouth, one by one.

And then he slowly moved down her body, his mouth and tongue drawing a delicious line down her center, to the hollow of her abdomen, and down again. He took the thong in his teeth and pulled it free of her body.

Hallie was breathing hard. She pushed her hands into his hair as she arched her back and drew one leg up. When his tongue slipped between her folds, she sighed, long and low, and gripped his hands, which he'd wrapped around her legs to hold her. He very deliberately brought her to climax, taking great pleasure in her excitement, aroused beyond his own comprehension at the way she bucked against him. When he closed his lips around her bud, she spasmed, and her body shivered against him, her pleasure infusing his blood. He rose up between her knees, pressed the tip of his erection against her wet body, and drew a deep breath in a Herculean effort to keep from being too rough, taking her too hard, too eagerly.

Their gazes locked in that moment. He could feel the flow between them, the silent communication that had never happened with anyone else in his life. Was this love that he felt running hot through his desire? Was it love that fed his desperation to do this right? Was it love that made the connection with her as important as the release? Was this the difference between sex and actual lovemaking? Because this felt different to Rafe. It wasn't just a corporeal thing, although his body was screaming for it. It was more transcendent than that. Important. Even a little unworldly, as he could almost believe he'd been put on this earth at this time to be with this woman. And the way she was looking at him—with affection, with hope— made him believe it.

It was such a tiny little moment, and yet he saw their future roll out before him, the years of happiness beginning with this very act.

And then he lost his damn mind and descended into fantastic, mind-melting sex.

He pressed inside her, a sensation so exquisite that he thought he might come at any moment. He managed to keep a lid on things, moving slowly at first, methodically, withdrawing to the tip, then sliding in again. Her eyes were closed, but her body moved with his. She gripped his shoulders, her hips lifting with each stroke. Her breath turned shallow; her body tensed around his. She arched her back in release, and raging desire exploded in him. He threw his head back, baring his teeth, letting loose a guttural growl of pleasure. With a final shudder, he collapsed to her side, his face in her neck, his heart pounding so hard he feared it might burst.

"Oh my God, Rafe," she said, and groped for his hand. "You know what? I think I sort of kind of love you right now. That was *fantastic*."

That was almost his undoing. Not that he believed she was making a declaration of romantic love, precisely. She meant she loved the sex. And yet, hearing those words on her lips was the stuff of this boy's dreams. He closed his eyes, held her tightly, and tried to burn every moment into his memory so that he would never forget how he felt tonight.

They lay there until the cold began to seep into the room, and Sulley was whimpering at the door. Hallie got up, slipped into her hoodie and the skimpy little thong, and disappeared. Sulley planted his paws on the side of the bed, and Rafe lifted him up.

Hallie returned with a bowl of popcorn and a bottle of wine. "I'm starving," she said, and crawled under the covers, curling into his side. When Sulley was convinced the popcorn wasn't for him, he curled up at the foot of the bed.

Rafe made himself get up, too, and built a fire in the room's fireplace before hurrying back to bed where it was warm. They watched the fire, snuggled together, eating popcorn, taking turns tossing kernels in the air to see if the other could catch it in their mouth while Sulley snored.

347

They talked about everything. How slow his Chicago project was proceeding. Her desire to practice ballet again and how she'd been thinking of going back to school. They marveled at how loudly Sulley snored for a puppy. They talked about spaceships to Mars—Hallie insisting it was a thing—and how vast the universe was with the discovery of even more new galaxies. They wondered aloud if Mr. Creedy's cows had gotten out since Rafe had fixed the fence, then giggled at how mad Mrs. Bachman would be if they had.

They kicked Sulley off the end of the bed and made love again when the moon started its descent into day, and spilled popcorn everywhere.

Hallie was the first to drift off, her eyes fluttering shut, a sleepy smile on her lips.

Rafe lay there a little longer, content in the quiet and stillness of this extraordinary night. He watched the embers of the dying fire and tried to think of the moment when their friendship had bloomed into something else. At what moment had they both felt the desire? He wished he knew, because that moment would mark his life forevermore. There was his life before that moment in time, and everything that would come after.

But for now, he had *this* moment, and Rafe knew it was the most contented he'd ever been in his life.

Chapter Twenty-one

Hallie was up first. She slipped out of bed as Sulley's eager tail steadily beat against the bedpost. She put her fingers to her lips, grabbed her hoodie and panties and sweats, and pulled them on as she made her way from the room on tip-toe, Sulley trailing behind her.

She was deliciously sore and strangely, happily, nervous. This felt a little like an alternate universe where she and Rafe were together.

Still, she felt exuberant this morning. Last night had been amazing. She'd felt like she was floating on a cloud of pure joy all night, and this morning, she was still floating.

She made coffee and took Sulley out, stomping her feet to keep warm as Sulley joyously experienced snow for the first time. She made him come back and fed him, then gave him a toy to gnaw on for a while. She poured two cups of coffee and went back to her room.

Rafe was lying on his belly, one arm draped off the end of the bed, his back exposed. Interestingly, he did have a tattoo, and it looked like a military insignia on his shoulder. She admired his back, broad and muscular, tapering into hips that looked sculpted from stone. Every part of him was strong and hard, and a delicious little shiver of memory of last night warmed her cheeks.

She went around to his side of the bed and carefully placed the cup of coffee beside him.

Rafe opened one eye.

"It's alive," she said in her best horror movie voice.

"Debatable," he croaked, and rolled over onto his back. The sheets went with him, and what was left barely covered him at all. He pushed himself up and blinked the sleep from his eyes. He glanced at the coffee cup. "Is that for me?"

"Yep. I bet you thought I was useless in the kitchen."

"I might have wondered a time or two," he admitted, smiling.

Oh, but Rafe was gorgeous when he smiled. His eyes shone with kindness. He was gorgeous naked, too. Hallie sat on the end of the bed, cross-legged, and pulled the covers over her legs. Rafe was left with a sheet.

"No fair. Come up here." He patted the bed next to him. "Where's the mutt?"

"Chewing on a toy." Hallie handed him her coffee and crawled up to situate herself beside him. Rafe kissed her shoulder before he returned her coffee to her.

"Hey, can you ski?" She was fishing—she wanted to know if he still intended to drive back to Texas today, but couldn't think how to ask him without sounding as if she needed him to stay. She didn't need him to stay—but she sure wanted him to.

"Yes. Can you?"

"About as well as I run."

"Excellent," he said, and sipped his coffee. "I love a good challenge."

Hallie grinned. So he was staying. This thrilled her to the point of excessive excitement. "Well, that's one thing I can provide by the truckload, Mr. Fontana. One challenge after another."

He laughed and put his arm around her, drawing her in close. "You don't have to convince me. You're about as stubborn as—"

"Hey!"

"But so damn *beautiful*." He kissed her shoulder again.

She rested her head on his chest. She could get used to this. She could get so used to this that she was imagining them in a little cottage somewhere, one big enough for just the two of them. It would have a room for her photography, and a room with a ballet barre. And Sulley, of course. Maybe a few cows. A pair of horses. She very firmly but politely ignored the voice in her head reminding her that she'd decided that she was going to get out on her own for once in her life.

They took their time getting out of bed, languidly exploring each other again, until the brilliant light of sun streaming in the windows and Hallie's gurgling pangs of hunger convinced them to shower and head to the slopes.

They had breakfast in town, stopped at the store for a few supplies, and by the time they reached the slopes, the sun had come out and made the day blindingly white. Hallie had her camera, and took shots of them skiing. Well, Rafe skiing. She wasn't coordinated enough to handle her skis and the camera at the same time.

They laughed more than they skied. Rafe almost killed himself laughing at how horribly she skied, bent over her poles, her skis in a snowplow. He skied circles around her. He held the camera and took a few shots of her, then skied more literal circles around her. He skied backward just in front of her, encouraging her to straighten up her skis. That proved to be a mistake—their skis got tangled, and they fell together on the slope, sliding off into the trees. They were laughing so hard until Rafe rolled her onto her back and kissed her.

It was, all in all, an absolutely perfect day on the slopes.

Later that night, when they dined in town, the waiter, making conversation as he opened the bottle of wine, asked what they'd done all day, and when he heard they'd been skiing, and Hallie had proclaimed it a perfect day, the waiter asked about the powder. Hallie and Rafe looked at each other and giggled. It was mutual—neither of them had noted the quality of the powder.

The only dip in the road was the slight argument they had when the check came. "I've got it," she said, her hand on the ticket.

"Nope." He put his hand on hers.

"Uncle Chet owns a share in the restaurant, Rafe," she said. "It's on the house."

He reached into his pocket. "When Uncle Chet invites me, I will consider it. But he didn't invite me, and I'm not taking a comped meal. Let go."

"What if I don't?"

He leaned forward, his eyes shining. "Did you have fun last night?"

She nodded.

"If you want to have fun tonight, you better let go."

"Stop twisting my arm," she said, and immediately let go of the check.

That night, they experimented with each other, alternately dissolving into fits of laughter and heavy breathing. To Hallie, it didn't matter what they did—every moment was sheer perfection and amazing sex. Rafe knew his way around a woman's body, and he wasn't afraid to show her.

The next day, they tried running, but they were both winded. "Altitude," Rafe said through gasps for breath.

"Super big hills," Hallie added as she leaned against him, her hands on her knees. Sulley rushed back toward them, his tail wagging. He was the only one who wanted more.

That night, they ate in, thanks to Mr. Collin's wife, who had left lasagna for them. After they'd done the dishes, they prepared hot toddies from a recipe they made up as they went along, and took them into a bath. They lingered there, making sudsy devil horns and mustaches. When the water cooled, Rafe built a fire in the living room.

Hallie dried her hair and joined him. She was feeling good and stepped into first position, pliéd, and then moved into second.

Rafe sat on the couch with his arms sprawled across the back of it, his feet propped on the ottoman. "What are you doing?"

"Dancing. Sort of. Trying out some moves." She moved into third position, fourth, then fifth, and last, stepped into an arabesque. Rafe watched her with an expression that made her feel strangely self-conscious. As if she'd shown too much of herself. "I know I'm rusty," she said apologetically.

He shook his head. "You have no idea how gorgeous you look."

She smiled gratefully. "My ballet teacher used to complain that I moved like wood and not water." She swept her extended leg in front of her and lifted her arms overhead.

"Your ballet teacher was either blind or crazy."

Hallie laughed and dropped her leg. "Come here," she said.

"What?"

She grabbed his hand and pulled him up. "You're going to be the hunter. I'm the swan."

"I'm the what?"

She positioned him, his weight on one hip, his right foot extended and pointed. Except that Rafe couldn't really point his foot—his toes did not seem to want to bend in a downward position. Hallie laughed as she bent one arm behind his back, then extended the other arm. She put her hand in his. "You are the hunter and you have captured me."

"There is no way I captured you standing like this," he groused.

Hallie did a double pirouette, then leaned toward him, her leg extended backward. "I bet you've never done *this*."

"I bet you're right."

She moved into a backbend, then pliéd again before lifting her other leg and extending it backward. She leaned forward again.

"You never said why you quit dancing. Why did you stop?" he asked.

She pirouetted. "I'm not sure, really." Pirouette. Plié. Relevé.

"An injury?" he suggested.

"No injuries."

"Well, I have one. Can I stop now? My foot is cramping."

Hallie paused to reposition his feet into first position. He complained that now he looked like a penguin. She stood on her toes and swanned toward him.

Rafe caught her by the waist when she twirled off center and very nearly crashed into him. "You should dance again, Hal. You love it so much."

Hallie stopped spinning. Her feet were beginning to ache. She needed pointe shoes to do this right.

She put her hands on her hips and studied him a moment, then took his hands and set them on her waist. His caramel eyes settled on hers. He pressed his lips together, as if he were biting back words. But then he caught her waist and suddenly lifted her overhead, eliciting a squeal of surprise from her before he put her down. Hallie slowly moved backward, her hand on his, bending as far as her stiff back would allow.

"Hey. You're going to fall," he said.

"Then don't let go. See how that works?" She lifted up and smiled.

He smiled, too—adoringly.

"This is the first time I've really danced since college."

"Seriously, why have you waited so long?"

"Good question. I don't know how to answer other than to say I wanted it for so long that when I washed out of ballet school, and then dance in college, I felt like I'd washed out of life. I couldn't face it."

He nodded. "I can understand how disappointing it must have been."

Could he really? He was right—her life was different. He probably had no idea how easy it had been to fall back to the usual. A life of privilege. Someone on hand to take care of everything. Some man's arm to take.

"I used to watch you," Rafe admitted quietly.

Hallie smiled curiously. "You did?"

"When I worked for my dad, you'd come out on the east lawn and practice those jumps and twirling around."

"Grand jetés and pirouettes."

"You were the most elegant, graceful thing I had ever seen. It was like a spot of beauty and wonder in a world where there were only men and scrub brush and animals."

No one had ever said anything like that to her. A smile was building in her chest and radiating outward. "I never knew you saw me."

"I wasn't supposed to." He caressed her arm. "But I used to live for those glimpses of you dancing on the east lawn."

He had loved her, and she hadn't known it. It was amazing to her. She rose up on her toes and extended her leg, then bent the knee and pirouetted, and fell into Rafe's arms.

"Did you do that on purpose?" he murmured, and kissed her temple.

"Busted."

They made love in front of the fire in the living room on the bearskin rug. And later, again in the kitchen. It was as if neither of them could be satisfied.

Much later, when they were in bed, and Sulley was on the floor with a new bone, and both of them had a book from her box, Rafe put his aside and traced a line between some freckles on her chest. Hallie smiled. She set aside her book, too. "We're ravenous, have you noticed? It's like we've been penned and we're just getting out."

When he lifted his gaze to hers, she saw something in them that made her shiver. She'd struck a chord—Rafe had been penned somehow.

She was still thinking of it the next morning when they went into town for breakfast—that he'd been penned, and she didn't really know from what, but she thought maybe from wanting her, and that astounded her. She couldn't imagine anyone feeling that way about her for so long. She'd never thought of Rafe as anything but a friend until the first time he came back from Afghanistan, and he was filled out with the hard lines and shadows and curves of muscle.

How was it for him, she wondered, when Chris had come along? Hallie had taken the path of

Chris because she thought it was the path she was supposed to take, and it wasn't until her father died, when she'd called Rafe, and they'd begun to talk again, *really* talk about things that mattered, that she began to wonder if maybe she'd had it wrong all along. Had she been wrong about every single thing in her life?

"What are you thinking about?" he asked, staring at her curiously from across the table in the pancake house.

Hallie looked at his eyes, his two-day growth of beard, and his lips. Those soft, pillowy lips that had touched her in places she didn't even know she had. Was she wrong now? "You really do get me, Rafe, do you know that?"

He laughed. "Yeah, a little, maybe."

"No, you do. You've made me open my eyes—"

His phone suddenly rang, startling them both. She gestured, indicating that he should answer. She herself had not turned on her phone since Rafe had appeared on the drive. She didn't want the world to intrude.

"Hey, Jase, what's up?" he asked. He frowned. "I can't hear you, man. Hold on." He covered the phone with his hand. "I'm going to step outside." He slipped out of the booth.

While he was gone, Hallie pulled her phone out of her purse and turned it on. When it came to life, up popped dozens of texts from Chris. For heaven's sake, he hadn't paid her this much attention in all the time they were together. What was his problem? He was the guy who suddenly became interested in a girl once she stopped returning his calls. Well, Hallie had no patience for that. To think she'd been so close to marrying that man made her feel a little sick. She would have walked up to the altar in her perfect dress, determined to make their life perfect, even though it wasn't perfect for her. Sometimes Hallie scared herself with how willing she was to ignore what she needed to be—

"Hallie."

With a start, she looked up from her phone. Rafe slid into the booth across from her. He sighed, looked out the window at the clouds that had begun to gather over the mountaintops. He sighed again, wearily, and said, "I'm gonna have to head home."

"What?" Hallie hadn't even thought about the end of this yet. All she thought about was the next day, and the day after that, and all the things she wanted to do with Rafe, and all the ways she wanted to touch him. *"Why?"*

"Something's come up in Chicago, and I need to get home to handle it."

"Is everything okay?"

"Yeah. I think. Just a problem we've run into."

Hallie nodded. She tried to think of what to say, but she was frozen. She couldn't grasp that this dream would come to an end. "When?"

Rafe grimaced. He looked at his watch. It was only ten. "Probably should go today."

"Today?" she repeated incredulously. This was it? This wonderful, soul-cleansing interlude of love was ending today? She wasn't ready for it to end. She couldn't absorb it, not like this, not so suddenly, not in a pancake house.

She buried her face in her hands.

"Hallie?"

"Don't mind me, Rafe. I just need to cry about something," she said, and bit back her bitter tears of disappointment.

Chapter Twenty-two

Hallie insisted on driving home with Rafe. He didn't see any reason for her to rush out of this bit of paradise. After all, Nick was looking for an excuse to fly. He was waiting on the call to pick her up.

"He's not expecting to hear from me for a few more days. And I don't want to stay here without you."

She was standing in front of him, dressed in jeans and snow boots, a puffy vest and a knit cap. It was hard as hell to say no to this woman.

"It's a two-day drive, Hallie."

"I don't care if it's a five-day drive. Why do you have to go right now, anyway?"

Because he was enough of a Luddite to have not set up PayPal or Venmo, or to trust any entity but a bank to send money. And Jason needed money. A *lot* of money. They had to come up with three thousand dollars to get the plumbing inspected and passed.

"Wait, what?" Rafe had asked when Jason first told him.

"What can I say? You gotta grease the palm."

"Yeah, but I thought we'd already greased that palm."

"Are you kidding, Rafe? They won't even come look at it."

It wasn't the money, although Rafe did not like spending his hard earned money on bribes. But he'd been as determined to save money as he was to keep his feelings for Hallie hidden from the world, so he had a lot. And he got that sometimes these things happened when you were building a new business. But something was beginning to feel a little off here. It seemed like too much palm greasing for a gym.

"I'm not at home," he'd said. "I'll get back to you in a couple of days." He also needed to get to Chicago and check things out for himself.

He was trying to convince Hallie. "I told you—we've run into a problem in Chicago that I need to deal with. Hallie, listen to me—stay and enjoy yourself."

"This place will never be the same without you. So Sulley and I are going with you. Unless you tell me no."

Rafe didn't see how in the world they would roll up to Three Rivers like nothing had happened. But he couldn't look this woman in the eye and tell her no. Frankly, he had the opposite impulse—to do whatever it took to make her happy. "Are you sure?" he asked her once more.

"I'm *sure*."

They made quick work of tidying up Uncle Chet's house and were on the road by noon. On the way down the mountain, they stopped at the caretaker's house. An old man with rheumy eyes and large-knuckled hands walked out to the truck. Hallie handed him the key. "We're taking off, Mr. Collin."

"I'll let Mr. Applewhite know."

"Actually," Hallie said, holding up a finger, "would you mind if I let him know? I want to surprise him." She smiled.

Rafe thought that was an odd request. Surprise her uncle with what?

Mr. Collin shrugged. "If you say so."

"Thank you!" she sang out, and waved as Rafe put the truck in drive.

He looked at her sidelong as they continued on. "What was that about?"

Hallie pretended to be digging in her purse. "Oh, I think it's probably best if he doesn't tell Uncle Chet I took off with a man in a pickup truck." She turned a smile to him. "You know."

He wondered if she meant she didn't want her uncle to know she'd left with *him*. This was precisely the sort of thing that should have worried him, but for the last few days, he'd pretended none of that was real.

They made it to Amarillo that night on the strength of license plate games, Hallie's awful singing of show tunes, Slim Jims, and iced tea. Five miles from the city limits, they saw a sign for a motel that was friendly to dogs, truckers, and children.

"In that order?" Hallie asked.

Rafe grimaced when he saw the place. He was fairly certain Hallie had never in her life darkened the door of a motel like this. But she went right on in, took a look around, flipped on the light in the bathroom, said, "Gross," and then stepped out. "Under no circumstances will I step foot in that tub." She bounced onto one of the two beds and invited Sulley to join her.

Rafe had stretched out on the second bed, his legs feeling cramped from the drive. He could feel himself dozing off when Hallie's phone pinged. He opened his eyes as she picked it up, looked at the screen, then tossed it aside.

He didn't ask her who. It was her ex again. He wanted to say that he didn't like it, but in no scenario did he have that right. Neither of them had tried to define what had happened in Aspen. They weren't exclusive. And the farther and farther they moved from Aspen, the more uncertain he was about what they were, exactly, and the less of a right he had.

Plus, he was leaving for Chicago. That hadn't changed—he'd invested too much of his time and money into that project. But that didn't stop him from hating the doctor with everything that he had.

He looked at Hallie. She was scratching Sulley's ears. "Do you remember telling me you were going to Aspen to get clarity on what was next for you?"

She looked at him with a funny smile. "Yes."

"Did you?"

Her smile faded a little, and she glanced off. "In some ways, yeah. In others, not so much." She stopped scratching Sulley's ear and looked at him. "What about you? Did you find some clarity?"

This was where his head and his heart were going to have a showdown. It was long overdue, really. But Rafe still couldn't grapple with his thoughts. He couldn't put them into any logical order. Or make sense of them and find a path through. "I think so, yes."

Her eyes widened slightly. And she grinned, resumed scratching Sulley's ears. "We had an amazing time, didn't we?"

That didn't sound like clarity. That sounded like she'd just gotten back from some trip, and now it was business as usual. That didn't sound like she was thinking about what had happened between them and what it meant. "We damn sure did, Hal." He reached across the space between the two beds for her hand.

Hallie reached for her camera.

Rafe mentally shook his head. This seemed all wrong, like an abrupt end to a movie. He didn't want what had happened in Aspen to end, but what was he going to do, invite her to Chicago to sleep on Chaco's couch with him? Make ends meet while he worked with underprivileged kids and worked toward his social work license?

But why not? He didn't care about the struggle he was facing if it was for her. And Hallie was not without her own resources if she needed them. Maybe she could find a dance class there. He didn't know how that worked, but his head was filling with images of her walking Sulley along the shore, of the two of them nestled in a cozy apartment.

"Hey, look at these." Hallie moved to the bed he was on, nudging him until he made room for her. She showed him some of the pictures they'd taken. There was Rafe, on his back in the snow. There were the pine trees and aspens, the snow glistening on the mountaintops. There were several pictures of Sulley, and a few pictures that Rafe had taken of Hallie, always laughing, always smiling. A dab of snow on her nose, her eyes scrunched up with laughter. Her ridiculous snowplow form.

And the last one. It was a picture of him, taken just last night. He was lying in bed, obviously naked, a sheet barely covering his lower half. He had curled his arm behind him to pillow his head, and he was looking at Hallie as she took the picture.

It was the expression on his face that jolted him—it was a look of pure adoration. It was the look of a man who had pined for a woman for many years. There it was, glowing out of him. "Come to Chicago with me," he blurted.

Hallie snorted as she flicked through the pictures. "You don't want me anywhere near a plumbing project."

"No, Hallie—I'm serious. Come with me. Live there. You and Sulley and me. You don't have anything to hold you at Three Rivers now."

She looked startled. "Are you serious?"

"More serious about this than I've ever been about anything in my life." He sat up. "Chicago is a great city. Lots of culture and things to do. I am sure there are dance studios all over town."

"Wow," she said softly. "I wasn't expecting this."

He wondered what she did expect. "Just think about it," he urged her. He pushed the camera aside and pulled her into his arms. "I love you, Hallie Jane. I want to be with you. I know it's not what you're used to, but we could be happy there."

"I want to be with you, too," she said quietly.

But she didn't say yes to Chicago.

The next morning, they were on the road by seven. Hallie didn't talk as much as she had the day before. She said she was tired and slept through the miles where the air turned warmer

368

as they passed from plains to hills. Rafe tried to talk, but his thoughts were descending into his own personal hell. The closer they got to San Antonio, the more uncertain he was. It seemed like Aspen had been a dream from which he was slowly waking, and his biggest fear—that he'd made a mess of things—was coming true. She was distracted. A little distant. He wasn't sure what to make of it.

Hallie drove the last leg, and pulled into the drive at Three Rivers Ranch at a speed Rafe would not consider safe. They sailed down and around the house to the garage area, where she hit the brakes a little hard.

Rafe suppressed a groan at seeing Nick's truck. Luca's, too. And great, just to round it out, Mrs. Prince was standing in front of a delivery van, its panel doors open to reveal dozens of vases filled with flowers. Mrs. Prince was giving the driver a piece of her mind, judging by how her hands were flying. Hallie put the truck in park and stared.

"Is that for one of your projects?" he asked.

"No. I'm not doing the deconstruction anymore, I'm doing the aftermath now."

"The what?"

"Aftermath," she repeated, and opened the truck door and got out. Sulley bounded out after her, racing for the fence line to bark at the horses grazing there.

Mrs. Prince turned around as Hallie walked to the front of the truck.

Rafe was slow to get out. He felt a little queasy. Like he was about to be punched.

Mrs. Prince looked at Hallie. Then at Rafe. Then at Hallie, her brows sliding down into a V. "Well, what the devil is going on here?"

"Rafe gave me a ride home. What is *this?*" Hallie asked, gesturing to the delivery van.

"*This* is your ex-fiancé's latest effort to impress you. Your grandmother hasn't stopped sneezing. She's allergic to marigolds, you know," Mrs. Prince said accusingly, as if Hallie had ordered marigolds from her ex.

"He sent me *flowers?*" she asked disbelievingly.

"Whole van is for you if you're Hallie," the driver said. "Where do you want me to put them?"

"You want me to tell you where? Up his ass," Hallie said, and folded her arms.

Mrs. Prince made a sound of surprise. "That's not exactly helpful." To the driver she said, "If you would be so kind as to unload them into the garage, we'll decide what to do with them."

Nick and Luca appeared now. Luca was holding Sulley. Rafe could not have asked for a worse scenario. Nick and Luca were giving him curious looks, and Rafe thought he and Hallie might as well have worn matching T-shirts reading "I slept with that one," with arrows pointing at each other.

"I must admit, I'm surprised to see you, Rafe," Mrs. Prince said, turning her frown to him now that the driver had his instructions.

"Hi, Mrs. Prince."

"Did you pick Hallie up at the airport?"

"What?" Nick asked. "I was supposed to fly up and get you." He sounded disappointed.

"Okay, would you all stop looking at us as if we committed some heinous crime? Rafe brought Sulley to Aspen because Rico couldn't, but I didn't like being up there alone and asked him to bring me home. That's it, that's all there is to it."

That was it, huh? Nothing to see here, folks. Move along.

Rafe glanced at Hallie, but her expression was shuttered. No matter what he wanted to believe was true between them, he could see the hesitation in her. It was undoubtedly the same hesitation that caught him, time after time. She was a Prince. He was a Fontana. This was never going to be real, and his instincts had been right all along.

"Speaking of that," he said, and walked to the bed of his truck, removed her things and Sulley's food, and set them on the drive. "Here you go, Hallie. I better get home."

"What?" Hallie said, turning to face him. "But—"

"Yeah, I have that Chicago thing I've got to take care of," he said. "I'll text you later."

Hallie watched him as he got in the truck. She was still watching when he turned the truck around. And in his rearview mirror he could see that she continued to watch along with the rest of her family as he drove on.

He drove almost blindly to his house, his mind working a thousand beats a minute. Angie's car was parked in the drive, so he pulled up on the road. He rubbed his face with his hands, tried to wake himself up. He was tired and confused, and the scrutiny of his own family required a whole different kind of energy.

He made himself get out and walk into the house as if nothing was up. As if he was coming home from the gym, or something equally benign. He was expecting a welcoming committee full of questions about where he'd been and what he'd been doing—he'd told his dad he would be out of town a couple of days, but didn't say more than that.

What he found, however, was his parents seated at the dining room table with the kids parked in front of cartoons in the living room. There was a somberness between them that alarmed Rafe. "What's going on?"

His mother turned a tear-filled gaze to him. "It's Rico."

Rafe's heart lurched painfully, and he felt like he was swaying on his feet, although he was standing perfectly still. "He's dead," he said softly.

"Nope," Angie said. "But he might as well be."

"He's in jail," his father said. "He's been arrested for public intoxication."

"*What?*" How was that possible? Rico had been home maybe ten days, tops.

"He's in jail!" his father repeated. He rubbed his face with his hands. "Stupid, stupid," he muttered, and stood up from the table and stalked into the kitchen.

"He made a mistake," his mother said.

"Yeah, he made a mistake, all right," his father said, and slammed the fridge door shut before appearing again. "I've got enough going on here with the Prince family falling apart, and now my own family. He's going to wind up in prison. He doesn't have any goals, he doesn't have any ambition—"

"Dad! He's got a disease," Angie said.

"What he's got is a lack of willpower."

Rafe's dad had never bought into the idea that addiction was a disease. For him, it was a choice—just don't drink. Man up. Take care of business. The blood began to drain from Rafe's face, swirling into hot indignation in his chest. Rico needed help, and he wasn't going to get it at home. Rafe knew what he had to do. But he resented it—all he'd ever done was help with his brother. And his family. His friends. Especially his father. *Look after your mother, look after your brother and sister. Help, Rafe. We need you, Rafe.*

373

His father wasn't through. He returned to the dining area, a lock of his salt-and-pepper hair curiously out of place and hanging over his brow, and gave Rafe a stern look. "Is it true? Have you been with Hallie these last few days?"

Rico must have told him. "Yes."

"You were with *Hallie?*" Angie exclaimed.

"Stay out of it, Ang," Rafe warned her.

His father dropped his head. His hands curled tightly around the top of a dining room chair. "You don't know what you're doing, Rafe. The Prince family will put on a good front, and they'll make you think you're their buddy, but when it comes right down to it, they're as judgmental as anyone you will ever meet—"

"Martin!" his mother said with alarm.

His dad looked up. "She's not your friend," he said. "Don't make that mistake."

"Dad, I—"

"I have worked for this family for *thirty* years, son. You might have a grand old time of it, but in the end, it's all gonna come out exactly like I'm telling you now—that family will not let her carry on with an employee's son for long. That's the way it works around here. We're probably going to be gone from here by summer, mark my words."

"Martin, you're borrowing trouble," his mother said. "The Princes have been very good to us."

His dad clenched his jaw and looked at the three of them. "I'm just saying that we don't need an excuse for Mrs. Prince to push me out, not with Rico in crisis. I've got no place to go at my age."

Rafe sighed. "Rico is always in crisis," he said calmly. "He doesn't need to be here, Dad. In fact, this is probably the worst place for him. He needs to be someplace where he can find something that interests him."

His mother shook her head. "And where would that be? We don't have the money to send him anywhere."

"I do," Rafe said. "He can come to Chicago with me."

His family looked at him with expressions of surprise and, worst of all, hope. A solution for Rico.

Rafe to the rescue again.

Rafe caught a flight to Chicago on standby that night to discover what the problem was with the gym and pave the way for his brother.

He wasn't much of a drinker, but he drank on that flight, stacking up the little bottles like a platoon. He was trying, without success, to numb his feelings. He hated himself for believing he could bring Hallie to Chicago and make a life with her there. He hated himself for believing he could escape the problems in his own family.

What he wanted was to go back to the days in Aspen when he could pretend that nothing else existed or mattered but him and Hallie.

Chapter Twenty-three

It had been two days since Hallie and Rafe had returned from Aspen, and she'd received a text from him that said only, Family issues. OMW to Chicago. Talk to you later?

What family issues? The Fontanas were the lucky, close-knit family that seemed to have a good time no matter what. The Prince family was the one with issues. She'd texted back: When will you be home?

Not sure. Will let you know when I can. Boarding now.

And that was that. She hadn't heard another word since.

Which would have been par for the course a few days ago, but then there was Aspen and, well, she was missing him terribly. She was having a full-on war with herself—she wanted Rafe. She wanted to be with him, she wanted to be in love . . .

But she also wanted to pursue the ideas she'd

slowly been developing. She wanted to figure out who she really was. To live, for at least a time, without anyone to depend on but herself. She needed to know if she could do it.

Hallie was mulling this over as she drove around town, giving away armloads of flowers. Things had changed between her and Rafe after Amarillo. Everything had been so perfect in Aspen, and when he'd asked her to come to Chicago, her first thought was a hearty yes. But then something had clicked in her head, and she'd wondered, was she really going to go from a broken engagement into a new relationship? Wasn't that exactly what she had said she would *not* do? Was she quitting again?

The thought had plagued her for the rest of the trip. She didn't trust her emotions. She couldn't say with confidence that she wasn't choosing Rafe because it was the easy thing to do. Part of her wished everything could go back to the way it was before she'd kissed him, because at least she'd understood who and what they were then. But instead, she'd kissed him, and somehow, they'd slid off into a ditch.

She walked into Jo's Java with flowers and put them on a table in front of the daily specials board. She'd been Instagramming them in the various places she'd dropped them off yesterday and today. Those pictures had elicited another round of calls from Chris who, mysteriously, didn't seem to be in surgery quite as often as he used to be.

She was tired of him, too. It was more than time to put an end to this ridiculous chase of his. It almost seemed to excite him. The last time he'd called, Hallie had answered her phone and asked if they could have dinner.

"Really? Are you kidding?" Chris asked.

"Nope. Not kidding. I'll come to Hou—"

"I'll come there. How about we go to Bliss? We haven't been there in a long time."

Because Hallie didn't care for that San Antonio restaurant. She'd told him that more than once. "Tomorrow night?" she asked. "I mean, can you get off work? I know how busy you are."

"For you, of course I can, Hallie. This is great. *Thank* you."

She wondered if he even noticed the irony in his declaration that he could get off work for her, when only a few short weeks ago, it was impossible. Well, Chris would not be thanking her when the evening was over.

"What's this?" Jo Carol asked. She stuck a pencil into her beehive and leaned over to smell the bouquet.

"They are for you! Courtesy of my ex-fiancé. He sent a truckload to my house, and I am spreading the love."

Jo Carol actually looked startled. "Are you reconciling?"

Hallie laughed. And laughed. "God, Jo Carol, you're so funny," she said.

Next, she went to Mariah's shop across the street.

"What are you doing?" Mariah said, and hurried out from around the counter to help Hallie with the box full of flowers she was carrying.

"Bringing you flowers. They were a misdelivery."

"A misdelivery! How are this many flowers misdelivered?" Mariah asked, and then caught herself. "Oh. You mean you are regifting from Chris."

"Okay, I am regifting. I don't want them and you do, and I need some jeans."

"Hello, Hallie."

Hallie hadn't noticed anyone else in the shop and whipped around. Genevieve Bertram was smiling at her. She was wearing a wool dress that fit her so closely it was impossible not to notice how ballerina thin she was. Hallie used to be that thin. She didn't think she wanted to be that thin again—it ought to be a full-on paying job to stay that thin. "Hi, Genevieve! I didn't see you there."

"How are you?" Genevieve asked. She glanced at Hallie's "Surely not EVERYBODY was kung fu fighting" T-shirt.

"Me? I'm good! And you?"

"I'm very well, thank you. You look great, Hallie. By the way, I didn't want to say it when

379

I ran into you at Thanksgiving in that crowded theater, especially while you were with that handsome man, but I'm really sorry about what happened to your, ah . . . engagement."

"What handsome man?" Mariah demanded.

Hallie shot her a look.

"Fine," Mariah said. "You can tell me later." She turned back to a few boxes she was unpacking.

"Thank you, Genevieve," Hallie said. "Better to know what sort of jerk you're marrying before you marry the jerk, I always say."

Genevieve tried to smile, but the effect looked quite pained.

"Your program was great," Hallie said. She meant it. Okay, she might have choreographed it differently, but she could imagine corralling all those kids had been enough work in and of itself.

"Thank you," Genevieve said, looking pleased. "It's been a *lot* of hard work. Remember Cressida Sharp?"

Oh, but Hallie remembered Cressida, all right. She still had the occasional dream about her. Cressida was a diva, a girl who had pulled on her big-girl panties and then had strutted around as if they actually fit. "I sure do," Hallie said, and grinned.

"She helped me choreograph it. And by that, I mean she choreographed the solo dances. I would have thought with all the solos she had back then, she would have learned at least a few things."

Surprised, Hallie laughed.

Genevieve smiled. "It's really good to see you, Hallie. I'm living in San Antonio now, so if you're in town and you want to have lunch, give me a call. Mariah has me on speed dial so she can lure me here with all her great sales."

"I would like that."

Genevieve started to walk away, but Hallie said, "Hey, before you go—I've been kicking around an idea sort of similar to what you're doing for Kidz Korner."

Something flickered in Genevieve's eyes.

"Not *like* what you're doing, I didn't mean that," Hallie hastened to assure her. "But remember the girl with Down syndrome in your program?"

Genevieve nodded. "Her name is Marnie."

"It occurred to me that there might be a lot of kids like Marnie who would really love to dance, but are probably never going to have the skills to dance onstage with a group like yours, right?"

Genevieve said nothing.

"Maybe they just want to take dance," Hallie said. "And I thought that maybe I could give them a place where they could learn to dance. Maybe even teach them? I don't practice ballet anymore, but I still know how. I'm thinking about going back to school to get a teaching certificate.

I thought maybe I could do something like that." She realized she sounded very hopeful, as if she needed Genevieve's approval. Maybe she did. She needed someone to tell her she wasn't crazy.

Genevieve blinked. "Where would you teach them?"

Hallie hadn't actually thought that far ahead, but when Genevieve asked, the answer jumped into Hallie's mind so quickly that she wondered if maybe it had been there all along. "My dad left me some warehouses on the highway between here and San Antonio that are sitting empty. I have a trust, I could convert at least one of them to a dance studio."

Genevieve nodded thoughtfully.

"See, I want to be involved with dance again, and while I'm never going to be a great dancer, I could still teach it. And I thought I could teach kids who might not get the chance otherwise."

"My niece is autistic and she *loves* to dance," Mariah said. "She would give it her all, I know that. She's always wearing a tutu."

"That's exactly what I'm talking about," Hallie said quickly. "I could even start a scholarship program for kids who can't afford it." That was another thought that just appeared on the end of Hallie's tongue.

Genevieve was still considering her.

"Does this sound . . . like a good idea?" she asked hopefully.

A smile slowly lit Genevieve's face. "It's actually kind of brilliant, Hallie. Kidz Korner isn't a dance company. That's what we did with them for one season. They'll be doing art murals next. But your idea is fantastic. And you know what else? You were a *great* dancer. You probably still are."

Hallie laughed. "Trust me, I'm not. I went to ballet school and was asked not to return, remember?" She said it so easily—how interesting that she could say that now without it hurting like it used to. Her complete humiliation was a distant memory now. Wasn't it Rafe who had said that grief had a way of making you see things like you needed to see them? Damn it, he was right again.

"I always thought you were a really beautiful dancer. Your lines are so fluid and elegant."

Hallie's eyes widened. "That's what I always thought about *you*."

Genevieve laughed.

"Were you always so kind, Genevieve? Was I just a self-centered little prig who thought only about herself?"

"Probably," Mariah said.

Genevieve smiled warmly. "I don't think my teenage self was particularly kind. The truth is that I was always so jealous of you."

"Of me?" Hallie laughed.

"Yes! You were pretty and talented and, my

Lord, rich like Croesus. It was a bit much at times."

"Still is," Mariah said, and playfully nudged Hallie with her elbow.

Hallie grinned. "You know what, Genevieve? I am definitely going to call you for lunch. We clearly have lots to talk about."

They left after exchanging numbers, and back in the car, Hallie texted Rafe. I had the most amazing idea. You're going to love it. Plus I ran this morning and I made it two miles before my lungs collapsed into ash. Improvement!

He responded, That's great. Keep it up. Can't talk now, in the middle of a big mess. Talk soon.

Talk soon is what she and her girlfriends said when they were through with the group chats. It didn't actually mean *talk soon,* it meant *I'm getting off the phone now, don't text me, I'm done with this convo.*

Hallie put down her phone. The cloyingly sweet smell of the flowers in the back made her feel a little nauseated. At least she hoped it was the flowers and not her intuition knocking on the door.

Her intuition was telling her something else entirely as she dressed to meet Chris the next night. She was seated on the edge of her bed, strapping on a heel, when Luca appeared in her doorway. "Where are you going?"

"Out. Why are you always here?"

"Because I miss you so much."

Hallie rolled her eyes.

"The horses are here, Hal. I rode out today to check on some things."

"Hey, can I stay at your loft tonight?" she asked.

"Why? What's up? Seriously, where are you going?"

"If you must know," Hallie said, and stood, smoothing the lap of her dress as she checked her outfit in the mirror, "I'm having dinner with Chris."

Luca's eyes nearly bulged out of his head. "Excuse me? You're doing *what?*"

"I'm having dinner with Chris," she slowly repeated.

"Hallie—"

"I'm not getting back with him, Luca. But he won't stop contacting me, so I thought I'd have a nice dinner with him and end this civilly. Preferably not while he's having sex with someone else."

Luca leaned against the door, mollified by her explanation. "What does Rafe say about it?"

The question caught Hallie off guard. She turned her head slowly and looked her twin up and down. "Why do you ask that?"

He shrugged. "Just wondering if Rafe had an opinion. You two have been pretty thick lately."

"We're friends." The words rolled easily off her tongue, then stabbed her in the gut. Was that her decision? They were only friends?

Luca chuckled dubiously. "Right."

"So can I stay at the loft or not?"

"Fine. Ella and I are at her house anyway. Just one question—is Chris staying there, too?"

"No!" she said, shocked he would even ask.

But Luca eyed her with suspicion anyway.

She would wonder later why she didn't just confess to Luca what was in her heart and on her mind. But she didn't. It was her little secret. Except that it was a ginormous secret, and it was coloring every moment of every day. Particularly because she didn't know where her head was.

And she couldn't get into it now—she had another man to deal with.

Chris was waiting for her at the door of the restaurant Bliss in San Antonio. He stood like a gentleman and smiled appreciatively at Hallie as she came up the walk toward him. "Gorgeous as always," he said, and took her hand, leaning forward to kiss her cheek.

Hallie suppressed a shiver of revulsion. She looked at him and forced a smile and wondered how on earth she'd once been physically attracted to him. He was a good-looking man, she guessed, but his eyes weren't as intense as Rafe's, and his physique not as spectacular as Rafe's, and his smile not as warm as Rafe's. Chris's belly was getting a little soft, and his arms, well . . . they were skinny compared to Rafe's.

But it was more than the superficial differences. It was the way Rafe looked at her, like she was the only person in the world. She had a picture of him lying in bed in Aspen. He had gazed at her with utter regard. She knew what that look was, and it was so vastly different from the way Chris had ever looked at her.

Right now, Chris was looking at her like a puppy dog. "I got us a reservation for dinner. We're a little early. Can I get you a drink?"

"Could we talk a minute?" she asked.

"Sure, of course," Chris said. He guided her into the crowded bar area and signaled the bartender. "Two martinis," he said, and then to Hallie, "What did you want to talk about?"

He reminded her of a kid who was eager to rattle off his Christmas list.

"Well, for starters, I don't like martinis."

He laughed.

"I'm not much of a drinker, to be honest."

"What are you talking about? We used to have martinis all the time."

Hallie winced. "I know we did, because *you* like them—not me."

Chris seemed confused. "Okay," he said. "No more martinis."

"It's not the martinis, Chris. It's me. Everything

we did was because you liked it. I'm not saying that's a bad thing. I'm just saying that I allowed it to happen because I thought I was supposed to. I thought I was supposed to suppress myself in order to be everything you wanted me to be. You know, the perfect wife, as described to me by my mother. Or . . . society."

The bartender slid the martinis across the bar to them.

"I wanted to make you happy, too, you know," Chris said defensively, and gave the bartender a twenty.

That was debatable. "But you didn't lose yourself trying to make me happy. That's the mistake I made."

He looked puzzled. "So what are you saying?"

"I'm saying that everything I did was because it met someone else's expectation of what I was supposed to do. But I don't think I ever really met my own expectations."

He frowned. "Could you be a little clearer? I'm not sure where this is taking us."

"Right, okay," she said, nodding. "I guess I'm trying to tell you that I've changed."

He laughed with a hint of derision.

"What's so funny?"

"You haven't changed, Hallie. A leopard doesn't change its spots."

His smile was so patronizing she wanted to kick him. "What spots?"

"I'm just saying you're a certain kind of girl. You were born for the life I could give you."

Well, those were fighting words. A life that *he* could give her? As if she had no say in it? That was exactly what was wrong with her and exactly the wrong thing to say. Hallie put her drink down. "Chris. I am asking, sincerely, from the bottom of my heart, that you not call me again."

Chris stared at her as if he didn't speak the language.

"I don't love you anymore. I'm not sure I ever really did."

His eyes widened. The bartender retreated to the other end of the bar.

"In a way, you did me an enormous favor when you fucked Dani. So thank you for that." She gave him a little hand clap.

Chris blinked. He shook his head. And then he laughed. "You really had me going."

"I'm very serious, Chris. To borrow a phrase from Taylor Swift, I am never ever getting back with you, and I need your shit-show of an apology tour to end. It's really annoying. It took me two days to pass out all those flowers around town."

"Hallie." He glanced around them. "You surely didn't drag me all the way to San Antonio to tell me you don't want to see me again."

"You were the one who offered to come here, remember? I didn't ask you to dinner to tell you I don't want to see you again, because I've already told you that. I wanted to see you to tell you that it's really, seriously over, and if you don't cut it out, I'm going to get a restraining order. That would not look good for your image, so I hope you will hear me this time, because I don't want to do that. But I will. In a *heartbeat*. I like you, Chris. I think what you did was shitty, but hey, I'm over it. And I'm over you. And I really need you to stop."

He slumped back against the bar, his expression blank. He stared off into space for a long moment. "I don't believe this. You never even gave me a chance to explain."

Now, *that* was funny, and Hallie couldn't help a small giggle. She leaned closer and said softly, "Your lily-white ass riding high over Dani did all the explaining for you." She straightened up again. "Seriously. Lose my number. Delete your account."

His blue eyes began to well with tears. He covered his face again.

"Oh," she said soothingly, and put one arm around him. "Don't cry."

"I'm not," he said curtly, and moved so that she had to drop her arm from his waist.

The hostess appeared and looked uncertainly at them.

"Hey, you want to have dinner?" Hallie asked him. "I mean as long as you're here. My treat.

I'm dying to know whatever happened to that nurse who was stealing OxyContin from the pill room anyway."

Chris sniffed loudly. He dug a handkerchief from his pocket. "She got caught."

"No way!" Hallie said, and linked her arm through his. "You'll have to tell me all about it." She nodded at the hostess.

Chris allowed her to escort him into the dining room.

She had a surprisingly pleasant time with Chris after the final breakup. They talked about his job, people they knew. The meal was excellent and the wine superb. At the end, Hallie gave Chris a cheerful pat on the shoulder, wished him well, and sent him off to his hotel. She walked to Luca's loft on the Riverwalk.

Once inside, she kicked off her shoes and plopped down on the couch. She pulled out her phone. It was eleven o'clock, but she texted Rafe anyway.

You will never guess what I did tonight.

Did you eat an elephant one bite at a time?

Nope.

Count your chickens before they hatch?

Ha. No. She included an emoji of a chicken.

March to the beat of another drummer?

She sent a GIF of a marching band. I ended it with Chris. I mean, I ended it a long time ago. But he hadn't, so I made sure he understood it's done. He won't text me again.

There was a long pause before the three dots cropped up. Rafe's reply was clapping hands. She was hoping for a little more than that, but she'd take it.

She texted, When will you be home?

Day after tomorrow.

Will I see you?

Of course you will.

She sent him a GIF of a girl skipping through sunflowers.

He didn't respond with anything else, which seemed a bit odd.

Chapter Twenty-four

Rafe swung by to see John Horowitz when he arrived back in San Antonio. He and Chaco had come up with an idea for how to train John. It would require some modifications to the training program, obviously, and some strength training for muscles John probably hadn't used in a while or that were underdeveloped. Rafe laid the plan out to John. John was giddy with excitement. "When can we start?"

"Soon. I've got to take care of a few things first."

When he arrived home, a very sheepish Rico met him in the drive. The two of them hadn't spoken since Rafe took his place and went to Aspen. Rafe looked his brother up and down. "So you're out of jail."

"Yeah. Dude," Rico said. "I'm sorry."

Rafe shrugged. "You're always sorry, Rico, but being sorry doesn't change anything. *You* have to make the change. You have to want it."

"I do want it," Rico said, and shoved his fingers through his hair. "You have no idea how much I want it. Or how hard it is. I think I've got it, then something happens, and I just . . . just can't stop myself."

Rico was right—Rafe didn't know how hard it was. But he was tired of the apologies and the promises to do better. He considered his brother a moment before saying, "I have an idea for you, if you're willing."

"What's that?" Rico asked warily.

Rafe had talked to Jason and Chaco, and they'd agreed with Rafe. Rico needed a big change.

He suspected Rico would jump at any opportunity to get him off this ranch. Hallie had been right about that—Rico was not cut out for ranch life. And Rafe couldn't *not* help his brother. "Let's go inside," he said, and put his hand on Rico's shoulder, squeezing affectionately.

When Rafe explained what he had in mind, Rico didn't hesitate. "I'll go. When are we leaving?"

"End of the week," Rafe said.

"Dude," Rico said. *"Thanks."*

Rafe didn't have much to say to that. He wanted to help Rico. But he resented that it had to intrude on his life.

He left Rico in the kitchen with his mom, talking excitedly about going to Chicago. According to Rico, he'd "always wanted to go there."

Rafe walked outside, got in his truck, drove into town, and parked in the Timmons Tire and Body Shop parking lot. He had missed Hallie something awful. Had thought about her every moment of every day he'd been gone. He didn't know how he was going to explain the new wrinkle in his family life. He still wanted her to come to Chicago, but he didn't know how he would make this all work.

He texted, What up?

> Looking for my pointe shoes. I swear I had them here.

> Can you come into town?

> !!! Are you back?

He responded with an emoji wearing sunglasses and a smile.

> Where are you?

Good question. Where was he? His heart was with Hallie. His head was somewhere different. Timmons Tire and Body. Beautiful afternoon. Meet me at the park by the gazebo.

Give me thirty. No emoji. No kissy faces, no GIFs of someone frantically finding something to wear. A simple *give me thirty.*

He tried not to read too much into it.

He was sitting in the gazebo in their bicentennial park when Hallie drove up and hopped out of her Range Rover. She was wearing jeans that accentuated her curves, and her strawberry blond hair hung in a braid over her shoulder. When she spotted him, she ran across the park, and he had to admit with a smile that her form had improved drastically.

He stood up when she entered the gazebo, and Hallie took a flying leap at him, wrapping her legs around him and kissing him hard. She lifted her head. "That's how they do it on *The Bachelor.*"

"I have no idea what that means."

She unwrapped her legs and slid down his body. "I missed you, dude. It seemed like forever! How long has it been?"

An eternity. "Ah . . . four or five days?" He put his fingers beneath her chin and tilted her head back to kiss her. He lingered there, his lips on hers, his tongue touching hers, and he felt a rumble in his body that went to his core. It was an earthquake. But he had to keep his emotions in check, under wraps. He had to do the right thing, to say this in the right way.

When he lifted his head, she smiled. "Did you fix your problem?"

She was talking about Chicago, but he immediately thought of his personal problem.

"Some of it." They'd paid for the plumbing inspection. But they'd run into some trouble with the electrical wiring. Chaco said he thought they might have to rewire the whole damn building. "How have you been?"

"Oh! *Busy,*" she said. She smiled.

Rafe pushed his hands into his pockets. "It's cold. Want to go to the taco stand? Or how about the Magnolia? It's nearly happy hour—"

"Wait, Rafe. I need to tell you something."

Rafe's heart hitched. *Don't do it. Don't say it.* "Listen, Rico relapsed," he blurted. He didn't know why he said it like that, other than he wasn't ready to hear what she had to say.

Hallie gasped.

"He was arrested for public intoxication—"

"No! He's in *jail?*"

"He's out now."

"I am so sorry. How did I not know this? I saw Martin yesterday—"

"That is not something my dad would want known."

"Oh." She stared up at him. "I'm so sorry, Rafe. I know how much you and your family have worried about him."

"Right," he said, and glanced down. "So here's the thing. Rico needs help."

"Sure."

"I'm going to take him to Chicago with me, and he's going to work with us."

Hallie nodded again. She swallowed. "Okay," she said after a moment. "That's great. So . . . you're *both* moving to Chicago."

"Yes. I know I asked you, and I still—"

"You know, that actually works out great for both of us, I think."

He felt suddenly incapable of movement or speech.

"I'm moving to Austin. To finish school."

Rafe was stunned. He couldn't think of what to say.

"Remember? I told you in Aspen."

"Yeah," he said. He put his hand on his waist. He turned away from her, ran his palm over his head, trying to absorb the blow. "Did you at least think about coming to Chicago?"

"I did," she said quietly. "A lot."

He looked at her over his shoulder. He loved her so much that he couldn't breathe right now. "You thought about it."

She sighed. She looked at her hands for a long moment. When she looked up, she said, "I *did* think about it. And I thought you were right, that I was jumping from a broken engagement into another relationship—"

"Oh my God," he muttered. There it was, the gut punch.

"It doesn't mean I feel any differently about you, Rafe. I love you. But I think I need to get out on my own. I need to do this, to accomplish something without anyone's help. I need to know who Hallie is."

"You can't accomplish that in Chicago?"

She pressed her lips together.

"Right," he muttered. He felt sick. He had skated onto the lake, and he had plunged through the thin ice, and now he was drowning. "So what, we just go back to where we were? After what happened in Aspen?"

"Aspen was amazing," she said. The tears were glistening in her eyes.

"Yeah, so glad you thought so, too," he said sarcastically. "I never should have gone. I never should have told you."

"But I'm so glad you did—"

"So you can break me now?" he asked hoarsely. "How can you just turn it off? *I* can't! I think about you *all* the time. I thought things were different now."

"*I* am different," she said, pressing her hands one on top of the other over her heart. "I am profoundly changed. But I need to do this for myself. I can't go from depending on one man to depending on another. I have never in my life been on my own, Rafe. I have never had to make it. Someone always made it for me. I need to discover this, and if I don't, I don't know what kind of partner I could be to you. I really thought you'd understand."

"What I understand," he said bitterly, "is that

I was right about you and me. I knew it could never go anywhere, not really. You were never going to be with a guy like me. Well, Hal, we've had our moment in the sun. Now I have my brother to think about, and a business I'm trying to get off the ground, and you are moving to Austin, apparently, and we need to step back and let things settle."

She looked stricken. "I'm not trying to hurt you, Rafe. I am trying to be a better person!"

He looked at her beautiful, lovely face and gave a small, sardonic laugh. "My old man was right."

"What?"

"Never mind."

"Rafe!" She put her hands on her hips. "I am obviously not explaining myself well. I'm doing this for *both* of us, don't you get it?

"You're not doing it for me," he said, the anger suddenly gone out of him. "But do what you need to do, Hallie. I would never be able to bear your resentment anyway."

"*What* resentment?"

"The resentment that would come. It might not happen now, but someday, down the road, when I couldn't provide for you in the way you wanted or be the high-society escort you're used to, when I couldn't give you the lavish things your father gave your mother, you would resent me."

"Wow," she said. She took another step back.

Her expression had gone from dark to stunned. "Is *that* what you think of me? Sounds to me like the real resentment would be on your end. Because I would *never* resent you, Rafe. Especially not for something as shallow as things."

He turned away a moment, trying to get his thoughts together. But when he pivoted back around, two tears had slid down Hallie's face. He crumbled. "No, no, no," he said. "Hallie, baby, please don't cry. I'm just . . . I'm disappointed."

"I'm not *crying*. When I found my fiancé in bed with a bridesmaid, I cried," she said. "Tears of sheer fury. But these aren't tears." She pointed at her face. "You want to know what this is? This is a leak from a broken heart. I'm leaking, Rafe, because I really do love you. I really *do*. I should have told you, I should have made that clear. But I love you so much, and I think that I have to figure out how to love myself, too, or I'm never going to be the woman you need *me* to be. Did you ever think about that? Because I don't want you to resent me either."

He felt his own heart cracking and leaking, too. He carefully put his hand on her elbow and slowly pulled her into his chest. He wrapped his arms around her. "I guess we're breaking up before we even start," he said into her hair.

"Ohmigod, this is just like *The Bachelor*, too," she said tearfully. "My life is one long episode of the fucking *Bachelor*." And then she began to cry.

He still didn't know what she was talking about, but he felt like he'd just been tossed into a dumpster to lie in the ruins of his broken heart.

Chapter Twenty-five

A stiff breeze kept snapping the Texas flag Dolly had installed over Charlie's grave. Like they needed to call any more attention to themselves.

Cordelia had on her sheepskin booties and a puffy jacket Charlie had bought her in Zurich one year. It was a bit of overkill—it wasn't *that* cold—but Cordelia could not seem to shake a chill that had settled into her bones with the first winter rain.

"Well, you won't believe what happened," she said to Charlie's grave. "Martin pulled me aside and apologized for his son. Can you believe that? I wouldn't apologize for our kids even if they murdered someone." She hesitated a moment to think about that. "Well. Maybe if they murdered someone. My point is, you defend your kids."

A lone hawk circled overhead, checking out the ground for something to eat.

"Weather is coming," she announced. "Rain. Might ice a little." She wondered if she could have a fire pit up here. She'd ask Martin about that when he'd had a chance to calm down from their latest spat.

"Helloooo!"

"For God's sake," Cordelia muttered. Here came Dolly. She had a thermos and a tote bag slung over her shoulder.

"A bit chilly today, isn't it?" Dolly asked.

"Yes, too chilly for seniors. You don't have to stay," Cordelia said.

"Oh, I'm all right. And besides, I like spending time with you, Delia." She smiled and patted the top of Cordelia's head.

Cordelia swatted Dolly's hand away.

Dolly settled into the chair next to Cordelia, the thermos dangling from her fingers. "What's in there?" Cordelia asked.

"A medicinal."

"What sort of medicinal?"

"The type to soothe a weary soul," Dolly said with a wink.

"My soul is not weary," Cordelia countered.

"Okay, then it sparks a perky soul."

Cordelia arched a brow.

"It'll warm you up."

"Do you have cups?"

Dolly reached into the tote bag and withdrew a pair of plastic coffee cups. She opened up the thermos and poured. Cordelia could smell the alcohol. Dolly handed a cup to Cordelia, tapped her cup against it, then said, "Now, what did you say to Martin that upset him so?"

"Oh, that," Cordelia said. "Can you believe that stupid man actually thought I'd let him go? He said between the money problems, and our argument about the horses, which, for the record, he won, and his son messing around with my daughter, he fully expected to be cut."

"We can't cut Martin," Dolly said.

"Well, I *know*." Cordelia sipped the concoction. It was spiked hot tea. "This is delicious."

"Good afternoon, ladies!"

Cordelia and Dolly turned their heads to see George struggling up the hill. "Are we going to have to put in a chair lift in for you, George?" Cordelia called. She stood up, opened up the third lawn chair, purchased at the end-of-season sale at Walmart. She set it next to Dolly. "Dolly makes it up here just fine."

George braced himself against a tree to catch his breath. "She's a fit and healthy woman."

"You should take up tai chi, George," Dolly suggested.

"I just might."

"What are you doing here?" Cordelia asked, and gestured to his chair.

"Dropping off some papers for Hallie. She's interested in doing something with those warehouses after all."

"What?" Dolly asked. "She's moving to Austin

next week. What's she going to do with ware-houses?"

"That, I don't know. She asked for the deed restrictions and I brought them down." He sat, and accepted a cup from Dolly. He sipped. He coughed. He sipped again. "What's Martin so mad about?"

Cordelia waved her hand. "I didn't consider his feelings."

"There's a shocker," Dolly muttered. "And he thought Delia was going to fire him."

"I'm not going to fire him, I'm not an idiot," she said to Dolly. To George, she explained, "He apologized to me for Rafe. Said he didn't think anything between Rafe and Hallie was appropriate given the Fontana working relation-ship with us. I told him to take his head out of his ass, he was being more uptight than me. He said he didn't think that was even possible, and that his concern was for his son, not Hallie. Well, that didn't sit well, so I said, 'Listen, Martin. There are two types of people in the world. The type that thinks young love is beautiful no matter who it is,'" she said, holding up one finger, "'and dumb-asses. And guess which one you're being.'" She snorted. "Last I checked, Rafe was a grown-ass man. And why would Martin apologize for anyone spending time with my daughter? So I told him it wasn't his business, and that I couldn't ask for a better companion for Hallie, and he said, oh sure, when they had their first big fight, I'd think differently, and then it would be the old heave-ho for the Fontanas." She shook her head. "Ridiculous. Why are men so ridiculous?"

"Delia, you'd be an absolute fool to let Martin Fontana go," George said sternly.

"Well, I *know* that, George. I told him he was a damn fool if he thought for one minute that I could run this place without him, and he'd be buried up here along with the rest of us."

"What'd he say?" Dolly asked.

"Not much. He got down off his high horse and swanned right out of there."

She noticed that Dolly and George were looking at each other with surprise. "What?" she demanded.

"Two weeks ago, you said you'd take Charlie's gun and shoot Rafe if you found out he was in Aspen with Hallie," Dolly reminded her.

"I say a lot of things I don't mean," Cordelia said defensively. "But the more I thought about it, the more I realized that outside of family, no one has ever stood by Hallie like Rafe Fontana has. He's a good man. Look at the way he's cared for his own family. He took Rico to Chicago to get him straightened out. He cared for his mother all those years when she was sick. He's a good man, and if he wants to keep Hallie safe and love her, I'm not standing in the way."

407

"They're in love, you know," Dolly said.

Cordelia looked at her. "Are they?"

"Well, *I* think so. They practically smell like it. I don't blame Hallie—he's got a great butt."

"Dolly—"

"But I don't want her to go to Chicago," Dolly said. "That's too far."

Cordelia shrugged. "I don't, either, but if that's where life leads her, who are we to say?"

Dolly reared back and stared at Cordelia. "What in blazes has happened to you?"

"Oh, I don't know. Could have been Wednesday night when George over here took me out for a drink and explained that I was a little snooty."

"I never said snooty," George said.

"You said I should live and let live."

"What I said was that you had to stop harassing Tanner Sutton."

George was referring to Margaret Sutton Rhodes's son, Tanner. Or, as Cordelia thought of him, Charlie's illegitimate son with his illegitimate lover. Who had once been Cordelia's best friend. And now Tanner was heir to the acreage on the west side. "Well, that's not going to happen—I'm not going to let him build apartments there. But I thought about what you said, George, and I decided you are right. Life doesn't always go according to plan. People need to be happy, and Hallie hasn't been happy in a very long time."

"Again, I was talking about you," George pointed out. "Not Hallie. I didn't know about this thing with her and Rafe."

"Same thing in theory."

"Well, look who woke up and entered the twenty-first century," Dolly said.

Cordelia didn't know if she even believed what she'd said to Martin and again to Dolly and George, but the thing was, she wanted to believe it. She wanted to believe two good people like Hallie and Rafe could be happy. Who was she, or Martin, to interfere? But that was a parent's nature, she guessed.

Run this ranch without Martin? Dumbest thing she'd ever heard.

Cordelia sipped more of the spiked hot tea. "I guess maybe a person can change after sixty years." She glanced at the headstone. "I hear you chuckling, Charlie. Cut it out."

No one spoke for a moment, until Dolly said, "I am never going to get used to you speaking to a headstone."

Cordelia held out her cup. "Top me off, will you?"

Chapter Twenty-six

Christmas was a somber affair for the Prince family, the first without their father, the first without the elaborate gifts they were used to receiving. They still had the towering spruce delivered from Colorado. It almost reached the vaulted ceiling.

Hallie's mother had brought in her interior decorator to trim the tree. Hallie had offered to do it, but her offer might have been half-hearted. She was in the middle of her move to Austin, and she didn't want to be bothered, if she were being honest.

She'd taken an apartment in downtown Austin, and although the drive was only an hour and a half from San Antonio, she'd been trying to establish this new reality for herself. She was trying not to go home every weekend.

She'd been to the Comeback Center on campus and had talked with Tasha, the counselor with whom she'd corresponded in Aspen. Tasha was enthusiastic. She explained to Hallie that much of the coursework could be done online, and really, there were only two courses that would require her physical presence. "You could do one in the spring, one in the summer, so you could work," she'd suggested. The other courses Hallie needed would be self-paced.

Hallie could have her degree by the end of summer. That was exciting. But she found life in Austin to be a little lonely. The city had a different vibe from San Antonio—it had a faster pace and a younger crowd, particularly on campus. At thirty, she felt like a dorm mom walking around campus.

She didn't know anyone, either, and didn't know where to go to make friends. How was it that she was so bad at this? A woman in a coffee bar explained it to her one morning. Hallie had bumped into her, and they'd struck up a friendly conversation as they waited in line for coffee. "Most people move here for a job," the woman said. "That's where they start to make friends. You're in school, right?"

"Will be," Hallie said. "I came here to get established before the semester starts."

"Oh," the young woman said. "Well, good luck." And she was gone.

Hallie needed more than luck. She walked Sulley along the Colorado River every day. She wandered up and down the eclectic shops on South Congress Avenue. And she read. She read everything from romantic comedies, to self-help, to spiritual guides, to thrillers. She read in the early mornings and the evenings. She got herself an actual library card at the Austin Public Library.

When it came time to go home for Christmas, Hallie felt almost relieved. She and Sulley had been in Austin a little more than two weeks, and she was feeling a little homesick. But she was also feeling enlightened about a few things. She and Sulley struck out on a pale blue Christmas Eve morning.

Her grandmother had dug out some of the family treasures—a Santa that had been handed down through generations, but was missing his bag and one shoe. A herd of reindeer for the mantel. Stockings for all of them, which Martin hung. Hallie looked longingly at the stockings hanging from the enormous mantel. They were all there: Grandma, Mom, Nick, Luca, Hallie. And Dad. Grandma had hung Dad's stocking.

They all felt the absence of Charlie Prince. Hallie missed her father desperately, but strangely, she did not miss the big-ticket gifts. No state-of-the-art drones. No cars, no motorcycles. No trips to Paris to shop or Louis Vuitton bags or exquisite jewelry. The holiday seemed calmer and saner without those things. From Luca, Hallie got a pair of pointe shoes. She'd complained about being unable to find her old ones, and with Ella's help, Luca had bought her a pair. From

Nick, a pair of cashmere lounge pants to replace the sweats he said he was sick of seeing. From her grandmother, a framed picture of her and her father that Hallie didn't remember, as well as a new chew toy for Sulley. And from her mother, a triple strand of pearls that her father had given her mother for their tenth wedding anniversary.

"Mom," Hallie said. "Are you sure?"

She smiled and nodded. "He would want you to have it."

The best part of the day was the meal. Just the five of them, as well as Ella and George. It was a remarkable meal in the history of the Prince family. For starters, Hallie's mother had cooked most of it, this time with the help of a cookbook, because apparently, in the two weeks Hallie had been gone, Frederica had departed.

"It wasn't as bad as I thought it would be," her mother announced.

That wasn't the only difference in her mother. She hadn't second-guessed Hallie about her decision. When Hallie had told her she was going back to school, her mother's only question had been, "What does Rafe think?"

"What does Rafe think?" Hallie had echoed, surprised by it. "Well, he's in Chicago. So I don't know."

Her mother's response to that was a single raised eyebrow.

Hallie wondered if maybe her mom's grief was

finally winding down to normal. Or maybe it was simply that she'd finally accepted that Hallie was thirty years old and was capable of running her own life. And yet, that was a little hard to believe, judging by the lifetime Hallie had spent with her mother trying to run her life.

Neither had her mother mentioned Hallie's weight or what she ate. But Hallie was trying to get some weight off for ballet. She wasn't losing anything in spite of her best efforts, although admittedly, her best efforts were pretty lame.

Over dinner, Luca asked where Martin was. "I tried to catch him in the office, but he hasn't been around."

"They've all gone to Chicago to spend the holiday with the boys," Dolly announced.

"So what's up with that?" Luca asked, but he was looking directly at Hallie. "Is Rico staying up there with Rafe for good?"

"I don't . . . no one said anything," she stammered. She could feel her face flaming. But no one pressed her.

The day, while quiet, was one of their better days since her dad had died. She was relieved there weren't a lot of questions for her. Maybe because her would-be wedding day had been planned for New Year's Eve. Hallie had forgotten it, really, because she was distracted by her obsession with Rafe and trying to start this new, independent life in Austin. But a couple of wedding gifts had arrived, sent by people who had not heard the news, and she was reminded again that just two months ago, she'd been devastated.

She was convinced that Luca, Ella, and Nick had analyzed her and had come to their own erroneous conclusions about what had happened between her and Chris when he'd come to town. She guessed that they believed Chris was the cause of her distraction. She let them think whatever they wanted—better that than them knowing she was actually grieving Rafe.

But her distraction was bigger than her broken heart. When she wasn't daydreaming about Rafe—trying to guess what he was doing or thinking of a text to send him or reviewing that afternoon in the gazebo, debating if she'd come on too strong, or not strong enough—she was working on her idea to open her warehouse.

Between Christmas and New Year's Eve, with George's help, she'd found contractors who'd had a look at the warehouses and submitted estimates for renovating one into a ballet studio. She'd even called Genevieve about that lunch, and had gone into San Antonio, had sat on a porch in a terraced backyard in Castle Hills, watching ducks swim around Genevieve's pond, and had asked for Genevieve's help. She didn't know how to find the kids she wanted to target. Genevieve was more than happy to help, but on one condition.

"Let me help you begin ballet again. You have to get over your feelings about your dancing, and I have a studio here to help you do that."

"But I'm in Austin now."

"That's okay. I'm in Austin at least once a week to see David's mother," she said, referring to her husband. "I could come to your place. It's a start, Hallie. Come on, let's see what you've got," she'd said, and had dragged her into her private studio at her house. Standing on borrowed pointe shoes, Hallie went through some poses.

When Genevieve saw how rusty Hallie was, she folded her tiny little arms and shook her head. "We're getting together at least once a week until you get it back. And you *will* get it back, Hallie. You have to believe in yourself."

Hallie was working really hard on doing exactly that.

Mariah put Hallie in touch with a social media marketing expert. "It's a must, Hallie," Mariah had said, and Charlotte had bobbed her head along in agreement. "No one does business without a social media presence. You've gotta go the whole nine yards. Tell her, Charlotte."

"You've gotta go the whole nine yards," Charlotte repeated obediently.

"I don't even have bids back on the warehouse yet," Hallie had said.

"So?" Mariah demanded. "You have to start building buzz *now,* Hallie."

Hallie rang in the New Year with Luca and Ella, but she left before the stroke of midnight because she couldn't keep her eyes open. They both gave her sad smiles, which Hallie assumed was because of their assumption she couldn't face the night that she was supposed to have had her big wedding.

In all honesty, she hardly gave it a thought. Funny how one could go from complete despair to feeling nothing about it in the space of three months, other than the feeling of deep, deep relief that she had not married Chris.

She was surprised when she received a text from Rafe just before midnight. She hadn't heard from him except sporadically, usually when she initiated it. Happy New Year. This was accompanied by a burst of fireworks on the screen. How are you?

Happy New Year! I'm good. You?

Good. Just wanted you to know I was thinking of you.

Her eyes welled with tears. She felt obliged to send him a GIF of fireworks in response. She typed, I really miss you, but then deleted it and typed, Thanks, Rafe.

He did not text back.

She left Three Rivers after the first of the year,

and headed back to her little apartment high atop the world in the middle of Austin. She and Sulley walked to the big windows with the sweeping view of the interstate—the river view had been insanely expensive, even for her—and both of them sighed.

She started the first full week of the year with renewed determination. But between a barre class and another stroll around campus, Hallie felt strangely empty. She wanted so badly to tell Rafe about it, to hear what he had to say. This was supposed to be liberating, but she didn't feel liberated. She felt lonely, and closed off from her family and her friends. And damn it, she missed Rafe like crazy.

She obsessed about what he was doing in Chicago every day.

She attended her education class the first day of the spring semester. When she looked around the room, she saw she was ten years older than these people. What had ever made her think she could pick up where she'd left off? No wonder they allowed so much of the coursework online.

She spent her evenings searching social media to see what Rafe was doing, which was useless, because he didn't post. She posted pictures she took around Austin on Instagram.

Halfway through January, Hallie was reaching the conclusion she'd made a terrible mistake. She was not the sort of person who could strike out on her own without anyone around. She *liked* having people around. She liked being near her family. She liked the ranch, and she did not like the middle of the city. She liked seeing cows and horses, and not a running trail so crowded that she couldn't make any headway on her pace.

She wondered what Rafe was reading. If he'd met someone. If Rico was drinking. She would text him, How is everything? And he would eventually text back, Good. How are you?

That was it.

She was desperate to know how he was doing, but he'd been so hurt by her and so distant in their texts that she feared his rejection. As the month crept along, Hallie began to think of ways to worm her way back into Rafe's life.

Near the end of the month, she was tired a lot, and she felt so *bloated,* in spite of having reduced carbs to trim some weight. And strangely, she was suddenly obsessed with cheesy Tater Tots.

Genevieve had been up twice, and they had practiced ballet in front of the view of the interstate. "You really need a studio," Genevieve had said.

She really did, but she couldn't find one that wasn't a ridiculously long drive across town in heavy traffic.

What she really needed, she thought to her miserable self, was Rafe.

The one bright spot in her new life was the

warehouses. The contractor she had decided to go with was affordable and ready to start the work. Hallie was excited about what he'd drawn up. Maybe Luca was right—maybe her father had left her these warehouses because he trusted her to figure it out. Hallie would never really know, but at last, she was grateful to her dad for leaving them to her. She was throwing her heart and soul into making it happen, all on her own.

She started going home for three or four days at a time to work on the warehouses, enlisting her friends to help and making plans for what she wanted to include.

When she wasn't studying for class, or taking her online course, she was lying on the couch, looking at the ceiling, wishing her neighbor would turn down the heavy metal, and thinking of Rafe.

Always Rafe.

And then she started to think about something else.

On the day she left Austin for home to choose fixtures for the warehouse, she and Sulley pulled into a pharmacy. She bought four pregnancy tests. One to find out, three to make sure.

Chapter Twenty-seven

Nothing could make a man despise a martial arts gym more than icy cold weather, constant plumbing and electrical problems, and a drain on his wallet. Rafe was losing his drive.

Between bribes for inspections, and the many required updates that came along with renovating a very old building to modern standards, and the rent hike that had happened before they'd even opened their door, Rafe and his friends were running on fumes.

"Man, I'll be honest. I've thought about going back to Pittsburgh," Chaco said over dinner one night. "I had a good job there."

"Look, we can make this happen," Jason said. "But we have to get aggressive in getting kids in the door, you know? And fundraising. My sister is going to help us with that. I told you, she does fundraising for a few nonprofits around here."

Rafe thought of Hallie. He thought about Hallie all the time. She knew about fundraising. He tried to picture her here, in this gym, in this neighborhood, raising funds. He didn't know what that looked like, exactly, but he knew she would be beautiful when she did it.

"I agree with Jason," Rico said. "A few road bumps, so what? We need to man up." He gave a fist pump in what Rafe supposed was the signal to "man up."

Rico had taken to Chicago like Rafe could not have guessed. He loved the old neighborhood, the hustle and bustle on the streets every day. He loved the cold. Rafe had long had the impression that Rico didn't like hard work—he'd complained enough about it at home—and he'd assumed he'd have to do a fair amount of babysitting and listening to him whine every day. But he was beginning to understand that what Rico didn't like was ranch work. Cattle and heat were not his thing. Apparently, gyms and cold were. He worked as hard as any of them.

Because Chaco's place was tiny, Rico was staying with Jason and his family on that awful couch, and Rafe was sleeping on Chaco's marginally better couch. Jason's mom had decided to teach Rico Spanish, and Jason was teaching his little sister and Rico martial arts. Rafe thought Jason's little sister had a crush on Rico, and at first he'd worried about that, because Rico could be a dog. But Rico was respectful—he didn't take that bait.

Sobriety had been a struggle for Rico, especially New Year's Eve. But Chaco had been through the same thing, and he was a great support to Rico. "Dude, anytime you have an urge, you call me. We'll go for a run or go get a slice and talk it through."

Knock on wood—so far, Rico had remained sober. He showed up every day, ready to work, and had good ideas. Rafe was really proud of him. This had turned out to be just the thing his brother needed, and Rafe was happy that he was able to make it happen.

But Rafe was beginning to wonder if this was the thing *he* needed.

He'd been planning this gym for years now. He'd believed it was the perfect solution for him—doing what he loved, and on the other side of the country from Hallie. It was still the thing he loved to do, and he was still on the other side of the country from Hallie, which was about as far as he could take his hurt. But it wasn't working. He didn't feel right here.

He didn't feel right in anything. It was like his life was an ill-fitting suit and he couldn't seem to adjust it to make it comfortable.

They'd agreed going in that Jason would be the manager of the gym, as he had the connections and was from Chicago. But Jason couldn't seem to navigate around any of the problems they kept butting up against, and it seemed to Rafe as if the management end had fallen to Jason's father. That was fine for now, but there would come a day when that would need to end, and he worried about how that would go.

The living accommodations were wearing on Rafe, too. He hadn't been able to find a job in social work that would meet the requirements he needed to obtain licensure. Either the jobs that fit didn't pay enough, or they didn't have the credentials for overseeing his work. He'd been surfing Chaco's couch for weeks, and it was getting old. Rafe had sacrificed his comfort during his time in the army, and now, about to turn thirty-three, he wanted his own bed in his own room.

All of these thoughts weighed on him, but the unspoken thing that kept him up at night was Hallie.

Sometimes, when Chaco was sawing some logs in the bedroom, Rafe scrolled through Hallie's Instagram account. She posted a lot of pictures of Sulley, who had already doubled in size. There were a few pictures of Aspen that would crop up every now and then. There were a few family photos—Luca and Ella, Miss Dolly doing tai chi with her friends. And there was one of an empty warehouse with the caption *What's a girl to do?*

Sell it, he guessed.

But most of the pictures she'd posted lately had been ones she'd taken as she wandered around Austin. In all of them, she was alone, smiling at her phone with some landmark in the background.

It was probably his own misery speaking, but her smile was not as bright as it burned in his mind's eye.

He and Hallie had exchanged a few texts over the last few weeks. Not many—he didn't know how he could go back to being chummy, not after he'd left Texas as a fraction of the man he'd been. And the texts were superficial, a lot of *how are you*s. They hid behind words that were easy to send—but without emojis and definitely no GIFs.

How he regretted going to Aspen. He'd existed all these years with his private fantasy—why couldn't he have let it lie?

Toward the end of January, his dad called and said his mother hadn't been feeling well.

"Is it back?" Rafe asked quietly, meaning the cancer. Meaning a third round for his mother.

"Maybe. Can't get her to the doctor," his dad said. "She's being stubborn, and I can't keep up with everything."

That was his father's way of telling him he wanted him home. He didn't know how to tell Rafe in any other way. "I'll take her," he said. "Rico and I will be home in a couple of weeks for his court appearance, and I'll get her to the doctor, Dad."

He could now add that worry to his nightly agony.

Just before they were to leave for that trip home, the gym hit another snag—an inspector informed them they didn't meet the ADA requirements for entry and exit.

"You gotta have a wheelchair ramp," the guy said.

"No one told us that," Jason said angrily, and looked around for the contractor. To Rafe, it was just another in a long line of mishaps and roadblocks, of giant flags waving at him, telling him to go home.

The next day, as Rafe watched Rico pack for home, Rafe surprised himself when he said, "I think I've had it with this deal."

"What deal?" Rico asked, his attention on his bag.

"The gym. The whole thing."

Rico looked at him with surprise. "Are you kidding me right now?"

Rafe shook his head.

Rico gaped at him. "Don't give up *now.* We're almost there. We're so close."

"I don't know, Rico—I've put a lot of money into this, and it looks like it's going to take a lot more."

"See? That's what I'm saying—you've worked a long time toward this."

He sighed. He felt weary to his marrow. "Sometimes, you just have to know when to fold a bad hand."

"Well, this isn't that," Rico said. "You just need a break. Look, we're going home for a few days. When we come back, you'll feel differently."

"Maybe so," Rafe said. But he couldn't shake the feeling that this project, initially conceived by three soldiers in Afghanistan, was beginning to feel too heavy. Like a years-long slog toward nothing. All the money he'd worked so hard to save was sinking into a black hole of constant needs, and they still had nothing to show for it, other than an unfinished building. But its biggest failing was that it hadn't achieved his secret goal of taking his mind away from Hallie.

They arrived in San Antonio to miserably cold rain that fit Rafe's mood. Rafe took the late afternoon to pay a visit to John Horowitz. John was home now, and had a physical therapist coming around to see him twice a week. But John lived with his mother in a tiny little house. It had been equipped for John's new reality, but it was an old house, and the rooms were small, the hallways narrow. It was hard for him to get around. There certainly wasn't enough space to do adequate martial arts therapy. Rafe thought that if he were around, he could make a few changes to that house to help John out. Take out a wall. Widen the door to the bathroom.

John was unflaggingly enthusiastic, convinced that he would be able to live without help one day very soon.

Rafe wanted more than anything to help John achieve that goal.

On his way home, he noticed trucks outside Hallie's warehouses. *What's a girl to do?* As he drove by, he noticed her car parked next to the trucks. It was the middle of the week. He thought she lived in Austin now.

He'd meant to text her and let her know he'd be in Three Rivers for a few days, but he hadn't. It had seemed pointless, really. But seeing her car spurred an overwhelming desire to see her in the flesh. He drove down the road another tenth of a mile or so, then turned around and went back, pulling in and parking next to her car.

He sat and stared at the warehouse. His gut was churning. He didn't know what to expect. Would she be happy to see him? Would it matter, because his chest felt like it was about to explode? "Yeah, well, you're here. No turning back now." He got out and went in.

The moment he stepped inside, he was instantly rushed by Sulley, who announced Rafe's arrival with a lot of barking, and then a launch at Rafe's legs, his tail wagging. Rafe went down on one knee to greet his travel buddy properly. "Hey, Sulley, how are you?" he asked, scratching the dog behind the ears. "I'm happy to see you, too, buddy."

Sulley pushed off from Rafe and raced away, probably looking for someone to praise his greeting skills. Rafe stood up and glanced down, and only then noticed that, apparently, Sulley was muddy. And now he was, too.

"Rafe!"

He glanced up from trying to get some of the mud off him. Hallie was standing in the middle of the warehouse, her hands shoved into the pockets of her sheepskin coat. She was wearing ear-muffs, beat-up jeans, and work boots. She looked surprised, but her happy smile glowed, and his heart was melting. His poor, beat-up heart.

"Hey," he said sheepishly. He felt uncharacter-istically awkward, and dragged his fingers through his hair.

"I didn't know you were in town!" she said, coming forward. "You should have told me!"

"Just got in. Did you take up carpentry while I was gone?"

"Sort of." Her smile deepened. "You have mud all over you."

"Sulley greeted me."

"He likes the mud puddles. Come in. I'll show you where you can clean up."

He followed her deeper into the warehouse, where workers were putting down some flooring.

Hallie led him into the offices and all the way to the back to a bathroom that was being enlarged. A wall to the open bay had been removed, and the opening was covered with heavy plastic. "What's going on?" Rafe asked.

"I am building a ballet studio. Surprise!" She pulled a piece of paper towel off the roll and stuck it under a sink faucet.

"Really? You're going to dance again?"

"Well, sort of. Genevieve has been coaching me."

Another surprise. "I didn't think you were friends."

Her eyes were glittering when she turned to face him. "Funny how things have a way of changing when you're an adult."

Yes, funny that.

She brushed the towel against his shirt. "She's actually very nice."

Rafe couldn't take his gaze from her eyes. "I was surprised to see your car. I thought you were in Austin."

"Oh. Yes, I am in Austin. In a way," she said with a flutter of her fingers.

What did that mean?

She concentrated on his shirt. "Oh, and guess what? Luca and Ella are building a house on his land. When they get married, they're moving into his loft until it's finished. And when it's finished, they are going to totally immerse themselves in ecological rejuvenation." She paused, her smile deepening. "That's a direct quote." She arched a brow.

Rafe and Hallie broke into simultaneous laughter. Hallie loved her brother, but she and Rafe had sometimes found Luca's enthusiasm for conservation amusing. "I guess the prairie chickens paid off after all," he said.

Hallie giggled, then pulled a sorrowful face.

"Don't make fun, Rafe. That has turned into a very tragic story. There are only about a dozen of them left, according to Luca. He's distraught. And vowing revenge." Before Rafe could ask revenge against whom, she said, "It's *so* good to see you."

His eyes moved over her face, remembering every freckle, the exact placement of her dimples. She had no idea what it meant to him to see her. "You, too, Hallie," he said quietly.

Her smile softened. "I've really missed you, you know that? *So much,*" she whispered.

Those words squeezed his throat. Rafe couldn't help himself; he touched her cheek. His heart had melted, and he felt like the rest of him was crumbling into dust again. *Missing* was too inadequate a word for the way he'd felt. An entire history that lived in him had been extracted, and left in its place was a gaping, weeping hole. "Same."

"I guess it would be inappropriate to kiss you hello?"

"I'm not sure that's a good idea," he said.

"Since when have I gone with the good ideas?"

Hallie. His heart was already broken. What was one more kiss? "I suppose I could allow it this once."

Her eyes sparkled. "Okay, here goes. Do you need to hold on to something?"

Only you. He shook his head.

She slid her hands up his chest, and around his neck. She pulled his head down to her, lifted her face, and touched her lips to his, so softly. So reverently. So carefully. His senses, which had lain dormant these last few weeks, began to unfurl. He put his arms around her waist. He drew her closer. He was falling back to another time, to Aspen, and all his emotions, all the desire began to wave.

But then Hallie slipped down and pushed back. She looked alarmed. "Oh no."

"What?" he asked, confused.

She suddenly turned around and retched into the toilet.

"Oh!" Rafe said, grimacing.

She retched again.

"Hallie! Oh no, Hallie, no." He had to turn around and face the wall, swallowing down the nausea that started to build. "Jesus, are you okay?"

Her response was to flush the toilet. "Sorry! I must have eaten something that didn't agree with me."

"Do you need to sit down?" he asked the wall, still afraid to turn.

"I don't think so. I feel much better. You can turn around now."

He heard the sink begin to run, heard her rinse her mouth. He slowly pivoted toward her. "Are you okay?"

She grinned sheepishly. "I think so. Come on. Let me show you around."

She pushed aside the plastic flap and stepped into the warehouse. The kiss, the moment, was gone. Rafe hesitantly followed.

She opened the bay door and said they were going to put in a big picture window. "It's pretty, isn't it?"

He would say beautiful. All trees and a creek, and even as they stood there, looking out at the rain-drenched landscape, a hawk perched on a fence post and calmly stared back at them. In the distance, a few cows grazed alongside goats. "That's Prince land for you," Rafe said. "Prettiest country in this part of Texas."

"That's Prince land?" she said, her voice full of wonder. "The ranch is too damn big."

Rafe laughed. He wanted to put his arm around her.

She showed him the flooring samples, and the mirrors they would install. "So who is going to dance here?" he asked.

"I'm so glad you asked," she said. "Remember the little girl in the Thanksgiving Day show? The one who made you cry?"

"I didn't *cry*."

"You cried," Hallie said breezily. "My idea is to teach more kids like her to dance. I've been in contact with a group in San Antonio that serves the needs of disabled kids. And I'm talking to the school district. I'm going to advertise, too, and get the word out, and Genevieve is going to help me. I'm excited, Rafe. You inspired me."

"Me?"

"Yes! By what you're doing in Chicago. But really, because you were the one who encouraged me to figure out what I needed and not what I thought others expected of me."

"I did?"

She laughed. "You did!"

Rafe looked around him. She'd accomplished so much in a short amount of time. "But what about Austin? Aren't you in school?"

Hallie didn't answer for a moment. When he looked at her, she smiled a little. "I'm enrolled," she said. "I'm learning a lot about myself."

That was not an answer, but he wasn't going to press it. The less he knew, the easier it was to keep his emotions in check. Or so he assumed. "This looks great, Hallie. Congratulations."

She smiled gratefully. "How about you? How is it going in Chicago?"

Rafe shrugged. He forced himself to smile. "It's going. Rico loves the work."

"Fantastic."

She asked about Rico, and Rafe told her how he was actually making it work, both in terms of a job and his sobriety. But the more he talked, the more he ached, and he finally said, "Well, it was great to see you, Hallie. I should probably go."

"Oh." She turned toward the door. "Right. Probably best. Talk to you later?"

"Sure," he said, and started for the door.

"Tell your mom I said hi!" she called after him.

Rafe glanced back. He watched her swipe up her camera from a bench on her way and walked to where the workmen were setting big mirrors on the walls.

He made himself leave. He felt strangely sad. He wasn't part of this, not even as a text advisor. Not even a little. She really had moved on with her life.

Later that evening, he looked at her Instagram. She'd posted pictures from the warehouse today. Mostly pictures of Sulley sitting on a tool belt. And the obligatory selfie taken in front of one of the newly installed mirrors.

For the millionth time, Rafe closed his eyes and thought of Aspen.

Chapter Twenty-eight

Hallie was definitely pregnant.

If the tests hadn't convinced her—she had an amazing capacity to argue what she wanted to be true as opposed to the truth displayed on four pee sticks—the morning sickness definitely had.

She was hiding her bouts of sickness, too, and that was getting difficult. She had finally convinced her mother that her general queasiness was the result of an intolerance to milk and milk products.

"Since when?" her mother had demanded.

"I don't know. For a while," Hallie had said vaguely. "I need to be careful."

She wasn't even remotely prepared for a pregnancy, and she'd been shocked by it, too. It figured that she would be in the two percent of the population for whom condoms were not effective. But even in the midst of her fluster, she felt surprisingly excited about it. Thrilled, actually.

Hallie desperately wanted to tell Rafe. She didn't know how he would take the news, but one thing she knew with all her heart—Rafe Fontana would do what he thought was the right thing. He would insist they get married. But Hallie didn't know if she wanted to get married. She loved Rafe, she really did, more than anything—but to get married because she was pregnant? That seemed exactly like something the old Hallie would do because it was easier. It was expected. But the new Hallie was perfectly capable of being a single mother.

Well, she hoped she was, anyway.

Of course she would love it if she and Rafe could raise a child together. But she didn't want Rafe to marry her out of a sense of duty. She wanted him to marry her if it was right for them both. At least after a period of proper dating instead of sneaking around. She didn't want any misguided notions that he was saving her, either, because she didn't need anyone to save her from this. She'd already figured things out for herself—she would push herself to finish the coursework before the baby came. She didn't need to live in Austin to do that—the two cities were close enough that she could make the drive to Austin once a week for class and do the rest online, just as Tasha at the Comeback Center had explained.

But Hallie wasn't moving back to the ranch either. She was doing this on her own terms. She *needed* to do this on her own. But if she did it with Rafe, even better. As she saw it, she had a choice between two positives: her and a baby, or her, a baby, and Rafe.

She talked to Ella about renting her little house. "But what about Austin?" Ella asked.

"I figured out I don't need to be there. I'm only going to one class on campus and the rest is online."

"Wait," Luca said, appearing from Ella's little kitchen. "You're not giving up—"

"I am not," Hallie said, bristling a little, although it was a fair assumption to make, given her history of giving up. "I have a very firm plan to finish school and open a studio, all by myself. I am changing my location. And if you guys are building a house, why not let me rent this?"

"Sure," Ella said.

Luca looked at his fiancée. "Don't you want to think about it for even a minute?"

Ella smiled at him and patted his cheek. "Nope."

Everything was falling into place, and now Hallie had to tell Rafe, and sooner rather than later. She just wanted to know how he felt about her first, especially after she'd hurt him like she had. So she came up with a plan to show him how great it could be, the two of them, if he still loved her. She was going to gently guide him into thinking it was his idea.

Just like Grandma had guided Grandpa.

Her first opportunity came when she ran into Rico at the ranch, and he'd gushed about how *amazing* Chicago was, and how *brilliant* his brother was for coming up with such an idea. Hallie had seized the opportunity to gush, too, telling Rico that Rafe had inspired her, and she was doing something similar. Except with ballet.

"Really?" Rico had seemed a little too surprised, frankly.

"Tell you what. Get Rafe and come and see. You guys can help me hang a few things."

So they came, and they were here now, walking around her warehouse. Rafe was a few steps behind Hallie and Rico, eying her with a little bit of suspicion and a little bit of amusement as she showed Rico every nook and cranny. "You know, when I found out Dad left me these warehouses, I didn't know what I would do with them. But they're so convenient to Three Rivers and San Antonio. And *cheap.* The renovation is hardly costing me a thing."

Rico and Rafe exchanged a look.

"Too bad you didn't have this in Chicago," she said breezily. "If you'd stayed here, you could have opened your gym right next door." She pointed to the east wall and the adjoining warehouse. "You could have had it for free!"

Rico's eyes widened. Rafe frowned. "It

wouldn't be free. There would be rent and renovation costs."

"Oh, Rafe," she said, laughing. "I own these warehouses outright. Who needs rent?"

She could have used the rent, but that was beside the point.

"I think there's already a program like ours around here," Rico said. "Didn't you work with them one year, Rafe?"

"It wasn't quite the same as ours," Rafe said. "And there definitely isn't anything like what we could do for wounded soldiers."

Rico and Hallie looked at him. "What wounded soldiers?" Rico asked.

Rafe shrugged. "Just an idea." When he noticed Rico and Hallie continuing to stare at him, he waved his hand. "My pal John Horowitz—he could use a program like ours."

"The guy with no legs?" Rico asked. "The one in San Antonio?"

"The guy with one leg," Rafe corrected him. "I told him I'd help him out. It's not impossible for wounded soldiers to practice martial arts."

Rico's brows rose to his hairline. But Hallie saw an opening—a door opened so wide that the sun was shining through it.

Next, she coerced Luca into inviting Rafe to Ella's house for dinner.

Luca groaned. "Don't get me involved."

"Involved in what?" Hallie asked.

"Hallie, just tell him how you feel about him."

"What? I don't—you are—" She choked. "He's just a friend," she insisted.

Luca rolled his eyes. "Whatever, Hallie. You invite him if you want to spend time with him. It's not like Rafe and I hang out."

"Well, maybe you should. He's a nice guy. And if *I* invite him, everyone will think it means something. Like it's a date."

"Oh, and we can't have *that*," Luca said, folding his arms.

"Your imagination is running wild, Luca. Just do it. Please."

Luca gave her a good once-over, then sighed. "Fine. But you owe me."

"You're acting like I'm making you walk over hot coals."

"Ella's not very social, okay?" he said, and walked out of her room. "But I'll do it!"

Rafe, Luca later reported, was reluctant. But he finally agreed to come when Ella asked.

Hallie didn't know how to take this report, but decided she was not going to be dissuaded. She would have called the whole thing off if she hadn't been carrying his baby. "I thought Ella wasn't very social," Hallie said.

"She likes Rafe," he said. "*Everyone* likes Rafe," he added, sounding a little miffed by it. "And she likes you, too, Hallie."

"Who doesn't?" Hallie asked, and batted her eyes at him.

So Rafe came the night of their little supper party, and Ella took him on a tour of the little house with the two bedrooms, the single bath, living room, and kitchen. The house had new floors, a new roof, and new paint, and the kitchen had been spruced up with modern appliances.

"Nice," Rafe said, looking around. His gaze fell to the door leading out of the kitchen to the back porch, where a thin screen separated them from a pig, a dog, and a couple of chickens in the background. "Are those the prairie chickens?" Rafe asked.

Hallie laughed. Luca glared at her. "Just chickens," he said somberly, and then launched into an explanation of how important prairie chickens were to returning this ranchland to its natural state. Rafe seemed interested, so of course Luca warmed up to him then.

Over burgers, Luca asked about Rafe's project in Chicago.

"We've run into some unexpected expenses," he said.

"Oh?" Hallie asked, perking up. For Rafe's sake, she didn't want to hope there was big trouble in Chicago. But she hoped there was big trouble in Chicago.

"The building codes and the system to get

renovations approved is insane and expensive," he said. "More than we bargained for."

"That sucks," Ella said.

"It does. It's lost a bit of its sparkle for me. Surprisingly, Rico loves it. It's the first time I've seen him excited about something, you know?" He looked up. "And he's sober. He's poured himself into the work and is learning about it."

"That's amazing," Hallie said.

Rafe offered to help Ella clean up. "Great," Luca said. "Hallie, you're with me. We have animals to feed, and if you haven't fed Priscilla, you're in for a treat."

"I can't wait," Hallie said. But when she stood up, she felt queasy. "Just a minute," she said, holding up a finger, hoping it would pass. Nope. It wasn't passing. "Excuse me."

She hurried to the bathroom.

When she finally came out, Luca was standing on the other side of the door, his arms crossed. "What the hell? What's the matter with you?"

"Just a bug or something."

"Really? Because I just watched you eat a cheeseburger in like three bites."

"I was hungry," she said, and looked past him to see if anyone was listening. "A person can't be hungry when she has a bug?"

"Hallie." Luca stepped closer. Hallie stepped back. "You know you can talk to me about anything."

Oh *Lord,* Luca had guessed the truth, and he was going to want to know who the father was, and she was going to have to lie because no way was she telling Luca before she told Rafe. "Listen—"

"Just tell me the truth, please, and I'll do whatever I need to do to help you."

"It's sort of hard to explain." How could she possibly explain anything with Rafe not thirty feet from where they stood?

Luca frowned. "So it *is* an eating disorder?" he whispered, looking appropriately horrified.

"An eat—" Hallie launched herself at him and pummeled his chest. "Are you insane?" She shoved him away, yanked on the hem of her shirt, and stepped around him.

"It was just a question," he said as he followed her outside to feed the animals.

"It was a stupid question!"

With the kitchen cleaned and the animals fed, Rafe thanked Luca and Ella and said he had to get home. "I'm taking my mom in for some tests in the morning." He grabbed his jacket and thrust his arms into it. "Thank you—I really appreciate the meal."

"Good luck in Chicago, man," Luca said.

"Wait!" Hallie said. "Can you give me a ride home?"

"I'll take you home," Luca suggested. "I'm going there anyway."

Hallie shot a look at her brother, but Ella, bless her, understood the girl code even if she didn't understand what was happening. "Actually, Rafe, that would be a big help. We'd drive her, but I don't feel so well."

"Is something going around?" Luca asked, looking between Hallie and Ella.

"Sure," Rafe said, because he was the sort of man who would not refuse the request of his host. He opened the door.

Hallie put on her coat and picked up her purse. "Thank you so much for everything," she said to Ella.

"We should do it again." Ella put her arm around Luca's waist and leaned her head against his shoulder. "Take care!" She shut the door, and they could hear Luca ask her if she needed him to get some TUMS for her.

Rafe looked at Hallie. "What's going on?"

"What? I need a ride, that's all."

"Uh-huh," he said as they walked down the porch steps to his truck. He opened the passenger door for her, and when she was in, he went around and got in behind the wheel. "Nice evening," he said. "I haven't hung out with Luca since we were kids. I really like him and Ella."

"Well, I obviously like them, too."

He smiled. "It was nice spending time with you, Hallie. I'm grateful that we can still be friends."

Friends. Fortunately it was dark, and he didn't see her anxiety.

"So Ella said you were going to rent her house," he said as they pulled onto the road. "What about school?"

"I'm not quitting! I have a plan, and I will finish."

He said nothing.

She looked at his hand. She wanted to hold it, to press it against her heart.

"I like Ella's little house. I can just picture it after you put your mark on it. Flowers hanging upside down from the ceiling. Broken champagne glasses. Fancy dresses used as planters."

"Ah, Rafe," she said. "You really do get me. And I get you! You should seriously think about using my warehouse space if the Chicago thing doesn't work out."

He chuckled. "The Chicago thing better work out—I've sunk most of my life savings into it."

They had reached the end of the county road, and Rafe put on the turn signal to turn right.

Hallie felt a little frantic. She didn't want to go home just yet. "Can we get some ice cream?"

"You want ice cream?" he asked, sounding surprised.

She didn't really want ice cream. "Yes. Dairy Queen."

He smiled. "If the lady wants ice cream," he

said, and he turned left and drove into Three Rivers, straight to the Dairy Queen.

The ice cream place was busy. Kids in red aprons and hats ran cones and floats out to cars. Hallie ordered an ice cream cone. Rafe declined. It was a busy night at the Dairy Queen, and the cone was taking a while to get to them.

"Do you miss Texas?" Hallie asked curiously as they waited.

Rafe looked out the driver's window. "I guess I do. It's pretty damn cold up there."

Another moment of silence ticked by. Then he asked, "How is it with you and the doc?"

"Done and dusted," Hallie reported. "I told him I'd get a restraining order if he didn't cut it out."

Rafe chuckled.

"I'm serious," Hallie said. "What about you, Rafael Fontana? Have you met anyone up there in cold Chicago?"

He slowly turned his head to look at her. "Seriously?"

"Why do you look like that?"

"Like what?"

"Like I asked if you were kicking puppies or something. You're a guy. Sooner or later that itch is going to hit, and I happen to know from personal experience that your itch is pretty insistent when it hits."

"Not fair," he said.

"Why not?"

"Because, Hallie, it's only been a few short weeks since you . . ." He pressed his lips together.

"You can say it," she said quietly.

"Since you sent me on my way. How's that?"

That was not what he meant to say, and she knew it. There were so many things she wanted to say to him. Like how she loved him. How she needed him. How her feelings for him hadn't lessened since they'd been apart, but had only grown. "I'm really sorry about that," she said softly. "*So* sorry. I thought I was doing the right thing."

"Don't worry about it," he muttered, and rolled down his window to a kid with an ice cream cone. Rafe handed her the cone, paid the kid, and then looked at Hallie. "Don't choke on it, now."

He put the truck into gear and drove while Hallie half-heartedly ate the ice cream she really didn't want now. Rafe was still nursing his hurt, and she didn't know how to fix it.

He turned through the ornate gates of the ranch, coasted down the drive, and parked near the front of the house so Hallie could pop inside.

She wiped her mouth with the back of her hand. "Thank you for the ice cream."

"Welcome," he said, inclining his head graciously.

They sat there, staring at each other, and it felt to Hallie like a million sparks were passing between them. A million unspoken words. She couldn't help herself; she twisted around in her seat. "Are you ever going to forgive me?"

"There is nothing to forgive," he said.

They both knew that wasn't true. "Are we ever going back to the way we were?"

Rafe smoothed a bit of hair from her face. "I don't know, Hallie. It would be nice if we could, but I don't know."

He had to know. She *needed* to know. "I really do miss you," she said, and then suddenly pitched forward and kissed him on the lips.

But when she started to pull away, he put his hand on the back of her head and kept her there, deepening the kiss, and shifting in his seat to meet her halfway. He kissed her like she'd kissed him the first time. As if he'd been lost without her. As if he'd been waiting for just this moment. The kiss was frighteningly arousing, and Hallie feared she might be only moments away from ripping off her clothes and straddling his lap. She slid her hand into his shirt, to skin so warm to the touch, and he responded with a tiny sigh of contentment—

Light suddenly flooded the cab. Motion detector lights threw the spotlight on them, and both of them gasped and wrenched away from each other. Rafe sat up, peering out the windshield. "Cat," he said.

"*Cat?* We don't have a cat." She leaned forward. She clucked her tongue as a big black-and-white cat sauntered by. "Mr. Creedy's." She pressed a hand to her chest. "I feel like I'm fifteen all over again and making out with Jason Park."

"You made out with Jason Park?"

Hallie nodded.

"I made out with his sister, Emily."

They both started to giggle, which quickly escalated into gales of laughter. Rafe put his arm around Hallie's neck and kissed her temple. "You're one of a kind, Hallie Prince."

"So are you, Rafe Fontana." She smiled at him, waiting. She thought this was the moment he would confess that he still loved her, and Chicago was too cold, and they could live at Ella's and raise a baby and a pig, and they would be so happy.

But he didn't say that. He reached across her and opened the passenger door.

"Is that it?" she asked.

He smiled so sadly that Hallie's heart lurched. "I won't make the same mistake again, Hal."

"Oh," she said weakly. "Okay." She looked at the door. "How long are you in town, anyway?"

"Another week. Mom has some doctor appointments."

"Well, could you maybe come by the warehouse this week and help me install the ballet barres?"

Rafe's gaze narrowed a little. "Correct me if I'm wrong, but don't you have an entire construction crew to do that?"

Rats. "I have an extra one I decided to install. It's in the garage. So will you?"

Rafe rubbed his neck.

"I'll take that as a yes," she said, hopped out, gave him a tiny wave, and ran into the house.

When she stepped inside, she paused just inside the door, her back to it, listening to his truck drive away.

Hallie closed her eyes. She loved him so much she ached with it. She wanted him to love her just like that, so hard that he ached. God, but she'd made a huge mistake. She'd mortally wounded him, she could feel it. She'd left him in the gazebo because she'd needed to figure out her path. Well, she had, and her path included him, but she didn't know if he would ever trust her enough to believe that it did. And even if he never did, she was going to have to tell him about the baby. She desperately wanted him to truly want to be with her before she did. She didn't want to spend a lifetime guessing if the baby was the reason he was with her.

She took several deep breaths, pushed away from the door, and walked into the kitchen.

"There you are."

Hallie shrieked, and clapped a hand over her heart. Her mother was sitting in one of the chairs near the fireplace in the breakfast nook. "You scared me to death!"

"Sorry."

Hallie dropped her hand. Her mother had a box on her lap. Hallie recognized it as the box Dad had left her mother. None of them knew what was in it, but whatever it was, it had made her mother cry from time to time. "What are you doing?" Hallie asked.

"Just looking at a few things."

"Are you okay?"

"Oh, I'm fine," her mother said. "This box used to tear me to pieces, but it gives me strange comfort now. Funny how grief works—at first it's like a knife, and you can't breathe, and you think you'll die. But with time, the pain dulls, doesn't it? I can actually laugh now about things Charlie and I did."

Hallie walked over and sat in the chair next to her mother.

Her mother smiled at her. "Tell me something, Hallie. Are you in love with Rafe Fontana?"

Hallie's mouth dropped. "No!" She didn't know why she denied it. Maybe because she didn't want to hear her mother tell her why she disapproved.

"You don't have to tell me," her mother said lightly. "It's just an intuition I have. That, and you were sitting in his truck outside for a while."

She was looking at Hallie so thoughtfully that it made Hallie nervous. "What if I am?" she asked flippantly. "Are you going to lecture me on it being too soon after Chris, or say he's not the right guy for a Prince princess?"

"A few months ago I definitely would have done that, wouldn't I?" she mused. "But now? I don't know. I guess I'd tell you to make sure he was the right one for you."

Hallie peered at her mother. She didn't say things like that. She said things like, *Who are his people?*

"You know, your dad and I had some pretty big ups and some pretty spectacular downs. If I have one regret, it's that I wish we'd been a little less volatile around you kids. And yet, in spite of everything, and all that he did, I never wanted anyone but him. He was the right one, and I don't regret the heartache he caused me for a moment."

"Are you serious? He cheated on you," Hallie reminded her.

"Hmm," her mother said, as if she hadn't thought of that. "Well, let's just say I am serious right now having had a couple of glasses of wine. I guess if you were standing on the outside of our marriage, you wouldn't believe that cheating Charlie was the right man for me. But he *was* the perfect man for me, and I want *you* to have the perfect man for you. If it's Chris, if it's Rafe, if it's Prince Harry, I don't care. I just want him to be the right one for you."

"This is pretty astounding, coming from you, Mom," Hallie said.

Her mother laughed and picked up her wine-glass. "Tell me about it," she said, and drank.

Hallie never did answer her mother whether or not she was in love with Rafe. But in hindsight, she didn't have to. Her mother knew.

Rafe was the right one, the perfect man for Hallie. She knew that now. She knew it based on how badly she missed him.

The only problem was getting Rafe to believe it.

Chapter Twenty-nine

Rafe didn't know if coming home was the best thing he could have done for himself, or maybe the worst.

He couldn't seem to get away from Hallie, no matter how much he needed to for the sake of his own sanity. One minute he was installing ballet barres, and the next minute, he was in a big-box home store helping her pick out wall art. That turned into dinner in San Antonio, which included a healthy debate on whether or not ballet was as hard as martial arts.

"Martial arts are combat, Hallie. Ballet is art."

"Oh yeah, your 'combat training' is going to come in really handy when planks of wood attack and need to be judoed."

God, he loved that woman.

It had made a mess of his brain. He'd been so hurt by her rejection, but his mind was willing to let him forget it. He could feel himself growing less and less interested in Chicago, too. It was beginning to feel like a chore he had to tackle. His lack of enthusiasm astounded him after he had put his heart and soul into that project. But it had always been a plan B. He had always needed to be someplace Hallie was not after she married. And when she started a family.

Jason texted him with regular updates—the electricity had to be rewired again. The plumbing for which they'd just paid an outrageous amount sprang a leak in one of the lines. Nevertheless, Jason said they ought to be able to launch in March. Three months behind schedule and thousands of dollars later. When are you coming back?

Rafe let that one go. He didn't know quite yet. Rico's court appearance was at the end of the week, and depending on what happened with that, it could be as soon as the weekend.

That seemed too soon. He'd taken his mother to the doctor, and the test results wouldn't be in until next week. She'd assured him she was fine, it was just a precaution, but Rafe wasn't so sure. She didn't look great. She had that look of fatigue in her eyes, the pasty skin that came with not eating right or enough.

One night, he'd mentioned to his dad that he was worried about insurance if he should get laid off. "If Mom's sick, how are we going to manage it if you don't have a job?"

"Oh, that," his dad had said with a dismissive flick of his wrist. "Mrs. Prince and I have had a meeting of the minds. I'm not worried about losing my job."

"What? When?"

"A month or so ago," his father said. "She admitted she can't run this ranch without me and isn't planning to anytime soon."

That news was a relief, and it only heightened his obsession with Hallie, always present in his thoughts.

Not that he'd changed his mind about the viability of the two of them. There were still so many things to consider. Mostly, his ability to trust her with his heart. But a lot of it had to do with his own fear of not being able to live up to what Hallie needed or wanted. She had lived a life that he'd viewed from afar, had been to places he couldn't imagine, had every privilege a person could have in this world. How could he compete? And the one time he'd tried to be the man she wanted, she had sent him packing.

But Hallie was different now. Something had changed with her, and he didn't know what it was. Maybe it was just as she said—she didn't need to be in Austin. She had set her goals, was accomplishing them by herself. But why had she come back to Three Rivers?

Ella had said something that night when he was helping her with the dishes. Rafe really liked Ella—she was quiet, and she seemed very perceptive. He'd mentioned how much Hallie and Luca seemed to like her little house.

Ella had laughed. She said, "Have you ever

noticed that they're both kind of desperate for a normal life? They had a lot of things growing up, but there was a lot of strife, too, and I have this feeling that they both want what the whole world wants." She looked at him, and her gaze pierced his in a way that he hadn't expected. "You know, someone who loves them completely. That's what matters to them, I think. Not the things."

It was what mattered to him, too.

On the day of Rico's plea agreement, the entire family went to court, prepared to tell the judge how hard he was working to correct his mistake. Rico's court-appointed attorney drew Rico aside, and when Rico returned, he was grinning. He said the state was offering a plea of guilty in exchange for probation, but that his attorney was going to request that the deal include approval for him to work in Chicago. As long as Rico had monthly drug tests and didn't drink and returned for status hearings, his lawyer didn't think it would be a problem.

Rafe's father's chin began to tremble.

"What?" Rico said, and put his arm around his father's shoulders. "Come on, Dad. I love what we're doing up there. It's a *good* thing. I've been working, like you want. I haven't been drinking."

"I know, Rico," his father said. "I feel like I'm losing both my sons."

The judge granted Rico's request. But any

deviation from the plan, he warned, would result in the revocation of his probation.

That night, Rafe wandered into Rico's room. He was already packing, even though they didn't leave until the day after tomorrow.

"Dude, you've got time," Rafe said.

"I want to be ready," Rico responded.

Rafe stretched out on Rico's bed. "Why do you want to be there so bad?"

"I don't know. It's just . . . Jason and Chaco, they aren't judging me, man. Here, it feels like everyone is waiting for me to fail, you know? And I like it. I like the work, I like the vibe." He smiled at Rafe. "If it weren't for you, I wouldn't have figured it out."

Rafe wished he could figure it out for himself.

"I wish I'd started way back, when you first tried to get me into a program, remember? But I get it now, bro. I can give back. I know that doesn't sound like me, but I'm different now. I'm twenty-nine years old, and I don't have squat. I want to change that. I want to change who I am. I'm sick of being a coward about life."

It was an interesting admission from Rico. He and Rico had more in common than Rafe had really understood. He wanted to change, too. He was sick of being a coward, too.

Rafe got up and walked to the window. He looked out at the night sky, darkly blue, a thousand stars shining down on them. You couldn't see the stars as well as this in Chicago, not with all the lights. "Here's the thing, Rico. Our program won't be able to support much more than Jason in the beginning. That's why Chaco has a job and I was looking for one."

"I can get a job," Rico said quickly. "I'll wash dishes—"

"So what if you took my place?" Rafe said. The words slipped out of his mouth before he could catch them back. He hadn't really thought through the idea clearly—it had just come out. As if his heart was doing the thinking now.

"Huh?"

"I mean, you'd have to get back here for your court appointments without me doing it for you." He turned from the window and looked at his brother.

Rico's eyes narrowed. "What the hell? You've been working on this gym for a long time. And you're just going to let me take it?"

"I don't know," Rafe said with a wince. "I belong on the ranch, Rico. This is who I am. I'm not feeling Chicago."

That was it. That was the crux of his discontent. He wasn't feeling it. What he was feeling was a need to be here. With his parents, his mother especially. As much as he'd resented their need of him, he guessed he'd given them every reason to expect it. He would never feel right about himself if he wasn't there for them.

And then, of course, there was this irresistible need to be near Hallie. It was happening all over again, his infatuation swelling and absorbing all his common sense.

Yesterday, she'd talked him into changing fluorescent bulbs in the warehouse—she insisted he call it a studio—and while he was up on the ladder, she took pictures of him. "Cut that out," he'd said.

"Make me." She'd taken another picture.

So Rafe surprised her by leaping off the ladder and grabbing her up, kissing the shout of surprise from her mouth.

That kiss, a playful one, quickly turned molten. His hand was in her hair, and she clutched his jacket. He could feel himself hardening, could feel the desire billowing, ready to set sail. He wanted her as bad as he'd ever wanted sleep or food. She felt that essential to him. But with a grimace, he'd made himself stop. What was different? What could he possibly expect from that?

"Don't stop," she said, and pressed against him. "We can go to my car—"

"We're not teenagers."

"Do you have a better option?"

He put his hands on her arms. That was just it. There *were* better options, but they were sneaking around like teenagers, stealing kisses here and there, because he couldn't bring himself to take that leap. "Not at the moment."

Hallie groaned. She pressed her head to his chest. "You're killing me, Rafe, you know that? You act like you want to be with me, and then you don't." She suddenly straightened up and stepped back. "You know what? I don't want to play this game anymore. I love you. I really, *really* love you, in case you haven't figured that out. I know I hurt you, and I know you think I'll do it again—"

"I never said—"

"You don't have to! I just know it. I don't know what else to say except that I love you so much, and if that's not enough, I don't know what is. I made a mistake, Rafe. I thought I was doing the right thing, but I have learned so much about myself, and the right thing for me is *you*." She turned around and walked into the offices and sat down on a box and dropped her face into her hands.

He followed her inside. "Hallie, I—"

"No," she said, and looked up. Her face was full of an anguish he didn't really understand. "Leave me alone, Rafe. Please."

He did as she asked.

But Hallie was right. This was ridiculous. *He* was ridiculous. He had to decide once and for all what he was doing. They could not go back to the way it was.

Maybe what pushed him over the edge was Nick.

On the day they found out that Rafe's mother's cancer was back—this time in the bladder—Rafe's dad lost his cool. "I can't do this," he'd said. "I can't run a ranch with half the people I need and take care of your mother at the same time. I need you, son."

But Rafe needed work. Paying work. "If I stay, Dad, I'll help you where I can," he said, because of course he would. That was what he did. "But I need a paying job. And not at the ranch." He wouldn't go on the Prince payroll. He was adamant about that. He still hadn't figured out how to navigate his way with Hallie, but he would not be on her family's payroll.

"Where are you going to get a job?" his dad had asked.

"I don't know. In social work. I just need to get serious about it."

But then Nick had asked him to come into the office to talk about a few things.

"About what?" Rafe said into the phone when Nick called.

"Life, man. Just come."

So Rafe went. "Martin and I need your help," Nick said flatly.

Rafe was already shaking his head. "I'm not working for you, Nick. I'm not going to put myself in that position."

Nick looked offended. "What are you talking about?"

463

Rafe hadn't wanted to say it to Nick, but he wasn't going to lie about it either. "Look, Nick. I have some pretty strong feelings for your sister."

Nick nodded but otherwise had no response.

"*Serious* feelings," Rafe said again.

"Rafe, come on. We all know that. You two are constantly together."

Okay, so much for his attempts at discretion. "I'm not talking about a casual dating thing."

"Well, that's great," Nick said.

Rafe sighed with irritation.

"What do you want me to say?" Nick asked. "I'd be thrilled—*thrilled,*" he said, tapping his chest, "if you were with Hallie."

It was Rafe's turn to be confused. "Why?"

"Why?" he said, as if that was a dumb question. "Can you think of a better man for her? Because I sure can't. So, okay, you don't want to be on the Prince payroll," Nick said, dispatching with that misunderstanding for more pressing business. "But what if you were on George Lowe's payroll?"

"The lawyer?"

"Hear me out," Nick said, and laid out his idea. George, a gentleman rancher, would hire Rafe, not only to run his small cattle ranch, but also to contract him out to Three Rivers. Rafe would work with Three Rivers Ranch, and for George's ranch as well. Not *for* Three Rivers Ranch. Not *for* the Princes.

"Ranch management," Rafe said.

Nick laughed. "Did you think we needed you to brand cattle? We need help running a cattle ranch, and you know as much as I do. Your dad's a great majordomo, but he's not a cattleman."

"But I just got my degree in social work."

"You'll still use it on ranchers, trust me. But I'm not saying you have to do this forever. Just help us over the hump. Surely there is a way to combine ranching and social work for real," Nick said.

Rafe didn't know how in the hell that could be done. Nevertheless, he couldn't quite grasp the opportunity that had just fallen into his lap. He didn't know how to reconcile all the effort he'd put into another career entirely with this one.

"Don't say no. Just think about it. George will get in touch in a week or so."

Rafe didn't need to think about it. A door had just opened, one he'd been standing outside of since he was twelve. He would figure it out. He would make it work, come hell or high water.

Chapter Thirty

Hallie's studio was just about finished. The big picture window had not yet been installed, and there were some things she wanted to do to the offices—specifically, turn one into a nursery—but she was ready to start building the actual program. She and Genevieve had been trading ideas over email all week.

Hallie hoped to have her first classes by late summer, as soon as she finished school.

Once the program was up and running, she was going to get back on that charity circuit and hit up all the organizations who had ever asked for a dime of Prince money to support *her* cause.

Her mother wanted to help. "You leave the fundraising to me," she said to Hallie. "Those society bitches will be donating before they even know what hit them."

"Mom!" Hallie said with a laugh. "Those are your friends!"

"Hallie Jane, you are so naive sometimes."

"I hope you get plenty of Janet Tobin's money," Hallie's grandmother said. "She's got too much, obviously, judging by all those Cadillacs she keeps buying. She can't even drive."

"Don't you worry about her, Dolly," Hallie's mother said, her gaze narrowing. "I have her in my sights."

Hallie's family was equally surprised and proud that she'd pulled this off, and so quickly at that. Hallie was a little surprised, too. But her ability to do it gave her hope that if she could set up a nonprofit to teach ballet to underprivileged and disabled children, she could raise a baby.

Speaking of which, she was going to have to tell them. She could hardly zip her jeans. Her morning sickness was hard to hide, as it seemed to hit at all times but the morning.

And, of course, she had not yet told Rafe. That was beginning to bear down on her.

She already knew what she wanted to say. "I know you'll want to do the right thing, but I can't do the right thing back if that's the only reason you are doing the right thing. I need you to want to be with *me,* Rafe."

Or something perhaps a little more coherent than that.

It made her feel sick every time she practiced it out loud, because she wanted so desperately for him to want her.

She planned to tell him tonight. She'd invited him to meet her at the Magnolia Bar and Grill for a drink she would not be having. But it seemed a public place would make it more restrained. Maybe she wouldn't cry. On her way into town, she'd stopped at her warehouse. She was so happy with the way it had turned out, and when the big window was in, it would be the best studio in all of San Antonio.

She was alone, and decided to practice her ballet while she had a chance and could still move. She was going through her ballet warm-up—first position, plié, second position, plié, and so forth, when she heard something near the front of the warehouse. She never got used to the creaks and moans of this place. She turned around, expecting a delivery.

But it was Rafe who was standing in the entry, watching her.

"Oh," she said, and brushed her hair back, feeling the warmth flood her cheeks. "What are you doing here? We're meeting at the Magnolia, right?"

Rafe moved forward. "I . . . saw your car and I, ah . . . I need to talk to you, Hallie."

Hallie's heart plummeted. She couldn't speak. *He was leaving.* He was going to tell her he would always be her friend. She didn't want to hear it. So she blurted, "Great! Because I have something to tell you. I am—" She paused and looked at something he was holding up. "What's that?"

"This?" He jingled it. "It's a hotel key. To a room at the Hotel Emma. Know the place?"

"Well, I do. But . . . what is it, again?"

"I have arranged a nice hotel room, Hallie, because somehow, we, two functioning adults, have managed to move back home with our parents, and I don't want to ravish you in your childhood room. Or mine. Or in a car. I want to ravish you in a soft bed with clean sheets."

Hallie's blood turned warm and gooey. "You're going to ravish me?"

"So hard."

Warm and gooey was turning to lava, and her heart was beginning to race. "But I thought—

"Forget what you thought. Hallie Jane Prince, I have loved you since you pushed me off the saddle stand."

"When did I do that?"

He put the key in his pocket and walked across the warehouse to take her hand. "Look at me. I love you. I have *always* loved you. I loved you so much that I joined the army because I couldn't have you. And I don't ever want to be without you again, okay?" He went down on one knee. Hallie gasped. "I want to marry you, Hallie. I don't have a ring because this part," he said, gesturing to himself with one knee on the floor, "is totally spontaneous. But it's right, because there has never been anyone else for me. And there never will be. Now, I don't know how you feel about—"

"Yes!" she shouted, and threw her arms around his neck. "I knew it! I *knew* you still loved me!"

469

"I have loved you so much and for so long that I thought something was wrong with me."

"Nothing is wrong with you! I love you, too, Rafe. I can't even find words to tell you how much. I just desperately needed to hear you say it."

"Baby, I will say it every day for the rest of your life if you will have me."

"Oh my God, this is *just* like *The Bachelor*!" she cried with elation.

"Who?"

"Never mind," she said, and kissed him, sliding down onto her knees, too. The kiss turned very hot very quickly, and she was moaning because she was so much more aroused in a pregnant body than she could have ever imagined in her regular body.

"What did you want to tell me?" he asked as he bit her shoulder.

"Later," she said.

"Good. Let's go," he said, and he stood up, swept her up off the floor, and then kissed her as he mummy-walked out of there with her in his arms.

Hallie was amazed by his preparation. "When did you change your mind?"

"It's a long story," he said. "I'll tell you over dinner."

He'd talked Ella into getting some clothes for Hallie, which included a dress that she could not zip. But it turned out she didn't need to. They couldn't get out of bed. They made love like they had in Aspen, two people who were desperate for each other, making up for lost time.

Much, much later, Rafe ordered room service and champagne. Hallie was wearing one of the hotel bathrobes and chowing down on the french fries she'd asked them to cover in melted cheese when the champagne arrived. "Don't make yourself sick," Rafe said, laughing as she shoved fries into her mouth. He handed her a glass of champagne.

Hallie wiped her fingers one by one on a napkin and set aside the champagne. "Speaking of sick."

"Let me guess—you're sick of cheesy fries?" He settled onto the bed beside her.

"Never," she said, and smiled. "But I've been sick. A lot."

"Are you okay?" he asked with a slight frown. "You're probably not getting enough minerals."

Men. "Rafe, remember how many times we did it in Aspen?"

He chuckled. He pulled her across his lap to nuzzle her neck. "Every time, in vivid detail."

"We did it a lot," she agreed, smiling at him. "Do you know that condoms are only ninety-eight percent effective?"

He laughed and kissed the hollow of her throat. He was not getting it. "Okay, how about this," she said. "You know what I'm going to do with that second bedroom at Ella's?"

He lifted his head. "Please don't tell me your grandma is going in there," he said, and moved lower, to the part of her chest he could reach through the gap in her gown.

"Not Grandma. A baby. *Our* baby."

"Oh you want to . . ." His voice trailed off. He stilled, his lips on her skin. And then he slowly lifted his head, his eyes full of shock. "Are you . . . are you *pregnant,* Hallie?"

She laughed. "I am *so* pregnant. I can't button my pants! And there really aren't enough cheesy Tater Tots in the world."

Rafe sat up. His hands went to the top of his head. He looked to the ceiling and drew a deep breath. "Why didn't you tell me?"

"Because." She suddenly wished she hadn't eaten so many fries. "I didn't want you to do the right thing out of a sense of responsibility. I was hoping you'd come around to trusting—to loving—me again."

He swallowed.

"Oh no. Rafe, I'm sorry. I thought you'd be happy."

Rafe lowered his head and smiled through the tears shining in his eyes.

"Oh," she said softly. "Don't cry."

"I'm not crying, *you're* crying," he said, and gathered her up in his arms and held her tight. "I didn't have to come around to loving you because I always have. I could not be any happier right now, Hallie. I could not possibly be."

Neither could she. She hadn't even known this sort of love was possible. She'd be happy to tell her mother that Rafe was the right one.

The absolute perfect one.

Epilogue

It was a beautiful evening at the ranch, a perfect evening for a wedding, and Cordelia was thrilled with the way everything was turning out.

Of course they had the wedding catered—she wouldn't have people in Three Rivers talking about how the Princes had fallen on hard times. No one could look at this spread and think for a moment they weren't as rich and privileged as they'd ever been. They didn't have to know she'd taken an old evening gown and had it shortened.

Luca was so nervous he made her laugh. She sneaked into his room, where he and Nick were getting ready. "Here," she said, and handed Luca a shot of tequila.

Nick looked at it as Luca downed it. "Should you really be getting him drunk before he takes his vows?"

"Just taking the edge off," she'd said, and had gone off, giggling at how stupid in love that boy was with Ella Kendall.

On the patio, Hallie was wearing a pretty dress that she could zip. She was five months pregnant, and if there was anyone in town who didn't know it, they'd be talking about it after tonight. That was right, everyone was talking about Hallie Prince again, but Cordelia didn't care. Her daughter glowed with happiness. Let them talk.

Her first ballet classes were starting next month. Cordelia couldn't imagine how she would teach at six months pregnant, but Hallie was determined. She'd finished more than half of what she lacked toward a degree and was on track to finish by the end of summer.

Rafe was going to open his martial arts and physical training studio next to her, the focus on kids and wounded soldiers. And he was in the process of getting his social work license, working with a vet program. "I'm going to need it with this crew," he'd said to Cordelia when the Princes and Fontanas had come together to celebrate the news of his engagement to Hallie.

Even Martin had come around. He'd grudgingly admitted to Cordelia that she was right, Rafe was good for Hallie, and Hallie was good for Rafe.

"I love to hear that I'm right, Martin. Feel free to tell me as often as you like," she'd said.

She was glad Rafe was staying for Mrs. Fontana's sake. She was going through radiation and chemotherapy for a third time in her life, and she looked exhausted in a dress that hung on her frame. Rico had come home, too, and it looked to Cordelia like he was a little fuller and stood a little straighter. The program Rafe had been building in Chicago was off and running, according to Rico. They had so many kids wanting to join the program that they were already thinking of expanding it.

When it was almost time for the ceremony, Cordelia mixed two gin and tonics and sought out Dolly. Not that she could miss her—Dolly was wearing the sparkliest turquoise dress Cordelia had ever seen. And then she'd decided to top it off with an orange fascinator. "Do you think maybe you're coming down with some form of dementia that makes you forget things like how to dress for a wedding?" Cordelia asked.

"What are you talking about?" Dolly asked, swishing her long skirt around.

"Let me ask it another way. Aren't you worried you're going to upstage the bride?"

"Well, that was going to happen anyway. Go big or go home," Dolly said with a wink.

In addition to Hallie, Charlotte was a bridesmaid. And so was Ella's friend Stacy, who was becoming a big country-western star.

Nick and Rafe were standing up with Luca. Rafe was terribly handsome in a suit. She understood why her daughter was crazy for the man.

And there was George, looking pretty spiffy in a suit, too.

"When are you getting married?" she heard a

476

guest ask, and turned her head. The guest was asking Hallie.

"Oh, I don't know," Hallie said. "We're going to run off and do it. We're thinking Vegas or Tahoe."

That was news to Cordelia. She wouldn't in a million years agree to it, but for tonight, it was all right to let Hallie believe that's what she was going to do.

"Ladies and gentlemen, if you will take your seats," the reverend said.

Cordelia watched as everyone settled into place. There would be no procession, so the attendants stood with the reverend.

Cordelia sipped her gin and tonic and noticed that Hallie kept looking at Rafe, and he kept stealing glances at her. Those two. They were so in love. They were lucky to have found the right person.

So were Luca and Ella. So many things had gone wrong in her life, but in this, Cordelia had done right. She had raised some pretty awesome kids.

You'd be so proud, Charlie.

"Please rise for the bride," the reverend said.

Ella began her walk down the aisle. She walked alone, as she had no family, but her head was high, and she was beautiful in a plain silk white sheath and carrying bloodred roses.

"Oh my," Dolly whispered. "She's beautiful."

Cordelia turned her attention to her son, and the look on Luca's face sent a ripple through her. He loved Ella so much.

And then she looked at Nick. Grumpy McGrumperson looked almost like he was bored. That boy needed an extra-big slice of cake with some happy pills stuffed into it.

But Cordelia forgot the woes of her eldest. She could hardly see a thing anyway, her eyes were so full of tears and a familiar ache of knowing what it was to love someone so completely like Luca loved Ella and Hallie loved Rafe.

And maybe Nick would experience it one day, although Cordelia wasn't holding her breath.

Books are produced in the United States using U.S.-based materials	Books are printed using a revolutionary new process called THINKtech™ that lowers energy usage by 70% and increases overall quality	Books are durable and flexible because of Smyth-sewing	Paper is sourced using environmentally responsible foresting methods and the paper is acid-free

Center Point Large Print
600 Brooks Road / PO Box 1
Thorndike, ME 04986-0001 USA

(207) 568-3717

US & Canada:
1 800 929-9108
www.centerpointlargeprint.com